GW00858943

This is a work of fiction. Names, characters, organisations, places, events, and incidents are either products of the author's imagination or used fictitiously.

Text copyright © 2015 Oli Anderson

All rights reserved.

Synchronesia: A Depressing Existential Novel

-OLI H ANDERSON

For whoever wants it the most.

Ask and it will be given you; seek and you will find; knock and the door
will be opened to you.
-Matthew 7:7

I am not what happened to me. I am what I chose to become.
-Carl Gustav Jung

What doesn't kill you makes you more miserable.
-Me

Chapter 0

You think this feeling's going to wear away one day, but it's not. It's going to last forever.

I used to feel the same way. By the time I'd realised, I'd been working there for a few months; an interminable run of being humiliated and demeaned and having to do the same thing over and over again for the sake of a few pounds an hour. I was beginning to not feel like a person any more, my hands cracked from the handling of too much junk, my inner nasal passages singed on a miasma of pale farts and body odour. I felt disenchanted and numb towards all things, rarely spoke to people any more. I was even getting used to the smell.

It had found me at the height of my desperation, after I got sick and had to quit my fancy job overseas, and move back to England to a cheaper place in a rundown city. I couldn't leave because I needed to visit the hospital so often and I was waiting for somebody I didn't know to die so that I could borrow something they didn't need any more. I saw a sign in the window so I went in and applied. I knew that I was overqualified and I knew that I'd get the job. I knew I'd end up trapped and full of hate but, because I had debts to pay, I went ahead and applied anyway.

The town we were all in was a dive, the kind of place where the billboards advertising new cars or breaks away were for the people passing through to someplace better, because nobody who lived here could afford anything. Some people dropped cigarette butts and unwanted food on the streets and the worse off smoked and ate them. There were proud old buildings made of big stones and embellished with carvings, but their insides were vacant and full of crumbling furniture. The windows had white writing on them that said 'closing down'.

I used to tell myself that these buildings were signs of a more prosperous past. These days, everybody of worth had upped and gone away, leaving only the needy and the confused like me behind. It was a bit like being stuck at the dead end of a garden party, where all the sensible people had gone home for the night and only the drunks had stayed behind to yell up and above one another and howl against the moon. Some people still tried to convince themselves that things were better than they really were. But these were usually just the people too proud to admit and face their own faults –the armies of the deluded, gilding their own cages, and synthesising pallid versions of happiness with which they would confuse themselves and everybody around them.

People out and about and on the buses would shout obscenities at each other and throw empty crisp packets.

All for no reason at all.

Chapter 1

I had an interview and they told me to start work the next Monday so I spent the weekend in denial. I couldn't believe that my life had reached its nadir already. Before it happened, I had been living a satisfying life of impecunious obscurity on the dole. Every Monday, my post office account would be accredited with the money I needed to hit the discount section of the supermarket and I'd still have a little left over for beer so I could drown my sorrows and try to forget about the world.

Sometimes, I would drink in the street, on the steps near the town hall, even though you weren't supposed to, and I'd try to imagine what it might be like to have a job with power on my side. One where I could walk with a stride and a bounce to my step instead of slinking through the streets with my hands in my pockets and my head down. I'd have an expense account and a private registration plate, eat in restaurants where you got served by waiters instead of till attendants, and have a driveway at my house instead of blinking light staircases and elevators that didn't work.

That Saturday and Sunday I did the best I could to find a way out of Monday's maelstrom. I had hated this town ever since I had arrived in it, the broken promises of half-finished buildings and talk of regeneration, the half-eaten fast foods that had been dumped on top of dustbins and telephone boxes, or the empty gentrified mills with smashed windows and keys stuck in their locks. And the people were even worse, spitting every other footstep that they took, talking loud and talking cheap, pushing, shoving, yelling at each other, like at the guy in the post office, or the bar tenders, and the bus drivers, each as poor and desperate and hateful as the next fellow. The last thing I needed was a job that would bring me closer to myself.

One night, I woke through the morning with a yen and a thirst. I climbed out of bed to the kitchen sink and drank speckled water through a dirty glass. I was drawn to a window that overlooked the yellow lights of the street just in time to see a white van pull up and a masked guy with a hammer climb up onto the roof. I watched him smash the windows of the building across the road and then drive off. I never knew why. Another time some guy down the road got shot. They cornered off the street and then they put a picture of him in the newspaper.

I spent those last two days lost within a haphazard panic, wandering in and out of backstreets looking for alternative work, something, anything, whatever would allow my ego to support the crumbling walls on which it now stood. I went to empty bars in search of hiring landlords, climbed steps to vacant offices, and paraded the vast aisles of white supermarkets in search of vacancies. But nobody wanted me and so there was nothing I could do. All that remained was to keep my fingers crossed and pray that fate would somehow save me from the slippery slope into hopelessness.

When I got back to the cold apartment I sat on the floor and trawled the back pages of the local rag for the scraps or scams or get-rich-quick schemes. All I could find advertised were people seeking girls to be 'models' or opportunities for cleaners that could speak foreign languages. I gave up all hope and decided to get drunk again instead. I might have even shed a few tears.

Monday came like a train without the brakes. I woke up earlier than I had in months, showered, and then looked at my reflection in a toothpaste flecked mirror. I threw myself a sardonic smile, knowing all the while that this experience was about to change me, and there was nothing I could do about it. Perhaps the charm and humour that used to reside within the younger version of myself would somehow work their ways back through the haze in my head or the languish in my belly. Only months ago I was young and healthy and running around the city, and yet now I felt senescent.

'The real world sneaks up on us like a killer in the night, pulling us out of the bliss of childhood and tearing open our eyelids to only harshness and the pervasive bitterness of incessant disappointment.' , I thought to myself.

And then I remembered that I had once considered myself an optimist.

The place was situated outside a shopping centre, and each morning to get there I had to walk past drones of other retail workers, dressed in uniforms, as though squirming children forced by sneering parents to wear lurid, itchy Christmas sweaters. Occasionally, at this time, you'd see a well-to-do face in the crowd, suited and booted with the old suitcase, eager to get out of there, away from the riffraff, back to the comfort of their offices and their water coolers and the cleaning ladies that they looked down upon. Music that I remembered from my high-school years as being subversive would play over the CD player as an innocuous accompaniment to people shopping or drinking tasteless coffee in the food hall.

I stood outside the shop with my new co-workers: a long-haired guy with tired, red eyes and an attitude, a thin-haired paunchy guy that dressed like an American truck driver, and a ginger-haired stoner. They all had pot bellies from too much TV, eating microwave meals, and drinking Pepsi. As the four of us stood about in silence we smoked cigarettes and curled our eyes. Occasionally, we'd try to make small talk, but it would only serve to fall flat and compound the intensity of it all.

To distract myself, I stared at a sign above the door that said:

'Arbeit macht frei.'

But I had no idea what it meant.

After a while, the long-hair with the attitude checked his watch, then pulled out an ominous and fist-sized bunch of keys with which he began to open the shutters. He had introduced himself as a measly shop supervisor but, you could tell from the way he walked, that he'd convinced himself he was supervising the whole of the nation.

I checked my own timepiece to see how I was attuned to the workings of these people. It was a watch that I'd picked up in China when I had been travelling, when I had seen the Great Wall slice up over the horizon, like there were no limits and that anything was possible. On its face was the official portrait of Chairman Mao, the Chinese big cheese, with the two hands taking the form of his arms, rising to salute and then contort as the hours went by. Red and lurid against his dirt green uniform, it had an innate kitsch built into it. Unfortunately, I'd broken it, drunk and falling in the road, and so one of his arms had fallen off, leaving it to count only the minutes and not the hours.

This constant counting of minutes had started to make me feel like I'd be waiting forever for life to pick up again: A constant sixty minute cycle of going around in circles and routine and waiting for something to change or kick up and out of there. I thought about body organs and getting on the move again, about feeling free instead of trapped. But then, I looked around myself, and realised that some people spend their whole lives feeling like this, and so I told myself to feel grateful for the good things that had happened to me, even if it did seem that they happened a lifetime ago, to the same version of a different person, one who shares memories and head space with me but nothing here in the 'now' and whom I probably wouldn't even recognise if I passed in the street.

The shutters opened and I crossed the threshold.

When you got inside, they made you empty your pockets and write down everything that you had with you, so that you wouldn't steal things. The tattered binder on which you did this was called the 'Search Log'. It was green and sticky. The procedure was simple enough, but people would write in the book with a flourish, as if they were the President of the USA signing a new Bill of Rights, as though they were doing something important just because it was official, and that everybody was going to crowd around them afterwards and shake their hands and take pictures for the paper.

It's the small people like us that make the biggest deals.

Because I was the New Guy, I went last; I wrote the following items beneath my name:

-I-pod.
-Nokia.
-£2.36

I had a copy of *The Catcher in the Rye* in my inner waist pocket, but I didn't have to write it down because they didn't sell books. Nobody had even seen one since high school.

There was a space in which you had to put the time you wanted your lunch. Here I had to write:

10 a.m.

All the other lunch slots had been taken.

I took my allocated lunch break. Though the town was bleak and dilapidated, it had a wide selection of pasty shops. As I stood about outside, smoking and deciding which one I should go to, a yoke of chavs passed me by and told me to get my hair cut.

I wondered for a moment if they were perhaps messengers of some divine force, imbued with the knowledge that we as humans are supposed to one day gain understanding of, their didactical invective serving as a gentle shot in the arm to put us mere mortals back on the right track.

Before I could ask them, their squat bodies and caps evaporated into the grey and amorphous cloud of the city's denizens. Up above, a group of youths were throwing stolen shoes at people from the top floor of the multi-story car park that overlooked the shopping promenade. It served to ground me and so I ceased my metaphysical musings.

When I went to the pasty shop I joined a long line of hungry people in tracksuits. Everybody that left the shop before me had crumbs around their mouths as they ate out of white paper bags. It was as if the humble pasty had brought people of all ages and nationalities together: white babies in prams had pasties wedged between their chubby hands, and so did black people in wheelchairs. I marvelled at the simplicity of it all.

7

I got back to the shop at 11.01 on the till clocks and was called over by the Supervisor to be castigated. Via a series of curt, staccato utterances and a tone that one may speak to either a dog, an illegitimate child, or a half-wit in, he demanded that I go and talk to him in a quiet section of the shop.

I knew this meant that he wanted to give me the introductory assertion of authority and I could tell he was the kind of guy that felt it necessary to do so. The ridiculous rules that held the place together and his relation to them were his only source of confidence; he was a martinet, purely because he was too stupid to figure out any other way of handling his authority without throwing it in people's faces.

'You're late', he said, before pausing, as if something magical may be about to happen, like a butterfly were to be born from a chicken's egg on the shelves at Tesco, or the traffic lights outside were to flash in new and exotic colours that nobody had ever seen before.

Then he stared at me through the insomniac, computer game addled red eye that has afflicted a whole generation. Waiting. I stared at Mao's arm and its full rotation. But eventually I was forced to say it.

I said, *'I'm sorry'.*

Morally and rationally, I felt quite confident that I had done little if anything wrong, but I had convinced myself that I was too world-weary and wise to play juvenile games with such an abdominous no-hoper. I walked off back to the shop floor, fully aware that my youth had left me, and that my life was over. A large part of me wanted to get out of there before things got any worse. But I knew I couldn't, because I had debts to pay, and I would feel guilty if I quit simply because of my proclivity to fallaciously believe it possible to be in control, if not of one's own destiny, then one's existence.

If there is one thing that can be said for sure about this life, it is that sometimes there is nothing you can do but eat a little shit for a while. Perhaps it's the only way you can appreciate the caviar that everyone keeps telling you is in the post.

I went back to the shop floor and attempted to alphabetise the stock on the shelves. Every time I thought I could see the top of the mountain some lowlife would walk in, with a banana or some other non-shop-safe edible, their sticky fingers leaving marks on the already dirty DVD cases and the crumbs from around their mouths and beards (regardless of gender), leaving wanton trails of disregard behind them on the floor.

Like a man tied to a tree as the house he has just built is set on fire, I could only stand and watch aghast as they nonchalantly reordered the fruits of my labour into systems of ill-reason and arbitrary assignment. For example, they would pick things up from the 'DVD Movies' section and capriciously reassign them to the 'Documentaries'. Titles that began with 'A' would find themselves in the 'S' section and vice versa. It was a never ending struggle for order in the chaotic world of human interaction; the next round in the eternal battle between Chaos and Cosmos.

I began to feel that I was just another soul lost in time, another one of God's shelf stackers, lost to the banality of it all, and the hell and the drudgery. Having convinced myself that my personal problems were much worse than anybody else's, I began to see myself as smitten with a secret disease and no way out of it. With each passing second I began to feel that perhaps the earth was about to open up and swallow me whole, so that piles of junk food detritus could fall down on top of me, like straws and ice, and the spit of strangers, and that I would be forever lost in the quagmire of anonymity, forgotten in the casket of eternity.

One day, the Shop Stoner approached and asked me if I could lend him twenty pence, an act which immediately piqued my curiosity because I had been accosted time and time again by drunks on the street who had made similar requests for the same denomination. For some reason, in all its heptagonal glory, the humble twenty pence piece had been exalted to a sort of *soup du jour* of things to be begged for within the city limits, like ten pence was too paltry and shameful, but that double the amount would allow one to maintain a degree of dignity without having asked for too much. Fair game for the penniless but socially self-aware.

I had liked to imagine that, somewhere within the walls of this great city, there was a secret door that only the bums knew about, and that, if you put twenty pence in the slot by the entrance, it would allow you access to a secret world in which all of your problems would be solved.

His answer, however, was far more mundane:

'Bus fare.'

Besides the Supervisor, he was the first of my co-workers to acknowledge my existence. I gave him what he asked for, and as a reward he opened up to conversation.

'How long have you worked here?'

'Two years, give or take'

'Do you like it?'

'Best job in town.'

'Where'd you work before?'

'MacDonald's.'

'Across the street?'

'Yeah.'

We both looked out across the road, where the staff at MacDonald's waved out to us with the familiarity of some secret brotherhood. The Stoner waved at them before melting away to the till area.

As he wandered off, I began to wonder why everybody was so poor. It had become a regular occurrence that staff members would be reduced to borrowing money from each other midway through the month, because their minimum wage pay cheques couldn't reach out past the finish line, and so they would be forced to protract and extend and lengthen in time the pennies in their purses. As a result, we had become experts at eating cheaply and unhealthily: two flapjacks for a pound from an adjacent health food shop, all of which tasted of the same, bland, powder despite being labelled in different flavours or colours that we couldn't care for or discern. Some of us would survive on MacDonald's breakfasts and coffee tokens, whilst others would run down to bakeries at the end of the day to buy discount throw-away foods, at lukewarm temperatures and with crusting edges. Some took on pound shops, or raided the discount section at Tesco, whilst others yet wouldn't eat at all, remaining reticent, hanging on until the first Monday of the month, so that they could stuff their faces for a day and then start the whole cycle on over again.

The wheel turns and the Earth burns but some things never change.

There was rent to pay on apartments and council tax so that the politicians could park their cars outside city hall and hire more traffic wardens to guard the rest of the streets. Electricity was up and so was water and people had birthdays and then Christmas would come and there was nothing you could do about it. Family members would get used to being disappointed in us yet nobody could understand how we could spend all our time working and being in a place we didn't really want to be with so little reward.

I wished there was a secret door, so that I could put my twenty pence into the slot and disappear forever.

Chapter 2

The place that I lived in had eaten away at my savings from the Old World and been sold as a 'luxury apartment', because it had been furnished with cheap furniture that was falling to pieces, and was close to the canal and the train station. In truth, it was just a cold old stone wall building full of drunk people running through the halls and where the corridors were without lights and where there was rubbish trailing down the steps like corpses left on mountainsides. You had to keep your doors locked at all times, even when you were in, because all the drunks and the thieves of outside would shake at the door handles, like furious, anguished burn victims trying to get away from it all. Dreams of elusion or plans of evasion pervaded, because life was cold and scary outside and nobody knew what might happen to them. It began to make me nervous. And my blood pressure was too high anyway.

I'd been living on my own ever since coming back. In the Old World, I had been engaged to be married, but when she found out about my illness and its implications our relationship became complicated and so we decided to throw it away, as though dumping old clothes into the ocean, but maintaining that we were doing something noble, like freeing a bird from its cage, or releasing a majestic zoo animal back into the wild. We reassured each other that it was fine, 'right' even, and then she accompanied me to the airport and kissed me on the cheek and I can still remember her lips wet with tears.

She cried but I didn't and then I disappeared through the gate wondering what the plane food might taste like and if I might be sat next to the type of stranger that would change my life. Someone with all the answers.

For a few months we shared emails about non-events, the kind of polite small talk that you'd make with an unknown at a bus-stop, but they tailed slowly away like puddles evaporating in the morning sun, until finally I was left truly alone; like a blank piece of paper in a warped plastic bottle out to sea; or a repressed love affair; a private, shamefaced dream. The last I heard she was engaged to a banker. Just like her parents had wanted.

So I keep telling myself that everything happens for a reason.

I had become so used to loneliness that it began to seem like an old friend whom I no longer liked but tolerated all the same. For years, I'd tried to convince myself that I would one day find a way to be by myself, so that I could write, even though I never knew what about and didn't really have anything to say. And I had always assumed that I would never be lonely, because I would have chosen to be living in solitude, instead of having it forced upon me, as though somebody with a flawed personality, or a case of the heebie-jeebies might, because I was an individual, built of strength and virtue, or so I had imagined, and so that parasitic need to cling onto others, which so many of us seem to be infused with, was not expected to haunt me. It had never occurred to me that true command of social isolation is contingent upon strength of character or true goals and motivation. And so, when I realised that I didn't have anybody, I could only turn inwards, towards those demons that come up in maudlin, hushed admissions of flaw and foible, so that I could berate myself for all the mistakes that had led me here. And convince myself that each action has a consequence. And that it was destiny. And that there could be no other explanations.

And in the midst of all this chaos, I began to notice that my senses were somehow intertwined, perhaps on account of their being too many stimuli in the vicinity; the constant bombardment of advertisements on the TV or in the magazines, or each time that you turned on the radio, or walked around a corner to be accosted by a barrage of assailants trying to sell you charity or new shoes or new ways of life that would solve all your problems.

In many ways, I felt like my circuits had been fried and that I had become the kind of person who no longer ran on oxygen, but upon electricity, because I was so dependent upon and in love with the modern times: the amenities and the colour TVs and the Internets and the constant communication and the shopping and everything else that comes with it, that I almost felt they were a part of me. And these colours and sensations would come to me at the strangest of moments; for example, when I was eating my daily dose of junk food and would associate the flow of the juice in a burger with a cool buzz of red in my head, or when I would drink water and hear the sounds of shattering glass, or when I would cross roads and see green men flash in countless other shades and feel a shudder down my spine because it was all too much to take. But still, despite these intermittent intrusions upon my psyche, I still felt lost and bored and broken, as though I were an inflatable toy that had been deflated and stuffed away in the back of the cupboard, or an apple that had been bruised in transit and then shoved upon a supermarket shelf; an autumn leaf that had fallen from a tree and been stamped upon into wet concrete, so that it can stay there and be stuck and remain in a state of austere inertia for the rest of its eternity.

I imagined myself at the end of an unwound ball of string, saturated and permeated with the sewer waters that I had been trying to vacation in, and I said to myself that, by looking backwards, I would somehow be able to untangle it all and find a reason for this perennial state of discontent. Yet, through the skewed vision brought on by the subjectivity of feeling sorry for myself, I could only ravel the string further. Eschewing sorrow and moroseness would prove to be futile I realised, unless I could convince myself that this was 'fate', and that everything was supposed to be this way.

When all we know beneath the moon has turned away from us, we have no choice but to turn to higher forces, but that doesn't mean that there is no longer a paucity of doubt in our hearts.

And anyway, Nature cannot make mistakes...

I had lived for months and seasons in the same routine: Wake up and listen to traffic reports on the radio, walk to work and lose faith in it all, eat lunch in empty market cafes over syrupy coffee, and then relive the past on an evening through hangdog masturbation, so that I could go to bed to toss and turn and see shapeless, wide-eyed dreams. I kept waiting for something to happen, a lesson to be learned, something that would give the answers that I'd been seeking. Why had this happened to me? What was next? In my old life, I had been complacently ignorant, living in the city, young and free and in demand, as I had 'genuine' conversations over 'real' coffee, bought from multinational chains. But nothing ever came. I stood as a dead pawn waiting to be turned into a queen, unaware that the game was already over.

And so, as the leaves fell from the trees and the sun forgot to shine, I gave up all hope, convinced that this was all I could ever be good for: hovering in and out of questions and answers, uncertain as to whether my faith was really mine or just some wall I had put up in order to shield myself from it all, relating to everything and nothing. I felt weary as though I'd seen the whole spectrum of life and each of the shades and colours it had to offer. But I didn't sympathise with any of them. I couldn't get out of my own head.

The only luck I seemed to have was that the job didn't require the use of a mind, just the flailing of limbs and the scanning of codes and hitting of keys with fingers, and so I was able to escape to some degree within myself. I knew about computers and video games what Bill Gates knew about cheap sex and broken dreams and so, as they threw cables in my face and spoke in esoteric languages that I couldn't understand - questions about control pads, or wires and adaptors and memory cards – I began to feel ever more detached from the world. It was a different planet, one where people went out in the day to find new ways of staying in their houses. A troglodyte nation that I couldn't get my head around.

Before, all I'd ever really done was to travel from place to place naively imagining that I was some kind of poet, or a Leonard Cohen gypsy boy. Now, all that was left for me was to swim in a sea of routine, waiting for old age to creep up on me, so that my body could finally sag and fade out completely, allowing me to be as forgotten in death as I felt I had become in life.

I was out of all circles, being only able to vaguely imagine the people I used to know and associate with getting on with their own struggles, as I had been left me to try and get over mine.

I knew it was only the beginning, but I couldn't *wait* for it to end.

All of this changed when I met a well-dressed man on the shop floor. He had a Half Wit with him that kept smiling, a simpleton that was in his care for the day, following on behind like some well-trained pet and grinning impetuously, as though our conversation was the most stimulating thing he'd ever seen. For all I know, it could've been.

Compared to the majority of customers, the Well-Dressed Man exuded a confidence that no doubt stemmed from his ostensible lack of financial problems. He marched around the disordered shelves of DVDs and video games as a Western tourist may some Indian shanty town, standing proud and unafraid, as though he had secret links to the consul himself, like he was immune to the reality of it all, yet still had a sense of ownership over everything surrounding him.

The clothes were rough and purposeful and in fabrics that were clearly built to last, ingrained with an old-fashioned sense of functionality and character, diametrically opposed to the polyester aesthetic that the yokels were wearing: the zombies over by the video games in their shell suits, or the old guy with the holes in his jumper and the stains on his pants drooling in his wheelchair besides the adult section.

There were people in the queue with mismatched colours, out-of-season prints and cuts, beer stains on their legs and fag burns about their bellies. The Well-Dressed Man stood there untarnished and colour coordinated, his hair rugged but still highly refined, as though he didn't need to please or answer to anybody, and so he had cut it himself. And down his sinewy arms coursed strong veins as though all of life itself were flowing through him, or a great river that could knock down walls. Set against the rubicund of his face were two world-weary eyes, like holes in the ocean floor, and around his neck was a golden rood that sparkled beneath the sterile indoor lighting of the shop floor. He looked at me as if he found me to be somehow incongruous. Then he opened up his mouth and blessed me with his words.

'Don't mind him,' he said, and he pointed to the Half Wit by his side. 'He's just sore because he lost a piece of his jigsaw.'

And when I looked I saw that the Half Wit had a plastic bag in his hands, one so cheap that it was almost transparent, and inside of it sat a jigsaw in a box, but I couldn't tell what the big picture was.

'Looking after half-wits is just my day job', The Well-Dressed Man piped up again, and then he stopped to think, as though he were pausing on a walk to sniff at a rare and exotic flower:

'I'm actually a Thinker.'

His matter-of-fact tone and the potency of his declaration awoke my curiosity. It hadn't occurred to me that there might be good wine in town. So far, I had only managed to taste the mould at the bottom of the barrel.

My stomach settled and I felt a great wave of relief as I looked up at him, the benevolent smile of the Half Wit behind him shining like the sun and thus causing my interlocutor to silhouette and stand in high contrast and at sharp angles, as though some holy edifice upon the top of a hill.

'I do a lot of thinking too', I said.

He paused but didn't look at me. For a few moments I got the impression that he didn't quite believe me. The silence between us was filled with the sounds of the sirens outside the front door, people shouting in the streets, another commotion between strangers. It was the city's version of elevator music, something that's always there but which you only pay attention to when suffocating in a dried up or awkward conversation. I stood silent and waited, pretended to refill shelves. Out the corner of my eye I watched the Half Wit rocking back and forth on his sandals. He was wearing white socks which, combined with his choice of footwear, I found to be particularly distasteful.

Finally, the Well-Dressed Man let the words flow out of his mouth, as though all morning he had been wanting to whistle a tune but had only just been able to remember what it goes like.

'Well...', he said, 'If you're as ardent a thinker as you claim to be, you must surely be familiar with the Big Guy Upstairs?'

As he uttered this words he fingered the rood around his neck. At the time I didn't think anything of it.

Unsure of what to say, I turned instead to the Half Wit, who was still rocking on his feet but now also chewing on the air around him. He obviously didn't have the answers for anything.

'A big guy upstairs?', I asked.

'Yes', said the Well-Dressed Man, 'Haven't you heard of him?'

'No, I'm afraid not.'

I began to instantly feel that I had been missing out on something.

'Well then, you simply must seek him out. He has the answers to all your questions.'

A pregnant pause interposed itself between us, an uncanny silence; the only sound that remained was the cacophony of sandal rocking against the angst being channelled through the shop stereo.

'Where can I find the him?', I asked.

His mouth opened up like a flower and emitted a beautiful, beatific smile.

'Why... He's everywhere.', he said, 'in everything, even right here in this very city.'

Then he took the Half Wit's hand, and left me alone to my labelling.

Chapter 3

I began to try and remember the last time I had felt anything. There had always been that crushing feeling of being an animal in a cage, but I couldn't quite fathom my animal nature. Maybe I was just a person.

For some reason, as we get older, our feelings become subdued, diluted almost, like that piss-pale orange juice that they give you in plastic beakers with biscuits at nursery schools, despite our knowing that the full on promise of the concentrate in the bottle offers so much more. When we are born there can only be potential, yet as our bodies grow and our minds become full of our pasts, we are watered down until we join the minions of the flavourless and the pallid and the confused. All of a sudden, there is no taste or demand for us anymore, and so we begin to fade away, once and for all, ceasing only when we are at our most ethereal, existing only in memories, in passing references, or, if we ever managed to touch their hearts, in the frames on people's mantles.

I'd spent the morning using tiny bits of clear tape to adhere the face plate labels on to shelves as I listened to a wall of sound on my headphones. The labels were designed to slide into a groove that was built into dusty units, on which all the merchandise was displayed, and they had the company's name and logo on them, along with some pseudo-virtue catchphrase about recycling. Most of the time, they'd be seen hovering about the floor, because a disgruntled public would pull and tear and ravage at them, and so most of them were covered in footprints or had been torn into hundreds of pieces. Some shelves didn't have them at all, but, all the same, I was determined to have the remainder stay strong and intransigent in their official roles, determined that the place needed order of some kind, despite my generally lax attitude towards it all.

Occasionally you felt a compulsion to do things like this, if only to get away from the till area and that inexorable queue of thieves and mooncalves slinking towards you with their garbage tucked under their arms.

It had been a busy morning, but I'd almost finished my taping task, and the shop was actually beginning to resemble something close to a place of commerce, instead of a bomb site being salvaged by thieves. Hardened balls of chewing gum remained stuck to the floor, but The Stoner had mopped and removed the debris left by passing shoppers, and even the objects in the window display were now beginning to hide their pre-utilisation behind a cursory shimmer, like polished toasters at a car boot sale.

Over the tills, I watched the manager being bellicose, telling people that if they didn't queue in the right place then he wouldn't serve them. They looked at him with furtive animosity, but they couldn't do anything because he had the money that they needed, and that was when I thought to myself:

In times of peace, the warlike man attacks the queue.

That morning, the light of the northern sun had an uncharacteristically pellucid quality to it. Deep shadows ran down the course of the shop, silhouetting those who walked through the doors as though golden nomads, and making the concrete slabs of the pavement outside shine with all the lustre of ice and magic. It was on mornings like this that the whole town looked beautiful and that, instead of the dystopian sinkhole that it appeared to be most of the time, became a functional haven of quiescence and tranquillity. The sun on proud faces and the clamour of people turned to murmur, as they sat about on benches and turned their heads to the sky; a noticeable change from the usual eyes to the ground, the general air of cunning and conniving, as though everybody was planning to tunnel their own way out of here, of escaping from all their problems.

And then a breeze picked up. It was rare that one would make its way into the shop, but this one had somehow found the strength to move in circuitous breaths about the walls, in and out between our fingers, cool yet somehow warm and liberating, opening us to each other, people smiling and commenting upon it instead of pining about their 'issues'. I watched a till receipt dance about the centre of the DVD section, an American Beauty plastic bag, and so I had to force myself not to be a cliché and project some kind of meaning on to it, as though some guiding force resided behind it all, and that we lived in the bubble of purposefulness. My playlist took a break between songs and, during the silence, I heard the laughter of a child. I looked around from the shelves to see a boy, maybe about two or three years old, running in and out of the rows of shelving units, completely unaware of the other customers in the shop. Some looked at him and others ignored him. Some smiled and others didn't.

'Crockett's Theme' from the original Miami Vice TV-show swam through my headphones. I knew it was unhip, but I had long since stopped caring. It reminded me a 1980s childhood, Saturday afternoon synthesisers and cheap special effects. I thought about weekends and what they felt like before I had to work on them; I remembered being scared of my father, before I realised that he was just a human and as infallible as anybody else. Bedtimes and home-cooked meals; being told to eat your vegetables; trips to the supermarket, belted up in the backseat of the car. Plastic, toys, and sunshine.

The sounds of the laughing child fell inwards to the breeze, his mother calling him over but to no avail. He sat on the floor and ran around in mysterious circles, oblivious to the pain and misery of those around him. And, as the music died, his mother dragged his limp body up by his thin arms. Then the breeze went away and the sun clouded out and the people were back to normal and the day continued.

I put the tape to one side and put my head in my hands as I leaned back against one of the dusty shelves. So suddenly it had hit me: I needed something to care about.

Chapter 4

It had been almost a year since I had come back after finding out about my disease. Though the doctors had said that I would be a list priority, due to my relatively young age, nothing had come, and so I had started to forget my reasons for being here. I found myself institutionalised, lost to it all like some barefoot orphan in the backstreets of some hypodermic city. The tastes of the disappointment and the waiting became as regular as air. And when I looked around me it seemed that everybody else was waiting for something too. I felt normal in the most eerie of ways.

I began to ache for intimacy as though a drug. The weight of an eternity on my shoulders was taking its toll: A new irascibility that I wore like a coat of wire, the ways my palms would sweat and I'd bite my nails without realising, only to later look down at cracked and bloody fingers and wonder what had happened to me. That final embrace at the airport had been the last I could remember, flash mob memories, swimming up to the surface, like old World War II mines lost out to sea. Prior to that before I was hospitalised, after a day at the beach. Back home. Listening to old CDs.

The voice in the back of my head whispered that I might like to end it all. Another wished that I'd died when I had the chance. I wasn't really living for anything anymore, it would say, just trying to change things. And it made me realise that I no longer looked forward to the future, just mooned down about the past.

I took a breath and counted to ten.

Images and faces and places rose up like decaying bodies with flowers in their pockets and empty smiles: A glint in her eyes as she crossed a bridge by the sea; the wind flowing behind her as she ran towards me. One time she got drunk and lay in the road and caused a traffic jam. Another time, down the underground, she held my hand and looked at me like it might mean something. I had wished the train would never stop.

The shop became my watering hole, leading ill-proportioned ladies to my front door, though none that I would've really opened it to if this hadn't happened to me in the first place. When we are desperate for one thing we will often deny ourselves another, and so I was prepared to let my ego slip, though it had slowly faded anyway. I took the plunge, into the darkest of caves, despite knowing that the torch had burned out long ago and that these needy people were revving themselves up to judge me for being slight of build and sinewy with my messy, needle-hole arms.

In the Old World, I had been used to superficial city chicks, the ones who wore makeup for trips to the convenience stores, or who knew about films and different blends of tea and read books about poverty, but only when they were out and about in public. They were the ones who would buy expensive clothes on a whim and embellish their tales with a false irony, acting free and spontaneous in pre-planned ways, because they were beautiful and knew that they would never have any problems. I missed the sense of reality that came from the superficial.

It was rare that a girl would come into the shop that would pique the interest of the guys who worked there. And even if this did happen they were never anything special. Maybe there would be the odd one or two out of term time, usually by accident, when the hotties hit home from the universities, rife with their Stockholm syndrome and slavish bouts of confusion, tailed by dumb and drooling, computer game addicted boyfriends who didn't know what they had on their hands. During the regular parts of the year, it was just more of the same: Too poor to concentrate on looking good, and too depressed to stop eating. I wondered if I would see myself turn the same way.

One day I read the free newspaper on the train. Tucked in on page six, beyond the weather report and the negligible novelty sections, there was an article about how the English working classes die twenty or thirty years earlier than those who had scaled the heights. I no longer wanted to live that long anyway, but it still grieved me that I might not have a choice.

I closed my eyes and counted to twenty.

The maze had found myself trapped within had invisible walls, Perspex or perhaps thin but impenetrable glass, and though I could see those living and walking around freely outside of its confines, I couldn't break through to express myself in the fuller terms that I would once have been able to. My bleached confidence, locked behind the counter with the pariahs and the clueless. The affected air of insouciance that seemed to once hold the key. Gone. People let you get away with what they expect you to be able to get away with. If you're dressed to the nines in your best suit you might be able to fool them into thinking that you're intelligent or that you've got something to offer, but if they look at you and see a tool behind a till then things aren't quite the same. Sometimes the customers would look on, low-life looking down on low-life, and they would say:

'Do they just let anybody work here?'

And I don't know why, but despite knowing that I was being insulted, I would hear myself reply:

'Yeah, I guess so', as my co-workers looked on disdainfully.

Chapter 5

There would always be the younger girls, the ones that could send us to hell and back, on account of their very beings. They were the ones who dressed tall and wore too much makeup, trying their bests to walk in tune to the curves of their new bodies. They were the ones who opened their mouths to still gurgle, or let out effervescent cackles that would ring out through the store like alarms we should all heed, but which some of us didn't or couldn't even if we wanted to.

But hell was probably over-hyped anyway.

I don't know how it happened, but it left me feeling dirty and strange. I was so desperate for attention from the opposite sex that I could probably have turned to Mary. And I needed a change in my routine to distract me from the waiting, because Mao's hand had turned transfinite degrees, but for months nothing had changed besides the weather.

This was how it played out:

It must have been close to Easter because I was wondering where my chocolate eggs were. I was half asleep, working the tills on some narcotic midweek shift. Nothing much had been happening except for more of the same, so when I noticed that some girl in the queue and her friend were apparently checking me out, I was too enveloped in the quagmire of minimum wage lassitude to do anything about it. I tried ignoring. Part of me convinced the rest of me that it couldn't be happening; maybe they were sharing a private joke of some kind, because they kept giggling; or perhaps I'd finally lost it completely and was projecting some twisted and repressed fantasy on to the faces of the general public.

Analogous thoughts continued. My eyes were avoidant of other eyes. I looked down and kept scanning barcodes, but when they eschewed the front of the queue because some other till monkey might serve them, choosing instead to wait for my own till to free up, I knew that something strange was about to take place.

I tried to swallow my tongue but it wouldn't fit, so I called them over in as gutter-free a way as I could muster. They approached me still smiling and I felt the sides of my eyes drying up.

As they walked on up, I determined that the fates had presented me with the classic teenage duet of a leader and her sycophant. Beneath her blonde hair, the Leader's smile was as knowing and as thin as the crack in an egg. She wore her low-cut orange top like a warning sign. A palpable tension spawned of reverence fell like a curtain over the serving staff, as we stood like hidden erections at choir practice. She was more confident than an older woman might've been but hadn't made it public yet, and as she passed me the empty box for a Sofia Coppola movie, it seemed as though we were partaking in something heavy and deserving of gravitas. The whole thing felt like a coming of age ritual; I opened it up to levity with a sardonic comment and a wry smile that I wore uncomfortably, like a birthday party clown in a business suit.

'I thought girls your age only liked movies about little cartoon animals that are trying to find themselves', I heard myself say.

They turned to each other for direction, laughed with their hands over their mouths in tentative stupefaction. The Leader recomposed herself by pulling her hair out between her fingers.

'I grew out of that weeks ago', she said.

And then I turned back inwards.

I explained that it might take me a minute to find the disk they wanted, because stuff went missing all the time; we didn't really know what we were doing. I made orphic jokes to obscure references. They didn't get them and I felt stupid. It seemed that all they were capable of doing was watching me sift through gutter piles of disks and sleeves and boxes about the floor, trying to dig out Sofia Coppola, whilst she no doubt sat oblivious in a Hollywood mansion somewhere, hanging out with people cooler than me and drinking champagne. I began to sweat and heat up and have minor palpitations.

Whilst I was down with my head in the pile of disks, I could see them leaning in close to each other and talking about something. It shouldn't have intrigued me like it did, but I imagined the warm breath passing back and forth between them. I thought about riding it.

Certain parts of the Leader were starting to get the better of certain parts of me, hanging there, like ripe apples on a tree in the middle of this desert, this dried up sea that everybody was drowning in together, yet too afraid or distanced to ask each other for help. I imagined my arms around her waist and that perfect curve of her back as I pulled her towards me.

When I found her movie, I put it in the box and passed it on over to her. Rated eighteen, but I didn't ask questions. The Sycophant was thin and freckled with pasty skin, fraught with anxiety. As I threw her change across the counter like James Dean might, The Leader threw me a know-it-all smile. I assumed it didn't mean anything, that she was just being young and confident, and that she would have smiled like that to anybody.

I really thought that when they left it would be the end of it.

Chapter 6

After work, burned by the horn, I bought into the whole 'going for a run' thing. I dressed down and dowdy, old shorts and a faded *Kiss* t-shirt, then I did the best I could to keep up the pace as I hit the other side of the canal by the apartment. To get there I had to cross a bridge. It was the revolving kind, but I wasn't expecting things to turn around any time soon. I was just killing time and learning to feel proud of the fact.

The sun filled the sky and took my breath away, which can perhaps account for why I began to wheeze so quickly. A few fields down the line, it occurred to me that I was even unhealthier than I had led myself to believe, and so I stopped running and began to walk. Real runners passed me by, proud like animals, with empty eyes and slick attire right out of magazines. The trails of dust that they left floating down and about behind them spread like seeds of doubt in my mind. I began to question my self-worth as I stumbled after them, clutching my belly, and cursing the absurdity of it all.

Coughing, I thought about cigarettes. I hadn't brought any, so all I could do was keep on walking. I didn't know where I was heading. The path led me through a village and up a hill.

For a few minutes, I stopped to gaze at the tattered yard of a ramshackle church besides a village green. Nobody had been inside for years, so my intuition told me, its old coats of paint cracked and flaked and falling intermittently to the ground. And, as curtains twitched in the windows of houses behind me, I felt eyes on my back. It was the first time I'd ever ventured to this side of the canal and the houses were bigger with elaborately groomed gardens and ostentatious ornamentation that projected images of stylised rusticity.

The cars in the driveways shone like they might in TV commercials and sported detachable roofs. And, despite the furtive peering out of windows and twitching of drapery, the surrounding houses each felt cold and unoccupied, even though they carried trinkets on their window sills - like little glass beads, or toys from overseas. Neatly-trimmed lawns and shrubbery seemed to pull me closer with one hand and push me away with the other. Yet, all the while, I knew that not all of these houses could be empty and that I was being watched and analysed as an intruder.

The village green comprised a few benches and a lawn full of clinical daffodils with nobody there to enjoy them. A footpath cut along behind the side of a bush and up into the woods, and so I climbed on, sweating, with the first sun of the year on my face, expecting to find nothing, but looking for everything at the same time. For the first time in weeks, I felt a renewed lucidity. The lethargy of mind and sluggishness that had defined the days since I found myself back in the mire of lower-class reality evaporated, as though I were shaking off and out of a dream, or as though I were a man just pulled free of the grip of a fever.

I forgot myself.

Following the path up into the woods, I found myself amongst the trees. Unseen birds scuttled under faraway bushes as they tried to forget about me too. And though I knew it was the work of nature, the forest carried a stillness, not exactly a state of peace or tranquillity, but the perfect sort of trimness that you might find in the set of a B-movie, where everything is placed exactly where it ought to be, and where each tree looks like a prop, or the shade of each leaf has been pre-determined by some great set designer in the sky.

Beyond and up from the woods, the world opened up into pastoral splendour and open spaces that I had not realised I had been surrounded by. I knew I had been living in the basin of a valley but I hadn't paid attention to the vastness of the hills. When we're lost in the city, we forget that we are borne of something this empty and mysterious, and we begin to think that down there with the sounds of the traffic and the artificial lighting is all we need, but as I sat myself on a hill covered in odd, sporadic rock formations, I fell recumbent against a blanket of warm heather and looked to the clouds, as sunbeams laved like lake waters against chalky shores. I listened to the silence and then my eyes took to the horizon. The whole city awaited in the distance and I began to remember and awaken.

Down there, I thought. Down there are all my problems. There waits disease and money issues. Dissatisfaction. Down there are the things that I need or that I want. There are people that can't be shaken from my psyche, because their very existence has left me weary and disenchanted, but whom I must either learn to love and tolerate, or learn to avoid and forget about. Down there resides ambition and aspiration and all that keeps me from it. There rests the past as I have lived it and as it is to be remembered. There wait the people that I have loved and have spent time with and maybe will do again sometime. Down there awaits the present and drudgery and whatever comes after it. Down there is a lot I have to work at.

I fell back deeper into the grass and the heather beneath me as I watched the cars on the road slide like skittles over ice, as shards of light reflected off of windshields, a light show for me alone. I thought about the people in the cars looking out at the hills and wondering whether anybody was up here. I tried to put myself in their shoes, see things from their points of view, but there were too many of them living free and out on their own time; things I had nothing to do with. I tried to get back in tune with my own life and then I closed my eyes and when I awoke it was dark and time to head home.

Chapter 7

A few days later, after work, I was heading home through the town centre. We were always the last shop to close for the day and so it was rare to see anybody about, except for the drunks in the doorways, or the chavs, and the hangers-on. Usually, at that time it would seem that a great storm had just taken the city; newspapers would litter the streets in discordant order; drink cans and cigarette butts would be blown up against the sides of the kerbs. They'd scrape along as the winds carried them away to wherever it is that the gutters lead to, and so I would feel a strange sense of relief because, until that moment, I had thought I had been living there, wherever that place might actually be.

I was tired from poisoning my already poisoned blood with too much coffee and nicotine. It was light out but should have been dark, because there were no people around, and the street lights had turned themselves on, flickering ungraciously, as though tuned into to the irregular pulse of whatever it was that had happened to this shithole town. The moon was out in synchronicity with the sun, as though it was scared to show up in solitude, and as I walked the incline to the bus stop, I looked to the sky as though wounded, because it reminded me that I was alone. My feet were swollen and heavy from being stood on end all day and my trainers were tight because they were too small; I winced with each footstep as I convinced myself that my pathetic life was even more unbearable than I had previously led myself to believe.

On each side of the hill were dusty, unlit shop facades; a town of closed doors where all the shutters were pulled down like poker faces. Strangers passed me by with their hoods up. They spat on the floor. I got to the top of the hill and then from around a corner, with unplanned fluidity, appeared the Leader girl and her Sycophant. They saw me and giggled. I was out of breath and so I tried to pass them by with my head to the ground. When they were a few metres past me and we were away from each other, the Sycophant shouted in my direction.

'My friends likes you', she said.

And so I stopped in my tracks and turned back round.

We hung out in the park that backed the school fields up on one of the estates. We had to catch a bus to get there. It was beginning to get dark, dying gradually, a light bulb on the dimmer. On the way we walked about strange neighbourhoods, where people had toys sprawled out about their gardens, where fences had been torn off hinges and empty cardboard boxes, which had once had electrical appliances in them, sat on unkempt lawns like abandoned corpses. One house we passed had water flooding out of the door, asparagus green down some torn up porch, a tired-eyed woman leaning lost against the jamb, watching her grubby young child dance barefoot in water that trickled down onto the street. I felt high and got stupid about things, showing off and dancing around to make sarcastic jokes about pointless observations.

They asked me to get some wine from Tesco so I did and then we bought some cigarettes and sat around smoking them together. I hadn't had red wine with cigarettes in an age. It went straight to our heads. Little girls were easy to please.

With their thin knees up against their chests, they sat gazing through self-conscious squint eyes, as they contemplated the things that had happened to them, or the places they would or wouldn't be going to in their lives. They affected earnestness and understanding about the world, talking about the boys they had liked and done things with, through giggled admissions and broken eye contact. The Leader smiled at me, her lips like hot tongs, and as I smoked a cigarette down to the bones and drank more wine from the bottle before passing it along, I forgot about all my problems for a while, and felt that I had found the solution to it all. When the conversation wore thin, I'd peel the label off the bottle, curl the bits of paper into little balls, and I stare philosophically into the distance. I could tell they really thought I was on to something.

They talked about high school or college or whatever it was. They rarely went despite the government's best efforts, choosing instead to hang around the shops in the city centre and gaze listlessly through windows. They talked about one of the catalogue stores; it had a lawn table and some chairs set up inside of it. They used to go sit there and chat about whatever it is that girls talk about. Sometimes they'd get thrown out by the security guards. They always went back though. An endless cycle. They knew everybody in town and everybody knew them.

As the wine kicked in, I could feel my head loosen up and my inhibitions fade away. I sat up close to and put my arms around the Leader. Her shirt lifted with the pull of her back against the wall to reveal her stomach; I lit another cigarette and pretended that I hadn't noticed that the Sycophant was starting to feel negligible. She sat with her arms folded and stared on straight ahead, keeping her lips pursed, trying to hide her disdain for it all. The Leader leaned in and kissed my neck. Her breath was warm but it sent a shiver down my spine.

I lit another cigarette and stayed up cool against the wall. Not a word, just breathing and living and taking it all in.

When the sun had faded away completely, we pulled ourselves up from the floor, and walked through the school field and across the tarmac playground to the school buildings. We were drunk and in high spirits, kept shouting something obnoxious, but I don't remember what it was. She held my hand as the Sycophant, now sullen and malevolent, followed on behind.

The bushes that lined the school buildings were brittle and the distances between them were measured and regulated. The moon lit the windows and threw our reflections back in our faces. I took a running dive and leaped into one of the bushes. They laughed. I came out with scratches and blood and shards of green stuck to my limbs. The pain started to sober me up a little.

I looked around and drank in my surroundings, walked up to one of the windows and peered inside the classroom, the whole of the world in miniature. I could see a rug on the floor by a tiny bookcase and a neat arrangement of tiny chairs and tables spread about the room. There was a blackboard covered in white dust and, up around the rim of the ceiling, was a pictorial version of the alphabet, all the way from 'apple' to 'zebra'. I tried to remember how it was different to my own primary school classroom but the differences were infinitesimal. Flashbacks of finger painting and story times and tepid bottles of milk and uniforms; I used to be so easily impressed by things, I thought to myself. Why does nothing surprise me anymore?

She came up behind me, still drunk and laughing, and pulled me by the T-shirt, away from the window. I'd left foot prints in the flowerbeds and breath against the windows. The gap between my T-shirt and the sweat on my back started to cool me down. I looked at her as she looked up at me. The wine had run out about an hour or two ago.

'Where's your friend?', I asked her.

'She got bored and went home.'

'Oh'.

I looked as though I might have been concerned.

'Don't worry, she does it all the time.'

Taking my hand, she led me over to an alcove between two of the school buildings. An automatic security light turned itself on as we slid down against the wall but it didn't faze us. She dipped into the pocket of my jeans and pulled out the cigarette deck, lit one and passed it over to me, then lit another for herself.

'I used to come to this school', she said.

She pointed over at the classroom unit next to the one I had been peering through the window of. There were pictures on the wall, scribbles; abstract works of unfiltered intuition and unbridled genius.

'Did you paint any of those pictures?', I asked.

She smiled.

'Yeah, that one of Buckingham Palace over there.'

'I thought that was a dog.'

She responded with a cursory laugh then took in a burn of her cigarette. I was starting to get a headache. I looked at the paintings stuck up against the windows for all the world to see.

'When we're young we're so unaware of the fact that our lives are already over.'

I let out a sigh as she looked on at me and laughed.

'You're weird.', she said.

'Yeah'

I slumped back further and looked at her chest again. I felt a twinge of compunction. My favourite food was in the fridge but I wasn't allowed to eat it. There was a silence between us for a while, and she must have felt my gaze on her, because she turned to me and said:

'You can touch them if you want to.'

And then the world froze.

I lay her on her back against the slabs of concrete outside the classroom doorway, just in time for the automatic security light to turn out. Darkness fell over us like a cloud, but I could still see her because of the moon, and her skin was cool to the touch, and she started to get little goose pimples on her skin as I listened to her breathe.

When I looked at her laying there she seemed so very small and so very young and inexperienced to me that it tore me down the centre, a part of me wanting to unveil what I had been dreaming of, but my conscience telling me otherwise.

'Go on', she said.

And so I tugged down on her underpants. Her top inched up and revealed the curves of her hips. I could see her belly button and she let out a sigh.

'You can touch them', she said once again, as though there was an echo.

My eyes moved to the curves of her chest and I slid my hands up along the sides of her ribcage. The skin was warm beneath her sweater. I was getting closer. She closed her eyes.

From the door that lay beyond the alcove I glimpsed a reflection of myself and what I might have been about to do. Memories of sanctimony before being sent back here washed over me like a muddy rain, as I remembered myself with girls my own age, and with relationships and conversations and less bravado. I knew what the right thing to do was but the brain in my pants was trying to convince me otherwise. I put my lips down towards her mouth. We kissed and I didn't feel anything. She moaned like she must have done.

Running my fingers through a strand of hair on her face, I slid it behind her ears as I gazed at her. Pulling away and sitting myself back against the wall, I took out a cigarette and began to smoke it. I looked at her and felt sick. The alcohol wore off with a snap and I stood up and pushed my soldier back into his barracks.

'What is it?', she asked.

I kissed her once on the stomach and then I left her there and went home.

Chapter 8

Life had become a series of self-betrayals and bitter tasting delusions. I tried to convince myself that I could still be somebody, get back on track, and, time and time again, I said to myself that one day things would pick up again, that I'd have the operation and so things would go back to normal, just like before. But I knew that I was just fooling myself; I knew that this was just a coping device, one to keep me going, because, in truth, I had no idea what the future might hold, and there was no point making plans if you might die tomorrow, because even the plans of the people who probably wouldn't pass away any time soon would most likely be derailed when they least expected it.

It seemed to me that despite being once known for loquaciousness, I no longer seemed to speak to people anymore, just the customers at work, so that I could ask them for money, or give them prices and tell them the locations of things on shelves, so that they in turn could waste their money and go home lost and alone to stare at their TV screens. Even if I did have the operation, I had changed so much inside that I would never be able to relate to the people I had known before, the city types with their mortgage plans and their ambition; the successful ones with their savings accounts and their fast cars. The past year or so had forced upon me a humility and a timorousness, and these newfound sentiments told me that we were each the same, each of us trying and wanting and in need.

All the same, the vicissitudes had slowly reached a stand-still. Nothing happened for days. At work, everybody seemed to have come to terms with the fact that they were there and so became subdued and introspective, less likely to flaunt their egos, instead just slipping into the throes of a silent and mechanical routine, doing the things that were expected of them without question or subversion. It was one quiet morning after another followed by dreary afternoons. If you asked the manager a question he would tell you to:

'Fuck off.'

Or:

'Get fucked.'

Or:

'Try harder.'

And I kept thinking back to the other night at the school, trying to figure what I might have been doing right now, if I had boned the Leader, instead of playing into my conscience and disappearing like a thief that hadn't stolen anything, or a fox that had left the chickens safe in the pen, choosing instead to slink away with its tail between its legs. Maybe if I had caught a glance of what I'd really wanted to see, it would've stirred something in me, and I would have found the courage to quit my life of drudgery, or perhaps it would have taught me something, and I would have been hanging out and making out with her now, instead of standing here emasculated behind a counter, with a barcode around my neck, silently looking for meaning in a place full of goods that nobody really wanted.

She hadn't come into the shop since. We never swapped phone numbers. I prayed that distance would help us to both forget each other, but I still had flashbacks at moments that didn't suit me, and when I was home alone I would think about her and then feel dirty and strange and have to wash my hands with alcoholic lotions. I kept my eye on the door to see if she'd come to give me a second chance, a way to change my mind. Mao was waiting with me, with his broken arms, and every time I looked at him he seemed to know what I was thinking and he would seem to wink at me, but not as though he was colluding with me, that we were in it together, but as though he found my behaviour to be worthy of his disapproval, and as though he knew that I could fail at any moment, and that he would be laughing when I did, because there was nothing I could do about it.

I had only seen the Well-Dressed Man that one time, over on the shop floor, the grin of the Half Wit, the clean plastic squeak of sandal rocking, and the smog of mysterious conversation up and above us all. And, though the whole exchange could not have lasted more than five minutes, the amount of time that I had since spent reflecting on his words was inordinate. I kept thinking about the Big Guy Upstairs and figured that this was just an eloquent man's way of describing a Fat Man. And, as I found myself out drowning in a well-thawed lake of intrigue, I began to become paranoid that I was perhaps the victim of some elaborate trick, that he had seen a credulity or innocence within me that could easily be taken advantage of for his own amusement; one that he had found risible in some way, and that he had been unable to resist reeling me in with his sartorial supremacy and well-veiled machinations.

There is a doubt that all of us at the bottom feel in our most private moments, myself being no different, and it pulled me down to the extent that it only seemed sensible to conclude that the Well-Dressed man had looked down upon me and seen a simpleton, or a foolish dreamer, one that he could toy with for his own gratification. Perhaps to him I was nothing more than a loner on the shop floor in need of a little stimulation: a shot in the arm or a kick in the pants.

Still, though these nagging dubieties occasionally got the better of me, I would at other times find myself taking reversed stance: believing everything I considered the Well-Dressed Man to stand for to represent the unadulterated truth. I realise now that these prolonged periods of gullibility came at those times when I was at my most desperate, on the days when I would leave the shop feeling consumed, believing that this was forever, and that the rest of the world was judging me for it and that I had failed to live up to all the promises of human splendour.

I hadn't been able to see that this period was just one of many small chapters in my life, and that with each day that passed the pages would turn, and that soon it would all end perfectly and with closure, and that there would probably be nothing to worry about, because it had been reasonably well-authored for a first-timer, and was over as well as it possibly could be.

Back then, during lonely moments, slinking through the streets with my hands in my pockets, or sitting meekly on steamy-windowed buses whilst trying to avoid animal confrontation, this promise of The Fat Man stood as the only diamond in the mine. If I could seek him out, I felt, I would be able to find the answers that I needed. And so, despite the reservations that I had on the days when complacency had taken my soul, the dream of keeping the fire alive would be fuelled on those rare days when I was able to shake away complacency, a snake shedding its skins and slinking off into desolate places, from the underbellies of rocks into the vastness of the desert, for better tasting food and a new way of life.

The remarks of the Well-Dressed Man would haunt me:

'The Big Guy Upstairs has the answers to all of your questions.'

As though his words were a ring of nettles trying to keep me out of a field, but that if I could build up the courage to panga on through the thicket, I would find myself out free and in the meadow, everything I ever wanted and all I would ever need right beside me; all the time in the world in my hands and no fear of it ever running out.

I took another breath and counted to thirty.

Once I had determined that The Fat Man was my only way to salvation, I knew that it would only be a matter of time before the signs led us to one another. Deciding that it was inevitable helped me to stop worrying so much, as though I had slipped over my eyes a pair of glasses that were designed to show me only the richer colours of the world and with a complexity that I had before managed to overlook somehow, perhaps because I had previously been too full of myself, or because I doubted so much, or because I had forgotten that good things can happen to all people, regardless of their station in life.

I began to notice within myself an acute and growing awareness of coincidences, small things that happened to me which seemed to be linked by some greater force, what I believe Jung had called 'Synchronicity'. These coincidences would be few and far between, and usually small, like how I would learn of a new word on one day and then the next hear it fall from the lips of a stranger, or like how I would perhaps read about or hear of some book by some author I didn't know, and then find either that book or one that was somehow related to it in a charity shop somewhere, or left on a dirty table in the coffee shop.

When things like this happened, which they seemed to be doing ever more frequently and with increasing greatness and intensity, I would treat the event with a sort of veneration, stopping to think and learn whatever lesson could be garnered from it all; I devoured books that I found in waiting rooms, and read reams of newspaper pages, left open and waiting for me on the public transportation networks of the city. Everything had something to teach me, or so I believed at that time, and so I followed attentively and kept my ear to the ground and my eyes peeled for whichever clue came next in the series.

Then I started working backwards. I thought about my meeting with the Well-Dressed Man. When I considered the probability of my having been out on the shop floor when he came in, or the fact that I was working in the very section that he was browsing in, it seemed phenomenal. Thinking of our meeting as being anything but miraculous seemed ridiculous, and of course, as his words had left me being required to seek out and speak with The Fat Man, I could not comprehend anything but this being the next logical step that the universe wanted me to take. I would put all my energy into finding him, believing that it was the only option I had left for finding meaning in my life.

Then, I began to look back even further. I questioned my disease and realised that before it had afflicted me I had obviously been living my life in a way that deviated from the path that I was destined to be walking. I began to feel thankful for the nausea that I felt, that each symptom was in some way a blessing, despite the pain and the turmoil. And then I would feel myself sinking into a well of self-abasement and languor, yet trusting in it for fear of not knowing what else to do. I thought back to my childhood and the anguish I had felt, but then felt it evaporate and dissipate as I realised that, without any of those things having happened, I would not be here right now, walking the path that I knew would lead me to The Fat Man's door. It was a path I had been following my whole life.

But there was a problem:

There were too many fat people in town. You could hear them trundling round every corner.

Chapter 9

I had always noticed that there was something inherently wrong with the majority of customers that shopped in the store. And, though I'll readily admit that nobody's perfect, it occurred to me that the people I found myself dealing with on a daily basis were especially not so. I've already mentioned the bulk of their foibles, each a fine wine cocktail of: obtuseness, odour, and obesity. Perhaps it was because we dealt in second hand goods, meaning that we were cheaper than other places, or because we were in a deprived area, where anybody who had made it to be over thirty years old had slowly witnessed their confidence ebb away or their idealism crumble like the old bricks that surrounded us all.

Whatever it was, it had left wan little clouds of 'numbness' floating up and about our heads, as though everybody had given up, as though their feigned indifference to it all had eventually encroached upon their souls in toto, so that all they had to do with their lives now was to play video games, or collect movies that they didn't really care about, but felt defined them in some indistinct way. The rest of the time would be devoted to stuffing their faces some more or consuming more sugars and fats and then smoking more cigarettes to take all the pain away.

One day I took the bus into town, I was going to the hospital. Slinking through the inner city, we passed the local business school, a renovated building in the tenderloin embellished with banners of false promise: *Local Enterprise is The Future* or *We Can Do It.* I watched two surly looking youths stumble out the building, blank-eyed and out of touch, getting down in a beat up boy racer, blasting out the latest and greatest in 1990s house tunes, revving up and out of there, and on to their enterprising futures. Spitting out of windows and on to the road, staring at the girls that they passed and beating their heads to the music, as an older, sweatier fat man, smoking cigarettes and wheezing with his shirt tight up around his no-neck sat watching them from upon a wall.

His pits drenched with the blaze of the saturated photo sun and broken marbles of sweat bejewelling his hairless, rubicund head, I gazed listlessly through the bus window, inexplicably overpowered by the scene. It occurred to me that he was probably one of the teachers, and that he would probably be dead soon, not just because he was so green and feeble, but because he had lost hope and lacked the animation of spirit imbued by purpose. He wheezed some more as the bus shifted onwards. Each of us could die at any moment, I thought, but few of us will ever change anything before we do so.

Behind the tills, looking for signs and waiting for clues, I began to notice that the way I treated the customers of larger proportions became more respectful. Should a fat man come to me, for example, armed with the bags of junk that I was expected to give him money for, I would find myself being more amiable towards him, sanguine and chirpy as opposed to the curt and muffled utterances that I dealt with the regular, thinner customers in. Though it hurt my pride to give the impression that I were actually happy to be there, I convinced myself that it was actually a form of insurance, just in case I happened to be talking to the man that I was one day destined to engage myself in conversation with: He with all the answers.

The last thing a pious man would want to do is inadvertently offend his God and so, in my own way, I began to consider myself as having become a man of piety, because I was walking the holiest of paths and I had a mission. And though my god did not yet have a name, nor for that matter even a face, I knew that he was somewhere out there, and that, if my faith refused to waver, I would be rewarded with a moment of his time. At the end of each transaction, I would linger for a few beats as I handed over change and receipts to the customers. Looking deep into their eyes for surreptitious signs of a connection, perhaps a hidden wink, or a knowing lambency, I would pause until they either broke eye contact with me by walking away, or asked me what the hell my problem was, as though I were some object of disgust, to be dissected and analysed in front of everybody.

Figuring that birds of a feather might flock together, I began to treat fat ladies with a similar degree of reverence, ever hoping that they would know of The Fat Man's whereabouts, and that I might impress them enough to introduce me to him. But, alas, despite of days and weeks and months of sugar coating, prostration and ingratiating obeisance, not one of them gave so much as a hint of knowing, seeming only strangely flattered by the veneration with which I treated them, waiting and breathing for more, and then leaving at pace when they realised I had no longer had need for them.

All the while, in the back of my mind, my eyes were awake to the opportunity of being reunited with the Well-Dressed Man, as though he might be able to offer me some sort of short cut, a ladder instead of a snake, a less ambiguous clue, confirmation that his words were the truth and not the folly of a mind more cunning than my own. Whilst sweeping up the crisp packets and biscuit crumbs from the shop floor, I would peer through shelves and watch the people deliberate over what they might be about to purchase, what they should spend their money on, all the while hoping that their choices would lead me to destiny's door, or that some new clue would present itself and make my life a little easier. But, as the seasons changed, I found that I was still not any closer; behind the tills, I would keep my eyes on the door, gaze forever out the window, as my ears attuned to the sounds of sandal rocking, a Native American with his head to the ground awaiting approaching bison, ready to run out and on to the street at the slightest hint of being able to get a step or two closer to the answers that I needed and the promises of eternity.

Chapter 10

My co-workers began to think that I was normal, because I started to do everything that was expected of me, like how I would laugh politely at their stupid jokes, or pretend to be an enthusiastic member of the gang when they held collective drooling sessions over women on the Internet, or when I joined in with the butch and the bravado, whenever we found a picture of the tits of some chick that had sold her phone to us and forgotten to wipe its memory first. I helped them to feel decent and normal about themselves, by buying into the tacit agreement shared between us that meant we would read into each other's comments before responding to them, replying with whatever tone or information was obviously required of us: approval, acknowledgement, understanding, a sense of allegiance or unity, of us versus them; that everybody on our side of the counter was winning the game and that everybody over there, on the outside, was clearly losing it or out of touch.

Our words were used to prop up the scaffolding of each other's delusions, as though we were parenting each other, because if anyone dare admit the truth about themselves, that they were just one in a group of failures, then they wouldn't be able to go on living like this, stuffed low down and dirty in this bin sack of complacency, and they might have to change some things about themselves, or they might have to start working towards something, or look at themselves long and hard and in the mirror, through the eyes of men instead of just dreamers.

Collectively, there was a sense that it was too late, that we were too old and too stupid for potential to still be a part of our lives, that society had forgotten about us like we had once forgotten it, and so now we were left to either go on pretending, because the hardest thing a person can do is consciously change, or we could accept that the only thing we had really succeeded in was removing all sense of purpose and wonder from our lives and continue to meander through this endless space, through this life of barriers and mind games and endless competition, doing things that don't feel right or natural, but which we had no choice but to do anyway, because everybody else was doing the same thing, even though they didn't want to.

First we are born, then we dream; we are forced to compromise, and then we become complacent until we die.

The pantomime played daily between nine thirty a.m. and six in the evening and we all had our roles to play. I stood back cool and aloof and ad-libbed in my role as the Mild-Mannered Gentleman, condescending politeness, so polite it becomes an insult, pushing my luck with dumb superiors, giving minimum effort to receive my minimum wage.

Though I couldn't allow myself to consider the manager to have any authority above me out there in the 'real' world, I would submit to his will down there on the stage, as though some tractable farm animal. Maybe it was so the public would come in and see that somebody was in charge when they saw him barking orders at people, that it would add the colours of life to the performance, an unquestionable degree of verisimilitude that couldn't be toyed with; I'd interact with my co-workers in the same way, listen to their shit and smile with a mouthful, but, should I bump into them out and about in the public sphere, the badinage would be gone, as though a fire had been left over night, and now there were only a few embers as forgotten memories.

Sometimes on your shift, you might bump into somebody in the back stage of the staff room, see them broken enough for candid conversations where the rules and roles had gone out of the window, where you were allowed to see each other as souls instead of barcodes, listen to their tales of woe, and share the horror of their lives for a few unsatisfactory moments. But it hardly ever happened.

At the end of each show when the shutters had gone down, we would check each other's wallets and pockets to make sure nobody had been stealing parts of the Mise-en-scène, and then we would courteously wave our goodbyes to the CCTV cameras that had recorded the day's performance, the insensate eye, storing our lives on video tape, should a discrepancy arise. We'd give stock phrase goodbyes and receive like or nothing in return, and then I'd mope out of the door and into the street, beneath the dramatic skies and the clouds that could swallow me whole, wander to the empty train station by the old bridge so I could sit on vandalised benches, and wait for something to come and take me away from it all.

I began to think of myself as an actor, saying lines that weren't really mine, mouth on autopilot, whatever people wanted to hear, so they'd zip it and leave me alone. I became skilled in convincing my body to react in ways that dissembled the contents of my mind, because if I didn't I would only be able to get through the day with a series of grumbles and mismatched undulations filling the air between myself and whoever I might have found myself engaged in speech with.

Nobody else seemed to understand the mysteries of life, not that I had the answers to any of them, but nobody else seemed even to wonder where we had come from, why, or how it might have happened. Instead, they seemed genuinely convinced that the purpose of our lives was to make failed attempts at dressing in the latest fashions, abide by the laws of temporary fads and trends, download music from the internet, spend their days floating in the empty spaces between the shops in the town centre, the insides of their own heads, the void between the blue lights of the TV screen, and the sofas that they sat on, where old crumbs from toast and biscuits sat moulding in the cracks between cushions

Without the masks of politeness or reserve, I could no longer speak with people, as though I was locked deep within myself, that outside the house the sun was shining, but in the living room was a deluge.

I didn't know where to turn. On the bad days I'd be near the end, on the good, I'd feel a strange elation when I walked through the streets, as though I alone might be on the verge of the discovery of some great secret, one that Joe Public was too slow to get his head around; the one that would set me free. Perhaps it was society that was the cause of my discontent, its structures, and the way it worked. I saw a new enemy in the face of anything that went against the natural order, things that didn't exist in the animal world, but which the human being had created, either physically or mentally - buildings, organisations, rules and customs, ways of doing things. I dug out an old camera and started talking photographs of street furniture, or abandoned buildings, hoping that analysis of the way we had chosen to develop our surroundings would tell me something about the mysteries of it all

Perhaps society would eventually collapse in the same way as those buildings, I thought, because they had both been built by the same force. Maybe the signs and signals and lights around every corner would speak to me, if I could just understand their language; I spent long nights on the linoleum floor of my kitchen, staring at them, digital photographs, wondering about the ultimate fate of the universe. It was hot so I kept the windows open.

There was a proud old building in the centre of town with rusting iron girders exposed like cuts through flesh to the bone. It used to be a theatre. Years ago, it had been closed down because people had become tired of pretending in front of one another, and so now they just walked past it as though it wasn't there. Homeless people sat outside it now and begged with torn paper cups from Starbucks, this particular area of the town having degenerated into a magnet for the kind of energy suggestive of dereliction or decrepitude, as if the homeless felt that they had finally found a place which made them truly feel welcome, where they could sit huddled into themselves, and where their forms could adopt the shapes of black plastic bags of unwanted junk that some virtuous office worker had dumped outside a charity shop one morning.

The Victorian walls of the building had holes in the bricks, chips missing, pushed out by weeds, and abraded edges . Yellow warning signs with black writing adorned the front and said: 'DANGER ASBESTOS!' or: 'DO NO ENTER 24 HR SECURITY' and carried silhouette pictures of stern looking men with glowing eyes and uniforms and torches and Alsatians by their sides. The colouring of the old dome roof had faded, like the untended photographs of some dead relative left upon your window ledge, and the bricks were beginning to see themselves go the same way, as though the whole of life had unexpectedly become anti-saturated, different shades of grey, boarded up windows and gutters that needed clearing, but probably never would be. Nobody knew what to do with it; just one big problem, right in the middle of the city, neglected by all, despite the secret awe that they felt towards it, a metaphor that nobody could understand, analogous to each of us that lived here, and just as ignored and uncared for.

One night, I approached with my camera. Across the road from the empty theatre was another abandoned building, not as old as its cousin across the street; screaming prefab, nineteen sixties concrete, flat and uninhabitable, except for pieces of machinery, and two-tone computer screens that flashed deep through the night like digital fireflies at the foot of some long abandoned mountain. I couldn't tell what the building might have been. It offered no clues. Regardless, I set my camera up on the wall around the perimeter and adjusted my shutter to capture what I would perhaps consider to be the 'essence' of the theatre across the street. It was dark and people streamed by as though shadows of the night itself; some were drunk, screaming in high spirits; some were sober and screaming for reasons known to them alone.

I set the shutter speed to sixty seconds, the camera resting on the wall around the non-descript building, taking in any light that it could find; stolen streaks from the backs of passing cars, out of synch traffic lights, or the burning embers of cigarettes in the hands of passers-by. Neon fuzz of mobile phone screens sent motes of light through the eye of the lens, as people walked down the street sending text messages, sharing trivialities, so they need not feel so alone. People poured out of pubs and crawled out of night club doors, or the backs of taxi cabs and into the night, drunk and listless and on their ways home. I kept my eyes open for salient fat people, but there were none that stood out as being the one with all the answers. If anything, everybody around here looked more lost than even I was, having stopped looking for answers long ago, and instead convincing themselves that distraction was the only way to saviour.

As the shutter made its way down to zero, I saw a man approach me beneath the street lights. He was haggard and attired in dirty clothes that he'd obviously been wearing for a long time; tracksuit bottoms and withered space age sneakers, juxtaposed against his primordial confusion and sluggish posture. Taking insouciant, almost French-like steps towards my place on the wall, he stopped sporadically to count upon his fingers, an intense but delicate concentration in his eyes as his lips trembled, and he craned his neck upwards towards the starry sky and attempted cognition.

There was a veil of stubble about his chin, though I didn't get the impression that this was a conscious fashion choice on the man's behalf, more like he had forgotten how to shave, so I imagined, or perhaps he had never been shown how, because daddy had run away and he had been forced to grow up hard and alone. His emaciated face and tired eyes lent credence to my musings, accentuating the image with the tale that they told of strife and worry, and of anguish and disappointment.

Anxious, I tried to direct my eyes away from his gaze and to focus on the light being exposed to my mechanical eye. I checked in on the viewfinder and saw that only ten seconds had passed. Time was dwindling like the dying ends of an uncomfortable telephone call. I looked up and he was still there and so I was forced to do my best and look right through him.

But before I had a chance to even blink, he had taken a place next to me on the wall. He didn't mention the camera, nor question what I might be doing. He didn't even introduce himself. Instead, he just said:

'I can't read or write.'

Then he pointed to the clock tower of the city hall, which stood behind us, a light house to stop the fools like us crashing into the banks of tardiness.

'Does that say ten o'clock?'

And I confirmed that it did. He thanked me and was about to leave, but then he saw the camera, that it was pointed at the theatre, and, for some reason, it made him stop in his tracks. Looking at me as a sick tiger might some rodent it may or may not want to eat, he inched ever closer to me on the wall. It was cold and our breath began to condense. He opened his mouth and tried once again to allow his brain to turn over the new information it had just processed but he couldn't find the words. Instead the two of us just sat in silence, staring at the camera between us on the wall, waiting for the remaining thirty seconds of exposure time to dry up so that we'd have something to talk about.

Cars and taxis and buses went by; I watched the traffic lights change. People crossed the road, some at the appropriate times, others in between traffic, darting with their heads forwards and carrying themselves as though they were invincible, because in their minds that's what they were, far removed from the realities of a physical universe. And then, finally:

Click.

I had captured the essence.

I reached out for the camera, quite forgetting about The Counter sat beside me. He was calm and poised, very Zen and quite motionless. Somehow, without my being able to pre-empt his moves, he snatched the camera away, before I could even find the time. I looked at him but his eyes told me I best not say anything; instead, I should listen to what he has to say and take it on board, like my life might depend on it.

It was a sign.

'If you want to understand the moment', he said, 'you are best off living it instead of toying with these infantile fantasies about being an artist, or about being creative, or about seeing the world from your own unique perspective. We are all of the same species and we are much more connected to each other than they would like to have us believe.'

I tried to take the camera from him. But he wouldn't let me.

'How do you know that if you can't even count?'

'Because there is only one of everything', he said. Then he paused, because he could tell I was the kind of person who was at the stage in life where pseudo-profundity would be instantly overwhelming.

'If you need to understand something, be it a building or a person or even a dream, you are best off seeing it from the inside.'

And then he turned the camera around and showed me that the picture I had taken was nothing more than a sheet of white, a blank screen from being exposed to too much for too long; a useless photograph on account of its looking too intently from the same perspective, finding the wrong kind of light in the wrong places, and assuming that it could capture the essence of anything from such a limited and extrinsic vantage point. He handed it back to me and I put it in the case before he had a chance to change his mind.

I stood up to leave, but he pulled me by the arm and back down to the wall.

'Have you got twenty pence, mate?'

I emptied my wallet for change and gave him all the twenty pence pieces that I could find in there, then I walked as quickly as I could to the bus station and got on my bus and went home.

Chapter 11

I bumped into the Sycophant in the town centre; she still had the same look on her face, like she was half expecting somebody to beat her in it, and so she kept looking around nervously, flinching, with her mouth agape and her eyes wide open.

I was on my lunch break, heading to get a pasty, something which recently I found ever more irresistible, and when we both saw each other I could see in her eyes that she would rather not talk to me, and I was tempted to treat her in the same way.

Unfortunately, my curiosity got the better of me and so I cut through the crowds of drones and foreigners and b-boys that populated the streets in the day time, and I stood directly in front of her, so she couldn't escape, and then I attempted to strike up a conversation, as though a match against a soggy box.

'Hey,' I said. But she seemed to be too busy to be bothered with small talk.

'If you just wanna know about the Leader, then you can ask me.'

And so I did:

'Yeah, what's happening with that?'

She looked at me and for the first time stopped being so nervous, like she was intent on telling me something, but couldn't quite figure out how.

'You should really call her and find out.'

And that was when I explained that I didn't ever get the Leader's phone number, although I didn't explain that it was because I had been too weak-willed to sleep with her, and that I had just run off and left her there at the school like that.

'Is she angry with me?', I asked.

'What do you think?', said the Sycophant.

Then she double-checked that I had the number and took her fraught face off through the crowd as though we were two people that had never met before and that nothing really mattered anyway because one day everybody would be dead.

I called the Leader on the telephone. From the way that she spoke I could tell she was in a room full of childish things, like perhaps there were posters on the walls of plastic pop stars giving the impression that they were down with the streets, or perhaps she still had stuffed toys or Barbie dolls set around her bedside table, and that instead of the bland patterns that real adults adorn their duvets with, she would have some kind of cartoon animal that was trying to find itself and a way to be accepted in the world, because in the eyes of her parent or parents, she was probably still a child, something to be protected and isolated, and had never left the realm of childhood for the one of phallic objects and wet vaginas and lust and smutty discovery out in public spaces. I felt dirty and ashamed.

It was about eight p.m. when I called her up. The Sycophant had most likely informed her by now that we'd exchanged numbers and I had been enjoying the thought of The Leader living in anticipation of my call, because I wanted to believe that I was still an important person; somebody of worth, or if not, at least somebody whose existence could still have a minor effect on the lives of other people.

She answered the phone in a tone that suggested certain dubiousness, a more high-pitched edge to her utterances than I had remembered, rising intonations and sticky inflections, as though an electric current was flowing through her veins. I sat back into the dusty chair of my living room, the lights out and the sounds of the geese attacking each other on the canal outside. I sat sideways with my legs over one arm of the chair and then I tried my best to act like I was in control of things, when, to be honest, I knew in the back of mind that I was far removed from the helm of the ship, and was much more truly lost out to sea.

'Oh', she had said upon recognising my voice, 'It's you...'

And I wondered if perhaps she hadn't been expecting my call after all, because she didn't sound particularly excited to be speaking with me. But then, it occurred to me that perhaps she was still embarrassed about how our last encounter had finished up. And so, to relieve the heavy burden of the past, I opened things up with a factitious nonchalance, as though I were totally fine with things, as though they couldn't have happened in any other way because that's just the way the cookie crumbles. I acted as though the past were irrelevant and that now was the only moment that mattered.

'I saw your friend the other day. She looked scared but she gave me your number.'

'I know...' said The Leader, 'I thought you might have called sooner.'

And then there was this pause, as though we were at a train crossing waiting for a train to pass, even though we didn't really want it to.

'I'm sorry about the other night', I said, 'For just running away like that.'

'It's okay. I thought it was kind of sweet in a way', she said.

54

I couldn't decide whether I wanted to meet up with her again. I knew that I shouldn't, because it would most likely lead to places I didn't need to be going. I was tempted to forget it all and make small talk about the weather, or about how my day had been at work, or about the guy that I'd met outside the empty theatre. But, before I got a chance to say anything, she said:

'I think you should know something...'

'What is it?', I asked.

'I'm pregnant.'

And she hung up the phone and I didn't know what to do.

Chapter 12

For the next few days, the regular haze that I bumbled from one place to another within seemed more fog-like, darker, mistier; a miasma of other people's cigarette smoke, fag ends, and conversations that never really began and didn't seem to end either. I didn't know what it could mean, that the Leader had fallen pregnant and had taken it upon herself to attribute the germination of the thing growing inside of her to be because of something I had done. I started to wonder if I had slept with her; I had often done things that I had failed to recollect, but never before of such magnitude, of such ill-lit proportions, or such gravitas. I became more introspective, my eyes looking at the world around me without taking it in. I stumbled and fell. Nobody noticed.

Whenever I tried to call her again, the sound of the ringing phone would suck the air out of my empty apartment. I'd sit in the chair, legs over the side and head against my hands; another thing to be waiting for and no control over the process of killing the time. I didn't know where she lived. I didn't know where the Sycophant might be. There was no such thing as email because the Internet had been cut off, and I had no time for delving into the mysteries of where people reside, or how I might go about finding them, despite this being the information age, where everybody else is supposed to be persistently accessible and under twenty four hour scrutiny.

At work, I resigned myself once again to the shop floor, a piece of dog shit on the soul of humanity's shoe, organising and filing and trying to bring order to the piles of dirt, and the fading, out-dated products. I felt right at home with everybody else's garbage. It became an extension of my true self.

During these periods of fatigue and under the cloud of lethargy, my ability to see colours became increasingly heightened, like how I would pick up a Bruce Willis movie from the ominous morass of shelves and see streaks of green behind my eyes, or how I would brush my hand over something directed by Michael Bay and see great fields of yellow against purple horizons, as I waited for whatever music was playing to stop, so that I could shield my eyes from the fuzz of white behind peoples whispers, or the intermingled neuron browns of police horse hooves in the streets and the silver streaks of a MacDonald's door opening and closing with careless abandon.

Nobody had ridden my back for months. Though I'd been living in Sartre's hell of other people, I had somehow managed to carve out a niche for myself, a safety deposit box to live in, right out in front of them all, where by the barriers of politeness or sarcasm alone I had managed to distance myself and keep the world at arm's length. Everything I had worked at had been perfunctory; a fake smile from behind dead eyes as I handed the change on over to some slack-jawed patron, the loose alphabetising of stock in the filing shelves, correct but not perfect, nodding and agreeing with everything that management said despite an obvious disdain. Blah. Blah. Blah. The days continued.

But, in my new state, I could no longer keep on top of things. My head was too full of questions and I was too tired of waiting to keep up with the bullshit that was supposed to constitute daily life, by which I mean those things like making other people feel like they're more important than they really are, or by paying your taxes, comparing yourself to other people, telling yourself that everything you've done to lead you here was the only way that things could have been, and so you'll act accordingly, to fit in with the rest of these screw-ups and really try to make it work. That phrase: 'make it work', just means that you're finally willing to compromise. And I wasn't.

Walking the streets on an afternoon, I would see cats asleep upon sun-baked shards of grass, beneath the shades of trees, or on doorsteps; I would see dogs down by the canal, jumping free and into waters. That spontaneity of the animal world, true spontaneity, not the marketed pseudo, saturated version that equates to impulse buying, is what distinguishes beast from man. I would think to myself that somewhere along the line, sometime long ago, the human animal had lost touch with his animal purpose, perhaps when he had learned to feel guilty for its selfish crudeness, its gnashing teeth, the blood on its lips; when he had discovered his arsehole. Somewhere along the line, we had become detached from whatever it is that we were, or what we could be, and now we were doomed to walk the earth until we destroyed it, feeling lost and incomplete and unsure of what to do with ourselves.

Once again, the Supervisor reared his sweaty head, seeing that I had fallen, yet determined to push me further. When you're down and you're weak, it is human nature for the rest of the herd to see how far you are really willing to go. Perhaps this is because they feel that one day you may bring something back with you, or perhaps it is just because they are confused, believing that you are in this competition with them, this great game, whatever it is, and so they will try their bests to break you, to vanquish any promise of their being something more than *this*, because they are scared of what that means for themselves. Knowing that I neither cared nor wished to retaliate, he would peer over my shoulder and scrutinise, bark orders as though they were bullets, belittle me because he knew I felt bad enough about myself to take it, and then he'd beat me with sticks, kick mud in my eyes, and press my feet into hot coals whilst he told me I wasn't worth a damn thing.

When people feel that they are broken or defective, they will try their very bests to destroy the things around them that they consider to be less or more so. Misery loves company and the Venus de Milo wants to break your arms; it's the natural way of the world, because we all want to believe that there's nothing more than what we have managed to build for ourselves, even if it is without foundation or because we didn't really work at it and just let it fall into place. We get older and we trick ourselves into believing that we have done our very bests, even though we know in our hearts that, in most instances, this is simply not to be the case.

I took each punch as it came, because I did not consider my working life to be my real existence, just a temporary imitation of a lifestyle until I discovered my true, higher self; the 'Me' that knows purpose and that is capable of finding the divine in even the most mundane of his actions. And so, for this reason, I considered each deflection that I encountered, in relation to the once youthful ideal I once harboured of 'now', the age I had found myself at, to be just another fork in the road, another trial, another tribulation, another obstacle to be overcome, just like in the movies. Despite it all, I had a vision of how the future might be. And I told myself it was good, even though in relation to the past the chances were minimal. My vision was the carrot and I was my own donkey and, if I didn't keep plodding on in some form or another, I would be whipped and left to bleed by the side of the road.

People become depressed in today's society because anger has to be turned inwards, because it is no longer acceptable to display it outwardly, and so we fill ourselves with an overflowing reservoir of emotions that we can't hardly handle, and eventually this cripples us, leaving us to stand in the road as the cars come hurtling towards us and the drivers beep their horns.

My ego had found a way to convince itself that some things were more important than others and, if I just kept my faith in the promise of The Fat Man, of the answers, then I would be able to walk away from all these issues and to keep my dignity intact as I did so. There were people that began to confuse my apathy for stupidity, or to think that I were some tractable object to be pushed around, and because I would do what was needed of me, instead of having that 'fuck you' attitude that everybody else learned from MTV, or the movies, it seemed to them that I had no plans for my life, or that I was wasted and confused and down and out, like everybody else secretly believed themselves to be. But I wasn't. I sucked it all in like a sponge, and then I redirected the energy into my quest. None of them knew that they were watering the flower that I had planted in my belly, the ragged-edged orchid that feeds itself on its own tears upon an evening, and so I kept breathing and flowing and taking energy from one place and putting it into another, and then I knew that, when it was time, I would be ready to truly walk away from it all. To close the door.

And now, to add to my list of questions, *'How can she be pregnant?'*, because I was certain that the doctors had told me that, because of the chemotherapy, my seed was on hiatus for at least another month or two, and I was certain that we had not slept together, even though I could remember her breasts beneath that shirt, and those hips up above the concrete of the school, and knowing that I had and still desired it.

My priorities were changing with each day that passed. Months ago this thing, 'life', had been purely about survival, but now the quest for the elixir had taken me down the sewer pipe, on an incontrollable current that shat Fat Men in my eyes, and mysterious finger counters outside of theatres, and elusive strangers in better clothes than mine. And, now this: a phantom pregnancy that I somehow knew I would be prepared to take the blame for. It was all too much.

My circuits blew some more; colours I had never seen before and couldn't even describe in words if I had wanted to; a whirlpool of dirty paint water, an acrylic oil slick. In times like these, when there are too many ways to head deeper into the maze, you can only wait for signs, and so that was what I did, convinced that destiny was my saviour, because I had nothing else to look forward to and no other way out.

I loitered about the shop floor, pretending to sweep, though the broom was covered in dust; pretending to reorganise shelves, when I was just reading the blurbs on the backs of DVD boxes, hoping that some sign imbued would show me a way out of here. On lunch breaks, I would try and call her. The times she didn't hang up straight away, I would leave messages on her answer phone, my voice becoming more agitated each time I heard that *meep* sound. All the way from:

'Hey, it's me... Gimme a call.'

To:

'Pick up the fucking phone...'

But it was always the same and she never answered. I'd look down at the watch on my hand, at Mao's broken arms, counting the seconds between minutes, waiting for something to happen, instead of trying to make it.

Then, out of the blue, it occurred to me that if you are waiting for a sign to come then you will not receive one, because I had once heard some clap-trap about how people who want something are unlikely to get it. And so, I decided to pretend that everything was fine, that I was not waiting at all, but that I was doing.

And I hoped that by doing this, I would be able to trick whatever force it is that sends these signs to us mortals, these coincidences, these turns of phrase which we imbue with meaning, or these random acts which can suddenly change our whole lives, into sending me exactly what I needed, because I no longer had morals, and so only chaos could guide me through my life. And I was prepared to wait for infinity to conquer the wilderness of desolation. Regardless of the cost.

I got sick of making the phone calls. I refused to do it anymore. I told myself that I should respect myself, even if I didn't have a need to, and then I marched about the streets with an inflated and false sense of purpose, having converted myself to the Church of Me, a statue of myself as an object to be worshipped, resting on some tenuous pedestal, ready to break, but unable to do so for fear of the consequences.

Chapter 13

Everywhere I went I saw babies: hanging out in push chairs in front of shopping centres, being pushed around by track suit adorned parents who blew cigarette smoke in their dear little faces, or popped illegal pills and tablets, but refused to use bad language in front of them for fear of being seen as 'bad' parents. They'd keep coming into the shop, families like armies, selling toys or movies that they thought the kids wouldn't miss any more, explaining that this nice man behind the counter was going to give them some money for it now, that they didn't need it no more.

Little girls would parade around dressed in Alice costumes, growing up and stuck down the rabbit hole, and I'd get shot at with toy guns, space rays and wild west, and so I'd shoot back with my fingers whilst parents looked on at me warily, like I might be the next serial killer they'd been told to anticipate, or another stranger with illicit motives, the fabled enticer with puppies, or candy, or other objects from nursery rhymes. The kids would lick at the shelving units as their parents looked on oblivious, then they'd mess up the shit on the shelves, but it was ok, because they were primitive and young and that was what they were supposed to do as the embodiments of chaos itself.

I'd look down at my hands, my swollen veins and the scars across my wrists, the cracked white must of my fingers, products of time and consequence. Everybody around me had once upon a time been inside their mother's stomachs; it was a fact that everybody knew, but ever since spilling out had done nothing but try and avoid or deny. I hadn't spoken to my parents in years. I wondered how they were doing.

After work, I returned to the old theatre; I knew that it was important to my quest, but I wasn't sure why. With all of the other objects that I had been seeking out lost to the mist, a visit to the theatre seemed to be the only logical step to be taken; I went back once the sun had gone down, when the dusk had set in, because I didn't feel that I could deal with people in the daylight, not without my mask to wear, adlibbing the role of God's Shelf Stacker, knowing exactly what to say and when, on account of the role's boundaries and limitations. At night time, I didn't have to be afraid, because I could see that everybody else was, by the ways in which they kept their eyes to the ground, or wore their hoods up over their heads, and puffed out their chests. There would be talk in strange languages and as usual they would spit on the floor when they passed, but at night time it didn't seem to be such an act of degeneration, because this was a big city, and the moon was out and this was exactly how you would expect things to be. Darkness is supposed to bring out the worst in us.

It wasn't late, but the traffic was down. The town was in pieces, anyway, and there was nothing to do on an evening, because all the pubs had run out of money and shut their shutters, and all the buildings that were still able to stand without scaffolding housed shops, like the one that I had found myself chained to, or the pound shops, where everybody bought their Christmas presents, or the mini-supermarket, by the old stone stairs, where the kids hung out after dusk and threw beer bottles at passers-by; or the 'Museum of Culture' that hung above it all, like some huge, ironic punch line, because we all knew that there was no culture, unless dwelling on the past is what counts, and hating the present is what constitutes it, and fear of the future is what we are collectively entitled to look forward to.

I stood in the road as the traffic slunk past and hissed like steam emissions at the back of some CO2 factory in a layman perception of China. I saw yellows and greys, mist on mountain tops, heard an eagle scream. The Chavs peppered the night in groups of three or four, scowling as they broke the night in.

From where I was standing in the road, the ancient theatre seemed even more imposing than before. The clouds shifted past behind it as though a painted backdrop and, for a moment, I considered that this play I was taking part in had extended its boundaries and had taken me out of the realm of the sublunary or the mundane and into the strange. Indeed, by now the play had become a living thing, a breathing organic entity that I had little or no control over. In fact, I began to realise, I wasn't in a play at all; I was the one being played, and there was little I could do about it. I thought back to the last time I had been in this place, the words of The Counter:

'If you need to understand something, be it a building or a person or even a dream, you are best to see it from the inside.'

And so, for lack of any other options, I decided to take heed of his word.

On the other side of the road, tied to a lamppost outside the theatre, were the dead petal remnants of a flower wreath memorial to somebody who had been run over by a car. I headed on over to see if the fragrance had lingered despite the shrivelled decay of fugacity, but the smell was only fetid and rotten, and the petals had become viscid, as though our memories are to be short-lived anyway, and then they become tarnished with all the intricacies of what must follow.

Lingering as though in need of being forgotten, the buses passed me by as I stared at people on the back seats, as the racer boys would shout out of the windows of their daddy's cars, and occasionally people would grunt to try and shock me, but I wasn't scared anymore because I knew I had more to think about.

I headed around the side of the building and was greeted with more of the same: signs showing that security guards with torches in their hands and dogs by their sides were awaiting intruders, that there would be prosecutions and criminal records that may affect my future employability. Here, by the back of the building, the lights were empty and vapid; just myself and my shadow congregating with a collection of empty bins, cracked paving stones, and broken windows.

I looked up towards the roof, straining my neck. More weeds around the perimeter, silhouettes before the light of the moon, and the back of the dome roof that stood still intact from the front of the building, was crumbled and long since fallen. I climbed up on to the top of one of the large bins, despite the odour of empty staleness, and as I climbed up and onto it, my hands and my knees found themselves seeped in puddles of day old rain water, and so I wiped it into my face to cool it down, because I was feeling hot and nervous.

The building had died long ago, but I knew that there were still enough bricks remaining for us to build a relationship. From where I was standing, down the dead end of the alley, I could see the shaft of lights from the main highway in the distance, and still people shuffled past in groups, or by themselves, and still the cars hissed by, and I felt the colours of all the world's motion. I wondered how I could get up and into the building; I considered my options from this new vantage point, a few feet higher, and it seemed to me that if I could shift the bin a few feet or more down the alley, I would be able to climb up to one of the windows, and perhaps remove the grill that covered the glass. The rusting bin grated against the cracks in the floor as I got behind it; I looked to the street lights, fearful that I had piqued the unwanted attention of passers-by, but the noise just made people move faster and disappear into the night time.

As I climbed and smashed the window, shards of glass began to fall to the floor. They tinkled and shattered and scattered amongst the puddles on the ground, my heart fluttering, as though there was a bird stuck in my chest and wanting to escape, because I had seen those signs with the dogs and the guards, and I didn't perceive myself as being brave enough to face their wrath.

I wanted to run, but it was a dead end alley and this made my heart beat tenfold, and so I stared into the lights, at the entrance to the alley - intent, like a rat in a corner. I thought I heard sirens getting louder, coming towards me, ready to take me, and I imagined what it might be like for me in jail, with my health condition. Panicked, I climbed inside the bin, despite the smell, and I closed the lid as much I could whilst still being able to peek out, and I waited as the sound of that thing in my chest echo bounced from the chamber of the night.

It was only when I had become quite satisfied that the sirens had melted into nothing that I pulled myself out and back beneath the window. Nobody came. Nobody would. I thanked the apathy that had taken men's souls, because I was certain that somebody had heard the noise I had made, but I also knew that most likely they didn't care. I paused and breathed and recomposed myself, and then I set about removing the knives of remnant glass from the windowpane, shimmied up the wall and pulled myself through. I felt a chill through my spine, as I thought about the glass I might have forgotten, but slid through without a scratch. As I wiped myself down and looked around at the place I had found myself in, I began to wonder what it might mean.

I just knew I was getting closer.

Chapter 14

The palpable warmth of the odour bowled me over with the intensity of its colours as the cracked glass, and the shards beneath the window, pane glistened beneath the moon. As pallid streaks of light broke down and out across the musky chamber, they sent out pale undulations and shimmering reflections that dwindled like dying fire flies at the end of some long-forgotten summer. I began to shiver and then I yawned at the same time.

Finding myself staring into the darkness of an ensuing corridor, with an intensity and ill-directed focus that I had seldom before experienced, I began to forget about and lose all consciousness of my body. It was as though, for a solitary moment or two, I had become my mind alone and so, thus transported to the nonphysical realm, I felt strangely at peace within myself and my situation, as though finally I had managed to realign myself with the path of paths and to walk in tune with the gentle beat that epitomised destiny's marching song.

Taking comfort in these metaphysical rationalisations, I slowly came back to down to earth, returning once again to the dualist union of a mind and body, intertwined and ensnared within the limits of the physical realm. Trying to focus on my hands alone, I stared at them listlessly in the dark as I reflected upon mental causation and the mysteries of mind-body interaction, the nature of how we interact with the world around us, and the fact that one day these hands will turn to dust, be food for the worms, and thus controlled by none at all, besides the elements.

If I could focus on my thoughts alone, I told myself, if I could stay perfectly and totally still, then I could convince myself that I had been living out this moment for all of my eternity, that I had just been born perhaps, and that this moment could be the seed from which the rest of my life would sprout. Once again, I took deep, almost inebriated inhalations, then I looked around me, in what little light there was, as I tried to understand the purpose of the womb I had found myself in and the gifts that it might have to offer.

As far as I could tell, I had come through the window at the top of a stair case, situated between at least two other flights of stairs. I stopped to think for a few moments, to make up my mind about whether it would make more sense to climb or to fall, and in the resulting silence of my inactivity, I thought that I heard voices floating up towards me from down below.

Down in the darkness, as though calling to me from the unknown future, I could hear the distant sounds of some indistinct tune. Upon closer inspection, I managed to determine that the ghostly air was almost militaristic in its execution, as though some lamentable exhortation were being amplified, or somebody were trying to incite something. But what could it be? And why? Its incongruity seemed almost unholy to me.

I held my breath, in both fear and anticipation, still as an old rock, almost paralysed as rampant speculations and trepidations assailed my sense of self-worth. Perhaps it originated from the outside world, out beyond the night, where the real world unfolds and the people go about their business. But when I put my ears to the broken window, I realised that this simply couldn't be the case. For those few moments even the sirens seemed to have ceased and the wind had stopped its hum; the traffic had given up hissing and the boy racers were on strike.

No doubt about it, the muffled commotion and mysterious exhortation was rising up towards me from the blackness of the basement. But it simply couldn't be, could it? This building had been closed for close to a decade, maybe longer, left broken and falling to pieces. Perhaps it was the security guards, the ones that I had been warned about outside, on the signs, with the Alsatians. But why would they be listening to this unholy music? And at such a volume? At such an ungodly hour?

Too scared to go down and face the unknown, but too curious to head back out of the window and into the mundane reality of barcodes and self-abasement, I took my first tentative footstep up towards the top of the building. The feeling that I was about to learn something of great importance, something that were to change me forever, began to tug on my sense of purpose as though the strings upon a puppet. Volition was just a word, I told myself, just like everything else. Everything is predetermined. There is nothing that can be done about it. It is already done.

As I held on, amidst the dark, to the side of an old railing, wet and unwholesome with years of dirt and negligence, the sounds of the marching music escorted me the whole while. Becoming fainter, the higher I climbed, it felt as though the air were getting thinner. And so, as I forced myself to continue up the stairs, I felt my breath become laboured and my legs become heavy, which in turn enervated my mind and reduced my false sense of security and purpose. I began again to waver.

Though I had seen the building from the outside a hundred thousand times before, and knew that there couldn't be far for me to go, I had to keep telling myself that I must almost be at the top. And, even though I felt certain that there couldn't be much farther to go, I somehow managed to convince myself that it might take forever, as though I were somehow an incarnation of Sisyphus but the rock which I had to contend with resided within and weighed me down completely.

I clambered the next flight in a mild panic, feeling more comfortable with my surroundings now, but still shrouded and encapsulated within the utter isolation of the darkness. My confidence fell away from me like a snap of the fingers; I had to reach out in front of myself and grasp for the stairs. Broken and loose and infirm, I began to tremble, because I had visions of falling, down through each flight of stairs and into the jaws of whatever it was that was waiting for me down there. Down in the pit down by the stage.

Slowly, after an interminable period of doubt and insecurity there appeared out of the darkness a delicate slit of light, cast about the floor as though the thread fine line between life and death itself, as though the threshold between now and all that I could ever hope for.

Still trembling in the inexplicable grip of fear, this light seemed to me to be the wry smile of saviour itself. I headed towards it on my knees, slowly and pathetically amongst the mould and the damp on the floor, until eventually I was close enough to ascertain that the source of light was the crack beneath a door. I pushed it gently and it opened almost as though it had wanted to, as if it had been waiting for and expecting me. As if it had needed me.

Suddenly, I found myself bathed in a light so bright that I could hardly believe it, and I crawled out onto the roof of the building just as the sun began to rise. Despite the tenor of the morning sunlight, the whole concrete slab of the roof was permeated with subtle shades of grey that lent the morning a pathetic and lifeless quality that made me feel inexplicably nostalgic for times and places to which I had no connection. I sauntered around as though I owned the place but harboured a complete distaste for it all, analysing the details and the design of the building, marvelling at the hollow backs of the domes on the roof - though they can be described as that only as a technicality. Truth be told, the contours and domes of the building which seemed almost majestic when viewed from the front of the building were actually flat from back here and propped up with brittle, wooden beams. It was as though the building itself was some kind of stage or movie set, a two-dimensional illusion that had been erected outside of its own means.

As these feelings of disillusionment encroached upon my psyche, I made my way, bleary-eyed and yawning once again, to the far side of the roof to see if I could find a vantage point that would afford me sight of my cherished city. Between one of the domes and a corner section of the roof, I looked down and out at a world oblivious; at the boy racers revving their engines at the traffic lights; at the drunks stumbling about and shouting at each other; at the homeless begging for change; the hustle and bustle of another day beneath the stars.

I wondered if I would be able to see the Counter, because I felt like he might be watching me to see if I had learned my lesson, but I knew that I probably hadn't and, like the rest of us, he was no doubt just peddling profundity anyway. I sighed and wondered what the point of it all could possibly even be.

I scanned the whole horizon of the town that was holding my head under water. From this distance it looked more peaceful, through the eyes of objectivity that I was afforded because of my height. But isn't it true that everything look better from the distance? Our dreams? The things we think we want or need? Mountains, maybe even the moon? As I looked over the old prefab office block across the road, the one that I had set the camera up outside of that time, I directed my gaze to the remainder of the skyline, thinking about how this whole place is just a toy box in which to keep all of my problems, and promising myself that one day I would leave for good, having put away these childish things once and for all, proud and strong and determined in my quest to become a man.

And then, after I had caught a hold of my breath, turning back to the roof over the vista, I became overwhelmed with the sensation that I had climbed these stairs to become edified. Things will only last forever if you want them to, I thought. And because I was tired, I slunk down against the wall over which I had just been peering, tired and lost, but somehow convinced, without the slightest trace of evidence of my own future success. Breathing deeply and completely now, I noticed something glistening on the roof just in front of me; drawn to it like a magpie to some shimmering but worthless thing, I crawled in the grey dawn towards it and realised that it was a piece of a jigsaw puzzle.

Knowing immediately who it belonged to, I put it safe in the bottom of my pocket. Then, as I lay down serene beneath the moonlight, drifting into sleep as though slipping into another coma, I thought to myself that I should be ultimately satisfied, for the clue I had been waiting for had finally found me.

When I woke up it was cold and early and the light was still grey because the sun had not fully been able to rise. The concrete that covered the roof had taken in and stored away the freezing temperatures of the night, and so I woke up shivering slightly, curled up foetal, wondering where my life had gone and what I could do to get it back. I had fallen asleep with my face to the ground, my arm underneath my head for support, and yet somehow I had still managed to get concrete imprints on my cheeks from pressing them in against the floor. I could feel the indentations with my arms, like the valleys and contours in an aerial photograph. I had become a dried up planet, uninhabitable and desiccated.

During the night I had dreamed about Her, my love from the Old World. We were on a beach, one that I knew we had been to in waking life, just before the doctors had told me that I needed to go home. In the dream, we were walking along together, holding hands, on the sand, but as we walked I suddenly felt a loosening of my grasp, and then I started walking towards the ocean, as though I were somehow drawn to it. For a time, I felt as though my body had been possessed, because even though I knew that I was heading for trouble, I felt that I should just succumb to it, and so I let my body lead the way as my mind shut down.

As I headed towards the sea, she began to cry out my name. Over and over again, my name ringing out and along the stretch of the beach, beneath the moon. Next I knew, I was in the water, and there was an undercurrent, and it started to pull my legs under, and so slowly I slipped. She watched me from the shore, screaming. Then, I got the feeling, under the water, that the ocean was formed of her tears. And I could imagine her stood on the shore still crying, and then her tears formed a stream that seeped into the ocean, and now I was here, drowning in them. And then it went black, as though a great shadow had faded over me, or as though I had faded away, or fallen into nothing. Then there was peace. And I woke up.

I sat on the roof, wondering what I might do to get out of here. Then I remembered the jigsaw puzzle piece in my pocket, and so I checked that it was still there, and when it was I felt nothing but relief. It felt good because I felt that I were a little closer to my goal, and I knew that it would be impossible to fail, because if you just follow the signs you will be led to where you need to be.

Looking over the side of the roof, back between the pseudo-dome and the walls, I saw the city come to life, the morning buses taking the working classes to their places of business, the middle classes in their cars, locked away from the world, and the rich in different towns completely, even though they owned most of the buildings in this one. There is something about moments like these, standing aloof and with a detached gaze, where this very detachment allows you to feel a connection of some kind, because you are taking it all in at once, in exactly the way that it is happening. I watched and reflected and the sun eventually became brighter and it warmed the roof and so I didn't feel so cold anymore. I felt as if though I were witnessing the genesis of something grand, something new and important.

There was a synergy to it all, as though each disconnected person that I could see down there, were somehow working in union with each of the strangers that surrounded them, epiphenomenal, like in the ways that ants will build a society when they work together, but if you get one of them alone it will not have any idea what it is doing. Indeed, the whole town from up here seemed to be welcoming me, and so I decided that it was time for me to go back down. Down towards the traffic jams and the council flats, but first to work, where I was expected to be in an hour or two. I looked at Mao to tell me the time and he told me that I would have to be quick.

I wasn't sure whether leaving the building now would get me in trouble or not. It was more likely that I would be seen climbing through windows in the daylight, but perhaps such behaviour could be pardonable - there were worse things that had happened in this part of town, and besides, what choice did I have anyway? I brushed myself down with my hands, wiped the asbestos of my pants, and then headed back into the stairwell that had brought me here, hoping that the daylight would lend it a more affable sheen.

When I reached the top of the staircase it was certainly lighter outside, so much so that I could see the steps properly, and so I didn't need to worry quite so much about falling down into the stage pit. I headed back to the window that I had smashed to get in here, and when I reached it, I realised that the music had stopped. Instead there was only silence. The shards of glass sat motionless against the window base, the reflections within them as clear as muddy puddles. I looked down the pit of the stairs, down there, towards the stage or the cellar and into the darkness. Like the death of drowning in my dream, and without the music, it seemed to be an even more hostile place, cold and uncertain. I slunk back over to the window and put my head out to make sure that nobody was there.

Traffic hissing on the road again, people passing aimlessly; when it was safe, I began to make my way back home, when suddenly I realised something: the big bin that I had used as a platform for climbing up here in the first place had disappeared. Once again I felt that flutter in my chest, as though the bird had returned, and I felt truly this time that it might actually escape, that it would be able to rip its way through my skin and into the rest of the world so that it could sound the alarm and let them all know I was here. In my panic I looked out the window and thought about jumping, but I couldn't because it was too high of a fall.

The freight train ran through the front of my mind, a red-tinged fear, bile and disgust. Somebody must have seen me enter the building. I turned back into the womb of the theatre and thought that perhaps if I dare head down into the darkness I would be able to find another way out, one at ground level and so I started to move down the stairs.

Each step that I took brought me a little closer to myself, because until that moment I imagined that I could've at least pretended to be a man. But with each footstep, I began to feel that I was becoming weaker, as if whatever was down there sat waiting for me, and that it was waiting because it was ready to beat me. This sensation became so strong, so overpowering, that once again I lost the ability to move. And then I felt tears streaming down my face, thousands of them, warm and salty and flowing. I pulled myself up the creaking banister and turned back around. I took a running jump, and then I fell through the window and into a heap amongst the puddles of the alleyway.

Chapter 15

I hadn't been to the shop for days but it felt like more. The smell of MacDonald's breakfasts and that cheap coffee and the cigarette smoke on people's clothes got the better of me and, as I looked around at the junk on the floor and the ever disordered shelves, I became instantly and inextricably overwhelmed by the sensation that the end was near and there was nothing to be done about it. They looked at me like there must be something wrong with me, as though I was a walking abortion, or an aberration; a rip in the Mona Lisa.

'What happened to your leg?', One of Them asked me.

I tried to ignore him and just get on with signing my name on the sign in sheet, the sticky green book that waited to learn the deepest, darkest secrets of my pockets; I faked a concentration, so intense as to be almost religious, and then I diverted my eyes and pretended I hadn't heard him.

'Seriously', said Another, 'It looks fucked up.'

And then, next I knew, there was The Manager, solicitous for a change, instead of throwing all that acid in my face, down on the floor, looking at the rip in my jeans. He saw that my leg was rent and that parts of it were still bleeding. Then he looked up at me and he said:

'Jesus, you should get to the hospital.'

Because he refused to break eye contact, I had to gaze at the floor and count the pieces of gum that were stuck to it. Underneath one of the shelves I noticed a baby's dummy. It was covered in dust.

They stood for a few moments expecting some kind of response, but I didn't want to go to the doctor, because that would mean that I would have to explain what had happened and I didn't want to lie. I kept my mouth shut and hoped for the best.

Gradually, they returned to their work: opening up the tills, making their small talk conversations about the TV shows they'd seen. Telling jokes. It was like they were a real team. A unit.

I tried to give the impression that everything was exactly as it was supposed to be. Brushing my hand up against my back pocket to make sure that the jigsaw piece was still there, I meandered round behind the till in silence and began to count up my change. I thought about germs.

Whilst I was counting, the Supervisor came up to me.

'You're late', he said. Then he passed me a piece of paper, which said *Employee Performance Report* across the top of it. When I read what he had written down there was something about me being late for work by five minutes, even though I wasn't getting paid for another ten, and it said that I would sign this piece of paper at the bottom to show that I understood what a terrible human being I was and that I would never do it again.

I printed my name and then stuck my signature down next to it. In the space that asked for confirmation of my job title I wrote '*Nobody*' and then I passed it back to the Supervisor as I watched him strut back down to the other end of the shop. I sucked it all in like a sponge and, because it made me feel heavy and incomplete, I had to lean against the counter for a few beats and put my head against my hands. Then the doors opened and a throng of customers that had been hovering about outside with bags of junk under their arms started to pour in.

'Next!', I shouted at them.

Then another day just like any other began and the remainder of my life became a little shorter.

The rest of the day was a blur, a progression of beeps and barcodes and mindless badinage. Customers would come in and expect conversations and well-serviced smiles, and because when they looked at me they saw a by-product of 'the system', I was expected to rummage through that shit-heap of silver disks, as though my own volition had been defenestrated, and now I was just an empty shell to be told which two directions to bumble in between. Somehow society had forced me to act as though I were actually happy to be doing this, to interpret that grimace on my face as a smile, and to mistake the despair in my voice for the giddy intonations of enthusiasm and zeal.

Nobody could tell that I was one step away from screaming, yelling that I just wanted to get out of here and that I wanted all of this to end, so I could go back to being myself again and saunter through a life of ignorant bliss. I began to feel more than certain that if it wasn't for the other people, every interaction that I shared with them, serving to force the lid back on, I would've opened up right then and spilled my guts to the floor. I was ready to crumble, but I didn't know how.

To pass the time, I reflected upon suicide, not that I was seriously considering it, but it seemed to me that, even if I did want to end it all, other people would somehow find a way to make it difficult for me. Life would be easy if other people weren't involved, was the way I saw it, and if death was its binary opposite, then surely it could be much the same way. If life is meaningless, so might death be, I thought. So why worry about consequences? I knew I had the strength of will to carry it out: perhaps I'd dive beneath the wheels of a bus, or slit my wrists in the bath. It couldn't be that hard. No, the real hill to climb, I suppose, would be going ahead with it knowing what other people might think of you after it had been carried out, not thinking that they had mistreated you in some way or been negligent and overly hurtful, but that you were weak and useless and selfish, because you didn't think about how your death would make them feel, how it might make them feel guilty.

But isn't that the problem with suicide? That we the living don't want those that we have failed to try and find a way to escape from us? Or that we would rather those who are going through each day, as though it is a mountain to be climbed, continue with their struggles, even though they are fighting with all of their might, just because we are afraid to question ourselves? Of course, that is only if our acceptance is related to their reasons for wanting to opt out. Maybe some of them just consider death to be a better option, and they don't want to hurt anybody or make any statements with their termination of the contract. All they want is peace. And if it means that there are less miserable or fucked up people in the world, then so be it. Let them leave us behind. For surely death is only another meaningless reward anyway, another empty kiss on the cheek, so that they can say something nice about us, and use our passing to put their own lives into perspective before they forget about us completely.

It began to make sense to me that, from an evolutionary perspective, perhaps suicide is a tool, one that has been given to us as a kind of gift, so that if we wish to end this pain and this constant pressure that seems to be coming at us from around every corner, we are able to do so. An intelligent creature should be allowed to end its own life if it chooses to because, after all, who else's life is it? Yet, for some reason, the majority feel some kind of ownership over the lives of individuals, to the extent that a man who wants to kill himself is bound to the feelings and emotions of strangers.

But why can't our lives be our own? Won't we ever truly be allowed to do what we see fit with them? Must we worry even to the grave what people may be thinking of us? Suicide doesn't have to be a 'fuck you' or an escape or anything with any negativity at all. It could be as simple an act as flicking off the light switch, or turning the TV to a better channel. But we are too bound up in the morality of a dead God to respect each other's choices. Live and let live is just one of many options. We could die and let others get on with their own lives, instead of holding them all behind with our constant bickering and our whining and our complaints and our needy quests for attention and our neuroses. We could give instead of taking.

It occurred to me, standing there behind the counter, watching the drones teem about on their quests for their food or money, that there must be hundreds if not thousands of millions of us that would wish to forget about our lives if we could. Those of us that are sick of being trampled on, those that are tired of being told what to do. And it's not just because we no longer have God in our lives, or because we live in dark days, or that the end is nigh. It's because those of us at the bottom have become tired, tired of rummaging through bins like foxes in the night, sick of being judged because of our financial status, bored of having letters from the taxman or the BBC tell us that we risk going to court because we didn't pay up on time or we don't watch Television. And they won't even let us leave it all when we want to? People shouldn't need people as much as they do. We're all leeches and we're killing each other anyway, vanquishing whatever is good in those that surround us, and not letting them escape from our egos because we are too afraid to do so ourselves.

I considered the alternatives, ways of killing yourself without anybody ever knowing. Perhaps you could die in a traffic accident, or have a misadventure and fall off a mountain. That way you'd get what you wanted and nobody would have to feel bad for it.

Things like that must happen all the time.

Chapter 16

I can't remember what time I took my lunch break; it was mid-afternoon sometime and the rain was falling. It brought a cancer cloud of grey down about the city, and as people ran under the cover of shop awnings or doorways, I walked around with my hands in my pockets, clutching the jigsaw puzzle piece as though everything depended on it, imagining that it had infused my fist with a neon energy, that it was the last bit of fuel in the engine. I looked out from beneath my hood for people that might be able to help me; I looked for signs. Though the rain was light, it wet me to the bone, and, as people in empty shops stood in doorways, taking in the unfolding scene, leaning, and colluding, I thought I saw the Sycophant amidst the crowds of tattered umbrellas.

She stood out because she didn't have one; walking along weather beaten, her thin hair sticking wet to her freckled face. I watched her dart down an old cobbled street where the closed down pubs were. I ran on after her. My feet plashed puddles and soaked the back of my tattered jeans.

The old street smelled like wet rubbish, quiet except for the sounds of the water breaking free of the cracks in the guttering on the peaks of crumbled walls, and, the yellowed stones of the old buildings, had turned a darker shade of almost green on account of the acid rain that was falling. Middle of the day, but I find myself once again alone, the familiar echo of the rest of the world getting on with its life haunting the unseen horizon. I stare through the cracked windows of the old pub, study the battered furniture that has gone rotten and weak from obsolescence, and then I head deeper down after the Sycophant, my stomach rumbling because it's lunch time and I am chasing rainbows instead of meal deals from chain stores. Another white trash flash of her tracksuit and I know she must be down here. I look down at Mao to see how deeply involved with my lunch break I am and then I wipe some of the rainwater into my face and stand there as I try to 'breathe with awareness' as I rub at the sides of my eyes. All things around me take on a strange softness.; I feel as though I am floating; another woken dream.

My attention is drawn to my leg, to the rip in my jeans. All morning I had walked with a slight limp, but now the laceration seems to have reopened, and a thin stream of crimson is coursing down over my shoes and mixing in with the rain waters, like some failed science experiment performed by a colour-blind biologist. I bend forwards and push into it with my fingers, right into the wound, hoping that the pressure will help it stop, and I even start shaking a little, when I think that it might not, imagining my blood leaving my body again to leave me dried out and limp like paper for the winds. I stand there for minutes with these thoughts on mind, and the whole time the street is empty, despite it being right in the very heart of the city. There is something about it which the rest of the herd are wary of.

I must have lost myself to my inaction, deep in the reverie, because, when I look up again, the rain has stopped and the sky is opening up to the sun again, and when I roll my eyes back over the old pub, at the boarded up windows from which the boards have been stolen, I see the Sycophant inside, sitting at a table and peeling the rust away from its aging legs, as though she were at a business meeting of some kind and she were a boss who had to fire somebody she didn't quite like. Her face had changed, as though the rain had washed away all the distress and the anxiety that had ruined it before, and even though her freckles were still there, her complexion seemed healthier with its rubicund tinge. She saw me looking at her and then nodded as though I should enter; I walked on over to the door, the flow of my blood no more than another tear in the ocean now, and then I pulled up a chair and sat across from her at the old table. We were both silent for a few beats. Then she started, no small talk or anything:

'It has surely come to your attention by now that The Leader is pregnant', she said, 'And though there is no doubt in her heart that you are the rightful father of her child, you will have hopefully figured out that she is not ready to discuss the matter with you any further than need be necessary. Of course, that doesn't mean that she won't be willing to at a later date, but, what it does mean, is that you are to be patient - that you must wait until the time is right. If you don't, then the ramifications could unfold in ways which could hurt not just you, as they most certainly would, but all of us. Everybody in this town and the next one and the one after that. Is that perfectly clear?'

I stared at her like an idiot might an abstract painting. I hadn't really listened to her speak before, because her personality had been subdued by the confidence of the Leader, and so the tone with which she spoke to me now, as though I hardly existed outside of her plans, made me feel shabby and small enough to be something that she had found in her food at a restaurant: A piece of hair from the head of a stranger; a wrinkled Elastoplast with a sticky centre. None of it made sense, not just this matter of the baby, but the ways in which my expectations of people in daytime tracksuits - the things they might be capable of - had been shattered. She spoke curtly and abruptly, like a hammer against a windscreen; I shuddered internally as though I'd just bought a one way ticket to comatose.

'Are you listening to me?', she asked.

I rested my hands upon the dusty table. People must have come in here in groups once upon a time; after work beers, preludes to night clubs on Friday nights. I didn't know what to say.

'Well?', she said again. And it made me feel that I didn't have a choice - that I simply had to say something.

'Well...', I began, 'I'm a little confused. You see, as far as I'm concerned I never slept with your friend. I mean, I can't deny that I didn't kiss her once or twice, but that was it. So as you must surely understand, these accusations about pregnancy really don't make any sense to me.'

She pulled out a pack of cigarettes and offered one to me. I'd been trying to quit again since the day after the night at the school, but it no longer seemed to matter now. I took one from the pack. She pulled out a fading book of matches from some long-forgotten restaurant and lit it for me. The smoke rose to the ceiling. I watched it rise and noticed that the paint was peeling.

'Why are you always hanging around town?', I asked her.

'I'm trying to find a job', she replied.

And for the next few moments we sat appreciating our cigarettes, like we might do in a regular pub, in a regular town. We sat as though we were sharing something, as though we had gained an understanding of some kind. I watched the rain water drip down the walls of the derelict building; there was a leak in the roof but nobody had needed to do anything about it.

I ran my eyes over the bar area, over the few empty glasses that sat waiting on the bar, perhaps the last drink of the owners before they packed up and left. The thin cloud of cigarette smog continued to rise above our heads; it looked like a thought balloon in a fractured cartoon, wordless like our vacant conversation, and trailing off into nothing like the one we'd just finished. I made musing sounds in an attempt to fill in the empty space. Then I thought of something to say, so I said it:

'Assuming that I am the father of this baby, when will I know that the time is right to meet it?'

The Sycophant took another crack of the cigarette. Her eyes rolled into the back of her head and then she took a handkerchief out from her pocket and slid it across the table on over to me. It was red and folded into quarters. There was something inside of it. Somebody had tied a yellow piece of string around it to keep whatever was held inside securely in place.

I looked at her for permission to unwrap it, but it wasn't given to me. She just sat there peering from beneath the straight cut of her fringe. For some reason her eyes had taken on a lifeless quality, but perhaps that was just because she was tired, or because the weather was getting the better of her, or because she secretly wanted to kill herself. She looked at me. I could hear the wheels of her inner-machinery doing somersaults but she wore a mask of placidity, like a Zen monk ignoring a fly in his eye.

'Do you think that you are capable of murder?', she asked.

I didn't know what to say.

The package on the table sat waiting like a train stuck in the station; I finished my cigarette and flicked the butt across the room. I looked out through the windows at the empty alley way; I could hear the sounds of the high-street up around the way. People were going about their business, as though that was all there really was to life. I thought about her question as I considered my relationship to the rest of the human race, and for the very first time since being born, I allowed these words to flow through my mind:

I am a murder.

Almost as though I were trying on a new pair of shoes in front of the clerk, seeing how they felt to wear, looking at them in the mirror. I caught my reflection in a cracked screen behind the old bar; the speckled veil of dust that covered it, I wore like warts. Though my new shoes didn't seem to fit perfectly, they weren't uncomfortable either; perhaps I would have to wear them in. And, as I stared at my face, I remembered what it had looked like before, back when I was young and optimistic, back when I believed that anything was possible, that change was inevitable, and that 'God' wanted more from me than just another pair of hands to stack the shelves for everybody else to take things from. Now, the face reflected back at me was gaunt, the hollows of my eyes black from ill-nutrition, a sickened and sallow complexion from too much coffee, and a lifetime of disappointment and cigarettes. Emaciated and jittering, I turned to the Sycophant to answer her question, but she already knew what I was going to say, and so she didn't give me a chance to answer.

'In there', she said, pointing to the red handkerchief, 'Is a picture of the man that the Leader wishes for you to *expunge*. If you do as she wishes you will be granted access to your child when it is born. If you refuse to comply you will never see the child, but proceedings will begin to ensure that the police learn of your illicit relations. The consequences of such could be very damaging, even for a person such as yourself, you are sure to agree.'

I sighed without saying anything. To be honest, I still didn't really know what was happening. As far as I remembered, sex with the Leader was as apocryphal as Elvis eating cheeseburgers on the toilet. But it didn't seem to matter; life was leading me down ever darker corridors. I had no choice but to follow on after it, blindly passive and willing and able to do whatever was required of me.

'Okay', I said.

Then the Sycophant stood up without speaking and left me as alone as I had imagined myself to be. I stared at the red handkerchief on the table in front of me, and even though it was so small, it seemed to consume all of the space around it. I sat in silence, in contemplative veneration; I knew that my future now had purpose, though I didn't know all the details. I reached forwards from the wonky chair, but just as I was about to unwrap the parcel my mobile phone began to ring. It vibrated in my pocket like a cicada in a shoe box. I answered it. It was work. They wanted to know where the hell I was because I'd gone outside the parameters of my lunch break.

I put the bundle in my back pocket, then I apologised profusely and pathetically, and then I left through the rain and ran back to the shop.

Chapter 17

That night I went home and climbed straight into the shower. The water dribbled upon me as though a fetish, but it was hot, and the steam cast itself around me as though some needy lover, and because I felt a true sense of isolation from the rest of the world, I felt at last that I could relax. I cupped the hot saliva in my hands and threw it over my face. Each time I did so, I closed my eyes and, for a few precious seconds, felt truly at peace, as though some fleeting form of death was pecking at my cheek.

Sucked up, turned out, and made to work, I lathered the soap into my pigeon chest with its visible ribs. I concentrated on the same parts of the same spots of my body, over and over again, the soap bubbles forming a superfluous second skin, and as I looked down at my sick frame, my sinewy arms and hairless legs, I reflected upon my corrupted inner, began to feel guilty, because I must have done something 'wrong' to end up like this. I tried to forget that I was thinking these things and just concentrate on the water. I splashed some more in my face. But I didn't feel anything.

When I heard the phone ring it was like a stranger had just climbed through the window. I didn't get out of the shower to answer it. I let the brittle assault of its tone ring throughout the house as the water splashed down the shower screen, and, when it finally stopped ringing, it seemed to me that time had stopped itself, and so I looked at the water droplets that had frozen around me, and I flicked some of them against the glass screen, and they shattered like flies against the wallpaper as I waited for time to pick up again. I continued to stand there, under the steamy dribble; I screamed because I knew that nobody could hear me and then I did it again, just in case they could.

Feeling that my water usage might be verging on decadence and that this might not be the only hell I ever end up in, I raised my hand to the switch and shut down the flow. I felt like I had spent the evening weeping and, now that I had finally been able to cease my tears, all that remained was a heavy but cool detachment from it all. It occurred to me that I had been thinking about murder, and I thought once again that if this string of words, '*I am a murder*', could pass through my mind, like a midnight freight train cutting through a local station, then perhaps one day it would be able to stop there, and whatever was on board would be able to alight and set up camp for a few days. Or perhaps it would even stay there permanently.

I felt eerie in the most normal of ways.

The towel was waiting for me on the sink, mottled and variegated like a stray cat, fetid and mouldy because I'd let myself go. When I put it over my face and dried my hair I felt like I might need to shower again; I stared longingly at myself in the mirror, my skin cold from the damp on the walls. Out in the hallway, I could feel the night air coming in off the streets and it made me shiver. As I watched myself tremble, I sneered at my own weakness, before heading out into the darkness of the hallway, my wet feet sticking to the ground as though they didn't want to be going any further, the dust from the floor sticking to the damp of my soles, and bringing me back to the horrid squalor of reality.

I looked around the kitchen, at the crumbs on the counter, the dirty dishes in the sink, and the clothes and the shoes and the odd socks strewn about the living room. The phone beeped to remind me that I had missed a call, but I couldn't remember where I had dumped it; I moved a few pieces of clatter out of the way, year old newspapers and magazines, cigarette graves made of fizzy drinks cans, then I looked out of the window, over at the forsaken buildings across the road. They were sucking up the yellow street lights; apart from the parked cars, there was nothing or nobody out there.

The handkerchief that the Sycophant had conferred upon me sat resting on the window side. I let it sit there like an unopened reminder from the electricity company. I was starting to feel that whatever was in there could only be bad news - even if it had come as a sign, even if I did secretly expect it to lead me closer to myself. I tried to ignore it, but it became another one of those little things that served only to suck the air from the room, to niggle away at me, and so I chose to suffocate a little more, instead of doing what made the most logical sense.

I tried to find my phone, figuring that the lesser of two evils would be the right direction to move in. I could remember times in my life when I had been too afraid to answer the telephone at all: *'If the phone rings, answer it'*, I had concluded. Do we ever really change? After a certain age? I figured that we didn't but kept on looking.

The phone beeped again, another cry for help. I was in a state of dishabille, wearing only my towel, and so my chest began to freeze. Shivering, I looked down at my abdomen and began to envisage the huge scar that was going to be there one day. I found the phone under a pile of dog-eared books that had collapsed upon the sofa; it sat beneath them with its plastic chipped and its battery dying. I flipped the screen and its neon blue set the room ablaze. It said I had a voice mail; I dialled the answer phone and this is what it said:

You have one new voice message, recorded... today at... 8:52 pm. Beep. Hi. It's Me. I hope you're OK. My friend told me about your meeting today, in the pub, and she said that you looked worried and that perhaps you were a little confused. She said you looked different to before... Anyway, I want you to know that there's no need to feel sad or worried or anything bad at all. I can tell that you have a lot of problems in your life, and that you're pretty close to giving up even, but this whole thing is going to work out if you just let it. If you do what I ask you to, I mean. I can tell that you just want to be loved and if you can do this for me then I promise to give you that in return. I'll be yours and I'll be true and I'll be faithful to you. We can live with our baby. We'll be together... Look, just do this one thing and it's all going to be over. Don't bother calling me back. I won't answer. I'll see you when the time is right. I love you, I think. Bye. Click.

I called her number but she didn't answer. It just rang like it wasn't designed for any other purpose, and so eventually I hung up, and I let my towel fall to the floor and decided to walk around naked. When I went over to the window sill, I saw somebody pass by in the street. Nothing more than another irrelevant stranger. My body leaned against the cold brick walls and it made my skin stick. I looked down at the red handkerchief with the yellow ribbon around it. I wondered what was inside.

Whoever had wrapped it had treated it like a meditation. The thin streak of yellow ribbon was wrapped around with perfect symmetry; the corners tucked together like black belt origami. I picked it up gently, with the reverence that it seemed to be demanding, and then I sat it in the palm of my hand and thought about the best way to open it.

I pulled at one end of the ribbon and then, with a fluidity as natural as the waters of a fall tumbling over the edge of a cliff, it came to pieces and the ribbon was released and the silken cloth began to unfold itself. Next I knew, I had in one hand the piece of string. In the other, was the blossom of the handkerchief, its four corners splayed about and over my palm like flower petals. In the centre, as though waiting for a bee to come pollinate it, sat an unmarked white envelope. I lifted it and let the handkerchief fall to the ground. Whoever had sealed the envelope had refused to lick it, and the back had just been placed gently inside, flapping around like a bad decision; I lifted the flap and took out a photograph.

Inside was a picture of a fat man. He was on a dirty bed without legs. He was probably the fattest man I'd ever seen.

Chapter 18

A day off. All the days before had merged into one. Nothing to do and nobody to talk to besides myself, my eyes glazed over as I examined the eclectic collection of objects festering before me on the kitchen table, and attempted to find some kind of connection between them all. But, despite my very best efforts, the jigsaw puzzle offered nothing besides an abstract array of rain washed colours from having being left on the roof of the old theatre for too long. It could be anything; I gave up trying. All the same, my faith that it held the key to my future was just as firm and unshakeable as ever before.

I looked at the picture of The Fat Man. Once again, trusting in the universality of all things, I knew that this was the man I sought; this was too big of a coincidence for it not to be meaningful in some way. I sat over a cup of tasteless instant coffee and swilled it about my mouth as I stared at him. His face was soft and leathery and round, and his innumerable chins sat beneath the sour expression on his face like great ridges cut into the side of some great painted mountain. Indeed, so sour was this expression upon his face that, as though etched in stone, it prevailed despite his eyes being closed. The picture had obviously been taken when he was unawares - when he was asleep or had passed out. Supine on the legless bed like some load that had just been dumped off the back of a truck and into the gutters.

'*Why would they want him dead?* ', I asked myself as the tepid coffee stained my teeth. More importantly, how would I go about killing such a thing? I suppose it would be fairly easy if he were bed-ridden, but before I performed the duty that was expected of me, it was incumbent upon me to seek answers to the deluge of questions that had been fogging my brain for the past few months. I felt a great sense of duty and responsibility swelling within my breast; I would have to be prepared if I were to perform as was befitting my calling. Nearly half the people that I had come across since arriving in this two-bit town wanted me to meet with, or to speak with, or to kill the abomination before me. I wondered if I were up to the task. I wondered what was in his head. There must be something of great importance contained within it. The solution to all my problems.

The composition of the photograph went something like this: The Fat Man was in a room laying on a dirty mattress, in the corner of a dusty room, littered with empty food packets, empty drinks bottles, and kitchen utensils. It seemed to me that he was asleep, naked almost, except for a huge sheet that somebody had wrapped like a nappy around his nether regions, and I stared in disbelief at his flabby, leathery, legs hanging over the edge of the mattress like the remnants of some long since demolished building, heavy, inert and inexorable. Though my reaction was slim to none, desensitized perhaps by a misspent youth of Internet and late night television, I all the same tried to convince myself that I was repulsed; I began to tell myself that he was a waste of space; a drain on resources that was killing the planet: Fat people are just a twisted by-product of our messed up society, I determined. Killing him would be a statement, a triumph for the human spirit. I would take the fall for it all and live out the rest of my days as a hero and then spend eternity as a legend.

Behind his bed there was a window, built into thin looking walls with peeling paint, another flimsy prefab construction. The discoloured old lace curtains were closed, and what little of the windows I could see were covered in dirt and a thin layer of residuum. There was a thin piece of string tied to one of the window handles that led to the big toe of his right foot, and I determined that this must be so he could open the window when the smell of his sweat became too much to bear, or when he needed the breeze to cool him down, or when he wanted nothing more than for the sound of passing traffic to send him back to sleep, so that he could recharge, and prepare himself for the next wave of microwave meals and carbonated downtime.

Because the window was so filthy, I couldn't see outside, but I could make out the vague outlines of rooftops, like jigsaw puzzle pieces themselves, and so I figured that he must be up high somewhere, looking above it all like some fast food satiated Greek god.

Around the bed, on the drink-stained rug on the dusty floor, there was nothing but junk: Empty food packets, instant noodle boxes, chocolate bar wrappers. What did this guy do for entertainment besides eat? How could he stand to live like this? Immobile, inert, and indifferent to it all. I had always considered such obesity to be a sign of smug complacency, but the more I looked at the photograph, the more I began to realise that there was a sadness haunting this man's days. Killing him would be a favour, like slitting open the belly of a beached whale to stop it from suffocating. Maybe he would even thank me first.

I put the photograph down and stood up and paced about the kitchen; I knew what I needed but I didn't know how to get it. It was the same old story, just like everybody else's: wandering through life waiting for some semblance of meaning to sneak up and shake you out of it all, hoping that things would somehow work out, even though you weren't really working quite as hard as you should do to make them do so; living each day like any other, instead of the last. Or thinking that this would be forever; failing to acknowledge that time would go on without me. My head was a quagmire of unpolished thoughts, faded memories, and poorly defined visions of the indistinct future. Just another one of the Hebetudinous; grasping for meaning in a room without furniture and no wallpaper on the walls.

Having decided that I needed some stimulation, I walked barefoot across the cold wooden floor, picked up the kettle, and tried to fit it under the tap. There were too many dirty dishes in the sink, so I couldn't. I pushed some of them out of the way; cheap red pasta sauce stains, remnants of things in packets, blackened carrot peelings and vegetable skins with the peas in the plughole. I found sanctuary within the sounds of the kettle boiling, knowing what the immediate future had in store, being encapsulated within an insignificant bubble of time that gave me room to breathe. And so, as the sounds of the filter heating up filled my ears and a steady trail of steam slunk out of the spout, I somehow managed to convince myself that I might be on to something. Everything would work out if I just kept calm and kept the faith.

The water inside the kettle began to roll and to boil and to turn with the weight of the whole ocean behind it. Of all the water on the Earth, I thought, I had taken to one side this portion and placed it under my control. I began to feel powerful. And then, finally, when the kettle started to sway from side to side, and the steam flowed tenfold, there was a CLICK, and the switch set itself back to its default position, and I felt that for once in my pathetic life I had reached a conclusion, a terminal state of closure and finality.

I picked up my cup from the sink area. It was clean but stained. I poured some instant coffee granules into the cup and when they had covered the entire surface area of the bottom, I poured the water. There was a splash and the granules began to fizz and I thought that I might have burned them and messed up the flavour, but then I thought back, to when I was younger, and I could remember somebody saying that you should always stop the kettle just before the water's boiled, because if you don't you'll burn the beans and your coffee will be no good. But I was bitter, like the coffee, no longer even spoke to this person, and so I wilfully ignored their advice, even though their words had been lodged in my head for the past decade or so, every time that I poured hot water over beans. Truth be told, I didn't care if I burned them or not. I just began to pour.

But then, when I was pouring the water into the cup, I realised that I hadn't filled the kettle properly, because my mind must have been wandering, and I was thinking about something else, crippled by fear most likely, doubting whether my plans for the future would prove to be fruitful, or reveal themselves to be of any worth whatsoever. And, as these thoughts took me, I began to feel that I was doomed. And they kept coming and there was nothing I could do about it. I began to dwell on the mistake that I had just made, not filling the kettle adequately, and I worried that maybe I was losing it.

But what could I do if I had? You are only crazy if other people say that you are. And so I turned on the hot water tap and I waited for it to run heated and then I put the cup under the stream and I had a tepid cup of coffee

---

Chapter 19

I had been awake since sunrise, my body attuned to the natural animal rhythms of the world, something that seemed logical and pure and true to me, honest even. We are all animals at core, when we boil ourselves down to just needs or desires, the tiny chemical reactions in our brains, our vertebrate sensitivity to it all. It had long since made sense to me to live like this, not in an antisocial sense, in a cave, but in a way that is true to the universe we live in, the natural order, the world without a God, or those interminable and incessant moonless nights that can make us feel so very alone.

Time continued to eat into my day off. The pressure to find something useful or meaningful to do became almost crippling. I couldn't permit myself to do anything if it were not linked to this strange, unfolding future that I had found myself attuned to. My latest and greatest obsession, clinging coldly to me like a succubus in the night, and lingering like a broken promise after daybreak. This is all I have, I thought, so how can it not be right? Nothing is as it is supposed to be, but nor can any of it take any other form. All we can do really is acquiesce. There is no volition in the bigger picture, but, if life is a game, then each move counts.

I leave the half-finished and unappreciated cup of coffee besides the picture of The Fat Man, then I rummage around for my keys, which I find between the cracks in the cushions on the sofa. As I walk across the room, I notice a ball of dust and hair ride about the waves of my motion. It lilts backwards and forwards, swaying somewhat, then it falls to the floor between the blunted sunrays coming through the window, sliding beneath the sofa to rot in peace with the rest of the dust, and the lost change and the biscuit crumbs. I wonder if this might be a metaphor of some kind, put my keys in my pocket, and then head out to the streets. On the way down the stairs, in the apartment block vestibule, by the ripped open post boxes and the piles of torn takeaway menus thrown away by disgruntled postmen, I encounter several of the neighbours, the nameless bipeds with whom I share communal spaces and council tax rates. As far as either of us seem to be aware, this is the first time we've ever seen one another; tension prevails and nobody says anything; eye contact is avoided at all costs, and I wonder why people must do this to each other, slither awkwardly about the cracks in the rocks, when we all dream and fuck and live and feel the same.

Out in the streets, the day flowers in much the same way as any other. Cars battle for parking spaces, people walk about with shopping bags; there is spit on the pavements and marker pen name graffiti etched into stone walls; office workers smoke in doorways and blow grey clouds of smoke into the faces of anonymous passers-by. And, up above, the sky seems so vast and so full and so imbued with drama that I expected something awful to be about to happen. But then it occurs to me that it is also pure and brilliant and blue, and that clouds must weigh so many hundreds of tons, and that something is keeping them up there, stopping them from falling. So it can't all be as bad as they all say. We are only doomed in spirit. Things may one day be OK.

I find myself at the bus stop. I hadn't been conscious of walking here, more aware instead of the desultory reveries into which I am ilk to fall, as though open manholes placed before my path. But when I see the shards of shattered glass surrounding the kicked-in bus stop, it shakes me back to consciousness of the moment and my reality, and I begin to stop dreaming and start doing, waiting purposefully for the bus to come and take me, to do what I must, so that I can live fully and die completely, as I believe is befitting a thinker such as myself.

My plan was rather simple: Head to the next town and think about ending people's lives without arousing too much suspicion. If anybody was to see me acting strangely in either town, they would most likely do nothing about it, on account of their desensitisation to degeneration, but if I stand out for some reason and they remember me, it seems better to be remembered by those who are far away. Back in school they had said I would never amount to anything, that I was a no-hoper. At last, I could feel that I was on the cusp of proving them wrong.

There is always something about bus stops that makes me nervous. Perhaps it is the fear of the unexpected, the fact that anybody in the whole of the city could be preparing to join in, to take a ride to the same place for different reasons, and that there is nothing you can do about it. Should the bus crash, or if the terrorists strike again, then these will be the people that you are going to die with, forgotten not as yourself but as one of them. Unless you were already famous or mildly renowned, everything that you had done before that moment would somehow mean nothing or be erased from the annals of your society.

I sat on the slanted metal wrung, which is supposed to pass for a seat, then I stared at my reflection in one of the unbroken windows, and I watched the people pass by in their cars until the bus came.

Nobody got off when the doors opened because they were all trying to get away too. As the ticket machine made its paper emission noises, I could feel the eyes of those already seated staring me down, like I was an outsider, a threat to personal space, liberty and territory, disconnected from the collective body. I made my way down the gangway, each step that I took heavier than the one before with the weight of their eyes upon me, the electric anxiety making my hairs stand on end, and the sides of my eyes swell with blue anticipation. Attempting to project an image of equanimity and self-control, I folded my ticket between my hands in a nonchalant manner, then slid it in to one of the empty card slits in my wallet as I went about the task of choosing myself a seat.

Just after lunch time, rush hour for the elderly, most seats were already occupied by little round faces, on top of which perched cotton wool hairdos. Dewy conversations steamed up the windows and I began to feel at home. Looking around me, I saw a young Indian boy with a tarnished red rose in hands. Alone and pulling apart the petals, a blanket of them rested on the floor beneath his feet. I carried on, past a thug shouting at two young children with deflated beach balls in their hands. He beseeched them to behave as he shook his fists. The excitement of the funfair must have been too much for him.

I took a seat towards the back of the vehicle, lacking the valour and strength of character required to go to the very end, yet far back enough to still feel youthful. The people who had free seats next to them peered into my soul, almost challenging me to sit next to them, but willing me not to at the same time. I walked away from them, thoroughly defeated in a battle of wits, until I had reached the last free seat, three rows from the very back. A foreign guy of indistinguishable ethnicity was sat in the window seat. He smiled at me and I noticed that one of his eyes was bigger than the other, both of them betraying the slight hint of madness. His hair was beginning to recede and he looked dirty. I smiled back in a cursory fashion, then I shuffled into the free seat next to him and kept my eyes to the floor, hoping that this was it, that I would be off the bus soon and wouldn't have to interact with anybody or anything else. The bus stopped at the next stop, somebody got off, a gust of wind fell about us all and swept the Indian boy's rose petals up and about us. Nothing made any sense.

The doors closed and the bus set off again. I stared down the driver in the rear view mirror and wondered if he was even more lonely than I probably was. He was too busy concentrating on the traffic to look at me, though perhaps he was avoiding me. I looked back to the floor, at my old school shoes with the holes in them, the flaking plastic soles, the knotted laces with the dry dirt turning to dust. I was forced to take a breath in order to recompose myself.

I will always hate being out and about in public, moving from one place to another, playing the role of just one of the many, another face in the crowd. Nervous people make me nervous. They make me feel edgy and strange and I never feel sure that I can take it very well.

I put my hands to my head and ran them through my hair. Sighed, but not so loud as to have everybody else on the bus hear me. I did it internally, back behind the walls of the glass maze. I wanted to shout out, up loud and above the heads of the rest of the passengers. I wanted to let them know that I was here. That I existed. But I knew that I couldn't because they would think that I was strange.

'Hello.'

It was the Foreign Guy of Indistinguishable Nationality. I had being trying to forget about him, because despite being just as desperate to reach out as the rest of us out and about the streets, I was picky about who I would reach out to. Most failed to meet the standards that I had set for myself, others I could tell would not approve of the way I had chosen to live my life and would reprove me for it, or they wouldn't treat me with the reverence that I felt I deserved, as though I were no longer an individual, or something to be remembered beyond the rest of the day's ephemera. It hadn't occurred to me at this stage that if everybody likes you then you are most certainly doing something wrong.

I pulled my head up from my crotch and sat backwards into the seat, slid down into it, vertebrae by vertebrae, lazy, as though my body were limp and being pulled down again by the undercurrents of my dreams. I wanted desperately to ignore the passenger next to me, as though he were just another voice on the radio in my head, another blip on the scale, another scratch on the record of white noise that was playing over and over again on limitless repeat. I stared straight and rigid, as though scouting the horizon for a signal of some kind, a letter from the President to be delivered by horseback.

Maybe the good news will come tomorrow.

Once again he broke the silence, as though the possibility of somebody ignoring him were not one of the available options. That simply wasn't the kind of world that he lived in.

'Hello', he said again.

And so I sighed in submission to the will of the Universe.

Because he sounded so very alone, and because he seemed so very persistent, I felt that I must acknowledge him in some way. Because he had chosen *me* to be the vessel into which he would pour himself today, and because I was already beginning to feel that I should be more open to new experiences, new people, and new things, and because I did not like the caricature that I could sense myself becoming otherwise, I plucked up the courage to reply. :

'Hi.'

And, even though I kept my eyes to the ground the whole time, he asked me if I had a girlfriend, and I tried my very best to explain to him that I didn't, but that once upon a time I had done. His English was short of the mark, uneven and unpolished, but I could see from the ways that his eyes rolled back into his head that he was trying his best to communicate with me, and that whatever he had to say about girlfriends was something he needed the world to know about. Sitting there, playing the role of Joe Public, threshold to the Rest of The World, I felt an obligation to listen as best I might, so that this man, wherever he might have been from, would not lose his faith in the rest of us, that he would alight this bus feeling secure in the idea of a world where you can open up to strangers and have them try their bests to understand you. I felt it mandatory to do so and I felt virtuous because of it.

'My girlfriend very happy', he say, 'every day sex two hours. She make good food.'

I give him the thumbs up, to show that I approved, and then I nod and I smile, just in case he doesn't understood.

'Very nice', I say. And I watch as his differently sized eyes flicker like the candles in a dust-filled church without a vicar. Then there are a few beats of silence, because neither of us can think of anything to say.

I begin to wonder if I haven't made a mistake, in communicating with such a specimen when of such a fragile state of mind. I look around the bus to see if any of the seats have cleared up, and indeed some of them have, but I don't have the courage to just stand and relocate. For some reason, I continue to feel that this poor man from overseas has a desire to talk to me, to be made welcome, and to feel as one. I tell myself that he would be offended and disillusioned if I left him behind. Shabby, incomplete and unworthy, abandoned in the Threshold to The Rest of The World.

After a few more moments of suffocating silence, he asked me where I was going. What he actually said was:

'You go where now?'

And for some reason I became intensely afraid. Why didn't I just stay at home today? Wasn't it my day off? Wasn't I supposed to be relaxing and recharging, so that I could go back to stacking shelves in peace tomorrow, fully rejuvenated and raring to go? I felt my t-shirt sticking to my lower back. I looked to the steamed up windows. The bus stuck in traffic, we drifted by a house with yellow tape around the front door and a police man standing sentry. Through the steamed up windows it was like gazing through fog, but, nevertheless, it was a scene of enough clarity to fill me with an ineffable and crushing sense of foreboding. The Man of Indistinguishable Nationality must have seen the consternation on my face, or perhaps it was the sweat on my brow.

'Too much murders this town', he said and looked at me as though he knew *everything* about my plans.

The colours boiled behind the screen of my eyes, as though there were a hound at my heels, sniffing me out before I'd had so much as a chance of formulating an escape plan of some kind. Before I had even done anything wrong.

This simple man with a happy girlfriend has outsmarted me, I thought. And then my breathing became heavy and I felt confused. I could feel my head darting rapidly from one side to another, swirling, as though I were a piece of paper being flushed down a stained toilet in the back of a library. All of a sudden I felt dizzy; I thought I might vomit. I leaned across the man, who was occupying the window seat, and used my thumb to draw a sad face in the condensation. He looked at me, a little scared and surprised, and I was happy because that had been my intention.

Nevertheless, still panicked, it occurred to me that I hadn't answered his question, about where I go now. Worried that it might be rude if I didn't say anything, I decided that the best thing to do would be to lie.

'I'm on my way to meet an friend', I told him, 'We're going to get drunk and meet some girls ...You know how these things are...'

And then I nudged him gently with my elbow, winked at him, as though there was some kind of private joke between us. But, instead of the male bonding experience that I had been expecting, he just looked at me, intently, like I had offended him in some way. Unsure of what else to do, I continued with the fabrication I had started to weave.

'We're going to go to this pub that we've been visiting together ever since high school. We grew up around here, you see. We're really very good friends.'

Still he said nothing, so I was forced to continue, as though on a motor. The nervous energy I emitted was like a few thousand cups of coffee

'It's nice to be close to people, isn't it? I would hate to be one of those people that have nobody close or special in their lives.'

I stared at him, finally making eye contact, begging him to make some kind of response.

But he had lost interest long ago.

Now quiet and subdued, The Man of Indistinguishable Nationality was leaning in silence against the steamy windows. Some more rose petals came floating down the way towards us, blowing down the gangway with the dust and the packets, and all the other items that the people on the bus had felt it necessary add to the public potpourri.

'Is getting hot', said the man.

And then I looked around at the empty seats, the ones that had been abandoned by those who had alighted with their shopping bags, or with their newspapers under their arms. Maybe I should take the chance to leave, I thought. To end this on a high, whilst I'm winning. But, before I had a chance to move, something was stirred within the soul of my squint-eyed interlocutor and, as he shook my hands without looking at me, he said:

'I go sit over there where is cooler.'

He arose from his seat, as though he wished for nothing more than me to get out of his way, as though I had just been wiped off of a blackboard. He brushed past me with a sense of determination on his face, without saying another word, to the free seats at the back of the bus, leaving me finally and forever again alone.

I shuffled along towards the window seat, the one he had been sitting in, and I kept my eyes towards the front of the bus, because I didn't want to make any eye contact with him, because there was no longer any need. Our relationship had ended and all I had left of him was the warmth that he had left permeated throughout the seat. I sucked it up as I bathed in the sweet memory of companionship.

I hoped that nobody had noticed that I had been abandoned, that I was a dull person and a poor conversationalist, but I could tell that they were all looking at me, and that they thought I was the Weird Guy on the Bus, and there was nothing I could do about it.

Chapter 20

Once the bus had pulled into the station I stayed in my seat, waiting for everybody else to get off first, so that I could keep my eyes to the ground and then slink down after them with my hands in my pockets and my head darting from side to side. Though I could barely see anybody from my hiding place near the back of the bus, the sounds of shuffling feet began to fill the whole vehicle as though smoke in a tent; old folks with their reusable shopping bags, opportunistic youngsters caught in the traffic and waiting for a chance to overtake; some of them push out of their seats to get away from the others, possessed of some demon that can't hardly wait to get off of the bus and into the rain, out into the high street, so they can bumble in between one another in the aisles of the pound shops, or so they can hold their noses behind each other in the cheeseburger line, and try to convince themselves that they are truly alive, that they are lucky, and that this is what they always wanted from life.

I sat patiently the whole while, the patron saint of serenity, earnest and true, with perfect posture and control and complacency. I became the surface of a pond without so much as a ripple; the last autumn leaf before the approach of a long, harsh winter - clinging to the tree, refusing to fall. I study the vagueness of my reflection in steamed windows, the condensation rising again over the sad face I delineated with my thumb. Then, when everybody else has clambered off and is a safe distance away, I pass down words of thanks to the driver, counting his change, and we speak as though we were once upon a time best friends. I head into the new town feeling strange and exotic and fresh, even though the weather is the same and the people are just as ugly and I still feel like the same person, knowing deep down in my heart that there's no real chance of anything changing today.

At the bus station tiny pieces of litter blow about the wind that comes uninvited through the automatic doors. Surly young men in tracksuits sit around on benches or stand about in circles, talking loudly and laughing cheaply, beating their chests and swinging from the trees as they show off before equally track-suited young women whose braless nipples pierce their t-shirts. Peppered against the crowds of youths walk the elderly; darting in and out of the crowds like the rabbits up on the hills, looking for rocks to hide beneath, away from predators, only they have their shopping trolleys and their walking sticks and their rickets and so stand out at the bottom of the food chain.

Some of them are visibly afraid, because here reigns only chaos and they are accustomed to a sterility of order. Their faces are riddled with fear, even though they try to hide it. Sometimes the youngsters, the rebels and the first world anarchists with their cigarettes next to the no smoking signs, lurch out in front of those that try to pass them by. One day, many of them will be old also, and most likely somebody will be tormenting them too.

The wheel is always turning.

If anything I lacked a concrete plan. I didn't know why I was here, just that I felt I should be and that if I stuck around long enough things would begin to make sense. Days before, I had tried on my new shoes, turning those words over and again, *'I am a murderer'*, and though they didn't fit perfectly at the time, the more I considered the fact that they might eventually do so, the more comfortable they seemed to have become.

The blisters were beginning to fade and I felt like I was walking on water.

I made my way through the town, my confidence growing the further I walked without anybody saying anything to me, trying to intimidate me, or breathe down my neck. Every town in this country is the same, I thought, the same shops with the same products at the same prices; the stench of the same fast foods with the same kinds of people hovering around outside the doors; the only thing that changes are the buildings, though only on the outside.

The company that I worked for, The Shop, they had a branch here too. I wasn't looking for it, but it found me, the store logo an apparition or an acid flashback from a B-movie, seeming to hold prominence over all that surrounded. I peered through the windows, the same bored expressions, the same lacklustre lifestyles and people queuing with crumbs on their vests and junk spilling out of their pockets. I felt a weight pressing down upon me, and so, before I got too depressed, I headed deeper into the jungle, like a hunter, out of his cave to find nourishment, so that he could drag his quarry back bleeding and then eat it in peace as he used his excrement to draw pictures on the walls.

I looked down at Mao; his good hand approaching the hour, I thought I saw the minutes change. Today would be my lucky day, I thought. Mao winked at me. I winked back and then made my way through the crowd.

Then my stomach began to rumble, pangs of hunger, an emptiness that woke me up a little and put me to sleep at the same time. My head felt light. It brought a surrealism to the situation, as though I were floating above these people, above all the shoppers and the loiterers and the malingerers

I tried thinking back to the last time I had eaten; it could have been the night before. I thought about a conversation I had joined one of the doctors in, at the hospital, and he had told me that if I became hungry then my bones or something could shatter, release toxins into my blood, and that this would cause my heart to attack me, and it would probably be fatal. In a state of panic, as these thoughts flooded my mind, I forgot that I had told myself I was no longer afraid of dying. I ran into the indoor shopping centre that awaited all who dare to leave the safety of the bus station, and, amongst the squat little security guards in their uniforms and the discount clothing stores, I looked for a food stall of some kind so as to take the pain away.

Suddenly, I realised that everybody around me was eating pasties, just like in the town that I had tried to escape from. They were eating them from the same white paper bags with the blue logo, as they took the same slow footsteps towards aimless destinations, and for some reason it made me panic even moreso, because the thought of everything being the same, so standardised, when it all seemed so alien to me, was too much to handle.

I sat on a bench outside a made-in-China shoe shop, gasping for breath as the cheap plastic frisson hung around my head like a cloud, and the anxiety of it all pulled the hairs out of my head, and my eyes began to water and everything seemed so much bigger to me and much more daunting than it probably should have been. Polyester people passed me by in packs; empty men and ladies with three-legged walking sticks, more old people with rickets scuttling like crabs, a great and unwholesome ode to life, all painted against a backdrop of dumb, fat children with snot on their nostrils, the hellish stench of synthetic materials and experience, dawdling, wasting and fading away with each rotation of an Earth lost in space.

I let out a scream.

For a moment, only silence prevailed, and then the pure confusion that is heir to animal madness, in which everybody around me seemed to pause, give up what they were doing, and stare at me with their mouths open and their eyes glazed over. Then, sensing that I wasn't the threat I could have been, they continued about their business, the show resuming, as though they had all remembered that time existed and that they were part of it, and that they had to keep moving to make it work.

I slunk back into the bench. My t-shirt rode up at the back, I felt the cool metal of the rung against clammy skin as though I were melting. Food, I kept thinking. Feed yourself. But I couldn't find the energy to stand up and become a part of the crowd. I so very deeply wanted to believe that I was better than these people, this dirty hundred dozen, the poor, the uneducated, whatever they were. I wanted to distinguish myself, to feel superior, to let the world know that I was only here because of consequence and necessity, instead of that I deserved to be, and that, if the universe had been just and providence not unkind, then I would have ruled over all of them and they would've thanked me for it.

Every footstep I took, seemed to take me deeper into the thickets, cutting my legs and my ego on the brambles, breaking me down. We are all the same at the end of the day. Living and dying and breathing in between. But, because I wasn't ready for it, because I suspected that they hated me, because I wasn't quite as undernourished, because my shoes gleamed just a little bit more, I would choose to stay inert, sitting here on the bench, until something came for me and took me away from them all.

I let out another scream, louder this time, more like a bark, more primal, to show them that I wasn't afraid of them, that I didn't care. Some youngsters walked past. They eyed me and began to laugh amongst themselves, as though I was the greatest joke of them all.

I barked again. But because they weren't expecting any reaction other than fear, they became confused. They threw their eyes to the floor, as though they had forgotten how to use them, and then they walked away in silence and I felt golden and complete.

My eyes closed as I leaned deep back into the bench. Nobody came to sit next to me. What a way to spend your day off, I thought to myself. Then I felt myself fading away, sinking to the bottom of an ocean of sleep, drifting to wherever it may take me, and not even caring if somebody might rob me as a punishment for nodding off in public, because I had nothing of value for them to take, and had long since learned to convince myself that self-pity was a virtue.

I woke up in the hospital bed, overseas. It was the same one in which the doctor had told me that I was dying, the one with the green curtains and the view of the city out of the window; the last time I had seen the metropolitan skyline, before I had been shipped back over to this country, like some faulty product being returned to Amazon, one that would only get a one star review, because it wasn't reliable and it didn't do what it said on the tin.

Despite my knowing that this was a dream, it still felt real to me, more real than my woken life seemed to in many ways. The colours were sharper and the edges were more defined and the people around me, the doctors and the nurses and a few of my friends and then Her, The One I Loved, were united by shared chemistry, a connection lacking in the world as I knew it now. Back in the unwoken world, people seemed set only on being in some constant, venal competition, instead of just being with one another or trying to see people as ends within themselves.

And so, suspecting that I would be unable to bask in these feelings upon waking, the whole dream scenario became tinged with a palpable and languid melancholy. I felt the sides of my eyes drying up, as though I was trying to stop myself from crying, and then I felt the tears trickle down my face. But at least I felt alive.

'I'm sorry', said the Doctor, 'but it seems that there's actually nothing wrong with you. Indeed, we have wasted your time and toyed with your emotions, and so for this we must apologise.'

I felt the eyes of The One I Loved upon me, smiling. I thought back to that time in woken life, when the doctor had told me the opposite of what he had just said to me in this dream, and when it had happened, I had become alarmingly overwhelmed with a potent sense of déjà vu, as though I had always known that this was going to happen, because I had always suspected that there was something wrong; I had long known that I was doomed and this would only be the start of it.

That time, She, The One I Loved, she had been crying too, and we both felt a weight on our shoulders, which we managed to share the lifting of. Now, in the dream, she started laughing, and so I began laughing too, and instead of the weight there obtained an unquestionable lightness and levity that filled our collective heart with joy. It lifted our souls to the ceiling, and as I put my arms around her, we climbed out of the bed and did a pathetic but honest little jig together.

Then all the doctors and all the nurses around my bed started laughing too. And so did the other patients. And it seemed for a few moments that the whole world had joined in. I looked out of the window, by the side of the bed, and I could see the taxi drivers laughing and the pedestrians strolling along beneath the scorching afternoon sun, laughing too. I smiled and then I shook the doctors hand and then I looked down and I was no longer wearing the hospital gown - I was back in my suit and tie. We started walking, right out of the hospital, down the corridor, by the endless bottles of piss sat on shelves and the constantly running water of the taps in the unisex bathroom. My soul began to soar with the release of infinite bliss. At last, I was heading home.

But then, then I remembered that this was just another dream that I didn't want to awaken from. This was only how I wanted things to be. And as soon as I realised this, everything started to crumble. I looked at The One I Love, who was holding my hand, but she had disappeared, and instead of laughing jovially, the cachinnations of the doctors and nurses had become heavy, like clouds that were about to burst, and they rang throughout the hallways and the corridors of the hospital building, and, when I looked to the windows, there were bars covering them, because I was dreaming in clichés, and then when the elevator finally came, just as the doctors and nurses were closing in on me, I saw that it had been bricked up, and I would not be able to leave.

They ate my flesh, and I felt the most penetrating of fears; forever defective and unable to do anything about it. Then I heard a voice and it said to me:

'Excuse me, Sir.'

And then it repeated itself:

'Sir.'

As I opened my eyes to the real world and I found that I was still on the bench. Instinctively, I checked to see if my wallet and my mobile phone were still in my possession, and, as though by miracle, they were. The only thing that had changed, it seemed, was that now there was a large man in a uniform looking down upon me, and, if the expression on his face was anything to go by, he wasn't very happy to see me. He had that empty look in his eyes, as though he lacked the basic cognitive capacities, but I couldn't tell him that because he was bigger than me and, most likely, he was able to get away with dishing out abuse to people as part of his unofficial job description.

'Excuse me, Sir. We've received several complaints that your behaviour has frightened a number of the other customers within the Kirkdale shopping centre. Also, I must point out to you that these benches are designed for sitting upon. Not for sleeping.'

I looked up at him from behind sleep strained eyes. He was wearing a tattered jacket, a few sizes too small and obviously not part of his official uniform because it had 'FBI' emblazoned in canary yellow on the breast. Though I couldn't see it from where I was sat on the bench, I could tell that it said it in even bigger letters on the back.

I wondered if I had gone to sleep in England and woken up in America, or perhaps in some unimaginative made-for-TV movie, in which I was playing the part of the hobo or the vagabond, the itinerant that seeps into the community and urinates in people's cars and irritates children on the way to school with his malodorous ways and messy hair.

'I'm going to have to ask you to leave the building, Sir', he said.

Then he reached out to pick me up off of the chair and escort me out of the building. And because I was so bewildered and still half asleep, I actually let him, blindly and obediently following behind him as docile and tractable as a cow. In fact, I was almost out of the door by the time I came to my senses. And as everybody gaped at me, as though George W Bush had just taken a shit on their freshly cut lawns, I managed to shake myself out my stupor, and thus say to him:

'But I am in need of victuals and refreshment, my Good Man.'

And, for some reason, that made him stop right in his tracks. The big lummox looked down upon me once again, because he must have been about twelve feet tall, and he said something that was too convoluted for me to remember verbatim, something about not using bad language in front of public officials, or whatever the hell he considered himself to be. He even pushed me back up against a wall, the window, actually, of a charity shop that sold jigsaw puzzles and broken tea pots to old people. Then he looked at me with his red eyes ablaze, incensed and disbelieving of the fact that I had dared to challenge his authority.

'Then eat outside, mate.'

And I couldn't hardly believe it, because I had not expected him to understand the word 'victuals', so convinced was I of my verbal authority. He shoved me out of the door and I felt my face burn and begin to redden as my false sense of superiority melted away like butter down the crumpet hole .

I watched him through the double doors, swaggering like the cock of the school through the corridors as he walked away, and my stomach continued to rumble and my throat began to burn.

Chapter 21

Hot and bothered, all concepts of fear and any sense of self-worth left long behind, I find myself at the mercy of a new and misplaced intrepidity. Back behind the bus station with the degenerates and the lowlife and the scum, I make eye contact as some of them make note of my altercation with the security guard and so look at me as though I could be one of them. The air between us thickens as I wait for something to happen, an exit sign above the door to turn on and start flashing, a shot in the arm, anything that would help me forget about my problems and lend a false sense of purposefulness to the immediate present.

They stood there with their tracksuit pants pulled up high and their chains around their necks, still strutting and swaggering like apes that had escaped their cages and taken over the zoo, and as I stared into the dead eyes of some swollen baby in some ancient and dirty-wheeled pushchair, I coughed on the clouds of smoke being emitted by the cigarette clutched between the grubby fingers of a young boy, perhaps around ten years old. Then I listened to the dregs of conversation and snippets of banter that floated above it all:

'Babies should come with remote controls', one of the Mothers was saying to anybody who would listen, 'why won't he shut up?'

And it all seemed so normal in the most eerie of ways.

For a few misguided moments, I toyed with the notion of heading over there and delivering a formal introduction, letting them know that I could lead them forwards, on account of my being slightly more educated and having read more books, that I could improve their minds, lead them onwards and upwards to greater and better things. I took a whole footstep in their direction before realising that it would most likely be a bad move.

As soon as I opened up to utterance, or as soon as I spoke with that plum in my mouth and those grammatically correct enunciations, they would realise that I was just another interloper, some busybody with too much time on his hands, another imposter with a heightened sense of self-righteousness and a proclivity to impose his will on the world.

The ten year old with the cigarette saw me and was able, with his childish intuition, to sense the wall of hesitation that I had built around myself. And so, in order to throw him off the scent, I leaned back against the automatic doors of the shopping centre and began to chant self-help mantras to myself, things about manifestation, or about the universe, about *amor fati* and predestination. Though I was quite convinced that I had managed to project an air of relative calm, like an ice berg that may or may not be about to crack into pieces and bring chaos to an already raging ocean, I didn't want to admit to myself that I was afraid. I didn't want to lose my wits completely. I wanted to make it home alive.

Once again, the whole of the world felt heavier than it was supposed to, and I could feel the glare of the Smoking Child etching cuss words into the surface of my skin.

Having somehow found the strength of will to put my feet back into gear, I attempted to get myself out of there. What I needed was a vantage point, a place where I could look down at the whole of this zoo, this safari park, at once, so that I could see what was what, and who was who, and where they each stood in relation to one other. What I needed was to be up high and out of view of them all, so that I could play the role of the voyeur, audience member to this pathetically written pantomime. I would watch it as objectively as possible, as a lesson to be learned, see what it had to teach me, and then make my judgements fairly as I dictated whose lives were worth living and who was just another blip on the evolutionary scale, another anomalous freak of nature, another accident that left the unity of the universe open to question. A test of my faith.

The hunger that I felt had not subsided. Instead it had permeated throughout my body, spread itself evenly throughout my limbs, and seeped deep to the pit of my stomach to squeal and to hiss like steam engines soon to be burned out of coal. And, on account of this even distribution of sensation, instead of that pressure in my head, like some extraneous and incongruous object in a microwave about to explode, I now felt a lightness and levity of being so complete and so pure that I began to feel as though I could float up above it all; as though I could choose to let go if need be, and that the waves of whatever truth I was on the verge of discovering would come sweeping over me as though rain after a lifetime of drought.

And then I looked down at my feet, and I couldn't believe what was happening, but the town beneath me was getting smaller and I realised that I was leaving the ground for the sky. Next thing I knew, I was miles high, sat on a cloud looking down on it all. The people down there looked like ants. For a moment or two, I felt like a Greek god, although to be honest, lacking a private education, I didn't know that much about them - except that they lived up on a mountain, looking down on people, I mean.

Whatever was going on, from up here, on my cloud, I could see the whole of the new town: the buses pulling up and into the station, regular and creaking, like the one I had climbed off of earlier, with the old folks and the people walking slow and languid like their will had deserted them. Down by the bus station, I could see the cloud of smoke that was being emitted from the smoker's area, down by the mass of pushchairs and jaundiced flesh and tracksuits. Then I saw the boy, the one that had been smoking, standing around with his troglodyte family members - guys in vests with the tribal tattoos down their arms, women in tracksuits with too much makeup on their faces - and as I looked at the Smoking Boy, I could tell that he had seen me and he was the only one who had noticed that I had managed to fly on up here in this way, even though I didn't know myself how I had managed to do so.

I gave him a polite little wave as my legs dangled over the side of the cloud. After all, even though he was smoking cigarettes he was still only a child, and so it seemed only right to expect that the innocence we naively imagine children to be imbued with to still reside within him. Truth be told, I expected him to be completely overjoyed by my whimsical gesture of good faith, I thought that it might give him a reason to live, that he would fling his cigarette to the ground and stamp upon the ashes. But instead he just gave me the finger. He flipped it right at me and then lighted up another cigarette. Perhaps he should be the one who deserves to die today, I thought to myself, because as we age the joy in our hearts tends to dissipate and he had already started out with so little.

But it wouldn't it be wrong to kill a child? Is there not infinite potential within each of them? The capacity for change? Or was that just another myth? Most likely, it would be wrong to kill anybody, or so they say these days. Life is priceless. But this was my destiny and I had to start somewhere.

I forgot about fear and anxiety and gave way to purpose. It made me feel strong again. I sat there looking down and thought about who I might be taking. There were so many options. It was like a pessimist working in an orchard and looking up at a tree rife with bad apples.

As seen from this perspective, the town could be taken at face value. Built deep in the recesses of a valley, with vast expanses of verdant hills barricading it on each side, it actually looked quite beautiful. In the upper echelons of the valley, in the areas affording the best views, expensive cars sat like polished statues in the vast driveways of opulent houses, and the buildings themselves were designed for pleasure and to be pleasing to the eyes, instead of the banausic tenements down the city, down the mouldy basin of the valley, in the houses for the immigrants and the tracksuits, cooped up and at war with each other like battery chickens, living only semi-free range lives with their semi-smashed windows and the anti-police graffiti on their doorways and the wire chain locks besides the keyholes.

'If life is as meaningless as they say then how can we say that anybody truly deserves to live?'

I watched people walk out and about the streets, a man with a torn paper bag under his arm full of used books, which he kept taking out and flicking through the pages of to read at snippets and try to find sense in them. Getting old, a mind clouded with memories, and his hair brushed up and over his bald patch; blue old jacket, tired old eyes, the way he fidgeted betrayed him, as though there was something he couldn't stop thinking about, like he had a sick relative in his family, some indisposed dependent forever on his mind, a coma victim perhaps or some atrophied train wreck in a wheel chair.

As a boy perhaps he had dreamed that life would be easy, that it would present itself on a plate with a natural cohesiveness and playful richness, that he would be solvent in every sense of the word, because life would hold itself together. Now, of course, he could only wince at the memory of such naïve thoughts, ones that had long since crossed his mind, because instead of life holding itself together, he had learned that it was he himself who was forced to act as glue, and that it took so much more strength to do so than we are told to expect of ourselves. Unable to find such resource within, he now took listless walks through the streets, flicking through the pages of books that people had given away, not understanding that most art only sells because it offers only the promise of an answer and never an actual solution.

'If all of us are seeking answers, does that not mean that there aren't any?'

Perhaps I should put him out of his misery, I thought, so that he might think that all that came before had been building up to this moment, so he can convince himself that, even if it wasn't worth it, that it at least made a modicum of 'sense'. But what if it didn't provide him with the necessary answers? He would be dying in vain and everything would be my fault and there would be little to be done about it. I decided to let him keep on walking in the rain, in his blue jacket with his tired eyes, forever with the hope that he would find the truth that he was looking for, flicking through the pages of dog-eared books, pretending that it was never too late for things to work out.

My search of the town continued as I looked out and about for an easy target, a person that stood anathema to myself - my bête noire. Essentially and unfortunately, however, at heart I was apathetic and at best I was dead inside; my life had not been lived upon the basis of a particular moral code or set of truths, and so the extent to which I could care about the actions of others, about the choices that they made and their lifestyles, was narrow and myopic, paradoxically, on account of being limitless and so encumbered by relativity. All that could really be done was to choose somebody at random, to find somebody who was just going through the motions, a soul who didn't care, a truly worthless and empty vessel just as jaded as myself.

A portly man with a cheeseburger in his hands, sweat stains on his T-shirt and crumbs of something old and out-of-date about his pants, took doleful footsteps down the towpath between an abandoned, smashed-up factory and a polluted river. I could tell immediately that he had given up a long time ago. He reminded me of, and perhaps even could have been, a man who had been a regular patron of The Shop when I was doing my time, a man infamous for his particular brand of malodorousness, because whenever he approached it would begin to feel like the walls had moved in closer and the stench of his hindquarters rubbing together would become too much for us all, and so the people working on the shop floor would come and hide as best they could behind the till area.

One day, on one of the rare occasions that I felt I might still be some version of myself that I might've liked to have permanently been, barbaric, brash, and irreverent, I asked him a question:

'Do you like this town, Sir? Because my personal opinion is that it stinks. I think it would be better if they dropped a bomb on it?'

And I remember that he looked at me, surprised that somebody was soliciting his opinions but more than happy to give them. Placing his DVDs delicately down on the counter, he looked at me as though he had been waiting his whole life to unburden himself and that finally he had been able to:

'I abhor this abomination of a place.'

There was such an vitriolic intensity to those words that it caught me off guard, because I had not expected this placid, bumbling man to harbour such enmity. Instantly, I felt ignorant and foolish for never before even having dared think that some amongst us are doomed to lives like this forever. Maybe I am too, I thought. It was still not out of the question.

To make us both feel better I said:

'At least it's not forever.'

But he just looked at me as though I might be dumb or incomplete. Because I should of realised that this man was a prisoner here and that I was not the tourist that I thought I might be. Because there was a very real possibility that this shit town vacation would be one without an end.

'It probably will be.'

He paid for his DVDs, movies that I supposed might be from his childhood, and then he slunk out the doors with his head to the ground and his smelly hindquarters rubbing together, and I realised that most people around us are already resigned to the fact that life is meaningless; most are just waiting for something to happen to them, so that they can die more quickly and with less hassle, so that they can get this whole inconvenience out of the way, because it is just another triviality that needs to be dealt with.

'Everything is dead, or dying, or waiting to die.'

I came out my retrospective reverie and returned to the generic person before me, the one with the cheeseburger in his hands and the grease on the pockets of his pants. I had been blessed with an omniscience, although there was always a chance that I had invented the facts, a layer of acetate that I had spread over the frame before me and painted faces and shapes onto. Yes, there stood another one, another waste of space, another victim of tragedy to look deep into the eyes of and see a terror and a yearning, like a gorilla that has been kept caged up in the zoo for too long and has become depressed because of a lack of activity. This man is waiting to die, I thought, and perhaps I could be the one to expedite the process, bring it swiftly to a conclusion.

My eyes must have glanced over thousands of them. People in cheap business suits, one size fits all, selling mobile phone contracts or unnecessary insurance to people in shopping centres. Their plastic smiles, their dead eyes. Charity workers on every street corner, each week appealing and accosting for a different cause, convincing themselves that they are interesting just because they are extroverted, preying on the indigent because they are the only ones who understand the virtues of helping people. Would it really be so wrong to butcher a chugger? What a town! What a life! So many choices!

If only I had a bomb…What would the world be missing if this town, or the next, were to be wiped off of the slate? What I would give to drop one casually over the edge of my cloud. *Give me the Tsar and I'll show you the stars.*

GIVE ME THE TSAR AND I'LL SHOW YOU THE STARS…

I came out of my reverie, determined to make a swift decision, resolved to do whatever was required of me. Once you have made a plan, no matter how ludicrous, you should stick to it. This is the only way of making progress in this world. I leaned forwards over the edge of my cloud, and then I fell forwards, down towards the earth, back towards the waiting area outside the bus station. I landed gently, but not so much that it didn't make my bones shatter, and next I knew everybody was looking at me, but they didn't say anything because they had never seen anything like it before.

I closed my eyes and tried slipping away from consciousness and towards nothingness. It enveloped me. Silence and darkness. And, for a few minutes, I thought I had found eternity, but I knew that not even that could last forever.

Chapter 22

When I awoke I could remember little of the darkness except for the nebulous tinge of its sensations. Though I describe it now as darkness, it was actually much more than that; it was a silence that had actually taken me, and I believe that what I saw was indeed the colour of such, the colour of possibility, the way that life could be lived without all of the external pressures and importunate stimulation that can neither be lived without nor escaped from in the phenomenal realm.

What enveloped me at that stage was a total state of serenity, a period of quiescence which I felt, at the time, would last forever. In fact, when I think about it, the very concept of time left me, deserting me like a bad parent would an ugly or unwanted child. And all those days gone before, the ones where my thought processes had been overtaken by sensation, where colours had shot down through my veins like some lachrymose rainbow haemorrhage, now those days didn't seem to pack the same punch that they had once been capable of doing.

Now, I found myself surrounded by colours of lesser hues, without lightness or darkness. Now or never and nothing in between, the cessation of existence, yet such a fullness of being that I never had felt before, or even realised could ever be possible. It was the beginning and the end of all things, though I realised that they were all happening and over and done with at the same time, and I awoke feeling fresher and more rejuvenated than I had in months, still lost and wandering, undoubtedly, but more confident than ever that I would one day find myself at the end of this journey in the place that my soul had been aching for.

And then, when I came fully to my senses, I was encircled by the bus station loiterers, the ten year old smoking another cigarette, his brutish family members with push chairs, and churlish babies with chubby fingers and chocolate stains around their mouths. Every single one of them was staring me down, keeping my body pressed against the ground, the plaster cast paving stones of a pedestrian street, the echo of footsteps as the more aloof members of the crowd passed me by. Everybody looked scared, as if they had never seen a person jump from the roof of a shopping centre before. It defied their sense of reasoning and logic. They stood scratching itches that didn't exist, fidgeting, anything to look busy because they weren't sure how to react to me, couldn't be sure of what I was capable. In many ways, it seemed to me, they were even more scared than usual.

I pushed myself up into sitting position and held my head in my hands for a few seconds. I massaged my two temples with the middle finger and thumb of the same hand and then I brought my palm to sweep over my face, rubbed my chin and played with the loose strands of hair on my chin that I liked to pretend were part of a 'beard'. I could smell and taste the metallic vestiges of blood and so I rubbed my thumb and my index finger together and, just as I expected, it was sticky and warm, and so I figured that I must have damaged myself in some way upon landing.

I ran my tongue over the ridge of my teeth until, yes, I realised, there was a problem. One of my front teeth was missing. The other one remained, but was much looser, so much so that I could make it move with just the smallest amount of pressure from my tongue. I thought about pulling it out, but from what I had learned in that place of darkness, in the open void between life and death, I knew that it didn't matter if I ripped it out or let it fall, because it would eventually end up in the same place anyway. I rubbed my eyes. They were wet, though not in a sad way.

My vision began to cycle through various states of disarray, of being blurred, an opaque screen, to a pellucid intensity that was all the while too much to get a grasp of. I looked at the circle of people around me, other passers-by, people using the bus station, joining in, wanting to see what the commotion was.

So much for being inconspicuous, I thought, and then I whistled a ditty to project an air of blendibility. Every so often, as my vision danced between a keen clarity and a dull discrepancy, I felt like I was a movie camera, zooming in and out of focus, and so I did the best I could to get a good look at this crowd of strangers from this cinematic angle down below. I had always wanted to be on TV or in the movies, to be culturally relevant. Maybe that was why I had never been 'happy'.

The laboured breaths I unleashed were in honour of the dreams I had let fall by the wayside, a fusillade in honour of the dead, a sky filled with paper lanterns set in flames. I became intensely worried that the Security Guard would show up again and ruin things for me. I had failed to kill myself and could not deal with the day getting any worse.

The crowd seemed to be closing in around me, hundreds of them with holes in their jackets and the stuffing falling out. Sweaty, dirty animals with their eyes wide open and their tongues hanging out of control. They stood staring at me, my broken bones encircled by their warm breath and their hostility as they mumbled amongst themselves and a great hush susurrus swept over it all like waves refusing to break. All the while, though I couldn't hear a word that they were saying, I knew that they were against me. I knew that I had done something that they couldn't agree with, be it watching them from the distance, passing judgement without interaction, or maybe just because I was thin and frail and it is one's biological imperative to nullify those that are even weaker.

And then it dawned on me that maybe it *was* possible for things to get worse, and that even though I had failed at finding a victim for my master plan, I *had* succeeded in doing something much worse: making an enemy of the crowd. I clenched my arms tight into my sides, stiffening my muscles on the bootless whim that somehow it might save me from what I anticipated must be coming. There must have been a hundred of them, give or take. And only one of me. The hunter had become the hunted. I took a deep breath and closed my eyes as I awaited the inevitable.

It was the Ten Year Old With The Cigarette that came for me first. Though my eyes were closed I could smell the tarnish of smoke and nicotine on his clothes, and as his tiny feet jabbed into my sides I could only shudder, because I knew that this was just the start of it and that once the rest had seen a child, a symbol of the future, attacking me, they would all follow suit. They began to shout, to roar as they lurched forwards. They said things that didn't make any sense. Get him. He deserves it. Sort him out. And before I knew it I was trapped in a washing cycle of fists to the head and the spin twist of blood in my mouth.

I stay there on the floor taking it all in. Blood. Bones crunching. A beefy woman with bingo wings rammed a pushchair back and forth against the flats of my feet, as the ill-looking baby within it cried out and above the crowd, as they smashed the heels of their shoes down against my limbs and watched my nose cave in beneath the swiftness of their kicks. Men and woman alike joined in to beat me down. I didn't quite know what I had done, but the fire in their eyes said they didn't like it, and so I knew that if I didn't stand up and try to run then that would be the end of me.

Which was, typically, when the English rain began to fall. Just as I opened my eyes and saw that there were even more of them than I had first anticipated. Crowds attract crowds and so as people got off buses they gravitated without volition towards the outside square. They saw boots in my face and the blood on my nose and assumed that I had done wrong. Somehow I managed to stand up, by grabbing a hold of their clothes and tugging on their sleeves. Between the punches and the smiles on their faces I heard the tail end of a conversation. Somebody was saying:

'Terrible weather for this time of year.'

'Yes, isn't it?'

And then came further blows to the side of my head as I stumbled in one direction only to have somebody punch me and send me staggering off in another. They thought I'd fall, but somehow I kept up the strength to resist. I swayed like a ship that was about to sink, but because these things take time, I knew I could last a little longer if I needed to.

I tried running away from them, up against the wall of the shopping centre, but there were far too many of them and they had the taste of my blood on their lips, and they grabbed me and pulled me towards them to be punched and kicked into others amongst them so that their friends could have a turn. A young buck that had just got off one of the buses ran up and pushed through the throng and smacked me right in the mouth. I felt my lip burst open and the blood flow into my mouth like a bitter metallic milkshake as everybody cheered for him. There was a complacent hubris etched upon his face, as though set in stone, as though he had been proclaimed the town hero and was posing for a bronze statue to be carved of himself and then erected outside city hall.

I pleaded with my eyes as I stood limp beneath the raindrops. We were back to our animal states, and the whole while, now that the pain I felt had become nothing more than a simple breeze that served to awaken me and heighten my senses, I kept thinking to myself. I thought, well, if this is as bad as it gets, not fitting in, then things really aren't that bad at all. An elderly gentleman in a sensible raincoat thrust his elbows into the side of my face and I felt my neck twist, the world a blur in slow motion, and a wad of blood and phlegm flew out of my mouth and mixed in with the rain waters as it swam about the puddles on the floor. My remnant front tooth, the one that had been clinging on by its root, fell deep and wide about me. An umbrella smashed against my stomach. I heard my ribs crack and then I fell back to the floor in silence, meditative, Zen-like, and broken.

The crowd began to settle, perhaps feeling that I would no longer be able to resist, that I had been pushed too far over the cliff to climb back up, that I was long gone and out of it. They became silent, perhaps in veneration for the imminence of death. Some of them went about their business, as though nothing had happened, pushing their shopping baskets, watching the handles of their plastic Tesco bags tighten and strain and cause their hands to fade out. They looked down at their shoes as they bumbled on by and the rain hit my temples, cool and liberating. I wished that I were back on my cloud, safe and away from these beastly people, instead of being down here at their feet, beneath the heels of their boots, subjugated like some rock throwing heathen before a mechanized army, awaiting their mercy as they themselves waited for destiny to decide what might happen to me.

I watched them from behind my half-closed and fully-swollen eyes. Some of them looked at their watches, as though my demise was not moving at a speed which they found to be convenient. They wanted for it to be over, so that they could go about their shopping, as though nothing had ever happened. So that they could go back to their bacon and eggs or their cheeseburgers; so that they could go buy some new cushions for the sofa; some trinkets for the mantel, or another TV, one to stick in the kitchen so that eating together wouldn't feel like such a chore. I squeezed at the bridge of my nose to concentrate the pain on a specific area. I tried to take a deep breath and count to ten but I lacked fluidity and seemed to have forgotten my basic sequencing skills.

I wouldn't be able to tell you how long I lay there, waiting for it. Long ago, two years previously, anyway, when I had first fallen ill, I had felt death closing in on me. Its black throes had seeped over my woken consciousness as though it were the last of the sands before the tide rolls home, and, as I fell into it, for that is what it felt like, a falling down, I truly thought that I my time had come, and that it would be over soon; I would be left alone with only this eternal silence by my side. But, as always seems to be the case, my time did not come. The One I Loved came bursting through the door, just in time to take me to the hospital, and so I was pulled out of drowning, saved from sinking, and the emptiness subsided. As I sat there on the floor, outside the shopping centre, my bones a mess and my skin bejewelled with sweat and the dry blood on my cheeks, I remembered these things and was made to think. Perhaps this time too I will be saved, I thought, because based on my previous experiences with death and dying that seemed to be the way in which things always worked out.

I looked at the crowd, tried to make eye contact with some of them, to find signs of life being valued as something more than just a commodity, or as just another thing to be taken away. Last time I had been at death's door, it seemed to me that I was fading away. This time there was nothing. No such sensation. Maybe they hadn't succeeded. Maybe I would live to see another day. A sense of balance and bittersweet serenity suddenly began to swell in my breast, because where I had once seen myself as a failure for being unable to kill myself, I saw that they too, this mass of people, had failed to do the same thing. I am invincible. I am invincible. I am invincible, I thought. And thus I found the courage to stand and face them.

The rain continued to fall about us as though any other day. I pushed myself up with trembling hands, half expecting my wrists to snap. And when I rocked back on to my heels I heard a collective gasp enkindled deep within the crowd, as though they had half expected me to topple back to the ground again, and this reaction was a just one because I could feel myself swaying like a tree in a storm, seeing that my sense of balance had been distorted by too many blows to the head, and my knees were weak from fear, and the rest of me no longer knew what the rest of me might be doing.

And it was in this tenuous and graceless manner that I fell forwards and tried to catch my balance; delicate steps and falters, a twisted ballet dancer with grazes on his knees. Amongst the crowd members, I could see the elderly man in the sensible raincoat; there was a look of malice about his face, a twisted lemon sucker punch mouth, bitter because he had been working hard his whole life to be a good, honest member of the community and punks like me kept trying to fuck it up for him. I recalled the crack of his elbow up against my face, cusped my jaw bone in my hands, thought about fractures and fissures as I continued to falter. Then I saw the ten tear old with the cigarette, sparking up another as he kept his eyes to the ground because nothing seemed to be going to plan.

The show was over. I forced myself to march on before them. Though they had done their very bests to keep me up against the wall, to limit the ways in which I could move and to prevent me from escaping, the rain had started to confuse them and so slowly they began to dissipate, those from the back leaving for the dryness of the shopping centre, because they couldn't really see what was happening to me anyway. My right leg deadened completely now, most likely by the woman with the push chair, I pulled it along behind me, as though a swollen corpse that I had just dragged out of a river, and as I moved towards those at the front of the crowd, not caring what might happen to me, evincing no concern as to whether life nor death might be around the corner, moving solely on the whim that survival would be the outcome, but at the same time not really being all that bothered about the fact that it might not be, I decided that I didn't care anymore. If I died I would most likely return to where I came from. And if I didn't?

'Well…That probably wouldn't matter either.'

The closer I got to the crowd, to the edge of the boundary that it served to form, the more it began to attenuate. I would hear them mumbling to themselves or to their partners, we'd better get to Argos before it closes, it's getting dark now, aint it, or whatever other bromides seemed germane to their survival plans for the afternoon, bored that the show was over, finally back to their senses after a few irresponsible moments of unrestricted emotion, the purging of anxiety that only a fist to the face of a stranger may serve to cure. Some of them though, they were leaving because they were scared, scared of the strength I had found, the power to resist, and I could see, by the jittered glances that swept across the floor, that they were feeling nervous and rueful and that I may have been blessed with the upper hand.

I edged right up to the vanguard of my circle of attackers. It comprised a number of them, each as burly and as hairy as the rest of them, men, women and children. They stared right into my eyes, the hebetude that glues their souls together causing their blank stares to form flat matte shapes, the lifeless, plastic eyes of children's toys, to point in my direction, and their mouths wide open, as though their brains had forgotten how to control their jaw bones. They stood there beneath my gaze, dazed, looking at me with entreaty, beseeching that I might go back and roll around anguished on the floor some more, so that they could go away with me still in that position, so that they could leave accomplished and having succeeded at something for a change.

I looked into the line of eyes for signs of life, like you might when you go to the zoo and you try to convince yourselves that the animals are really contemplating and that they have profound thoughts to keep them occupied and that is why they are so silent and so tranquil. They surrounded me, but I had such faith in my mission and The Fat Man that I knew they would let me pass. I walked into them but they stood intransigent, as still as the benches with the graffiti on them and the names of strangers on abraded plaques, as immovable as rocks that form the base of mountains, dullards with too much time on their hands and no sense of what to do with it.

'Excuse me, please', I said to one of The Faceless Many.

But they did not speak, instead they just allowed their chests to inflate, one at a time, and then they folded their arms and muttered collectively and disappointedly, as though their dreams had been shattered in unison and they had only just taken on board the idea that the future may fail to live up to their childish expectations.

One of them stood before the others, King Gone, and he curled up his lips in purple disdain and looked at me with a frown on his face and a tear in his eye.

'It's not fair', he said.

And so we shared a silent moment of reverence for all that had happened between us. A few buses backed out of the station, some pigeons flew on overhead with traces of pasty around their beaks. I craned my neck to the heavens and could feel the leaden lights of a flattened skyline shine dull down upon my face. For a few moments, I felt noble, standing there outside the shopping centre, the automatic doors opening and closing like a tubby jogger trying to catch his breath, there beneath the signs and by the vending machines and the window displays.

'I know it isn't', I replied.

Then I tried to force my way through them but, again, they wouldn't let me, and they pushed me backwards with their girth and their ignorance, even though it was clear that I was pained. I held on to my leg and winced, so that all aspects of my being and physiognomy would drill the point home.

Helpless and hopelessly aware of the situation's futility, I stood back and sighed, the apathetic suspiration of a jaded teenager stood before out-of-touch parents, the sigh of a mathematician trapped in an elevator full of accountants. I was in the habit of letting contention turn inwards and against me, to beat up against the shore of my ego, to make me feel small and inferior and defective; this time, however, perhaps on account of no longer having anything to be ashamed of, I felt my anger being deflected away from my inner space and being directed to the outside world, into the tangible place of things and people and then into that of abstract ideas and collective notions. Refuelled, I moved ahead in strides, convinced that this was my chance to break through the maze walls, an unsullied confidence in my own survival, no fear of pain or disgrace or social alienation - I had already been tarred with the poopy brush, and so it didn't matter what might happen next.

The dolt that was nearest readied his fists as I limped towards him. Those besides him did the same. Usually I would have flinched in situations like these. Today I would sign for the delivery.

'Let me through', I said, 'this has gone on for long enough.'

'Why should we?', they muttered amongst themselves, and that was when I noticed that the Security Guard was stood as part of the crowd, watching with a smile on his face.

'Because I am murder', I said.

And I looked at them knowing I that I could happily take the lives of any of them, knowing that there were no longer any mental blocks keeping me civilised.

I pushed my way through, and they opened up, not quite sure how else they might go about things. Some of them seemed about ready to weep but I didn't stop to comfort them. I returned to the bus station, to float across the unpolished floor with the dust and the crisp packets and the hardened lumps of chewing gum, and then I sat down on one of the metal benches by Terminal E, the place where the bus was coming to pick me up, to take me back home, to the place where I would be wiser than I was before, because I had learned more about life than I had realised possible, and I knew how fragile and precious we all were, about how we could be broken, that life is just an illusion, a game in which we try to prove that we have the strongest will or sense of purpose. And I knew that when I got back to my home things would start to make sense to me. Because in a world ruled of chaos it is possible to fake an understanding of anything.

Chapter 23

I made it back home, to the town I lived in. It felt different to before: smaller, less intimidating, and though the walls of buildings still seemed to close in and about my neck, I no longer felt that my breathing was restricted, or that the whole of the world was forcing itself upon me. I moved with a nimbleness and a grace, a ready alacrity, despite the limp, my forsaken front teeth. And as I walked beneath the artificial yellow of street lights, the cracks in paving stones passing me by, I felt casually imperturbable, less agitated, not so wary of the fact that some wry smile hobo might jump out to steal my change, a cool disregard for the riotous sounds of the drunks in the night, as though I had maintained a modicum of omniscience, and that I knew how all things could unfold, and how I would be able to interact with them when they did so.

'The vagabonds will be washed away with the rain', I thought to myself, 'the dipsomaniacs will set the world on fire'.

Walking as proud and as tall as my limp would allow, I attuned myself to the rhythmic cracks of my bones as though marching music. And as I approached the charmless façade of the old mill building, the lines of target market parked cars in the road seemed to be waiting for something, as if there of their own volition, a mass exodus perhaps, instead of having just been left floating in space by more potent forces. Indeed, it now seemed as though all things were riddled with a certain weightiness that they lacked beforehand, packing punches in the night that left great sense of expectation, as though something monumental may be about to happen. I began to feel that the seams in the fabric of all things would once again become less disparate and that, somehow, all of the individual objects surrounding me would make the same kind of sense, because they were one and the same anyway.

On one of the big old stones built into the wall of the building somebody had graffitied. It said:

TREES ARE NO LONGER POETIC; DREAMS ARE NOT PROFOUND.

And I thought about it, then I looked around at this place in which I had found myself. At the urban lights and the traffic signs. At the Union Jack hub caps of rusting cars and the grease in unclean windows. The neon signs of ill-positioned factories out on the horizon, out over the hills, in the spaces between the buildings. Behind me, at the top end of the street, a building under construction was covered in scaffolding and a huge canvas sheet that flapped about the wind. Not a single tree in this wasteland mass, this monument to human development, manipulations of space, room to breathe in and float through, dumped here over time.

Perhaps this is the only poetry we have left, I thought to myself. Then I laughed because I wasn't a poet. I continued limping down the street, not a single other person in sight, until eventually I reached the door that would let me into my apartment block. To the broken elevator. The blinking lights.

I twisted the key, it clicked, and I went inside.

I dragged myself up the stairs, stopping for breath because my lungs were filled with water, pulling my dead leg behind me as though it were a sack full of puppies that I were being forced to throw into the river and drown. Both arms on the old balustrade, the dank of my skin gives birth to a shrillness that rings throughout the building, as though nails down a board, a psycho in a shower. Thank God I live on the first floor, I think. If I were to make it to the second I would die. I would collapse completely. This would be the end of me. The textbook dénouement to set my skin on fire.

The pain in my leg stirred again, perhaps to remind me that I was wasting my time with pseudo-intellectual thoughts when I had more important things to be thinking about. Like how I was expected at work tomorrow. Like how they needed my arms and my legs and the human capacity for remembering stock phrases and trite responses to trivial utterances made by different people in the same tones of voice. God, it was too much to bear.

'I stopped and hung my arms and my head down against the balustrade. Imperfections of polished wood cool against my forehead. The lower floors between the grills of railings. If I had the strength I would fling myself over. If I'd had the courage I would've done it a long time ago.'

The door opens, as if swallowing me. I float down to the dusty floor of the apartment; a blanket of used underwear and odd socks, a veil of sporadic food packets and whiskey bottles, fallen leaves in the autumn of my life, because that thing on the horizon is the icy smell of winter, and over those snow-capped peaks, beyond a cerulean freeze, awaits only the end. Each second passed is another one wasted. Soon I will be gone and back to the rest of it.

Perhaps it's because of the mess that I don't notice. Perhaps it's because I'm tired and I can't think straight and nothing makes sense anyway. For the first few minutes, I stay on the floor; motionless, the corpse of a corpse, stopping to catch its own breath, mind too tired to make itself up. Last reserves of strength went into pushing the door closed, then I lay there on the cool wooden floor, hoping that my body will somehow use this space to repair itself and that I will feel whole again and ready to go before my time is up.

The thing that catches my attention though, is that, even though it's usually cold in here, it seems more so than usual. Something doesn't feel right and so I shiver on the floor for a few moments wondering what it might be. Sneaking in via the main room, as if the walls don't even exist, is a steady breeze, chilling to the bone, and so I have to pick myself up again and drag myself into the living room slash kitchen, which the estate agent had said would be convenient, but which actually just serves to make all my clothes smell like microwave curry.

I turn the light on, look about the floor at the crap which is strewn everywhere; my worthless collection of books, the ones that have taught me nothing about life but were hip to get into, the ones with torn covers and cracking edges, the ones that I'm pretty certain I'd left on the shelving unit. Now they're down on the floor, down with the rest of my junk, the few DVDs that I own, pictures of people I used to know, commemorative coffee cups designed by Hollywood celebrities with their personal mantras and words of wisdom mass printed in impersonal copies of personal cursive.

For a few minutes I have to force myself to try and remember if I had left things this way. The old Hollywood cliché. I have been too mesmerised by the sprawl on the floor to pay any real attention to the rest of the room. I had forgotten about the breeze. But, when I look up, I see that two out of my three windows have been smashed and that a note has been blu-tacked right in the centre of the unbroken one in the middle. I float on over, too dazed to pay attention to any of the junk on the floor, and so some of it cracks as I stumble over it, but I don't care, because the plot is getting thicker and it takes precedence. I peel the note from the dirty glass as I shiver in the breeze.

In purple felt tip pen, somebody has written the words:

'Just do it'.

So I go into the bedroom, curl up, and try to sleep. I have to prepare myself for what's to come.

Chapter 24

I wake up and all of a sudden it's Tuesday morning. I'm expected at work in a few minutes but, from the most primitive level of my being, I've lost motivation and I can't be bothered anymore; I'm no longer afraid of or concerned about what the rest of the herd might think. Long forgotten are the rules of the game, cast off is the straight jacket, abandoned is the act; no more will I efface myself to facilitate the transaction process, succumb to the whim of mealy mouthed strangers, pick things up and put them down. And, for some reason, it all seems to be intrinsically linked with time, histrionic metaphysical rants, on account of the fact that I'm constantly waiting for something: waiting for the phone to ring; waiting for an answer or two; waiting for 'God'; waiting to die; anything to get this stage of my life over with, to get away from this place, out of the gutter and up to the stars.

'And they say that change is within us, that it doesn't matter where or what we are, that the roots of change, redemption, reside within us. All the same, I have become jaded and disillusioned, because the whole notion of hope does not take into account people with lives like mine, and so I am left out to dry. It's just a matter of time, I'll tell myself. Just a matter of time.'

But this is despite my beliefs and my relationship with time; the surprise I feel towards the vacuum in which it moves, the speed with which it falls out of reach, and moves away without trace. Why must it be that when I think I am on the verge of catching up with myself I find that I am further and further away? Why must it be that we are weeks or years behind, that certain parts of myself, such as my mind and my psyche, are moving ahead at speeds we do not have ways of measuring yet, and so when I feel that I am in some way balanced, it turns out that I am actually just getting used to myself, whatever thing I have become for this season, so that I can change again and move onto the next stage? Is it the human condition that we can only learn in retrospect? Why is it always 'too late'?

Some of them say that life moves in cycles, that each rotation is another lesson to be learned. It is death and rebirth and changing of the seasons. It is being one thing one year and something else ten years down the line. But I no longer see it the same way:

People change, but not on purpose. They are broken. People are changed by the things that bring them to their knees, or which derail the train. And so for many the safest way to play the game is to play it slow, stay on the tracks. Don't give up on dreams by never having any. Don't give up on yourself by never believing in it. This is the only way it goes after a while, no matter how spirited we may seem to the outside world, we all feel this way in the end. If you don't yet you probably will soon.

After a while, you're nothing without your idiosyncrasies and your routine. You need a mask to keep the chaos under wraps. Another compromise.

When I look in the mirror, the one in the bathroom, the back of my MP3 player, I tell myself that to live an honest life, one requires no plans at all. To live an honest life, all one needs to do is keep reacting to events out of one's control, because if life is out there looking for you it will come and find you And if it doesn't want you, well, it'll allow you to be just like everybody else, to float around pretending that you're in control of things, waking up to the same ring of the same alarm every morning, the same odd numbered times to bring you out of your slumber.

Life is for those that deserve it. Those kings amongst men who can climb out of barrels and will dare to break through glass walls and to transcend all of this whatever it is, these eyes to the ground, this pretence, acting only as is expected and never as is intended. We have been told what is acceptable in what situation and so we take heed. This is not living. In the real world, in nature, there is no need to pretend. There is no place for it.

'Maybe we'll see you in the supermarket every Saturday morning, your partner trundling along behind you, bloated, out of sync, afraid. Maybe you'll have a few kids, unappreciative, fat, snotty. You'll contain yourself within a cursory bubble of activity, reading the newspaper with an intent look upon your face, even though you can't fully grasp the implications of what they're saying, the back of cereal packets, vapid conversations about the weather or last night's football. Perhaps we'll get to watch you crumble, trying to not let your body slip away and failing at it, embarrassing yourself in front of YouTube exercise videos upon an evening, hoping that your will won't atrophy, telling yourself that you can save it, pretending to be still young and alive so people won't treat you like you don't exist and you can still give into your whims without having to worry about if it's becoming of you.'

Part time, languishing on a twenty hour contract, more time out of work than in it. Why must it still feel like the majority of your time is spent in the workplace? Flailing about it the water, waiting for savior, foundations of worldviews shattered, and heels of boots up asses. The night before I'd been too tired to sleep; it was as though my body lacked the energy to switch itself off, and so I stayed there in bed, forced inertia, trying to convince myself that I would fall asleep soon, that I didn't need the toilet, and that my mind was playing tricks on me.

Behind my eyes, where the darkness should have been, the void in which our dreams reside, I instead catch glimpses of the past as I would like to forget it. And the whole while, dead to the world, that broken window breeze sweeps in and about me, crashing the party; it fills the room, leaves me feeling violated and uncomfortable. I'd like to ask it to leave but I'm too faint-hearted.

It remains there in the corner, staring at people and drinking all the beer. I don't know what I'm thinking. Blank and afraid, I can feel the hairs on my arms begin to stand and on it all goes. I wake up in the morning with dry eyes and fragmented narratives running through my head. My thought process resemble shards of frosted glass, all over the place, not letting enough light in. Jesus, Lord, someone save me, surely this will all be over soon. I can't keep living like this. My ego won't survive.

I check the time on my mobile. Nine fifteen means time to be at work. Fuck it. The martinets and their myrmidons will be waiting with their cocks in their hands, but it doesn't bother me like it once would have. Today somebody else can bend over for them. My life is my time and most debts are nullified when you die. I give some rumination space to this idea of freedom. I need theoretical justification of whatever mistakes I am about to make. Don't know it for sure, but here's what I get up to:

True freedom is the letting go of the pressures other people put on you. It's not riding across the Chinese desert on an expensive motorbike. It's not jumping out of an airplane and convincing yourself that you've succeeded in looking the reaper in the eye. One day the desert will end and you'll be back with all those problems that you thought you got away from. One day you'll die anyway, even if you did feel for a few moments that you had found a loophole of some kind. True freedom, true release, is knowing that you can deal with all of the external pressures coming from those around you. It's knowing that you can look your boss in the eye and tell him to go screw himself without getting fired, being able to deal with all of the shit that society has dumped on your ass without letting it beat you. Accepting that some things are out of your control, and that you can't compare yourself to other people because of this, because you've known that you've done all that you can and still don't hate yourself for it. That is a freedom that some men can only dream about. It's a trigger against your own head pulled without regrets; an alcoholic who understands the implications of all that he has lost but smiles and sips down another all the same. The last cigarette of a lung cancer victim will be the best he's ever tasted. A successful suicide is a point for the one man team.

Instead of rushing, knowing that I was late, I stopped and took the time out for a leisurely breakfast. I spread lashings of butter over mountains of toast, limped down to the minimart to stock up on coffee, and then filled my pot to get the jitters back. Later, I showered until my skin burned, breathing in steam like needles, smothering myself in Congo from Tesco, a derivative shower gel with subtle musk leanings, applied it to myself like a pig greasing itself up for a banquet. I felt light and fresh and ready, slipped into clean clothes, and when I left the house, the autumn breeze seemed to be calling out to me, whispering that everything was going to be okay and that I didn't need to worry no more. The chances of a schizophrenic killing a person that he or she doesn't know are about the same as they are of winning the lottery. Perhaps today would be somebody's lucky day, I thought. All their dreams will come true, all the things they ever wanted for themselves.

Two hours off schedule by the time I got to the train station. A voice announces that the rail company apologies for the inconvenience that it has caused me, that the train into town would be delayed by approximately 12 minutes. When I do the maths it's more like 13. You can't trust anybody these days, especially those with access to PA Systems.

'This area is patrolled by security forces 24 hours a day.'

'If you see any suspicious objects please report them to a member of staff.'

In my state of anxiety I began to think about the Leader. Regardless of whether the child was mine or not, and assuming that nothing went wrong with the pregnancy, this child would be brought into this world, void of emotions, a triumph of logic over intuition. This is not a world for children. Not really. And this makes sense if you consider that we only spend about ten percent of our lives being young, and that the rest of our days are spent reminiscing upon this time. Wondering how things could have been if our parents had been richer or more understanding, if we had only been forced to do this instead of that. I felt a shiver down my spine. That is the mystery of childhood, that no matter how bad it may be, we would not really have had it any other way, for to do so is to deny ourselves, a butterfly spitting down on the caterpillars.

The train pulled up into the station. I walked down the platform with my ticket in my hand. A group of heavies employed by the Rail Network stood waiting at the end. By the looks in their eyes I could tell that they were out for the kill; that they wanted somebody to try and run away from them; that they wanted somebody to refuse to pay them, so that they could feel powerful for a few seconds, instead of just being complacent scumbags with lousy jobs and no friends.

There were three of them all together, an athletic black guy who obviously worked out a lot, a plump woman in a luminous orange work overall, and a nervous skinny, drippy man with long hair and a ticket machine in his hands. The majority of the people getting off the train walked through the barrier with their eyes to the ground and their tickets to the sky. You could tell they felt demeaned but were used to feeling that way. And, as they walked past, the Plump Woman in the orange overall thanked them individually, over and over again, spitting out the words 'thank you', like some convoluted gratitude machine, until eventually all meaning had been eviscerated, and all that remained in its place was an empty stream of gibberish, a spoken tongue that lacked incite or cadence or meaning. She may as well have just dribbled on everybody.

Though I had already bought a ticket I decided to start running. I was curious to see what might happen, because my spirits had been dampened by the dehumanising sluggishness of the queue, and I needed to see the limits of the power that these people held over me. As the Plump Woman was thanking a group of people in cheap polyester suits I began to run; my body hadn't entered this mode since I had attempted to run up into the hills behind my house, and because it was still relatively early morning and I was still half asleep, I fell under the impression that I had entered some ethereal dream state, where the boundaries of reality lacked form, and, as I overtook the polyester people before me, I felt the strange undulations of manic euphoria sweep over me, as though I had somehow freed myself, as though my amygdala had burst into flames and my neurons were ablaze, enough to set the whole city alight, and raze it to the ground.

When the Plump Woman saw what I was doing she pulled a whistle out of her pocket and began to blow on it, her cheeks bursting forth like swollen gonads each time she exhaled, and her lifeless eyes betraying themselves, using the last of their energy to exude the lurking glimmers of unadulterated excitement. She had been waiting for this moment for years, I could tell, and so at last I began to feel like the Hero, sacrificing myself and my security in order to help realise the dreams of another. A second whistle, somewhere off in the distance, pierced the calm of another grey morning. The air was crisp, it turned my breath to the clouds; the more civil members of the British commuting public looked upon the scene with bewilderment; I let out a battle cry and then I attempted to run through the barrier.

At first, I sensed with an electric and almost morbid intensity that my fellow, fare paying, commuters were on my side. Though they shuffled about with newspapers under their arms, as tractable and bovine as animals at the unfortunate end of an electric prod, there still remained a magnetism, the last traces of the living sparks that caused the hairs on their arms to stand up in excitement, and their eyes to open wide and alive, fuelled of a hare-brained lambency and anticipation of all and any deviations from the daily routine.

Some of them looked at me as though they wished for nothing more than for me to be the winner, to prove to the money men, that the little man still has a soul, even if we have forgotten what to do with it, and that we do not wish to spend our days being ushered into offices via dilatory forms of transportation. We do not need cursory apologies to be blasted into our ears every few minutes by unsympathetic, robotic voices. We want to be human again; even if this malady is the product of our collective efforts.

People began to move out of the way as I ran. Some of them, I'm sure of it, whispered words of encouragement beneath their breath, even though they feared being heard by those around them. For years they had spent their morning traipsing on through here, subjecting themselves to this diurnal diminution for as long as they could remember. The Plump Woman belly flopped forwards and tried to catch me in her arms, but I darted quickly and away from her grasp. Agility. Alacrity. Let's dance, my tubby lover. And as I imagined myself as a misplaced gazelle, running across the tundra, the pedestrian nature of my dull life dissipated, as I moved dissolute and unrestricted by morals. Failing to have caught me, the PW could only stand in the shadows, fruitlessly blowing on her whistle, as the world become a motion blur; I looked back behind me and watched her. I was free in the long grass, alive beneath the new dawn of a morning sun. Yet, carried away by euphoria, I had forgotten the lion at my heels.

Out of nowhere, another network goon; the aforementioned Athletic Guy with his muscles, and now a fire in his eyes - as though he had been betrayed in some way. But, despite the malice that he must have felt towards me, there remained a smile on his face - a beatific radiance, as though he had suddenly remembered that life involved sensation over insentience. His chiselled jaw sliced through the grey morning, adding a strange definition and contrast to the softness of the flabby office workers that dribbled on past with their umbrellas, and their suitcases, or the free newspapers still tucked under their arms like family heirlooms.

I prattled forwards like somebody with an inner ear problem on a bouncy castle, tuned into the jeers of paying commuters, those who had erroneously assumed that I was without ticket. Though I had previously convinced myself that they were with me, the tables had now turned. They wanted me to hang for my crimes, to burn; it was even possible that they had led me down the road to failure. They began shouting, throwing vituperative words of advice up and above one another:

'Get a job, slackass!'

'I pay for my ticket, scum boy. What makes you any better?'

'Get off the rock and roll and get real, white trash!'

And then the Lion lunged forwards and scraped his claw up against my sides. Somehow I eluded his advances. Even with a limp, according to Wikipedia, the top speed that a gazelle can run at is 20kmph faster than a lion. Perhaps that accounted for it. Or, maybe it was the surge of adrenaline which made me leave my limp behind. Regardless, I slipped out of his grasp and kept running. But I knew he would make a return. I cast my glance over towards the Plump Woman; she stood there forlorn, clutching her whistle, limp-wristed and inconsolable in a state of existential exasperation. She eyed me with the defeated look of a child that didn't get what it wanted for Christmas. I extended my hand and gave a wave but she didn't return the gesture.

Though I felt that the rest of my Englishmen were disappointed in my behaviour, I still felt that I was doing them a great service. Those poor fools had failed to realise that there was more taking place than meets the naked eye. They couldn't comprehend the bigger picture, didn't know that they were slaves to a system that doesn't care about them. They were destined to die still struggling. As long as I could convince myself that I didn't want or need a damn thing then, regardless of whatever might eventually happen to me, I would escape the same terrible fate that had befallen them.

'SO LONG SUCKERS!', I called out to the world.

I shook my fist as I did so, a series of uber-animated gesticulations, an attempt to bring one final camera flash of attention to myself, a terminal fusillade of praise to accompany the applause that resounded in the back my head. The truth of the matter though, was that even though I had deluded myself into thinking that people gave a damn about my actions, I could tell in my heart or hearts that I was nothing more than a minor annoyance. By the end of the day, they would have forgotten about me, convinced themselves that I didn't exist - that I was just another figment of their empty imaginations.

Chapter 25

Fading forwards, stumbling towards the town centre, I wondered why my tiny but significant act of rebellion had been met with mirth and malice, instead of the reverence that I had become more than convinced I was entitled to. Those people, those crowds, those commuters, I thought, each would love to have their wicked way with me. And so, as I clutched my uninspected train ticket as though it were my heart on my sleeve, I headed into the town centre, under the portentous shadows of old buildings, looking up to the sky and the clouds for a change, instead of down and out at the lead balloons weighing down my size nine shoes.

All the while, the usual mass of anguished faces, tracksuits, and tired eyes passed me by: senescents on benches; middle aged men in teenage clothes; caps, cigarettes, and beer cans; bucktoothed women pushing petulant kids in pushchairs; tabloid newspapers taken out of back pockets and being read with integrity.

I meandered onwards, past a ruinous husband and wife team burger van, beyond the Daily Mail immigrants selling made-in-China hats and cheap umbrellas, all the way to the centre of the high street, where the shop stood, waiting for me. I looked around for some form of distraction, but everything was so achromatic, so colourless and confused.

The phone in my pocket must have been about a hundred years old, but it didn't matter because nobody ever called me. Most of the time it was turned off, to keep the battery from dying, so as I turned it on and waited for the interface to load I looked around about me, looking for signs - which was when I saw The Jock in the crowd.

He had that look on his face, the same snarl that he'd had in high school, thirteen-fifteen years ago. Now though, it seemed like it had been watered down from overuse, lacked the intensity it had back in the day, and his eyes had gone the same way, beaten in by all those harsh realities we were warned about. If he saw me he didn't recognise me, or, if he did, he didn't feel like saying anything. I only recognised him because he was with the girl he'd been dating all through school. She looked exactly the same as she used to do, only slightly inflated. Apart from the remnants of the smirk on his face, The Jock had pretty much changed completely, no longer any hair between himself and the heavens, a transubstantiation of muscle into body fat. He wandered along dejected, as his sloppy girlfriend followed him like a cloud on the horizon, yelling at him the whole while, telling him how useless he was, how stupid - right in front of all these people - whilst he visibly tried to stop himself from turning round and cracking her one in the face.

The phone finished its load up as they melted away. It said I had a message. Actually, it said I had a few of them. I pressed the appropriate buttons and put it to my ear. Forcing myself to be my higher-self, doing what rationality would perhaps deem just and responsible thing to do, I attempted to tune into what was being said to me. But, alas, seconds into the first of many messages from The Supervisor, having reverted to his dog-addressing-retard-chastising tone of voice and genuinely convinced that 'supervise' is synonymous with 'superior', I found myself return the phone to my pocket, as though all along I had been a mime artist and it had never existed. I stood lost and dreaming amongst the crowd as I gazed into the open door of the shop and recoiled in fear at the sight of disks piled high on counters and the Macdonald's coffee cups with the free coffee stickers missing; at the junk on the floor, trampled upon and forever disregarded by the indecorous and impoverished members of our classless society.

I took a deep breath and pondered the meaning of my existence, lifted my shirt up a little, and stared into the fleshless navel of my fleshless belly so as to be both pretentiously self-referential and pseudo-profound. It occurred to me that, in the eyes of those around me, I must look as sick as I felt, and, having realised such, I decided that what I needed most of all was food, that somehow eating would be the only thing that could save me and help me blend in. I scuttled past the entrance to the shop, mere inches away, my inner masochist hoping that one of them would recognise me, so that I would be dragged into a back room somewhere and beaten, so that they would bring me kicking and screaming back to reality, so that I could return to the same page of the same book as everybody else. But none of them saw me, because they were all too busy scanning and pressing buttons and handling dirty money.

My scuttling led me in the direction of a supermarket in the seediest part of town, a place where the hobos would hang, and the junkies would lean against the walls of the cash convertors and the massage parlours to stare at passers-by and ask for spare change.

'Have you got twenni' pence, mate?'

I used to live in fear of this part of the town, but now things seemed different to me. It was as if the place had swallowed me whole, as though I had become integrated and assimilated and acclimatised. In the broken window of a closed down shop, I noted that my appearance had changed and I looked now like any of the other saturnine characters surrounding me. Life had beaten me in some way, because I had left the zest and liberty of youth, and chosen instead the mundane world of grief and unpaid bills and holey clothes that covered wounds that would not heal and would not go away.

At the top of a hill, I came to a shoe shop; another one of those plastic boutiques where you immediately assume everything is made in China, because of the chemical stench that hovers outside the doorways, because of the standardised fit of the shoes, the bargain basement prices, and the sacrifice of beauty for utility alone. The smell brought back my sense of colour; inexplicable pink hues and white line skyscrapers in unexplored and exotic countries; memories of Childhood and hot shot balls of galvanic gaseous orange; epileptic lights down my spine, and a blood rush to the head that made my toes tingle and my heart ache.

As I passed the shoe shop, enshrouded within the auspices of these sensations, a proud Asian lad came out with some shimmering patent plastic upon his feet; a sort of fake plastic vacuum that reflected and irradiated all and any light in the vicinity. This footwear struck me as so incongruous and unwholesome that I immediately felt a deep sense of pity for the boy, all the more so that he seemed happy to be wearing them, strolling almost majestically and completely unaware of his surroundings, strutting about in his tawdry plastic skids, as though the King of the Pavement. Despite all of my problems and all of the things that I had to worry about, I felt such a sense of relief that I'd never be found dead in such shoes that it almost brought me to tears.; it was the first time I'd felt sorry for anybody besides myself in years. I marvelled as he took a flimsy plastic bag with his old shoes in and dumped it into a bin before disappearing into the high street and out of my life for good.

I continued dreamily, past the mobile phone shops and the queues of people lining outside the chip shop, until eventually I had reached my destination. The supermarket doors opened of their own volition and I glided on through as though on ice skates before picking up one of the wire baskets with yellow chipped plastic on the handles. A security guard with a dutifully religious neck beard stared at me as I went through the barriers.

Pausing by the exotic fruit section, I hoped that my presence and attention to detail here might be enough to convince passers-by to think of me as sophisticated and urbane. And so, as I looked around to determine who would be sharing the afternoon's shopping experience with me, I pretended to examine the dragon fruits and the persimmons for imperfections. My fellow shoppers seemed to be nothing out of the ordinary, quite the opposite in fact: the usual Chinese housewives with placid children sat in trolleys full of bleach and mushrooms; stray middle-class white women that had come to the wrong supermarket; shadowy figures in black and white tennis shoes; and a down and out with a can of beer in his hands and a five o' clock shadow that was a few hours too early.

I picked up a lychee, ran my fingers over its skin, and felt a cool hiss of steam coarse through my veins, as the memories of exotic vacations and island motorbike rides infused my vision with pink mist. I put the fruit down and rang my fingers through the rungs of the empty basket, stared at my feet against the speckled polished floor, focused on the random stains and balls of dust, and the cross-eyed but muscular shelf stackers who were carrying boxes of bananas as though they had all the time in the world.

My stomach rumbled so I picked up the pace, floated through the aisles of pizza boxes and sandwich meats, and the mountains of hairless, antiseptic flesh that loomed high above on either side. I began to feel the twinges of a nascent intuition and so I stopped still in my tracks amidst the people bumbling up and down the aisles and the flesh in the boxes and the tin can music being pumped over the stereo speakers as the soundtrack to my complacency. I have finally made my way into hell, I thought to myself. This is it: little packages of meat with shining plastic dressings; soulless foodstuffs; aisles of chemical sustenance; and the speckled floors and workers in uniform. It all made so much sense. I became suddenly and incontrovertibly convinced that I had died on an operating table, or beneath the wheels of some bus - with a knife at my wrists - and now I had awoken to my reality to writhe languid for eternity, as the Muzak Holdings company played my funeral dirge.

A sophisticated packet of pork and apple sausages jumped into my basket, which tilted and needed readjusting because of the new distribution of weight. I began to wonder who might have held the basket before me, how dirty they might have been, whether it was anybody I knew, or if they could change my life. Then I turned the corner to the discount aisle, passed a selection of low salt cheeses on special offer. And that was when the day *really* began.

In a town afflicted with poverty the majority of us are basket carriers; it takes a fine class of person to be able to fill a trolley. Pushing one frivolously about is akin to driving a Rolls Royce into a council estate, so when I strolled nonchalantly past the fancy biscuit section and saw The Sycophant loading one up, it sent a shudder down my spine, because I knew immediately that something strange was afoot and that most likely I would be drawn into it.

An animal startled, I ran and hid behind the discount pasta sauces at the end of the aisle. When I was quite convinced that she hadn't noticed me, I stood with a packet of instant soup in my hand and feigned a scholarly interest in the nutritional information on the back of its label. With surreptitious solicitude, I watched her with the irrepressible feeling that at any moment some great truth might be revealed to me. Robotically and mechanically, she put two kinds of every biscuit into a trolley already overloaded with carbonated drinks - listlessly, as though performing some routine task that she had done a few thousand times before and had long since become bored of.

I continued to read the label with superficial fanaticism, so that any passers-by would not be awoken to the true game that I was playing. As I did so, the names of chemicals and preservatives set my mind ablaze: I saw a vision of the black smoke of mountain bush fires float up above the horizon, I heard the birds calling out in pain, and then the crack of their wings fluttering through trees.

The Sycophant was wearing her workaday raiments; the skinny bleached jeans with the faded shins and her oversized running shoes - not because she was fashion conscious or living in pursuit of a healthy lifestyle, but because she wanted to blend in and be left alone- and the ensemble was completed by one of those white puffer jackets with the yellow cigarette smoke stains around the pockets that the bad girls like to wear. Her fringe hung flat over her forehead, greasy and broken, and her freckled face sat beneath it, wan and confused, as she drifted amidst the flat lights of the supermarket at the mercy of the trolley, which seemed to be leading her places instead of having her asserting force on it in any way.

She drifted down the aisle with her mouth ajar, catching flies, whilst, over the radio, the Supermarket FM, the shoppers were collectively informed that we were in a select and exclusive group of consumers that were entitled to a discount on spring onions and pink dressing gowns. I got a boner. Then, as though to finish me off, they treated us to some more elevator versions of radio songs by Elton John and other musicians that I had only ever heard long ago at the weddings of long lost relatives. I looked around me, taking in the sights and sounds of the modern world with an almost childlike sense of wonder and detachment. Old people were tapping their toes to the innocuous beat; snot-nosed children were riding in trolleys. The Sycophant continued moving and drifting, picking up chocolate bars here and there, and then adding them to the piles of foil wrappers and primary coloured plastic bottles with the bubbles rising in her wonky-wheeled trolley.

I decided to make my way down to the next aisle, to shadow her steps and figure out what she was up to. I manoeuvred my basket with dexterity, slid it around and in between the herd of passing shoppers as though they were inanimate objects in my path, like rocks or pieces of old furniture. And, as I turned into the aisle, of canned fish and vegetables, I almost collided with a thug in a football shirt, a typical bro with too much gel in his hair and a pot belly and gaps in between his displaced teeth. In a moment of jarring stupefaction we both raised our hands as a symbol of nonfrontation. When I thought the moment had passed I looked down at my basket and continued on my way. But, just as I was about to vacate the aisle, he called out behind me:

'Fancy a bum?', I heard him say.

Then, beclouded in an ADHD peal of laughter, he marched off with another bro that had magically appeared at his side.

A cloud of existential anxiety brought me trembling to my knees. If it hadn't been for my mission to stalk the Sycophant lending me a temporary sense of purpose I don't know what would have become of me. I regained my composure and pursued her up and down the aisles.

As I was peering at her through the gaps between the shelves, I noticed that The Neck Beard Security Guard was watching me watch her. He was a-peeping at me from behind a pile of special offer baked beans and whispering into his walkie-talkie, slowly and laboriously, as though some sort of post-stroke Dirty Harry. I could see him thinking hard as he tried to form a sentence. In a cunning attempt to make him lose the trail, I picked up a can of premium canned lobster. Once again, I read the list of ingredients, and I think he must have fallen for my ruse, because he scratched his beard as though quite satisfied, then he whispered something into his walkie-talkie, and strolled off with his chest inflated and full of purpose in the direction of the fresh fruit and veg section.

I looked back to try and spy The Sycophant, but the guileful minx had faded to dust. I took my sausages out of the basket and put them on the shelf by the cans of tuna, then I deposited my empty basket in the middle of the aisle floor, and tip-toed as quickly and stealthily as I could down towards the checkouts.

When I got there the continuation of beeps and mindless chatter hit me like fireflies at the bottom of a mountain, a bumblebee symphony, and for a moment I was so overcome with the potency of the various sensations that I could only stand there, vulnerable and exposed to this unceasing bundle of new information. It was only when I realised that I could be seen in this position that I was able to tear myself out of this eyes open coma and to get out of everybody's way. I hid behind a column with a mirror on it, trying not to look at myself and at what I had become. In the reflection, I could see that Neck Beard was eyeing me again in the distance; I picked some discount DVDs from a basket and pretended to be reading plot summaries.

The same old Hollywood bullshit.

The Sycophant was bagging up her bottles and her biscuits, and the till attendant smiled at her with genuine reverence, as she handed over a shiny piece of golden plastic with the word 'Visa' written on it. Scanning took place and buttons were pressed. The beeps and the keyboard clicks hit me like a monsoon, as I had flashbacks of being back at work, and out of sync again with my life's true purpose. And, then, with the same ghostly nervousness as always, The Sycophant entered her pin number into the card terminal; she placed her bags, stretched at the handles, into her trolley, and I watched as she wheeled it out of the store. A breeze came in through the double doors as she left amidst the traffic and the clouds with their promises of rain.

I returned the DVD to its basket just in time for the Neck Beard to come up behind me and put a hand on my shoulder.

'Fancy a bum?', I said.

Then I ran out of the door, still hungry, wishing I had bought some food when I had the chance.

Chapter 26

Time had dwindled, instead of having overflown, and the rain clouds loomed in fragments, black and bleak and broken. I watched the Sycophant load her bags into the boot of a taxi and then slink anxiously into the front seat. Despite the dearth of time's passing, the streets awaited greyer and heavier than ever before and, as the taxi edged spiritlessly into the snail trail of moving traffic, metres per hour, heading down towards the heart of the tenderloin, I felt my lungs collapse with the grim foreboding of everything that was about to occur.

On the pavement besides me a small riot was taking place. As it turns out, the Sycophant had abandoned her shopping trolley, and so as soon as the locals realised that she had neglected to collect her pound coin deposit, a disorganised melee broke out which saw a number of umbrellas waved up and against the dour faces of its participants, as a panoply of language colourful enough to be used as the confetti at a whore's wedding bombarded the eardrums of all and any who might pass by.

Galvanised by the discordant energy of the commotion, I decided suddenly and intuitively that the most sensible thing to do at this juncture would be to follow the taxi on foot. And so, despite the incessancy of the pain and the hunger in my belly, the storm in my stomach, I focused on my footsteps and marched off after the taxi into the depths of the one-way system, amidst the car horns and exhaust emissions, towards the unknown future with the broken promise of its answers.

Late into the noon, sky light fading, street lights humming, the air felt heavy and the surrounding passers-by and the workers seen through shop windows seemed tired and distant and worn. Another apparition perhaps, I thought I saw the back of the Sycophant's thin head through the rear window of the taxi, crawling along behind a hatchback with two meek and hunched over old lovers in the front, lost and out of place in the big city. They had kids in the back, the offspring of offspring; a confederation of sedate and senseless people numbed out on harmless conversation.

I held my breath as I tiptoed past her, as though it would make a damn bit of difference. Truth be told, I was scared of her, despite her frailty and her nerves; despite her innate servitude towards The Leader and her sacred cause, there was something about The Sycophant that terrified me. Nothing unholy or evil; something worse than that; something very real - a subtle underscore of terror that left me overwhelmed with an incredible desire to have her destroy me, to have her list each of my character defects with the precision of some precocious child, but to reveal them with a supercilious nonchalance, as though she knew I didn't matter, as though brushing a crumb off her sleeve and onto the un-mopped floor of a greasy spoon.

A man with a rat for a beard and an old navy waterproof approached me from deep within the mist. Though his eyes told stories of knowledge long forgotten and imbued him with a profound sense of confidence in his reality, he seemed only to have verged upon on the cusp of actual understanding, stumbling as though forever dizzy, stopping and starting to organise his thoughts. With every passing movement, it seemed as though he was trying to recollect something, his eyes not searching but distant and, as I stared deep into the pit of his toothless black mouth, he looked at me as though I wasn't even there.

'You got twenty pence, mate?', he asked.

Hungry but virtuous under duress, I fulfilled his wishes by delving into my unspent dinner funds. But before I could get a chance to ask him what he intended to do with his shiny new twenty pence piece, the rain had quickened his pace and he'd vanished into the crowds of people hiding beneath their soggy newspapers, or with their jackets pulled up over their heads, and the grim looks on their faces, as though the rain was toxic and increased their chances of getting cancer.

In helpless dismay, I release a sigh at the thought of all the opportunities that have passed me by, as I check the progress of The Sycophant in her taxi - still making a steady but slow pace towards the centre of the city, and sandwiched now between the same old hatchback with the elderly drivers in front of it, and a steamy-windowed bus to the rear, drifting listless in the mist. Shapeless masses ruffle behind Plexiglas windows; the bus driver, hot and bothered in the front seat, loosens up his collar and opens a window to let in the air.

Back in the streets, a baby in a pushchair lets out a raucous mass off energy that makes my insides turn to mucus. Discomfited and discombobulated by the rain that falls, mummy pushes it in and out of crowds, around and through puddles, and, each time it opens its mouth, I am stricken by an iron that burns white against my skin and reminds me of The Leader.

I remember that night at the school; just the two of us beneath a flood of halogen. I think about her body and how I could've made it mine, about the curve of her back and the sweetness of her lips and the softness of her skin. For a few moments, I forget about the rain fall, where I am and what I'm doing. Instead, I become a walking recollection, back there at the school for that moment; the same sensations and textures, the same stale smell of smoke on her breath, and her cool lips stained with cheap red wine from the Tesco discount section. It's strange to me that she's pregnant, and even stranger that she would designate me to be the father of her child, although perhaps not. Perhaps the bona fide daddy doesn't give a damn and ran away. Perhaps she's just trying to give me something to live for because she saw something in me that nobody else could see.

More of that Hollywood bullshit.

'But maybe that's what we're all secretly looking for.'

The sound of a horn drags me back to the currently accepted version of reality.

Somehow, I have moved unawares to the middle of the road, right into the stream of traffic. The Bus Driver is snarling at me, and, up through the big steamed window, I can see that the heel of his palm is placed flat and unwavering against the horn. Behind him, veiled by a misted screen of pattered raindrops, standing in their sensible coats with their watches and with their buttons neatly done up, are a number of passengers, looking, staring, tearing into me; turning to look at one other and to tut and mutter amongst themselves in bitter disapproval.

I stand insensible, my legs unable to move, refusing to respond to mental compulsion, as though a man in a coma, unable to speak or even blink, but maintaining the will to live as his family debate about whether or not to flick the switch. An inner monologue scream for them not to do anything, to let me be, to think about the potentiality that still resides and defines, another shot at life. I. Don't. Want. To. Die.

'But only because I don't know what death is.'

The horn continues to ring out as a linear spasm of sound envelops my body. And then the other horns of other vehicles slowly join in with the performance, as though these vehicles are a part of some great mechanical chorus of geese, subservient to the will of the single deck conductor and its monotonous cry.

In the back of her taxi, The Sycophant stirs but pays no heed to the surrounding furore. I try to move my legs, but still they disobey, and so all I can do is stand there as the horns keep on coming and the bus driver's face increases in redness and intensity, and I am lost to the incomprehensible horror of it all. Redder than red, he lets his foot on and off of the brake and causes the bus to lunge forwards and dart back again, in an attempt to cattle prod me into action. But it doesn't work, and so I remain wide-eyed and in vain, hoping that a skyhook might fall and disentangle me from the futility of my situation. But I know very well how unlikely this is and that I must fight a losing battle with myself if ever I am to flee.

The throngs drift past on the pavements; traffic lights flick in and out of sequence; horns honk. Rain falls and the traffic refuses to move; I begin to get the impression that people are latching on to me as a source of drama, purely to add some motion to their days.

Helpless, I watch the bus driver get out of his seat, press a button somewhere, and open the door. He unlatches the gate that separates his seat from the gangway and then he climbs out of the bus and begins to approach me. The people on the bus are riveted and those in surrounding cars use their cuffs to wipe the condensation from their windows and get a better view. I gaze over the sea of traffic at The Sycophant in her taxi; she's lost in a phone call and oblivious to her surroundings.

The Bus Driver is the kind of man who if pushed could destroy. He tries to be reasonable and he is, cheerful almost, but I can see behind his eyes that, if I gave him a window to climb through, it would most likely end up shattered.

'We got a problem, 'ere, matey?', he asks, as little, crystalline beads of sweat form on his brow.

153

I stare deep into his face, transfixed, like a rabbit frozen before a predator; gazing at his bulging eyes, and his subtle smile; the perennial dipsomaniac drinking glow from too much work, and the heaving swell of his chest, caused by a chronic shortness of breath. In any other situation I suppose I would be able to find a reason to feel superior to him and so wouldn't have a problem with him, but as things stand I remain rickety and honest and weak.

'Well?', he asks.

But I can't answer because my body is still frozen and I don't know why.

The line of traffic behind the bus is getting longer and the drivers in their cars increasingly irrational and irritated. They beep some more to put the pressure on and so the Bus Driver, a man of old world values and ideas about life and masculinity, begins to get nervous. The beast within him stirs.

'Playing silly beggars, eh?'

And so, before I know it, he's pushing me off of the road and on to the pavement, as though I am a torn coupon from the newspapers being carried by the winds, or a soggy piece of toilet paper swept passively down the u-bend. He returns to his bus and the passengers applause. No bow, no smile or nod of the head; he gets back into his seat, rolls his sleeves down, and starts up the engine. The door closes with a hiss and then the bus lurches onwards, catching up with the traffic ahead.

I stand dazed on the pavement as I watch The Sycophant slide right by, unaware, oblivious to the fact that I'm standing here still and inert and hungry, pretending that I haven't noticed that the people passing me by are trying not to look at me

---

Chapter 27

By the time my legs had returned to me, the rain had stopped falling and it was almost dark. It was that time of the evening when the street lights warm to life, not yellow, but red, as though some ominous sign that the sun's vitamin smile might be about to slip out of the sky, or that the earth might burn and so we can all take a day off work tomorrow.

A city can only really be itself in the night time, a synthetic construction, or a tavern of design, with its lights and its neon signs, its traffic signals and window displays, alive to the shadows of spectral passers-by. I stand frozen to a shimmering wet pavement, basking in the smells of post rain petrichor, ever hungrier for answers and salvation, my eyes affixed on the Sycophant and her taxi, until they meld into the mass of toy cars down the bottom of the road, and I no longer know where she might be heading or what to do with myself.

Nothing better to do, nowhere else to go, I stumble down blind towards the general direction that the taxi took itself. Hopeless, listless, marching through the faceless streets; down by the shutters and the flickering street lights, I soon find myself hidden amongst the shadows, across from my place of employment, as the manager and his underlings stand with their hands in their pockets, or their sets of keys jangling in their hands, and the roll up cigarettes in their mouths as a simple reward for a long day of exertion. Dim-witted and tired and broken, I hear the security alarm set itself, and then I watch as my co-workers go their separate ways with their eyes to the ground and their hearts on their sleeves - young, numb and full of odium.

Hiding behind a lamppost like some kind of diffident dog, I felt a great shiver down my spine as I saw the manager in his torn jacket, standing there with his shoe laces untied and the fly on his half-mast trousers unzipped, like some overgrown child wandering lost about the gloaming. The same old crumbs and stains on the same old sweater; even from back here in the dark, they stand out like the remnants of dead galaxies in the night sky. I shivered again as a terrible thought overthrew me.

'They didn't seem to be missing me.'

Jolted into a sudden paralysis by an inexplicable and unholy sense of dread, I stood cold and small and alone in the world. Reality had all of a sudden chosen to present itself transparently and, as I saw my situation for the barren and untidy wasteland that I myself had failed to cultivate, I began to feel as though the skeletal hands of Fate herself had torn my eyes wide open and forced me to stare into a pit filled with my own shadows. Though this lucidity lasted only for a few footsteps towards the centre of town, its effects were still potent enough to leave a chip in the teacup. And so, for the first time in a long time, I considered the possibility that I might fail in my quest, that nothing was guaranteed in this life, or any other, and that the chances of things getting worse were just as strong as the chances of them getting better.

Gradually, the wave receded, just as quickly as it had enveloped me in the first place, and I found myself making a conscious effort to realign myself with what I considered to be the roots of my destiny; looking out for signs and symbols, convinced that The Fat Man, wherever he might be, would be able to answer and explain all and everything, and that the quest would be worth the sacrifice.

With each footstep that I took in this new direction, savouring the flavours of my self-delusion, I felt warmer and increasingly at peace within myself, as though I were moving into a union with God, into the Holy presence, right here beneath the matte yellow streetlights and the moonless sky, besides the golden arches of the burger bar, and the disjointed reflections in painted windows. My great realisation at this time was that 'God', or whatever he might be called, was insignificant in himself, but that the answers one might acquire from him were invaluable. After all, what is a God but a device to make sense of the world? To help us escape the heaviness of uncertainty? To provide a justification for this thing called 'life' and a method of living it? The awareness of this fact filled my heart with bliss. I felt suddenly elated, a marker pen thick contrast to the consternation just moments before, all at the thought of one day finding purpose.

'If God doesn't exist then he can be anything you want him to be.'

The voice in the back of my head informed me that our emotions are only ever relative to their opposites in polarity. After feeling such intensity of negative emotion - such loss, such depravity, such depression - their positive equivalents, when they found me, could only be equally as overwhelming. I felt like a man in arid farmland as a raincloud appears on the horizon and thus the joy of expectancy added new colours and fresh wine to my cup. And, as I walked through those streets, across the old granite slabs, beyond the holes in the road and the sleeping construction machinery, I knew that life was beautiful, and I knew that there was no true evil in the world, because everything was relative.

Mao was smiling at me from my wrist. 'It was only a matter of time', he seemed to be saying, 'Only a matter of time before all of your dreams come true'.

I let loose a feathered sigh, as I looked around at the others out and about the streets, and wondered if they were just as confused about life as I felt myself to be. At the bottom of a cobbled street hill, besides the boarded up banks and closed down record shops, a group of staunch looking people in white coats stood waiting for trouble to start. I remembered that I had read about them in the newspaper; The Street Angels, a group of charitable vigilantes that had taken it upon themselves to bring order to the streets at night, to protect the weak from the strong, and to engrain a sense of reckoning in a town where 'justice' was a dirty word.

The Angels stood beneath the shadows of trees, five of them all told, huddled together in the cold as the condensation rose up and off of their breaths, into the air and up to the heavens. In all honesty, their concern for this place seemed most incongruous to me, a person, like nearly everybody else I had spoken to in this town, that had become hopelessly aware of his situation and his ability to do anything about it. In many ways, I had accepted my fate with weak knees, and so the sight of anybody who might try to resist the natural transpiration of life's great tapestry seemed alien and strange to me, even if I was mildly afflicted with the same sense of respect towards these people that one might feel for anybody who works tirelessly in the attempt at fulfilling some impossible dream.

And so, with these thoughts in mind, I began to hope that some trouble would unfold so I could watch them in action; to see how far they were prepared to take things. Though I didn't understand them, I felt an overwhelming sense of curiosity towards them, a sense of awe. These meek, book reading sons of guns standing strong and alive in the night time –they moved me in ways I couldn't comprehend.

As I wondered if I shouldn't stir things up a little bit, by yelling something offensive perhaps, or by throwing rocks or roof tiles from a distance, I felt my legs carrying me down the hill towards them, dragging my swollen shin behind me, still sore and rent and lacerated from my climb out of the window of the old building and the kicking I had taken at the mercy of the crowd. Then, I noted that I held my hand to my cheek, curled my face in a look of masked anguish and brave tolerance, as I moved ever close towards them, with a tear in my eyes and a heaviness to my breath. Another step closer to deliverance, I could feel it.

One of the Angels looked into my eyes as I approached. Staring at me through a thick slab of glass, beyond the thick plastic rims of her spectacles, intent and concerned and oh so *alive.* As I winced in pain, she released an audible gasp that set my soul ablaze, then, as she leaned forwards, as if to save me from my falter, I began to feel safe and warm again – as though I had finally made it back home.

'What has happened to you, dear boy?', she asked, even though she was probably a few years younger than me.

The other members of her clan gazed upon me with a similar affection; I took a deep, difficult breath, grasped at my chest as though it were tightening and in pain. Then, I looked at them as if they were my saviours, because I suspected that was what they wanted to be, and, if there is ever a sure fire way of getting what you want, it is to give others at least a part of what they think they want beforehand.

'Are you real angels?', I sighed.

Then I swooned into her arms, into the folds of her white puffer jacket. Her stocky chassis supported my sinewy frame without effort.

It was getting colder now and I could see the clouds of condensation forming more thickly beneath her nostrils. Her skin looked warm and red and clammy to the touch. *Alive.* My vision was blurred, and the moisture around my eyes turned the street lights into tiny stars that floated inches above me, like some spectral phantasmagoria that made the whole situation seem more real than even the most vivid of my dreams.

'What on earth has happened to you?', asked an urgent young man with good posture.

The only male amongst the group, some kind of mutton stud, he began to take charge, to get carried away and bark orders at people. The Angel, in whose arms I still found myself to be ensconced, ignored his commands to prostrate me upon the bench to the side of her. Instead, she left me swaying in the cradle of her arms, as I looked up at her with my eyes half-closed in a state of bliss.

'Let him be', she said, 'for it would appear that he lacks the strength to even move.'

I winced some more.

For a few precious seconds, we stayed huddled as a group in this position. The strong arms of The Angel held me in their eternity, whilst the rest of her crew looked upon me with solicitation, occasionally pausing to reflect upon the nightscape, to scan the increasingly desolate streets for signs of discord, for crimes to solve, and people to save.

In the cradle of her arms, I found myself analysing her round face, the lines of municipal tree shadows splayed across it like hand prints on a rippled derriere. I had heard a theory once upon a time that, of all the animals, a person's visage most often resembles only that of a pig or a rat, and looking up from this angle, at her non-proboscis, her stubby pug of a nose, I decided that she fell neatly into the former category. The thick rimmed jam jar bottom glasses, I have already described, but the more I gazed upon the night sky from beneath them, the more I was able to ascertain how the world must seem to an Angel. The nebulous forms, the magnified lights and sensations; from down here, in her arms, I was only afforded a glimpse, at best a fleeting glance, but I knew that this was the secret of her power. She didn't say a word, just held me. This was her purpose and she was alive; proud and strong and intransigent.

I closed my eyes and remained there for a few more instants, quite motionless, rigid as a plank, concentrating on my breath and my breathing and the sensations of being here, of still being alive. I tried to lose myself to the darkness, to the all-consuming, enveloping everything that I had found myself subject to that day outside the bus station. But, try as I might, I couldn't connect. Too many extraneous thoughts and feelings ran through the corridors of my mind. I began to stir and make noise. The other Angels darted to my side, looked down upon me as though I may be about to say something meaningful and profound, teach them something abstruse, the kind of platitude that only a cripple or an invalid can utter with conviction. I let them wait for a few seconds, their freezing breath hanging about in layers outside the proud stone old buildings and against the street lights. I heard cold footsteps ring strange and true in the distance, counted them internally, and savoured their resonance in the back of my mind.

I readjusted my distribution of weight, dragged myself in increments up to a standing position, and caught my breath as they continued to look upon me.

'What on earth has happened to you?', asked the Mutton Stud for a second time; he stared intently at me, but, when I didn't answer, began to nervously finger the angel logo on his breast pocket.

I ran my hands through my hair, squeezed the bridge of my nose, waited a few moments before responding so as to add an element of suspense.

'I've been mugged', I replied, 'Round the corner, near the train station, by a man with shoe laces untied, stains upon his jumper, and biscuit crumbs in his beard.'

They gasped in a state of incredulity, as though a great injustice had been served. The Angel with the pig's face pulled me up tight against her bosom; she rubbed her hands through my hair, tenderly, matronly, and I felt as though I had returned to some place long ago forgotten, to a part of myself that I had been hiding from myself. I felt the tears well up in my eyes and saunter down my cheeks, as the salt hit my lips, and I tasted infinity.

'I've never been so scared', I lied.

And then the Angels began to cry with me; the saviours and the fallen, weeping in the same spot, unified in terrestrial time and space.

Indeed, it seemed at once as though time had frozen, just as the bells of the city clock did knoll, their sonorous chime ringing deep and alive, and consuming the whole of us all in a protracted running off of the hours. The world around us imbued with a sepulchral tranquillity, a moribund calm, it was only the tears that slid down our ratty piggy cheeks that denoted our inner motion, our sentient desires and miseries, the lifeblood flowing through our veins.

I seemed to have stepped outside of myself once again, standing back on it all, looking at the tableau vivant that the six of us formed, The Angel and her side kick, their three stock character associates with bland faces and a lack of memorable utterances. Some people are born to flesh things out, to make others seem more interesting, and, I know that comparisons are odious, but as I stood there watching myself in her arms, comparing the perceived version of myself - the one in my head - to the one that stood before me, I couldn't help but wonder if this was what I had been longing for all along; the touch of a woman and the sensation of warm breath that leads to a sense of shared catharsis.

Tears flooded. We grimaced together, felt alive, took the moment and made it ours. It didn't seem to matter why it was happening, just that it was; we were sculptures of ice slowly melting. I returned to myself and my senses, felt her hands running through my hair again, as I looked up at the veneer of dry tears on her face and its slick reflectivity in those omnipresent yellow street lights. I pulled myself into her arms and sobbed, let it all out as I held her onto her for dear life.

The other members of the group began to melt at increasingly rapid rates. They wiped their eyes and their red faces with their sleeves, readjusted their clothing which now felt sweaty and incomplete. My face still buried in the arms of an angel, I felt the hands of the other's begin to stroke my back, my legs, my hands, anything that was available. I became a patient in a hospital bed again, fondled by solicitous relatives; I became a blind man being healed by a prophet.

The Mutton Stud pulled me gracefully upright to attention, wiped the tears out of my eyes with his fingers, and, fighting his own battle with all things lachrymose, he said, faltering:

'My child, there must be something we can do for you.'

And then we paused.

I held my stomach as I told them tales of woe and hunger. I tried to hold them back, but the words came anyway, and I heard myself saying that the mugger had stolen my money, each penny that I'd earned and worked so hard for. Then, I told them that I had been on the way to buy a birthday present for my dear old grandma.

Oh, it was all so terrible! Why did life have to be so unfair all the time? We all try so hard and we all work so much and we all do all that we can and, still, the punches keep coming and the kicks to the teeth, and the knocks that we don't deserve, but are forced to take on board anyway.

I stamped my feet on the floor in an impetuous fashion, as if life was all too much for me. They groaned and looked at each other, and I wondered whether poverty could really have affected my moral compass so profoundly.

'Let us call the police for you', a Stock Character in the background said.

There was a brief pause to acknowledge that things hadn't quite gone to plan.

'Oh no,' I declined, 'I couldn't. I fear that the pressure and the paperwork would be the end of me.'

And, instead of getting suspicious, they looked at me as though I were brave, as if I were taking it on the chin like a True English Gent. They looked at me as though I had exactly what it takes, as though I were the high priest of tenacity and mental fortitude, and of all the other skills and qualities that are needed to survive in this cruel, modern world.

Slowly their wallets came out of their pockets and I felt bank notes being thrust into my hands. I shook and gesticulated as a sign that I couldn't accept, but still they kept coming, and so, eventually, I acquiesced, taking a couple of pounds from each of them.

Looking at them each for a final time, intently, right in the eye balls, as though we had shared something, a connection, something that would last forever, I noted the viscid tear trail on my face crack and open dry and warm, as I felt an insincere smile envelop my face, and I wondered what would become of me.

We shook hands and shared valedictions.

I put the money into my wallet and knew that all of us felt better for it, for we had each fulfilled our purpose.

Chapter 28

I can remember hearing or reading somewhere that each of the living creatures on our planet, be it a butterfly, or a humming bird, or a killer whale, will have, over the course of its lifetime, the exact same number of about a billion heart beats. A butterfly may only live for between two and four weeks, a killer whale for between fifty and eighty years, but, whatever the lifespan, the approximate number of times that the hearts of these creatures will beat will be the same, the whale's heart taking eighty years to do what the butterfly's does in a month.

When it comes to modern human beings, we are a deviation from the norm, an anomaly, with the number of heartbeats in our lifetime averaging around two and a half billion. It should be noted though that the life span of our early ancestors was much shorter, suggesting that in our natural evolutionary environments, back in the necessity of the wild, we would share the billion heartbeat rate of other species. And, I have often wondered if the same logic regarding heart beats over a set period of time can be applied to our modern state of health, because, on many an occasion, I have felt my heart beating and smashing and pulsating through my chest; felt my pulse swell up around my neck as though I might suffocate; or heard it in my ears, as though the universe were about to implode. Does it mean that I will die quicker? If the theory is correct, then perhaps it does. The sands of my hour glass are extra fine, flowing quickly and with silky purpose, and, the reason for this, I like to believe, is that those of us who are in tune with our calling, or in touch with our destiny, are the ones who will die earlier; we get to cross the finish line first, as a reward for our supreme efforts, and divine attention to detail.

If I sip politely from a cup of whiskey, then its effect on my heart are unlikely to be too extreme; if I go down like a fiend upon a bottle of the same, then my heart will let me know about it. Perhaps when I am overjoyed my heart will dance in my chest, or if I should find myself overawed by fear, lost in the woods, or terrorised by burglars in the night, my heart will tremble with me. If I avoid these extremities, walk a middle ground of balance, play things safe and do them the 'right' and 'civilised' way, will I live forever, but be treated to a long but boring existence? Is death the price we pay for the colours of experience?

The only thing I can state with any degree of certainty is that, as I limped away from the Angels, the pounding in my chest brought me ever closer to eternity, and I felt the impendency of my own demise with such an acute and fantastic degree of sensation that I became almost entranced. The impetus for this, I am sure, was a coalescence of fear and euphoria - the fear of getting caught, most certainly, but also a euphoric awareness of life's possibilities - an overpowering sensation that I was pushing my pathetic life to its limits and that, even though I was living in a box, so to speak, I had somehow found the fortitude to climb free of it, to open my eyes to the fragility of existence, no longer being pushed down, or made afraid by rules and conventions, quashed by the trammels of society.

I continued walking with my hands in my pockets, clasping the bank notes from the Angels as though they had spiritual significance, holding them as though freshly printed, despite the crinkles and tears in unimportant places. And, as the night began to emerge from the necropolis of another dreary day, I watched with fascination as lardy women in high heels and low cut skirts began to caterwaul on heat, to scream unspeakable obscenities at the taxis in the road, or amidst the vortex of lonely peoples, trundling home from work with dour looks on their faces, and crooked, aching backs, due to days of sedentary seclusion in windowless office blocks. I watched them aghast, out on hen nights or office birthday parties, heaving and swelling and spitting furious, intoxicating vitriol at random passers-by. Bad boys drive by in their daddy's cars; music blaring; purple iridescence. The crossing lights showed red, but people continued to run in an out of traffic anyway; I crossed with them; a car beeped at me in a kind of electric shock yellow.

Down and across the city square, outside the town hall - my limp miraculously cured and my gait as right as rain now - I considered the fact that those who refuse to believe in their own destiny do not really believe in themselves, that they are passive to the whims of chance, that they are utterly lost in the face of the chaos and the meaningless of it all. I stood stupefied, gazing at the disarrayed masses about me, and knew almost instantaneously that the majority of these temporary arrangements of matter had never even reflected upon the subject. Perhaps these words will sound superciliousness or serve as an example of unwarranted haughtiness, but I mean them only as undiluted observation. Regardless, it certainly seemed to me at that time that those of us who do not believe in destiny are without belief in the fundamentals of even our own existence, of our place and potency with relation to the scheme of things as a whole. Boiled down and rarefied to the most basic of principles, it seems quite unlikely that you can get anywhere without a belief in yourself, without a simple awareness of the importance of your being; I guess what I might be trying to say is that a man who thinks he is here by some great accident is less likely to feel a sense of entitlement than a man who thinks he was placed here to be king.

Looking around me, at another empty-bellied night unfolding in Hell's arsehole, I felt a sudden sense of entitlement myself. I rationalised and thus convinced myself that I had created this situation with intention, volition, and design. I told myself that, yes, I had made these things happen, because they were exactly what I needed, exactly what Destiny's doctor had ordered. I was a genius. A king. I would own it all because nobody else wanted to.

I stood slack-jawed and motionless in the centre of the square as I tried to take it all in. The news report was playing on the big screen TV; the clock was ticking on the city tower. Out over yonder, hovering in the background like some drunken, gormless whore at the tail end of a Bacchanalia awaited the Old Theatre. It had only been a few days since I had last ventured within its walls, yet it seemed like an eternity. I wondered if I would find the courage to go back in there today, to brave the bin water and the broken glass, to go down the stairs and march with whatever demons were awaiting me.

For the past few days, whenever I had thought about going in there, when my memory rewound itself and I found myself watching tapes of that horrible moment in the darkness, I had shuddered until I was made empty and unwell. Now, however, that fear seemed to have dissipated and I felt as though I could do anything. I am invincible. I am invincible. I am invincible, I thought. And, thus, I marched off towards my destiny, ready to face whatever God might throw at me.

For a few moments I found myself in a state of non-control, my body drifting towards the Old Theatre once again of its own accord, as if I were some sort of disinterested observer, simply watching the destiny of another person unfold unalterable before me, as though some movie I have seen a thousand times before, but somehow imagine that it might be about to end differently to how I had remembered.

As I picked up speed and my legs began to charge towards the Old Theatre, I looked down at my feet, moving with a neat sense of rhythm that embodied a new but as yet unclarified sense of purpose. And, as I watched the same old drunks in the alleys, and the same old miniskirts battling in the traffic, I realised that I was somehow above all of this, that I was somehow superior, because I was taking it all in at once, as a full-on objective observer, instead of with that Regular Joe subjectivity that gets the others through their days.

The Theatre was getting closer to me, almost as though it were being pulled, reeled in by some invisible but significantly sized piece of damp rope. I was close enough now to touch the exterior walls and so the roughness against the back of my hands set my skin aflare. I looked about me and found that I was standing in the spot where the beggars do their begging, by the malodorous piss stench doorways, in an Elastoplast alcove, the place where dreams go to die or memories try to be forgotten, to be sealed off for eternity by signs that say 'No Entrance' or to warn you that the CCTV has got the insensate eyes upon you.

Down on the ground, legs crossed, staring stupefied at the old holes in my shoes as a day's worth of debris and detritus sweeps about me, I find myself begging for change. There I am, throwing longing looks at the legs of passers-by, spitting out diffident mutterings of the same empty words, *'spare change'* - over and over again - as though I have some kind of speech impediment that people are too decorous to pay any attention to and which stops me from ever really 'connecting'. Most of them pass me by or try to ignore me - a few are even sympathetic enough to provide me with a smile - but none give any of the good stuff, and so, deep down, I'm left with the impression that they'd prefer it if I would just cease existing altogether.

And, so, I begin to forget for a few moments that I do actually exist, feeling a familiar chill as the reality of myself and my situation starts to melt away. My mouth on autopilot, I hold out my hands to repeat those same empty words, *'spare change'*, as if it's the name of a familiar dog I'm calling in for the night. But, when he doesn't come running, when there's no tongue hanging or tail wagging, I begin to get the feeling that he's run away for good, and as despondency falls about me, I have to force myself to be strong and to act like everything is fine. I tell myself that I have been here forever, in this very spot, and that for the very reasons of familiarity and routine there is nothing to be afraid of - there can be no spare change because all of it is needed. I stare mad and blank into the night, resting against the cold old walls of the theatre, attempting to use its strength to stop myself from falling to pieces.

As my back slides up and against the frigid bricks, I remember being back in the school yard with The Leader. I think once again about her hot tong smile and her knowing eyes; about all of the infernal things I could've done to her body but didn't. There's some flaw in my personality, I decide, some barrier or genetic deficiency that leads me to get close to women time and time again, but always for fear of commitment, or of being seen as the Bad Guy, causes me to leave, before too many emotions get involved, or too many expectations that I will inevitably fail to live up to.

'If only I could plunder as ruthlessly as the beast within.'

I felt almost as though I were being punished for this impuissance, that this whole situation was a product of my personality defects, and my anxieties, and my reactions to them. I knew this baby wasn't mine and I knew that The Leader and The Sycophant knew that I knew. But I also knew that they knew I knew they knew but that we all knew I wouldn't say anything, because I was weak, and I had nothing else to die for, and I would do anything just to go along with the flow, anything to let me trick myself into believing that destiny would have its way with me and that my short, pathetic life had meant something to somebody – even if it was all a lie. Yet, why submit to the unknown if not a lover?

More strangers passed me by; I sat gazing up at them, putting on my second show of the evening, right there outside the old theatre. I kept a bleary-eyed lookout for disgruntled Angels, fearful that they would see me begging here after I'd taken money from them, and thus become aware of my ruse. All the while, that flavourless speech impediment phrase floated out of my mouth, and up in between the faceless shadows and figures that continued to pretend I didn't exist. I sat back against the Theatre with increased force, pushed myself into the crumbling walls, the dry sand concrete, almost as though I wanted to become a part of the building. The old edifice looked like I felt, though I hadn't fully admitted this to myself yet; I was still convinced that destiny was something that could be relied on; I was still convinced that everything was going to work out fine; in the sense that it eventually ended, I guess it's fair to say that it did.

The light metallic sound of a twenty pence piece landing amidst the mishmash of cigarette butts and crazy paving between my knees brought me back to reality. Whoever had thrown it walked deep and far into the nighttime and, as I had been lost to a state of reverie, dreaming about an end to this torturous existence, I had failed to pay sufficient attention to those that had passed me by. I looked up to catch a glimpse of the good-natured soul that had deigned to share the wealth and, as I looked to the swarms, to the anonymous masses, I thought that I saw the figure of The Well-Dressed man hovering about the crowds.

Once again, in comparison to the mooncalves blotting his surroundings, he stood taller and leaner, carried himself with a rare grace, as though a deity sifting through the clouds. And as I watched him walk away, wrapped like some kind of expensive gift in his superior garments, it seemed as though a fog fell about the city, and we were all like ships lost out to sea, moving in and out of the smoggy yellow clouds lighted by the flickering and broken street lights.

I stood as briskly as I could; ready to make my pursuit through the mist. To be honest, the lethargy had taken a hold of me again, and I didn't feel like very much: My lungs were full of fluid and my heart of poison, and as I tried to catch a glance of the fading figure, I thought I saw the robust shape of The Half Wit next to him, but of course, in the nebulous haze of my tired mind, I couldn't be sure, and most likely never will be.

Just as I was considering pursuit of the fateful duo, in hope of relieving myself of some of the questions that had been sat on the tip of my tongue for the past few months, another stranger approached me - a surly youth with deadened eyes and a twisted spotted mouth. He moved towards me with a smile on his face as I sat in the doorway, although I suppose now, in retrospect, it would be more accurate for me to say that it was a smirk. His motions were fluid, quick, predestined perhaps, and he came floating towards me as though on a rowing boat that had been kicked by a dirty boot away from the shore, or as though he were on wheels of some kind, with a fluent, linear motion fixed upon the direction of its target. A target, it would seem, that happened to be me.

I noticed with some consternation that, as he approached, he failed to look me in the eye and instead focused on the ground about him. In many ways, he gave the impression that his actions were of a man coerced by some unknown force, as though he felt some kind of inexplicable compulsion of which he had already become quite ashamed; I remember he mumbled something to the effect that I should get a job, and as he said it, his twisted mouth became more distorted, and I noticed that in his unsanitary cakehole sat a disarrayed line of blackened and unsportsmanlike teeth. Even in the dimming lights of the fog stricken street, I could see the jewels of rotting food stuck in between the gaps, a congeries of semi-chewed shades and varied textures. And when he punched me in the stomach, telling me once more to seek some kind of employment, I could only concentrate on the irregularity of his deformed, lacuna of a mouth.

Softly, I fell to the floor, as though in some kind of daze, some dreamy, serene state, high on antihistamines. And, as I hit the moon chilled concrete of the piss stench doorway, I watched him and his tracksuit bottoms disappear into the fog. I wondered if he would able to find an NHS dentist out there somewhere, one that would solve all his problems and help him deal with some of those anger issues, then I collapsed in a heap and forgot about life for an indefinite amount of time.

Back down to the doorway, jaded now anyway, and with no appetite for conquest or adventure, I sat with my head against my knees as I tried to get over the sensation of having had the wind knocked out of me; as I closed my eyes, I felt my eye-balls roll back into my head as the bricks walls of the building slowly turn to dust and then...nothing. Where my back had once been supported I felt a familiar sinking feeling as my body began to convulse and I became consumed by the edifice. As I slipped into a fugue, I felt for a few moments that everything was at peace in the world; it seemed so natural and so golden and so just to me that I fell back as though sinking into a blanket after months deprived of sleep, as if finally reaching home after a long journey, as though set free from a cage and soaring glorious through the skies.

The quality and sensation of the darkness was different to the nothingness that I had experienced previously - in death - or in other encounters with those all-consuming emotions that had eaten away at my connection to things. Indeed, this particular brand of darkness, if 'darkness' is indeed the correct word for such, was not death itself, but something much more final than that; death, though its consequences last for an eternity, lasts itself for but a solitary moment - just as birth is a measurable point in time, followed by the rest of your days on this here earth - and though I would never presume to be able to say what might happen to you when you do die, what comes next, I can say with all sincerity that the sensation I felt at that moment awoke me to an infinity of being, a world in which the linear quality of time as we are used to it, was replaced with a world in which everything that has or ever will happen occurred at once, a beautiful, vertical symphony of every possibility, opportunity and happenstance.

I began to feel that this and any other moment you may care to mention had taken place infinite times throughout the course of eternity, as though the very core of my being had been infiltrated by an unyielding and inexorable omniscience of everything the future could possibly have in store for me. Slowly, in ever increasing crescendo, I heard that same marching music that I had heard before inside the building; its regular rhythm consumed me, encompassed and encroached upon my consciousness, as though a wasp laying its eggs inside the stomach of an unsuspecting caterpillar. And, though I could no longer see my body, I became bitterly aware of the fact that my feet were tapping without volition to the beat.

Perhaps even more strangely, I began to feel that I wasn't marching alone, but as a solitary part of a larger unit, of a great but lifeless army, some sturdy and timeless force that had contributed to the formation of the ages but that had slowly been forgotten about in the face of time's passing tides. I had joined the ranks of those hundred billions who had died before me, marching indefatigably towards an inevitable destiny, without a conscious sense of purpose, but with an unshakable faith in the wonder of it all.

I couldn't tell you how long this sensation lasted in its entirety - this march to nowhere except to where I already was. When I came around, the first light of day was breaking through the clouds, and in the municipal trees, the birds were starting to communicate with one another, although I arrogantly assumed that they were singing for me alone. The streets almost cleared of people now, I began to feel once again at ease. I observed the few that were stumbling home with hangovers, not having slept after a night out on the tiles; laboured breathing, heavy from too many cigarettes, their stomachs rumbling and desirous of beds to sleep in; of lights that weren't so bright and which didn't hurt their eyes.

Forcing myself up by pushing my hands against the gritty, tarnished ground, I noted the indentations on my palms from a night on the concrete. And, as I attempted to regain my bearings, I watched the routine of the city fall into place like some ill-choreographed ballet performance that the audience had only turned up to because the tickets had been free. Between my knees sat the few coins that had appeared in the night time, a collection of nugatory denominations, battered and worn around the edges – scratched-faced monarchs like hypodermic cocktails upon my psyche and making me weak to the knees; I put the intermingling of ill-gotten lucre indiscriminately into my pocket, and then I rifle about the cigarette butts for those that show signs of life, but as I don't have any matches, and they've all been smoked to the bone anyway, I give up and decide to try and drag myself up somehow. My body stiff from the cold and a night of contortion instead of sleeping, I rub my eyes and allow the sun to shine down.

Amongst the cumulus of dust and junk upon the floor, I noticed something that looked very much like a sweet or a candy, some other breakfast treat whose surprise manifestation before my eyes has lent it an air of compound delectation. As my stomach rumbles and I begin to lick my lips, I look down at the mysterious package, wrapped in cellophane to keep the germs and the scum away (which obviously didn't work because there I was), and I brush the coins and the change out of the way to get a closer look. The package had been adorned with Chinese writing, characters that I can't quite fathom or understand, but of which I was quite certain were of vital importance to my quest and which just so happened to look like this:

自殺

I supposed that it might have been the name of some restaurant that I didn't know about, but I concluded that it was more likely the key to the long-term happiness – a doorway to the answers I had been so long seeking and yearning for. Regardless, as I brought it closer to my face and peered through the cheap plastic wrapping of its stereotypical made-in-China gaudiness - red and gold borders, tawdry enough to start a house fire – I become instantly and irreversibly overawed with another sense of foreboding that once again set my heart a-pumping and made the blood in my brain hurl and swish, as though a baby that had crawled inside of a washing machine. The cookie inside was cut like the moon, hollow, thin, and as I bit into it I found a thin slip of paper. It had a message on it that said something along the lines of:

'All paths are predetermined.'

For a few silent moments, I sat in a contemplative state of veneration as I gave serious consideration to the message, took it to be almost gospel truth, as though an angel had just descended from the heavens and delivered it to me on a Post-It note from God himself. And who am I to say that such is not the case? I thought about the jigsaw puzzle piece that belonged to the Half Wit; I thought about the Leader and her baby and The Sycophant; I thought about time and my place within it and what it would mean for all of this to be over one day and for myself and my identity to be lost to the emptiness of human recollection.

Finally, I stood, looked ahead of me at the road increasingly flooded with traffic as the hum and the buzz of activity brought the day to life. Scanning the trail of the road up into the upper areas of the city, I determined that this must have been the same road that the Sycophant must have travelled in her one way taxi. And so, looking down again at the slip of paper in my hand, I stuffed the last crumbs of cookie into my mouth, and set off into a world of shadows, lost to the glare of the morning sun, in the same direction as the unknown future and the one way traffic on the road.

The early worker drivers in their cars looked passive and weak from sleep deprivation. Litter ran once again down the sides of the gutters, carried on a wind that wished to be elsewhere.

At the end of the road, just as it began to bend into oblivion, I noticed that I was in a part of the town that I had never been in before. A large building stood grand but semi-dilapidated before me, a block of run down council flats, or so it seemed, but for some reason with a sign that had probably been there since the seventies on the side of it that said 'Bingo' in a tasteless array of colours. It was at this moment that I began to get the most overwhelming sensation of déjà vu, as though I had experienced this moment, not just one, but many more times previously, and that something of great importance was about to happen which would have a lasting effect on the course of the rest of my life. A red car passed by with an uncomfortable hiss; an unfamiliar woman across the street seemed oh so familiar that I almost fell over as she opened up her spotted umbrella - even though it wasn't raining - and as I watched her set off in the direction of the city centre, I became fully aware that even the most seemingly insignificant encounters in a lifetime are precious on account of their fugacity.

At the stairway entrance to the tenement, besides the gaudy opaline bingo sign, precisely as I suspected I would, I witnessed the Sycophant emerging with a few bags of rubbish in her hand and her tired broken eyes evermore so, on account of whatever activity she had undertaken to while away the night-time. Out the door at the front of the building, then down the steps - the same clothes she'd been wearing the day before - she seemed even more tired and drawn than usual - traumatised almost, although I couldn't say why. I thought about calling out to her, giving a friendly wave, but I managed to resist just in time, knowing that she would find my presence, in this place and at this hour, to be peculiar to say the least. Besides, I did not want her to know that I knew she was linked to this place; it would be anathema to the grand design of the great plan.

As the Sycophant faded languidly down the street, the déjà vu sensation began to melt away. Without looking, I folded the slip of paper from the cookie and slid it into my back pocket besides the jigsaw puzzle piece. I pulled out the picture of The Fat Man, which I had been keeping in my wallet and I looked at it again; at his leathery skin; at the bed without legs; at the packets and containers surrounding him. Through the window of his room I could see nothing but the vacuum of the sky.

I remembered the words of the Well-Dressed man on our first encounter.

'The Big Guy upstairs has the answer to all your questions', he had said.

And I knew now that they would soon be answered.

Chapter 29

I remember as that day progressed, as morning turned to noon, the tenor of the daylights began to take on a crystalline and pellucid quality that reminded me of how I used to feel years ago, when I would wake up human and refreshed instead of half-vegetable and asleep. Illuminating the sides and windows of buildings as though great works of art, unyielding glaciers upon swollen seas, the brilliant red sun cast great, flat shadows about those who walked the city. And, for a brief moment or two I did feel human again, pausing to reflect, as I basked in the simplicity of it all. I convinced myself that today's clarity was a reflection of a newfound peace and understanding, a renewed and almost unwholesome sense of confidence that I was nearing the end of my journey. I knew now what I had to do and how to go about it; no longer afraid of dying because I knew in my heart that death is the only thing that unites us all, I smiled at those who passed me by, completely aware that despite all and any differences, our time is now, and so we will always be connected.

Many great men have lived before us, but they are dead and we are not.

Streets which had once looked oppressive to me in their unfamiliarity seemed radiant with welcome grace. The angry smirks and grimaces of passers-by, the faceless many, seemed warm now with a gentle affection; something that seemed to be saying we are in this together, you and I, for we are all brothers and sisters separated at birth.

Perhaps this optimism could be attributed to the weight that had been removed from my shoulders. If I were a priest, for example, try as I might to maintain an unshakeable faith in our lord and saviour above, there would always be some kind of doubt, the devil on my shoulder, whispering deep and long into the night within the shadows of incertitude. This being the case, I could never be sure that whatever I was submitting myself to, letting speak through me, was really something that existed outside of myself. Though I may feel some connection to a higher force, some deity that makes me feel things are just and righteous, purposeful and ordered, the opportunity to view this God, my master of creation, would never present itself in any tangible or concrete form that would allow me to empirically verify my most precious of intuitions. Maybe I would start to think that I had been afflicted with some nefarious madness, doubting myself with an ever increasing intensity with the passing of the days, until eventually all that would remain would be an empty tracing of what once was, for I would have separated my soul from my body, and been left with only a shell, brittle and weak and indefensible.

Indeed, now that I was almost certain where The Fat Man resided, I felt confident that everything I had been working towards over the past few months would prove to be fruitful. I felt as though I, and I alone, had been able to seek out the patterns in the chaos, that I had lighted upon conclusive proof of a God's existence, and that if I just kept on marching to the beat of destiny's drum, following the signs and keeping up the faith, I would be able to speak to him, face-to-face, to ask him all of the questions that I have spoken about so many times before. Finally, I could die happily and alone, safe in the knowledge that everything had been perfect, that all had been worth it, and thus my time on earth had not been as wasted as I felt it to be. I was a thinker –that was for sure; now I would turn the process of thought into action and use it to turn the world around.

I headed down towards the centre of the town, through a circular system of underpasses, as the inner city dankness emanated from the dirt-tiled walls with their council-approved graffiti murals. Almost in a reverie, I began to wonder how I might appeal to the good nature of my God once down and before him on my knees. Thus, it occurred to me that the situation would no doubt require some sort of largesse with which to curry his favour. But what would be appropriate for a situation so divine? I considered the nature of the beast, his ample girth and leathery thighs, and I wondered if I could perhaps perform some kinds of sugar ritual sacrifice upon a donut or a cream bun in his honour. And, for a few moments, I seriously deliberated upon this pathetic notion, but as I left the tunnels of the underpass and returned to the cookie-cutter radiance of a perfect day, it seemed to me so trivial and so self-centred that I gave up on the idea completely, for it would be me that received the benefits of devouring these sugary delectations and not the destined saviour of my dreams.

I needed to think bigger.

To win the blessing of my God, I would have to do something so remarkable, so unprecedented, that it would be written down afterwards in history books - an act of such magnitude that the plebeians and the small folks and their booboisie friends would spend the rest of their lives talking about it, paying attention to the lessons bestowed upon them, as though engraved in stone upon the top of the holiest of mountains. And, so, the idea struck me that I must supply my God with food, but quantities much vaster and even more prodigious than that of which I had seen the Sycophant purchasing that time in the supermarket. What was required here was nothing short of a miracle, a display of such unwavering faith and dedication that it would push the boundaries of nature to its very limits, something so profound that it would change things forever, despite leaving them the same in their definitiveness.

Of course, to do something like this in a society such as ours, there is no avoiding the fact that money is required and, as I was unsure whether I even had a job or not anymore, I would not be able to rely on a pay cheque to achieve my goals. The obvious and most sensible thing to do would be to head into the direction of the shop and speak with the manager, but, as I had not returned any of his calls since the day or two before, I would most likely be received with an animosity and ill-will that I simply couldn't be bothered to make myself available for; perhaps, if I am honest, I was also too cowardly for such confrontation. Regardless, I tried to convince myself that it wasn't an option and so continued to bumble oblivious into the afternoon crowds, scratching my thinning head of hair as I did so, and muttering insignificances to myself that I now struggle to remember. As I headed deeper into the town centre, avoiding the gazes of members of the public and disgruntled gang members, the clouds suddenly became overcast, almost as if were snarling at me balefully, in disgust at my inability to make up my mind, despite erstwhile swaggering with pride because I claimed to know what my final goal was.

It was at that very moment, almost as if the sight of such clouds stimulated an afflatus within me, that I realised what the most obvious thing to do would be; I would take out a loan and, of course, because of my impendent expiry, I would not have to face the usual trouble of having to pay it back. I rubbed my hands together in a perspiring state of glee and smug self-satisfaction, proud of myself for having come up with such a remarkable plan. Perhaps in the next life, I would be the CEO of a Fortune 500 Company.

In a ruinous and abandoned quarter at the top of the town, one that had never seen the steeple of a church nor the domes of a mosque, awaited the prefab shop units of the moneylenders, with their crumbling facades, and the single-file queues of dead-eyed, needle hole junkies standing with doleful expression outside their doors. Smiling faces and money-filled clenched fists adorned window posters advertising opulent lifestyles: flat screen television sets and things to plug into them; cameras and jewels; cruises away from the grey of the rain; a gaudy and tasteless imagining of wealth that could only really appeal to those without it. I waited a few moments until my nerves had subsided and then slinked to the back of the queue. Surly men with shaved heads and face tattoos tried to stare me down, but because I was already looking at the floor it didn't make much of a difference.

The 'shop' was little more than a 'room'. Divided in two by a thin, cardboard wall, into which had been implanted a thick door with a set of heavy duty locks and a key pad, it was no more welcoming than it needed to be. To the side of the door was a bulletproof window with bars behind it, much like a bank, but with more signs to inform people that alarms were in operation and that they shouldn't attempt to rob the place. Behind the bars of the window, sat on, what I ascertained from her half-moon revolutions, must be a swivel chair, was a particularly burly specimen of human female, whose job was to call forth the pugnacious looking people in the queue with a *canis unfamiliaris* cigarette bark.

Some of these patrons were amongst the toughest men in town, solid as old rocks, but before the Burly Woman, they cowered and grovelled like schoolboys, muttering with contrived and ingratiating tension as their faces became red and their breath became flustered. Once she had them in this state of subjugation she examined their provisional driving licences and, should it meet her fastidious standards, gave them a loan with a criminally high rate of interest. They would smile pathetically and thank her ever so much for doing so then bow and slink back out of the door and into the high street; I began to feel that maybe my own place of work hadn't been so bad after all.

Up above us all, like some peeping tom in the trees, peering into the bedroom window of our underwear drawer financial dealings, was a CCTV camera. Violated by its presence, I became convinced that it knew of the illicit criminal thoughts that were turning my brain to mush. Nervously, I began to hop from one foot to the other, even going so far as to consider running out of there once and for all, but as I turned around to do so, I noticed that an unseemly queue of people had grown in silence behind me and, as the thought of passing such a group of reprobates empty-handed was too much to handle, I remained firmly where I was.

Most of them were too busy expressing their distaste for the waiting times that they were being exposed to, as though time had become some kind of toxic radiation, to have noticed my transgression, but I still felt as though I had failed in terms of fortitude, and so I looked to my feet on the ground and wondered how I had been reduced to such calamity. I swivelled back on my feet and faced the front of the queue again. The Burly Woman called me forth and I marched up to the window with a slight sense of pride, as though I were an eminent scientist, who was finally about to receive a prize or some kind or recognition for a lifetime of hard work.

Having clearly decided that I was dawdling, the Burly Woman barked directly at me, telling me, I think, to hurry up, and so I began to feel the transitory sense of pride I had felt, just moments before, to wither like a decaying piece of fruit that had fallen from a tree. Finally stood before her, I was able to treat myself to a clear look at her face, which in many ways reminded me of a wrinkly dog, perhaps a pug or bloodhound, although not, I was beginning to hope, endowed with the sagacity that is associated with the latter of these species. She had those same dead eyes that were quintessential to the faces of so many around here and I got the impression that her diet consisted of little more than coffee and cigarettes, because deep down I could see that she was jittery and her hair was yellowed from the tobacco fumes. We stared at each other for a few moments, like two neighbourhood pets that are unfamiliar with each other and have not quite decided whether a stand-off is to be required. Though she couldn't see my hands from her position behind the counter, I had actually placed them over my bottom, for I was at that moment so convinced that she may leap over the counter and sniff at it that it was the only thing I could think of to do to instil within myself a sense of security.

'What the hell do you want?', she asked me.

She was relatively polite, I thought, considering how horrible it must be for her to spend all day in a place like this.

'Well, Madam', I said, 'A loan, if you please.'

I said it in as charming a way as I could muster, realising immediately that I had fallen into the same trap as the oleaginous macho men that I had heaped scorn upon just moments before. I sighed as I realised once again that all I was really capable of doing was disappointing myself. Nobody could leave this place with their dignity intact, that was clear as day.

She explained to me quite forcefully the terms and agreements of the loan, asked to see some identification, which I happily provided from my wallet, and then told me that my application had been accepted and interest would be added from that very moment.

'Fine. Fine. That's fine', I said through a shit-eating smile.

Then, I signed my name, as though upon the Magna Carta or some other magnanimous document that I would be remembered for being associated with, then I asked her the most important of all questions:

'What happens if I die?', I asked.

'You'll be forgotten', she barked.

Then I walked out of the door with five hundred pounds in my pocket and a renewed but transitory sense of self-worth.

Chapter 30

I looked down at my feet and realised that they were taking me in the direction of the supermarket where, only the day before, I had seen the Sycophant. Head down, eyes to the ground, I held on to the money in my pocket as though my life depended on it, trembling at the thought of the shady street people surrounding me attempting to get at it. But, despite the fear that I felt, a resilient pride began to swell in my breast in honour of my fiscal superiority and so as I began to look upon them disdainfully, I knew very well that they could smell the wealth on me but only dream of the crisp feel of the freshly pressed pound notes in their grubby hands as I complacently passed them by. As I sauntered in this fashion, I began to wonder what the maximum amount of calories I could buy with five hundred pounds might be; The Sycophant had bought biscuits and fizzy drinks yet I was determined to outdo her. This was a holy war.

I suddenly found myself over-analysing the contents of store windows as I drifted on past them. Over yonder was a discount store with taped up windows and, as I floated by on the other side of the road, I found myself questioning the contents of the seedy plastic tubs piled up besides the spit and the chewing gum wads upon the pavement. Out-of-date biscuits or expired multipacks of crisps sold three packs for a pound and I could imagine the dirty lips of The Fat Man curling with pleasure as I gave these to him. But, then, I thought it must be sacrilegious to give him something out-of-date, and was thus impelled to keep on walking, to keep my eyes out for other collations perhaps more pertinent to the cause. I passed fried chicken outlets and kebab shops; a man selling baked potatoes out the back of a van; a hotdog vendor with an Elastoplast over his nose and crumbs in his moustache. Everything seemed so hopeless, so I looked to the skies with a dour expression upon my face, and questioned the purposelessness of it all as I cursed the day I was ever born.

At just that moment, however, a round lady walked by with two or three round children waddling along behind her. Though they were muttering amongst themselves in a rather ugly dialect that I couldn't understand, the joyous expressions upon their little round faces as they tucked into their hot beef sandwiches, purchased from a gypsy caravan vendor down the street, said all I needed to know. As they walked past me I watched the red juices of the meat pour down their cheeks as they slobbered upon their fingers and churned and screwed their faces. Truly, this portly single-parent family was in an unquestionable state of blessed radiance, a state of complete satisfaction. The mere sight of it did make my heart rejoice.

As the smell of the beef lingered in the air after them, the subtle hints of onions and ketchup as potent as a perfume counter in a discount department store, it became so overpowering to me that I stopped right there in my tracks, enveloped within the inner city dreamscape of a hot beef afternoon. Once again, I paused stupefied, watching the world unfold before me, watching the little people get on with their lives, with their shopping bags, and their insignificant dramas, and their dull conversations. And, as I stood fathoming the redolence of the beef, which seemed to me in my synesthetic state to be all the colours and sensations of a great oasis in some formidable desert, I had once again the strange sensation of déjà vu - the sublunary tranquillity of the mid-afternoon scene seeming to me once again oh so familiar.

A balding and contumacious looking man with a chip on his shoulder walked by drinking milk from a carton; a truck with a large picture on its side advertising butter cruised down the road as though out of control. In both of these cases the image of a cow seemed to be the most salient feature of all, dancing quite happily through verdant fields of luscious grass, as though calling to me from some paradise afar. Immediately and irrationally, the appeal of such an idealistic and bucolic scene inspired within me the sudden whimsy that I wished to be a cow myself, to spend my days in a bovine stupor, eating grass and ruminating, forever away from the troubles of the world and society. I could think of nothing nicer.

Coalescing almost incestuously with smell of the cooked beef, I felt at that moment that the universe was trying to tell me something, informing me that I would not find any of the food I needed in this place, because none of it was good enough. If fresh food was my quarry then surely there would nothing fresher than a bona fide living beast! This became so obvious to me that I couldn't quite understand why it hadn't occurred to me sooner. What I would have to do was find a cow, a real live one, and when I delivered that to The Fat Man I would be sure to win his heart. I would be sure to be blessed with all of the answers that I could ever need.

I began to run home, as quickly as my tired feet would take me, not because I expected to find a cow once I got there, but because I wanted to change my clothes, so as to be dressed as best befits a ritual such as the one in which I soon expected to be partaking. As has already been observed within these pages, I am not the best runner in the world, and will certainly never be the fastest, but as I ran through the dilapidated streets of that once great city, the adrenaline pumping through my vessels and my neurons aflame, I began to feel as though I were truly unstoppable. I felt alive. Perhaps we have also observed by now the uncanny ways in which incongruous actions in uninspired places will find themselves on the receiving end of stares and mockery; and this is exactly what happened, as I ran through the streets with a mad gleam in my eye, and the conviction that my future had already been decided by some benevolent force.

For sure, as the sound of my footsteps pounding amidst the old stone pavements began to resonate throughout the city, willing me to go ahead ever faster, to catch up with myself and my destiny, to rebuild my life and to get back on track, I felt the unsportsmanlike glares of pedestrians upon my back as though there were a sniper on my tail with an itch to pull the trigger. I heard their tutting and their vituperations with displeasure, saw the unabashed looks of disapproval in their eyes, watched their mean mouths tighten into disgruntled grimaces, as they shook their heads, and pointed and raised their fists in the general direction of the silly bastard gallivanting aimlessly before them. Indeed, it was only the exhortations of my own footsteps that gave me the power to ignore the suspicious looks encroaching upon my personal space from all directions, those gazing upon me quite understandably, but nevertheless infuriatingly, assuming that anybody who would run through the town centre during a dreary afternoon perhaps had something wrong with them.

A gaggle of old ladies came out of a market place coffee shop just as I made my way by. Once they had seen me with my sinewy frame at loose ends, my arms and legs a-flailing and what I hoped was a dead-set sense of certainty and determination in my eyes, the maundering sounds of their conversation stopped almost immediately, and they stood looking at me with their mouths agape as their concepts of social decency were left in tatters, and their flabbers became gasted once and for all. I looked at them standing there with their mouths open, mildly confused but utterly judgemental in their approach to dealing with things. Surely they'd seen a person running before? As they glared at me with malice, I felt a great sense of injustice stirring deep within my loins. I glared back at them with the intensity of a thousand burned-out suns and broken supernovas.

The absurdity of their confusion began to seem so odious and distasteful to me that I did the only thing that I could think of to do. Perhaps it was because the smell of the beef was still in the air, or because I had cows on the brain - at that moment nothing I did seemed to have been born of any logical impetus - but as I got closer to them I found that I was slowing down and, then, next thing I knew, I was lowing, lowing like a cow, right there in broad daylight, there outside the city market.

'MOOOOOOOOOOOOOOOOOOOOOOOOooooooooo', I said, and then I said it again, only much louder.

I'm sure you can only imagine what happened next. The old ladies took umbrage at this peaceful act of mooing, perhaps considering it to be a threat, or an act of terrorism, of some kind. Indeed, they became quite flustered, so much so that their faces began to redden, and some of them even raised their umbrellas in my direction and shook them in a jeopardising manner. Usually, these kind of threats would have disconcerted me in some way, especially from a specimen so innocuous as an old lady, but I was so excited at the thought of my quest, and at having finally found a sense of purpose, that it didn't bother me at all. In fact, I found it rather amusing; I let out a little laugh as I continued to run in the direction of my apartment.

Occasionally, to bring back the sense of jocularity that I was beginning to feel, perhaps what would be described by some as a case of manic euphoria, I mooed arbitrarily at others that passed me by: like the man on his bicycle, for example; an elderly Asian gentleman stepping quite unsuspectingly out of a taxi cab; a child in a push chair; and a plump lady with a feather in her hat about to tuck into an ice cream. Observing their reactions to my lowing elevated me to a state of unmanageable excitement; I felt like a bladder that was about to burst. And, as I began to imagine how people would react when I brought a real cow into this environment, I felt the depth of my determination swell to newfound proportions. I became a bottle rocket shooting for the moon.

What a day it was turning out to be! What a life! I knew I was winning for sure!

However, my excitement was not to last forever. When I got to the familiar edifice of my apartment block, I noticed that outside on the pavement were a number of black plastic bin bags. Many of them seemed to be open and the contents, which seemed to be clothing, books and other familiar looking objects, had been scattered about the street as though a tornado had just made its way through a caravan site. In my excitement, the light of my consciousness failed to shine upon these items, and so, lifelessly and robotically, I pushed open the communal door of the building, rushed past the decaying post boxes in the vestibule, tried to ignore the smell of garbage emanating from the basement, and pulled myself up the stairs to the first floor on which my apartment awaited.

It was here that I began to get the strange sensation that time was not what I considered it to be, that, ineffably, it had drawn itself out and distorted itself into some sort of strange phantasmagoria, and that the image that was constantly showing itself before me was different to the one which appeared before everybody else. It was as though, all this while I had been watching a movie whilst all the others had been watching a TV show. I suppose that the last time that I was here must have been the other morning when I woke up late for work and decided that I wouldn't go in. A lot had happened since that time and I felt that something had happened to me that were irreversible. I had changed.

As I approached the door and began to remove my key from my pocket, right there beneath the blinking lights of an empty corridor, I began to get the feeling that I had been away for a period of time much longer than I had realised. Tentatively, I put the key to the lock, only to realise that something was amiss - the key no longer fit in the lock. I looked around for an eviction notice but there was none to be seen. This wasn't like the movies or the cartoons where some rabid landlord leaves a red 'Evicted' sign pinned to your door, but I knew deep within my soul that must be what had happened. Perhaps I should have opened some of that post that I'd received. As an act of propitiation, I let out another lowing sound, more lugubrious this time, dyspeptic, as though I had eaten something that didn't quite agree with me and I couldn't figure out the effect that it might be about to have on my body.

Forlorn, I turned and marched back down the stairs, one heavy footstep at a time, histrionic motions and occasional pauses in art pose attitude – 'The Lonely Man', 'The Scream' - just on the off chance that somebody was watching from a distance and would take pity on me. But, alas, nobody came and so I continued out of the door. On the way out, I put my keys in a random post box, then as the big wooden door of the gentrified building closed behind me, I knew that it was the terminal sound of finality and closure, that I would never be going back, and that, from this day forth, my life would never be the same. It seemed to me as though destiny really did have something in store for me, or at least that it wanted me to continue down the path to obsolescence.

The sorry state of my belongings, scattered willy-nilly about the streets, only served to compound the disdain that I felt towards it all. Most of my valuable possessions had been stolen by the more impecunious and less scrupulous members of the public, but a few of my treasured items remained, and so I began to feel reassured that all was not lost. I gazed in disbelief at the streets that surrounded me: over there in the gutter was a pair of Marks and Spencer's underpants bought for me by my grandma one distant Christmas; behind the front wheel of that rusting Fiat Punto was one of my spoons from Ikea.

Scattered in sporadic formation across the width and breadth of the street were things that shared a connection to me, random objects from unrelated times of my life, now unified in their desolation. Another suspiration as I decide to embrace the moment, just like I had read about in my self-help books; almost at once, my despair was transmuted into happiness and I began to feel as though these streets, once so cold and so distancing, were now my home. My sense of belonging and entitlement redoubled to inordinate proportions. All at once I felt at home in the world, but with the same sense of wonder that pervades the best of our childhood memories.

I poked at the plastic bags with my feet to see what was inside them. Most seemed to contain clothes that I had been quite willing to forget about, things that were too big for me, or too small, kept only for sentimental reasons, and so I concluded that I would be quite happy to leave them where they were, rotting miserably in the gutter of gutters here outside my ex-apartment. In fact, I was just grasping for the mental fortitude to walk away when I saw out of the corner of my eye that in one of the bags was a black item of clothing that would perhaps carry the air of solemnity and gravitas required for the ritualistic evening that I envisaged to be store.

Having removed the item in question from its flimsy plastic bastille, I held it up in front of me for inspection. Yes, just as I thought, this was the suit I had once worn in my old life, back before the ceiling had come crashing down and left me to fester in the basement. As I could recall, it had a button or two missing, but as I brushed off some of the dirt and residue that it had picked up during its time on the streets, I realised that it would do just fine. It would serve as an honest declaration of the reverence I felt towards this most holy of causes.

Rummaging through the same bag for the matching pants, I was lucky enough to find them almost straight away, as if it had been predetermined, and so Destiny herself had guided my hand within the depths of the plastic bag. The tattered pants also had a button or two missing, but I felt that I would be able to cover that up easily enough by simply wearing a belt. Removing the clothes that I had been wearing up to that point, a pair of jeans that didn't quite fit on account of my being so thin, and a baggy t-shirt, I replaced them, together with a creased shirt that I found in one of the other bags, with the buttonless suit of my dreams. Instantly, I felt almostas though I were my Old Self, pretending to be winning, pretending to be going places; I flashed a winsome smile to my reflection in one of the broken bottom floor windows of the apartment block, stuffed the five hundred pounds into my pockets and, then, leaving my belongings where they were, for the birds or the tramps or whoever else might want them, I vacated the street for a final time as I tried to ignore the crushing sense of defeat that I felt within the scheme of things as a whole.

Though it was by no means late enough to be getting dark yet, the bright lights that had seemed so irradiated with meaning that morning were starting to disperse and be replaced with the thick outlines of clouds that dominated the horizon, casting a grey mystery over all that worked and lived in the city. My plan now, of course, was to head on over to the village on the other side of the canal, the place where I had once been jogging, because I knew that, if I continued just a little further up into the hills, I would be certain to find a field of cows from which I would be able to pluck a most comely beast indeed.

Thinking these thoughts, it occurred to me that, if I were to succeed in discolouring the beast's volition to the degree that it would follow me on my quest, I would need a rope or a leash of some kind. But, rather than turn back into town, and lose the sensation that I was actually making progress, I decided instead to just keep my eyes out for suitable materials on the way, to let destiny furnish me with the tools required for success.

I took a huge sigh as I marched forwards. In my crinkled suit with the missing buttons, I was sure that everything would work out.

And, to a certain degree, I guess it did.

Chapter 31

Over the bridge, I did the best I could to ignore the twitching curtains and ice cold glares emitted from behind the dusty windows of the tiny but expensive houses, to distract myself from the lemon-mouthed old folks, sitting like corpses with beady eyes and mean mouths, in fading pieces of furniture. I glared with electric anxiety at my surroundings: looked to the sky and analysed the clouds; brushed my hands through the leaves of trees; contemplated the colours of flowers in fastidiously manicured gardens. And, as I considered the placement of gnomes under bushes and bird baths and water features besides pedicured lawn plants, I recoiled at the sight of the shimmering, varnished fences protected by reams of barbed wire and glass that glistened in the sunlight.

All the while, I entertained doubts about myself and my soul and my situation, but as I was too preoccupied with my desire to get my hands on a Holstein heifer to pay any real attention, I was able to let these thoughts roam onwards, free to take their place in the mortuary of my mind.

Before long, I was dragging myself up a path that led into the woods, which I remembered would take me deep into the hills and around into the fields where the beasts did graze. Last time I had come this way, everything seemed to have been in its proper place, each leaf and blade of grass positioned, it seemed, by some great set designer in the sky. And, perhaps because it was approaching autumn, the leaves having begun to fall from the trees in droves, carpeting the ground and covering the dirt path to the extent that I could barely see it, the woods now looked as though they had come into their own, as if the skeletal hand of death itself had swept over everything in sight, leaving only the bare essentials of what needed to remain.

Loose leaves blown by the wind; the end of the line. I wondered if I myself were being blown by a similar Aeolian force, if this place were the one that all the gutters might lead to. And, as I thought these thoughts, a great and cynical sense of peace swept over me, safe in the knowledge that the seasons were cyclical and therefore so was life; whatever happened next would be for the best. I felt like a cliché.

Another platitude right out of a bad Hollywood movie.

Up amongst the trees, in a forlorn glade where children who had no doubt long since grown up had once played, remained a solitary oak tree on which a piece of rope with a stick tied to the end of it swung ghostlike in the breeze. Upon encountering such, I realised almost immediately, and without surprise, that removing the rope from the tree would furnish me with the leash required to guide my anticipated bovine beauty down towards its destiny in the heart of the city. These thoughts were accompanied by a great surge of empowerment, for once the cow was attached to the leash, its destiny would be in my hands and mine alone.

Assuming it were a tractable cow that I encountered, one that were willing to follow wherever I might lead, the fate of the creature would be up to me and me alone. I trembled at the thought of such divine responsibility. Indeed, though I had already decided that the brute's demise was a prerequisite of appeasing The Fat Man, the excitement I felt came from knowing that I would be leading it to that end, that I were to take my place as an agent of fatality, and that by leading it in this way, I would be able to understand the workings of whatever force were leading me in like manner, with an invisible leash, but to the very same end.

Though the base of the old oak tree was encircled by rusting cola cans, torn crisp packets, cigarette butts and the torn away pages of seedy magazines, all of the implied corruption of spirit was nevertheless nullified by the fact that that something so innocent as a swing had been erected here. I hitched my legs up over the knotted wooden seat as it tipped from side to side beneath the weight of whichever leg I put upon it, but eventually I found myself being held quite sturdily, wearing my only suit, as I began to swing languidly in distorted circles, humming a melancholy tune to myself, though hardly being aware of the fact, gazing at the leaves on the floor as they were carried away forever by the winds.

It took a few moments before I was able to grasp the reality of my situation, step outside of myself once again and take it all in for what it was. There I was with my head bowed, like an overgrown child scolded for doing something that is really not that bad but which he has decided to feel guilty about anyway. I reflected on the incongruity of my business suit, recalled the meetings that I had been to whilst wearing it, the handshakes that I had made – all of those things that had once seemed so important, so pivotal to the course of my life, seemed so decadent and uninspired to me now that it made me wonder how I would feel about my actions at present way off into the future. All that was really in store for me now was one final transaction, perhaps the most important one of all.

Lazy I swung in another languid circle. Then, just as I was about to stop myself with my foot and climb off of the swing there was a large cracking sound and I watched myself tumble to the ground, as the branch that the swing was attached came crashing down from above, falling next to me, and causing the leaves on the ground to float through the air - as though in imitation of the circles I had been making in the air myself just seconds before.

I sat motionless on the floor for a few moments, confused. Then, when I had found it within myself to recompose myself, I stood up with a frown on my face and a throbbing in my heart, as I wiped the dust off of my backside and grimaced at the shame of such gracelessness. With some effort, I untied the rope from the fallen bough then stumbled off bleary-eyed in the direction of the fields, trying once again to find the path through the fallen leaves as I did so.

Eventually, I approached the rocks that I had sat on once before. They looked the same to me as always, but I remembered reading that all things are in a constant state of flux, and so began to wonder if there were subtle differences that I had not been able to pick up on. I sat down on the smallest of the rocks, rested a moment to catch my breath, and, as I looked down the valley at the city, I remembered how I had once thought to myself that all of my problems could be put in perspective by looking at them from a distance.

Behind the rocks were some of the quintessential building blocks of life here in this part of the country: stones, rabbit holes, and sheep. I climbed up a knoll behind me that was crested with a dry stone wall; my breath was starting to dwindle, but as got my foot in the grooves and looked on over yonder, I saw that I had come at the right time: The field was full of cows.

At the sight of such, I lost myself completely; aware of the sensation of standing there on the hill, but feeling a total lack of control over my body, a lack of ownership almost, as though it were no longer mine. It seemed to me that the cows were innumerable, so much so that, if I were to try and count the spots on their hides, I would not be able to do so in this lifetime alone. As I stood gazing at them, I could almost feel my eyes dilate. I could feel the hairs on my arms begin to stand, the sweat on my palms. My throat became dry as my mouth stood agape. I fell to my knees, weeping as I kissed the ground beneath me.

For a brief moment or two, I felt a return to peace, but then I remembered that, even up here, in the here and now, this place was as much a part of my problems as anywhere else and that I would never be able to distance myself from them because it was really within me that they resided. My body became me once again and, as I turned to face the horizon, the cityscape panorama offered from up on high, I looked down at the familiar buildings, the mazy streets and snickets, the cars on the road from A to B, and was struck by the sensation that after a little while our lives become nothing more than self-contained units of familiar people and places, and that familiarity breeds contempt, for others at first, but then inwardly, contempt towards ourselves.

This epiphany, the realisation that this place, which had once been a kind of sanctuary, was connected to the bigger problem as a whole, made my insides feel like collapsing, almost as if they weren't there anymore. I cried out and I screamed, but, because I was so high on up and alone in the hills, nobody heard me, except for the cows. There was another second when I thought about giving it all up, but to do that, I realised, would leave me with no choice at all.

I put my hands on the cold stones of the old wall, hoisted myself up and, rope in hand, began slowly to approach the cows as the tears continued to stroll down my face. I tried to force a repression of this realization - that my unhappiness was inescapable, that it was fundamental to existence - and as I did so, I felt a surge of adrenaline rush to my brain. Lightning flickered on the horizon and even today I can't be sure if it really happened or if I was just imagining things.

Though I knew that I was looking at nothing more than a field full of cows, a regular sight indeed on the outskirts of a backwater town such as this one, I felt so in awe of their holiness, that they seemed to me superior beings. Unaware or unbothered by my presence, they stood oblivious, chewing the grass in perfect harmony with each other, not a word uttered between them, but a complete sense of understanding and community based on a mysterious, wordless language that I couldn't understand because I hadn't spoken it in so long. It was almost as though they were members of some kind of exclusive club that I had not been invited to; I felt another tear slide down my cheek as I realised that I was still crying, crying more than I had done probably in all of my life up until this moment.

A palpable tension filled the air. When they saw me, an unfamiliar member of an unfriendly species, marching towards them as though I owned the place, they began to scatter themselves in groups throughout the field. Little by little, I watched them, moving out of the path they anticipated I would take; moving and stopping, moving and stopping, each of them with their eyes on me, lowing disdainfully in my direction, as though warning me not to get any closer. Regardless of their threats, I stood noble and proud before them in the field, still with the tears streaming down my face, but not as voluminously now. As I wiped my eyes with the back of hands, my vision became less blurred, and I felt sure that I would be able to recompose myself.

I looked about me.

Because I had stopped moving so had the cows. The majority of them were on the other side of the field now, as far away from me as the boundary of the stonewall would allow. A few still stood before me, not exactly within arm's reach, but within a distance that I could cover by running and not having to pop a lung. I kept my fingers crossed as I looked around to make sure that there were no bulls in here with me; I had neglected to consider that a possibility. Luckily, there were only heifers. None of them were with calf and so I assumed that I would be safe. The lowing continued as the electric tension filled the air and the evening crackled with life and excitement and anticipation.

At the far side of the field was a gate. I couldn't see from here whether or not I would be able to open it, and so, deciding that this might be something worthy of knowing, I began to tiptoe around the edge of the wall in its general direction. It was on the way across that I began to feel a profound sense of fear and solitude, as if these cows, should they want to, could turn the years of evolutionary superiority against me, back me into a corner, and milk me for all I'm worth. Though they remained poised where they were, their lowing became ever louder, instilling within me the fear that they were plotting against me, making plans for attack. And so I started to tremble; to seriously regret having ever entered their domain.

In a way, I felt like I was the only human being remaining on the face of the earth, and this sense of desolation was so crippling that I felt my energy reserves deplete and another great heaviness sweep over me like a whole winter's worth of bad weather. I felt a pounding on the back of my head, a pulsation explosion just above the nape of my neck. In a moment of madness, I became convinced that this was my soul, fearing for its own realness and trying to escape through the backdoor.

As my fingers stiffened and my toes set straight, I forced my eyes to the ground and moved in increments towards the gate on the other side of the field.

If an eternity can be measured in inches then that is how long it took me to get there. I reached the gate still trembling, practically fell against it, clenched at the metal rungs with my bloodless fingers. As my shivers turned to convulsions, the quivering of my body caused the gate to rattle. At first, it was barely audible, a voice behind you in an empty room - a stranger's whisper. But, slowly, the longer I stood there, the louder it became, until eventually the rattle became a clang, and the noise resonated throughout the fields and over the hills.

As the tension between the cows and I grew tenfold in its intensity, so did the fear I felt, even more so that I couldn't let go of the gate. As the clang continued, my breathing became heavier, and some of the cows, I could hear, were beginning to panic, get worked up, and slip into a frenzy. They started lowing again, louder than ever before; I tried best I could to still myself, to bring an end to the infernal cacophony of my metal paroxysm. I closed my eyes, focused, opened them again, and looked at the grass. Tried to count the blades in vain as my head began to swirl and my stomach churned and I just wanted to end it all.

I was forced to continue in this manner until I felt sane again. The dim of the clang became a rattle and then a hum and faded to zero. And, as I uncurled my fingers from the rung of the fence, I felt as though my whole hands had frozen. Even though a few of the cows continued to make noises with the murmur of their conspiracy, I noticed suddenly how silent it had become, now that there was a void filled only moments before by the clang of the gate. This silence brought me again to my knees, relieved that the great wave of fear had passed me by. I pulled great clumps of grass and earth from the ground, threw them up in the air, and watched them scatter amidst the field.

When I stood up again and examined the gate, I found that it wasn't held shut with a lock or a clasp but with a piece of rope. It was long enough to serve for a leash – Plan B in case my rope swing remnants should fail me. Deciding that it was now or never, I took a look behind me to check on the cows. Though their lowing had not ceased they seemed to be less disgruntled by my presence. Regardless, I suppose because I was outnumbered, I became paranoid, further convinced that there was some bovine machination in the works, and that it was I and I alone who were to be the victim of this most heinous heifer subterfuge. Indeed, I'm not ashamed to admit that as I stood there with my eyes on them, I could hear them whispering. They thought that I couldn't hear them, because they were so far away, but I could, as if the voice was my own in my own head.

They were saying things like:

'We're gonna get 'im, ain't we, girls?'

'Yeah, of course. Who does he think he is?'

And:

'Slap him with your udders, love.'

My throat dried up in in anticipation of whatever might be about to happen next.

The greyness of the clouds in the sky and the promise of rain on the horizon made the green of the fields seem ever richer. I stood transfixed with my hand on the rope but my eyes to the scene, that of the cows stood as if posing for a coffee table portrait, the wind whipping through their tails, the regal sheen of their coats making them seem almost proud, much more than just the common cattle that our derogation has deemed them to be. I began to wonder if I was doing the right thing. As my glance passed over the eyes of the tranquil beasts, I was able to sense a life force within them, not so much a personality, not even a soul, but something more fundamental than either of these notions, something purer and more refined - the will that permeates all things, or the necessity of whatever unfolds out of human control.

The tears had stopped flowing now and the gate was opened.

For a few moments, it seemed as though all the world had paused to catch its breath. The wind stopped, or lowered to an imperceptible degree, and it made me realise that it had been there all this time, up here filling the spaces between man and beast. Now, it had come to rest, bringing us with it into the same state of serenity, of anticipation for what might happen next.

I moved with delicate footsteps away from the gate and towards the cows, who I had hoped were getting used to my being in their living room. Though I had unshackled the gate from its chains I had not opened it fully; I would save that moment until I had a cow by the neck and could lead it at my will. Then, I found that I was kicking off my shoes and removing my socks. I couldn't tell you why, I just assumed that it would transport me to some primordial plane of being, some place where the innate hunter - the congenital savage within me - knew what to do, how to go about catching and taming one of these wild beasts. Success in such matters was within me, I knew; it was part of the human psyche.

The city no longer existed, because now the hills were my home. Supermarkets and convenience stores and corner shops were extravagances of the imagination. I lunged forwards, towards a cow that had been ruminating quite peacefully. When it saw me it darted backwards briskly, its flanks shaking, the other cows looking up and watching with some concern.

The grass felt cool against my bare feet. I bent my arm and wrapped the rope around the elbow of my right hand and the wrist of the same. I was pretty sure I'd seen this in a movie at some time and so I felt a degree of professionalism, as though I had already earned a certificate of some kind for performing similar actions beforehand, and was thus making the most of my talents and aptitudes.

The other end of the rope still had the branch seat of the swing attached to it, and so I swung it around my head, moving gracefully as I could towards the next cow in range. When I got close enough, I released my grip on the rope and watched the wood shoot out through the air and into the direction of the cow. I felt a sense of pride, as if I were making the best possible use of the skills given to me as a bona fide human being, as if I were using the intrepid daring and know-how that had allowed us to flourish throughout the ages.

Watching the wood hurtle through the air, I became quite convinced that it was going to wrap itself around the neck of the poor animal, and so when it hit the beast on the side of the head and made it scream in a way that I had not previously realised cows were capable of doing, I was marginally surprised. This sense was redoubled when I noticed that some of the surrounding cows seemed to actually be offended at what I had just done to their friend.

I reeled in the rope as the cow ran off to the side of the field with the others of her caste. Quite at a loss as for what to do, I did the only thing that I could think of, which was to head up after them in their corner of the field, but as soon as they saw me approaching they began to move out of my way and into another corner, the group of many now becoming a single herd, which seemed to move with only one mind and one objective. Twenty or thirty minutes must have passed by the time I gave up chasing them like this, stupidly thinking each time that they would not be able to outsmart me and that I would be able to gain the upper hand.

Finally, perhaps maddened by the lack of success and the niggling realisation that these reasonless creatures might actually be smarter than me, I decided that it would be best to change my tactics. Upon thinking these thoughts, the wind, which you may recall had reached a state of quietude, came back with a vigour and potency that would be hard to match in the tropics, or in any other place where they weather is more romantic than it is here. Waking me up to the dreamlike quality of my situation, I felt the legs of my trousers flapping back and forth as I looked down at my feet, at the grass between them, and the soft coating of drying mud that had covered my toes and seeped beneath my nails.

The cows too seemed to be awoken to a new lust for life as the wind began to bluster, and as they were looking around curiously at each other, no doubt forming even more devious layers of subterfuge, I noticed with alarm that the gate had been able to open itself with the help of the breeze.

Fearing that my hunting ground were about to become infertile, I ran with the last of my energy towards the gate. As I did so, I felt the softness of cow droppings beneath my feet, cool and moist and liberating. I stopped for a moment to catch my breath and wipe my feet on a none poop polluted patch of grass, and, as I was rubbing my foot back and forth, I noticed that the cows were running towards me, or perhaps more accurately, to the gate stood behind me. Some of them, I assure you, looked me right in the eyes as they came bounding onwards. I turned to see if I could beat them to the gate, but they came too strong and they came too many, and so before I even got there they began to slip, one by one, between the cracks and to be lost to the open expanse of the hills out yonder.

By the time I reached the gate, the fastest of the cows had already slipped out of my grip. I tried to close it, but the remainder of the cows had long ago taken a disliking to me, and so they didn't back away - like they had before - but indeed started to make moo at me, with increased degrees of both volume and aggression. Perhaps it was stupid of me, but I tried to close the gate, and as I did this one of them came right up to me and nudged me with her head.

I fell to the floor with the force of it, before I even had a chance to close the gate properly. The cow that butted me pushed me up now against the side of the dry stone wall, so hard in fact that I could feel the bricks digging right into my back, and then I felt her feet upon me, kicking, and then it seemed like the others were coming towards me to join in with the same. A confederation of knees and hooves engulfed me, as udders and tails encroached upon my very being. The sounds of the mooing became even stronger, almost as if the stench of the death's imminence had driven them into a mad cow frenzy, as though I were a heretic being stoned by some primitive believers, as though I were a witch being dipped into a pool to be drowned, as though I didn't quite fit in and so something had to be done about it.

Between the ground and their udders I could feel that the cool of the wind that was still blowing. It added a drama and a serenity to the intensity of the moment. Some of the cows defecated in their excitement; I put my hands over my head to shield myself from the butts and the kicks that kept coming - one to the arm, one to the leg already lacerated. A final smash came against my head and I thought that would be it, the end of me finally, but then, just as I felt myself slipping back into unconsciousness, I noticed that the sounds of their cries were getting quieter, that there were fewer of them.

I pressed myself into the wall and closed my eyes, convinced that I were about to sleep for the longest time.

Chapter 32

A most abject and overwhelming sense of failure brought me back to reality. It was still light, so I couldn't have been long gone, but my head continued to pound and throb, and the intensity of my beating heart served only to be compounded as I looked around me at the field, once abounding with cows, now turned to nothing more than an Eden abandoned; a desert of grass and clouds and empty spaces, where all the promise and potential of life had once resided as though half-forgotten retrospections.

The gate remained wide open, taunting me almost, moving ever so slightly in the wind, but even out in the hills, and upon the most distant of the visible roads, I could not see a single one of the cows. They had eluded me; they had won the battle. Their will had been stronger than mine, and, now, all I could do, if it were not my calling to lead one of them onwards to greatness and eternal renown, was to return to the city with my own tail in between my legs.

So that is exactly what I set off to do.

Worst case scenario: perhaps I could go and ask for my job back in the shop. Perhaps I could contact the landlord and tell him I was sorry, give him a sob story of some kind, and take out another loan. I still had the five hundred pounds in my pocket, so not all hope was lost. And, who knew, maybe when I returned to the city below, I would realise that I had learned something from this whole experience, become wiser and more tranquil and even edified– illuminated with all I may need to make things work out, after all.

Even so, despite these vague and only mildly conciliatory thoughts, deep within the pit of my soul, I knew that I would gladly give everything and more for another shot at pleasing The Fat Man, finding The Cow as I had first envisaged, and scoring another home run with Destiny. I pulled myself and my mental contusions up against the dry stone wall, clutched at the rope with the same sense of desolation that had defined the rest of my life, and then wandered barefoot across the field in search of my shoes.

Down in the valley, the toy cars were lining up behind each other, and so I figured that it must be some time around rush hour. It would be dark in an hour or two and I would be out homeless for the night; I would have to hurry back or risk the chill of the hills and the imminent health detriments that accompanied it. In a rather melodramatic panic, I kicked my foot from side to side, shifting the long grass out of my way as though it were aflame, but there was no sign of my shoes, no matter how hard I might search for them and, thus, as my hopelessness redoubled my motivation began to diminish. I continued in this ilk for a far greater amount of time than would probably be rational, but eventually, the lethargy and a great sense of frustration encroached upon me completely, and I convinced myself that I had found the courage to forget about them.

'Man is born free and yet everywhere he is in shoes.'

I marched out of the gate barefoot, wondering if I would be able to find my way back to the city, and, as I meandered through the desolate hills, I noticed with some small comfort that the path back down had been well-trodden, and so I felt not so alone.

In the distance, I could see a generic looking country road, which I figured I would be able to walk down and save myself some time. Despite the sense of being defeated, perhaps on account of too many kicks to the head, I felt nothing but appreciation for the beauty of my new surroundings, for the fern plants and the grasses and the curves of the hills and the horizon. Even the pellets of sheep droppings seemed perfect to me in the wholeness of their being. Old and abandoned farm buildings peppered the hills, and, as I passed them, I noticed myself nodding in approval, muttering comments to myself about their pulchritude and the beauty of simplicity. Perhaps I had gone mad, but, in my suffering, I somehow felt that I had reached a transitory state of *satori*. It was the only explanation.

I tried not to think about the future; I tried even harder not to think about the past. I must have read a million self-help books in my lifetime that told me to concentrate on the beauty of 'Now', the gifts that only the present moment is capable of offering mankind, and so I paused to contemplate as I swung the rope back and forth between my fingers like a pendulum, following the direction of my thoughts, as if by some strange magic. I tried to focus upon its rotations, to convince myself of its profundity and the idea that there was some great mystery to the world, that not everything could be explained by or reduced to the material, that there was and is something greater than each of us combined. But I felt nothing, no admiration, no sense of wonder, nor even the slightest sense of astonishment. There I stood before myself, just another nonentity attempting to convince himself that there were unfathomed aspects to a dull and predictable lifetime; I needed there to be something more than the reality that stood before me; I felt as though I were losing my faith.

The failure at not finding a cow had brought about in me a heavy sense of dejection. The thought even crossed my mind that there was no such thing as fate, that destiny was chimerical, that all of the things that had happened to me could not be explained when looked at objectively, because there was no unifying pattern, that it was only chaos which ruled our lives and chaos which brought our lives into being and it would be chaos, the very same, that would end things for us and without purpose or design or volition. I felt sick to the back of my stomach.

Looking at myself, at the pitiful waste of space that I had become, I thought about taking the rope to the nearest tree and hanging myself upon it. But something within compelled me to continue forwards, perhaps so I could find a closure of some kind down in the city - the final punch line to the sick joke that my life had become - the final twist in the tale that would kill me with its irony alone; I continued to follow the country road down the hill. Houses began to appear hidden amongst the trees.

Whenever I came to a turning or a fork in the road, I would choose the path that led me down, because that would be were the city was and that was where I needed to be. Despite the months and weeks I had spent lamenting my existence in such a place, I now wished for nothing more than to be back there. Down as far as possible, so I could curl up and die and forget about myself for a while.

It was down one of these country road turnings, that I began to feel a sense of release, as if I had been freed of the shackles that my beliefs had held over me. Though I was still disappointed, I was quite happy in a way that I had found myself to be lacking in discrimination about certain matters all along, and I decided that perhaps I would be happy now - now that I had shed my skin and given up on destiny.

The abrasive textures of the uneven road cut into my feet, so much so that when I looked behind me, I could see tiny irregularities formed of my own blood glistening as the sun set, a Hansel and Gretel death trail leading me right back into the woods from which I had tried to escape. Thinking about destiny's trammels, the coincidences and the connections I had made between the random events that had taken place in my life - the Well-Dressed Man, The Leader and The Sycophant, Babies and cows and old buildings - I couldn't help but laugh, so loudly in fact that if anybody had driven by and seen me they would have suspected, quite rightly, that I was beside myself. My reasons for laughing though were very simple: looking at the rope, at the battered relic from some stranger's childhood, I thought to myself how crazy it was that I had only a few hours before imagined that I would be walking home now with a cow attached to it.

Working back from that thought, I reflected upon all of the incidental happenings and activities that had led me to believe in the first place that a cow was what I needed. Standing there, in the middle of the road, my feet bleeding, my only suit dirty and with missing buttons, I couldn't help but feel that I had been nothing but a fool. I suddenly saw everything with crystal clarity, as though a mist had finally been lifted and I could see my situation for what it was. There was no destiny after all. This disease and everything else that had happened to put me in this situation, they weren't happening to me because some force was leading me somewhere or attempting to teach me a lesson, that was ludicrous. I understood now, finally; there was no destiny, only coincidence and chaos. I was lucky that I hadn't managed to get my hands on a cow after all, or who knows what might have happened. I had followed the chain of coincidence as far as it would take me and this was the end of the line. If destiny did have something in store for me, it would have to do something pretty grandiose to put me back on the same path.

I continued thinking these thoughts as I meandered on down the road, stopping every so often to laugh at myself and the ridiculous ideas that had polluted my mind for the past few months. As soon as I got back into the city, I would make a new start. Whatever the Sycophant and the Leader had planned for me, I would try and ignore by avoiding them. It was as simple as that. Perhaps I could contact some of my friends from the Old World, try and find a job somewhere. Maybe I could try to find a nice girl, speak to the doctors and move out of the city. I was the cow and I was the leash; I could take myself wherever I decided, regardless of the limitations I felt were imposed upon me by external forces. In between the laughing I took in deep and calming breaths. It almost didn't matter to me that I had lost my shoes.

It is hard to be honest with yourself about your shortcomings, perhaps one of the hardest things of them all. Nobody likes to change their ways if they can avoid it and so it is only if life pushes us around from one place to another and actually makes us change that we can develop in any meaningful way. There are those rare ones amongst us who can improve themselves without external help, but they are the exception. The rest of us would remain the same forever if we could help it.

The roads soon evened out and when I looked up behind me I could see the hills that I had just stumbled down from. I had used so much of my energy that I was no longer aware of the sensations of being awake or of being tired, just of being, and so the winds through the trees and the song of the birds seemed so perfect to me, so much in harmony with my optimism, I felt that even in chaos there could be a unity of some kind. A few fields over I could see the canal, the familiar sound of the geese slowly ebbing into my consciousness, the odd figure of a man throwing bread to the ducks. Even if there wasn't any order in nature, in chaos, it is our job as human beings to impose a sense of such upon it. All it takes is a little time, space and causality. I felt that, despite everything, I had found a purpose, not just for myself, but for the whole human race. For those brief seconds, which felt like minutes, everything seemed to make sense to me.

Oh, if only life really were that simple...

It just so happened that the road on which I had been walking was furnished with curves, and so, though I could see over fields and up above hills at the countryside scenes to either side of me, I had been unable to see what the very road I had been walking had held in store for me all along. Perhaps you will be not surprised after coming with me this far to learn that fate is inclined to play games with me, pushing me back and forth like a parent that does and then does not want the love of its child. As I say, I had been completely ready to give it all up, walk away and leave it at that, but as I got around the curve of the of the road and found myself looking ahead, I could see that there was traffic congestion of some kind, and that there were people in and out of their cars, and that something much heavier than I could ever imagine was in the process of taking place.

From where I was standing, I could see that the road branched off into a T-junction, but that there seemed to be a three way blockage on each of the turnings in the road, each a few cars deep. Now that I was closer, I realised that what I had taken as being the sound of geese was actually the petulant sound of car horns being beeped on repeat. A few of the driver doors were open, and as I got even closer to the scene, I noted that there was some kind of commotion unfolding just in front of the cars, where it appeared that several people, mostly men, were shouting at one another at the crux of the junction.

From the distance at which I stood I could hardly see a thing, but, suddenly overwhelmed by the peculiar sensation that my world were about to come crashing in, I picked up my pace and took bounding strides towards the scene. I had reached the last of the cars now, the one at the back of the queue, and as I passed it and stared inside the window at a thoroughly fed up woman in the front seat, I got the feeling that she had been here for some time, as though she had been waiting for something, but didn't know what it might be.

It was at exactly this moment that something seemed to 'click' or change. The sky was brooding; I became aware of the pain and the dizziness and the throbbing in my head, the sting of open wounds from kicks to my ligaments; I realised, I think, that I was not alone in the world, even though I felt it sometimes. Because, wherever I go and whatever will happen, there will always be moments like this - moments that involve meeting with and interacting with the herd. I touched my bleeding broken face, down and dirty within the vertiginous throes of anticipation.

Despite everything, all of the lucid thoughts that had flashed through my mind just moments before, I began to get the feeling that whatever was taking place was taking place especially for me. Try as I might to deny the fact, I just couldn't shake it. I couldn't relinquish the feeling that this was a turning point, not just literally (although it certainly was), but a turning point in my destiny, irreversible, inducible of lasting and seminal change.

There were still a few cars in front of me, but I was close enough to see that a group of men, obviously the drivers of various cars spread about the narrow roads of the junction, were huddled around something in the road, something bigger than them and far more obstinate.

'It's come down from them bloody hills', one of them said.

Followed by a murmur of general concurrence from the others.

And, upon hearing these words and taking on board the full weight of their meaning, I found myself once again vacillating to other side of the spectrum of belief, lost deep within the clutches of another mental tremor, a plenitude of electric sensations and emotion. I thought I saw my life flash before my eyes and maybe it did. I looked at some of the people in the cars as I manoeuvred on by, women and children mainly, and they looked at me as though an abomination, the women at first seeming horrified, and then covering the eyes of the children with their hands and bidding that they look away. My bare feet battered I ploughed onwards. I knew what was awaiting me and I might as well just get it over with.

Gathered in front of the cars was a circle of men. They looked alike despite the differences and stood in the middle of their circle was a cow. Part of me wanted to believe that this was just a coincidence and nothing more than that. Part of me wanted to believe that here in the countryside things like this must happen all the time, and it wasn't destiny or any other force that had brought me and this creature together, but chaos, the simple fact that anything is possible in this world, and so there was always going to be a chance of something like this happening. But try as I might, this was not something that I could accept.

The situation began to unfold in such a way that I was dragged into it, and even now, thinking back, I cannot think of any other way in which things could have turned out, leaving me to believe only that there is one road our lives can take, but a variety of different ways on which to travel it.

One of the men, red faced and flustered from attempting to move the cow out of the path of the traffic, saw me approaching with the rope in my hands and assumed that I had come to help them. Accepting that I must perhaps be somebody of bovine authority because of my suit, ignoring the stains and the cracks in my face and seeing only what they wanted to see, the men allowed me to approach the cow, quite stubbornly standing there, despite the noise of horns being pushed by impatient wives leaning over from passenger seats, and to have me try and put my rope around its neck.

I have never been a man's man, on account of my illness most likely, but as I noosed the neck of the beast with success and began, quite naturally, to march off with it in the direction of town, the men cheered me on and, I'm not ashamed to say, I felt quite the flush of pride. I thanked the men for their understanding in as ceremonious a way as I could muster, hoping to continue with the illusion that I were in some way affiliated with the cow so that they would not object to my leading it away, and I think it must have worked, because not one of them said a word.

I had walked a few metres before any of them had even said anything of any relevance, but then, noticing that I was barefoot, one of the men, the one with the flushed face, which was still red now, said to me something that took a moment for me to grasp an understanding of. He said:

'It's good to see that one of you are wearing shoes', a comment which caused the others to chuckle like good neighbours as they got back into their cars and prepared to drive away.

For a few seconds bewildered, I realised that the only other being that he could have been talking about was The Cow. Perhaps because I had been too busy focusing on getting the rope around her neck, trying to look official in front of the fellas, I had failed to notice. But when I looked down at the animal's hind legs, I nearly fell dead in shock.

The beast was wearing my shoes.

Chapter 33

Leading my new friend by the rope leash, just as nature had intended, I realised, that in the very back of my mind, I had known all along that this would be the outcome. Truth be told, I felt as though I had been performing this action over and over again through all of eternity, that even the new things unfolding before my eyes were not quite as new as they could have been, that they had happened before, and there could no longer be any surprises, just an empyreal appreciation for the purity and chastity of the moment, a heart-swelling, chest-inflating beauty that empowered me with each bare footstep towards the town centre.

The Cow, acquiescing to the demands of my rope leash, plodded languidly besides me, giving into my whims and caprices with an indelible respect. It was as if she understood the workings of our relationship fully, the path that it would take, the things that we would get from and give to each other. We were a perfect couple, united in our differences and brought closer by desire.

Parading down the narrow country roads that would lead us into the city, we could hear the sounds of the car horns hooting, the drivers of the cars we had just left behind battling each other to be the first to turn into the roads, and I truly felt as though these sounds were the vestiges of my having been there. I felt as though I had left a lasting trace, proof that I actually existed, my name etched into a bench with a pocket knife, my phone number scrawled across the toilet door of the public library with a permanent ink marker pen. And so, as I stood there beneath the clouds, feeling as just and noble as a king, The Cow lowing as though inspired by and appreciating the sentiment, I looked down at my feet, no longer bleeding, the sensations of the ground against them no longer as abrasive, and I reflected upon our game plan.

At the rate we were moving, it wouldn't take us long to get into the city. Every town in these parts is built into and cradled between hills of some kind, and so with only an hour or so of walking it would be possible to get back to the outskirts, and then the suburban sprawl, and then, finally, once and for all, to the urban centre itself, with its crumbling walls and its broken bones; its lassitude and empty promise.

The lights of day were still shining, despite my prior assumption that they would be gone by now, that they would have been replaced by darkness, and that the sun would have set for the final time upon my days of vacillation and uncertainty. I knew now, deep in my heart of hearts, that whatever days would follow this one would be defined by the glory of certitude, my conviction, the assurance that I would feel with each of my actions, because I would now have the full weight of the universe behind me, for I was a saviour and a prophet and maybe even the Messiah. Unlike so many others, I could say with confidence that I had a purpose, that I had a reason for being here; I wasn't just another tourist like all of the slow motions bumbling around the city with their eyes to the ground. Nature wanted me dead but destiny had kept me alive and very soon I would find out why. When I looked to the sky, it seemed to me that the sun were still shining for us alone, that somebody or something up there was carrying a torch through the labyrinthine corridors of the night to guide our way. Angels were watching over us. I could feel it.

The Cow looked at me, wondering what I must be thinking as I reflected upon the same about her. If she could have read my mind, or even just formed rational thoughts, she would have learned that I was reflecting on my desire for this moment to last forever, that I felt a great sense of achievement, even though my feet were scarred and I was officially homeless, my vagabond status now signed, sealed and certified. I felt an almost translucent incredulity, doubting what was real before my eyes, namely, that I had set out to do something and actually seen it through to completion for a change. If, in my life, I could put one of the many moments into a bottle and keep it with me forever, this would certainly have been it.

In my short lifetime, I had rarely felt these kinds of emotions, a sense of pride and purpose that lent a ready alacrity to my thoughts, a clarity and vision, and as I did not know whether or not such feelings would be transitory, I wanted to bask in them for as long as my eternity would allow. I felt such an inflated sense of pride when I looked at The Cow, into the deep, knowing simplicity of her eyes, that I become over-awed by almost parental feelings of sentimentality.

I felt that this beast was a part of me, as we all are with everything, and it seemed so plausible to me that she knew what we were doing, and that she had accepted it, that I felt a tear come to my eye, almost as if I had some kind of challenged or deformed offspring that had just won the egg and spoon race at the school sports day, bringing me weakened to my knees.

I considered that perhaps I should give her a name, but decided against it, for there are no names in the animal world, devoid of human concepts. Names are for things that choose to or have been chosen to dwell in the world of man - dogs and cats and other vermin, machines sometimes, boats and planes and motorcars. I wanted to make myself feel like I had entered her world, and I felt proud, because, despite the limitations caused by her position within the food chain, she had made it this far and would now be sure to reach her full potential.

Cars passed us by. We had to pull ourselves up against dry brick walls so that they could squeeze on down the narrow roads. Drivers swerved with saucer eyes, and from out of back windows, I saw passengers turn to face us, visibly perturbed that there was a cow wearing shoes. Their sense of alarm reminded me how removed I had become from the regular world of offices and commutes and television spectacles. This was my life now, and all oh so normal to me in the most eerie of ways. As far as I was concerned, her shoes seemed to be the most congruent of all the things in the world, bringing out the colour of her eyes, accentuating her form and her shape, defining her as a person. I wished I had some rubber gloves to slide over her hooves at the front and complete the ensemble.

And, then, civilization presented itself to us once again. Trees dispersed and found themselves replaced with derelict council tenements and tiny houses, dwarfed by the lorries and the trucks that passed them by on the busy roads which would lead to bigger places down even bigger dual carriageways and then motorways. Kids ran around in groups, the younger ones playing and laughing and gangs of the older ones standing around and skulking under trees, or in corners, or in other desolate places where the smells of angst lingered and refused to be forgotten. But, despite the throngs and the buzz of animal activity, the atavistic aggression permeating the air, nobody paid us any attention. A few of them saw us, no doubt about it, but they looked on with indifference, which I was glad about, because earlier I'd had presentiments that we would be set upon, that The Cow would be hurt, or even worse, that we would be separated from one another, after a lifetime of work and causality setting the ball in motion and finally bringing us together. I had feared that these surly youths in this rancorous part of the city, would be the first crack in the ice berg, sending us drifting in different directions out to sea.

As we walked on, still clouded beneath the promise of these unrealised fears, I tried my best not to look across the road at the children smoking cigarettes. They were perching them between their lips, hands free, just like James Dean in old photographs, and, through their teenage squint eyes, they looked at me askew, saying nothing, just standing there, trying to intimidate us with the silence. I remembered earlier having naïvely thought to myself that if it had come to a moment like this, when we had encountered children in the city, that the smaller ones would come up to us and try to stroke her hair, or touch her sandpaper tongue with their curious, life-seeking hands. But the reality that faced us now, was that there was nothing about the situation that enticed them. Perhaps it was too close to reality, too close to the natural order of things. I couldn't explain it if I tried.

They noticed us without particular attention or awareness, lost deeper within the well of their problems and the travesty of their lives than those in cars who had turned their heads and allowed their mouths to fall aghast. I stroked The Cow on the cheeks, touched her ears. I noticed that there was a fly in her eye and so I blew on it gently, as though a lover whispering sweet poetry into her ear from a million miles away, and then I watched the fly fade and buzz away into the riddled haze of an industrialised skyline, the red bricks of small houses, the smell of burning oil and gasoline from passing tankers, cigarettes and marijuana buds, and the strident sounds of alcohol.

Perhaps it's because I knew at that moment that there would be no turning back, because I knew that I was in safe hands now, I found myself taking the borrowed money that I had stuffed in my pockets. At first, I took one note at a time, and I held it between my fingers up high above my head, and I would feel the wind or the force of passing traffic try to rip it from my hands. I would let it waft and flap beneath the street lights and then, when I felt that it couldn't take it any more, I would let go of it and watch it float off into the road, under the wheels of cars, stuck to windscreen, and escaping off and away into the unknown future.

I my mind I became a composer, a twenty pound note symphony floating up and away, one after the other until crescendo, and I could feel that the smile on my face was a mile wide. When the children saw me they came out of their hiding places and ran towards us. They asked me excited questions, darted in and out of traffic to pick up banknotes still dancing like ghosts in the road. Getting attention was an expensive business, but I needed to feel I was on to something. When I got bored of them I left them where they were. We had a job to do in the city, and so I stroked The Cow again to let her know that we were on our ways.

I didn't want her to feel any discomfort, I didn't want her to be harmed in any way. I wanted to watch her grow and blossom and succeed and become everything that I felt she could be, all of the things I had wanted for myself but had never been able to achieve, because of life dragging me back down or derailing me, or any one of a hundred and one other excuses that could be used to rationalise my position in this cold, cruel world. I put my face up close against hers, felt the moist, warm bursts of breath from her nostrils. On the road, the trucks continued to roar and rumble by; people in cars, on their ways home from work, stared straight ahead subdued, listless and feigning ignorance of the honey we were making right before their eyes. We were nearly in the city now and I would be glad of being there.

We came to a round-about congested with traffic. The lights of indicators flashing and of traffic signs flickering in and between instruction shook me out and away from repose, woke me again to the sensations of electricity and the shock bursts of colour and theatre of mind that made my reality seem all so unreal to me. The multi-colour curtain fell behind my eyes and, because I did not feel as though I had the energy to stand there and deal with such things, I pulled The Cow by her leash and we darted in and out of the traffic in the road. The cars honked more when they saw us approaching, I guess because they feared for their paintwork as we squeezed in between them and then up onto the embankment of the grass knoll roundabout. A synthetic island in a whirlpool of machines and impatient drivers and a million different radio waves and MP3s being played through the cracks in unrolled up windows.

My intention had been to lead her up and over the knoll, down the other side so that we could take the main road into the city, and get things back to where they should be. And it was right here, at this juncture, that The Cow resisted my pull for the first time, an incident that made my heart shudder for fear of the implications. It shuddered so much and with such resounding intensity that I was certain it would bring me a step or two closer to death, to the end of all of this, even though, truth be told, I would've been quite happy to forgive her and spend the rest of my days huddled up snug against her hooves.

The more I tried to move her, the more interested in the council allotted grass of the knoll she became, and, so, as she paused to chew at it and no matter how much or how hard I pulled at her leash, I couldn't get her to follow. As I tugged on the rope, she would pull back against it with all the might of her thick neck, and I was honestly panic stricken because I realised that she was stronger than me and it was only because of her desire to cooperate that she had followed me this far in the first place. I tried pulling a few more times anyway, but all I got to follow me was the same sense of despair and resistance, the feeling that it was she who was taking me places, not the other way round as I had originally led myself to believe.

I gave up and let her chew on and ruminate as cows are apt to do. We stood lost in the middle of the roundabout as the cars tried to slither by and some of the drivers even rolled their windows down and asked me what the hell I was doing, but I just thrust banknotes into their hands and tried to ignore them, and eventually they were forced to follow the line of traffic and drive off anyway.

The grey sky seemed fraught with tension. I began to feel like I were some object on display in a museum or in a gallery full of images that I couldn't quite understand. It seemed to me that this roundabout were the stage and I were a player, and those rotating round in their cars were the audience, and The Cow and I were putting on a show. The simple black and white shades of her skin seemed so real to me against the synthetic metallic shades of the vehicles passing us by, and the reflections of flickering traffic signs and dusk red street lights in their bonnets, that I began to feel like a walking palpitation. I felt the rope slacken, and I knew she was ready to follow me again, and so we moved on across to the other side of the roundabout, and we weaved in and out of the snail trail of traffic, and before we knew it we were back on track to the town centre.

By this time, the roads were beginning to clear of commuter traffic and so the steady stream of cars on the roundabout was replaced with sporadic but steady light trails that passed us by like apparitions. Some of them honked at us as they went by, others threw things out of windows as their radios blared - butts of joints and cigarettes; roaches and food packets. In this manner, we continued until it seemed as though the town centre had risen up from out of the ether. Slowly, we passed by the old clock tower lights of the city hall, beneath those proud old stone walls of so many old buildings and their histories, through construction sites with wailing machinery and cracks in the earth that could swallow you whole.

Up until this point, the journey had been an indiscrete dream, a fog of fast food takeaways and empty shops, a mist of time compression and extension, red horn, and tail lights floating off into oblivion. For a while, we walked down back streets and through multi-storey car parks, blue with the light of the moon. We walked past shops with their shutters closed but windows lighted, cracks in pavements outside of banks. We saw drunks asleep on benches and phone boxes and bus shelters where the glass had been smashed. In time, we stopped to catch our breath and as The Cow chewed upon some street furniture grass, I came back to my bearings and realised that we were around the corner from the Old Theatre. I stood and rubbed my head, let loose The Cow's leash because I knew that she wouldn't run away, and then I emptied my pockets and wallet and looked at the picture of The Fat Man, the jigsaw puzzle piece, and the Chinese cookie slip with its symbols and advice.

I took a deep breath and counted to forty.

When I'd recomposed myself, I looked down at the watch on my wrist. Before, whenever I had looked at it, I would see Mao's one remaining hand eventually move, or twitch, but now it was in a state of total repose, a limp-wristed state of obsolescence, facing forever upwards just after five minutes past whichever hour it happened to have once been. His face had the same stoic expression upon it as always, but he no longer seemed to be in either collusion or competition with me. He was gone and there would be no bringing him back. I rubbed the tip of my index finger over his face as though to close his eyes.

The clock tower of city hall seemed to be mocking me, looming above from up on high, knowing now that I was forever a part of the same time zone as everybody else around here. I pulled my fingers through my hair, forever caught in the same cycle, the same trap as all of the other dirty and ungoogleable people in this town. I took the watch off of my wrist and threw it as far as I could across the city square; I heard it smash and shatter into pieces in the indistinct industrial darkness and then I turned to face The Cow.

As I looked at her standing there, the familiar quality of the yellow street lights made me feel once again at home, or at least in some place familiar, and so that warmth instigated within me a flood of emotions that made my heart overflow with love. There beneath the pallid moon, redundant by human intervention, I once again felt those feelings of paternity, a swelling pride and desire to be all and everything to this living thing stood dumb before me. I took a step closer, feeling now more than ever that time was just a label, and that my history was now and my future was the same, and that all of them would be forgotten with the passing of the rest of it. Time will outlast us all, I thought. But how could I know for sure? Maybe it was within us.

Question marks make all kinds of things seem profound.

I saw in her eyes a desire that I could remember having felt myself during my youth, a desire to be released from myself, a desire to get out there and to really connect with whoever might happen to be around me, to have them truly understand, to have them know more about me than just my name, or my age, or the part of town that I live in. When I looked at her, I saw all of these things and more: the face of every girl I ever loved, the curves of their bodies and the flow of their hair. I felt and heard the words that had been whispered to me in states of intoxicating splendour and moments of union; every promise ever broken; every mistruth made ugly; every lingering utterance fresh off the lips.

In the spaces that filled the gaps between the lifting of her head from the grass to bite at it and raising it to chew, I felt great waves of confusion and stifling panic ricochet up and down my body. I took a step closer towards her and placed my arms around her neck. At first she was unresponsive, shaking her head, stepping backwards, but when she began to understand that I meant no harm, she returned to that quintessential bovine state, embracing me with her passivity and melting into my arms, like her own hotter butter might on the knife I later intended to slit her gut with. As I thrust myself into her, holding her as tightly now as I could muster, I noticed in time a cessation of grass crunching, and I knew that she was feeling everything that I did, because she had not reached down to replenish her supply.

We stood there like this for a while, each of us taking in and familiarising ourselves with the energy of the other. I buried my face deep against the thick skin of her neck and its hair. I stroked her gently as I listened to the regular rhythm of her breathing, then I went in for the kiss and placed it gently behind one of her ears.

I was sure I had never felt this way before.

Chapter 34

People glided by oblivious, their eyes to the ground, hypnotised by the steady rhythm of their own footsteps; the bells of the clock tower chiming once again and calling me home; I pulled myself deep up against her, wishing I were inside.

I continued to focus only on her breathing. In a world of traffic signals and blaring music, underwater TV sounds through muffled walls, and the haze of voices through the windows of restaurants and bars, her breath seemed to be the most calming and regular of all the things in the world. It seemed to slice through all of the disparate ideas that distanced me from my surroundings; calm and unchanging; stable yet alive.

When I finally let go of her and turned around to face the world again, I was surprised to see the spectacle that has amassed before me. Instead of the desolate streets that I had expected to be greeted with, I found myself facing a healthy throng of people, of varying ages and dispositions, a variety of classes and statuses, and of varied calibre of physiognomy, standing quite close to me, but not so close that it was uncomfortable. Many of them were standing with their mouths agape, and all of them in silence. They stood looking at me with great anticipation, a necessitousness in their eyes, not because of monetary issues (although for a good few of them this was certainly the case), but because of a depravity of the 'soul' - if such a thing can be said exist in a time as insensate as all this. They wore a collective veil of sadness, one that filled the metres between us with blackness, and the tired eyes and the pale faces hiding beneath reminded me of a funeral procession, as though life had disappointed them in some way, and now they were in mourning for whichever dreams or ideals had been snatched away like eggs from a nest before their very eyes.

I stood for a few moments, assessing the scene, stroking the Cow to reassure her that everything would be okay and that there was no need to fret at the sight of such an un-baying and apathetic mob. She put her head to the ground and took in another mouthful of grass. I reached out for her leash, holding it gently between my fingers, and then, without a word, I turned my back to The Crowd and began to head across to the town square, towards the Old Theatre, and then to where The Fat Man lived, so that I could put an end to all of this and to all of my problems and forget about the world. She followed me as I had intended, plodding along slowly, and it felt good again, as though I still had at least a modicum of control over whatever might blossom forth.

My plan had been to walk on in this manner and forget about the Crowd almost completely, but when The Cow and I had walked a few metres off yonder, I began to hear a muttering and murmuring amongst those we had deserted, and when I turned to face them, I found that they had moved into a grid formation and that they were shuffling along behind us three files wide. When the Cow and I stopped moving so did they, and when we began to plod along again they followed behind, keeping the same distance as they had done before, as though the set space between us had been determined by official decree, and that anybody who overstepped the mark would be desecrating the holiness of our ritual. I said nothing and continued ahead to the city square with them in tow; on the big screen television there was a Chinese gymnast twisting herself into a hernia; a line of young men had been stood in front of the screen, looking up in wonderment at her leotard, but when they saw me walking by with The Cow, with the Crowd behind us, they assumed that something momentous was taking place, and so they assimilated and joined in with the procession.

We walked past pubs and coffee shops with open windows or verandas and patios and people sitting outside despite the chill of the evening. I pretended not to pay any attention as some of the patrons put out their cigarettes, or took the last swigs of their drinks, and drifted listlessly into the mass of people behind me, becoming absorbed within its silence, and adding weight to the thunder of its footsteps.

To the side of me now was a construction site asleep for the night. Its machinery stood there immovable against the cracks in the earth and the crumbling bricks and soil that had been torn out of the ground. I began to panic, feel anxious; I don't know why. I stood still where I was and then I looked behind me to the crowd, grown in mass and size. As they saw me turn around they stopped dead, the diminuendo of their footsteps a fallen house of cards scattered beneath the streetlights. And, then, they looked at me once again, standing in a variety of shapes and sizes, but each with that same curious and supplicating expression that seemed to beg of me more than it would ever be possible to give.

It was as if they had projected upon my actions a weight and significance that could mean anything and everything to any one of them. As I looked at them, I got the feeling that many of them had been locked inside the same routine for years, drinking in the same bars and coffee shops, smoking the same brands of cigarettes, finding new ways to convince themselves that the conversations they were having were not the same ones that they'd had a million times before. As they looked at me, I began to feel like a whore who had shut up shop for the night, but had for some reason forgot to turn out the red light, and so the punters kept coming back to knock at my door.

Regardless, I had at last found myself at the head of the crowd instead of under the heels of its boots, and, as they looked at me, as though I were delivering the news that they had been waiting for their whole lives, I began to feel that, finally, I might have a shot at being a person of worth. A surge of power, chaste as the devil, ran down my spine to the tips of my toes. I wondered what this message I had to deliver might possibly be, what the majority of people would like to hear; it would probably have something to do with them being a better person than they think or have been told that they are, or being more beautiful than they have been led to believe, but somehow this seemed trite, and so I had to keep on searching.

I wondered if it was reassurance that they were looking for, to be told that things were going to work out, and that they didn't need to change their ways, but I didn't want to lie. Maybe it was the strangeness and incongruity of the image I created, standing there with The Cow, but they looked at me as though I was really on to something, and so I took in a deep breath, clasped my hands around The Cow's leash, and then stood there listening to the hum of the traffic, and the crumbling of bricks, feeling that this was a once in a lifetime opportunity to set the genie out of the bottle and have it soar free above the clouds.

I put my head down next to her ear and began to whisper:

'We have the power to change lives. Whatever we tell them, they will carry to the grave.'

But she just stood there without saying anything, and so I racked my brain for something profound and fundamental to deliver, because I knew that was what was required of me and I didn't want to disappoint. I thought back over books I'd read and movies I'd seen; I tried to recall the lyrics of the most romantic and inspiring of all the songs I'd heard, but none of them seemed universal enough to appeal to the gallimaufry mass of people stood before me. All the love songs I had heard only really spoke to me when I was falling in or out of love, and, from all the wisdom in all the books I had read, I had only taken that knowledge which articulated better than I could myself what I already knew - that which offered reasons or excuses not to change my ways. I thought about using corporate logos and mantras, something generic, but which would seem profound in the light of certain context. Yet, no matter how much I thought, nothing came; my mind was an empty canvas, and my soul a damaged brush that had not been washed properly; it had become brittle and strange, and could paint nothing worth hanging on the wall.

The building site was fenced off with a chain link fence and so, in a moment of nervousness and electric anxiety, I found myself fingering at it as I hopped from one foot to the other, as though it would bring me back to a state of calmness and control. Every few seconds, I would catch a glimpse of somebody in the audience, like the buck-toothed photocopy salesman in his pinstripe suit, or the old man with a plastic bag full of vegetables from Tesco, the scurvy looking woman in the back row with her mouth slightly agape - a gormless expression that reminded me of my high school girlfriend and made my heart melt with both shame and nostalgia.

In each set of eyes I found that same freak-me-out supplication and it broke me because the pity I felt only served exaggerate the pressure to give them what they wanted. I removed my hands from the night-chilled metal of the fence and then did the best I could to exude an image of purposefulness and charisma. I tried to find a space to stand where the street lights would light my face as though I were the final hero that the Earth deserved.

I have never been able to stand in front of groups of people and talk. And, so, as I stood there before the masses, I had to fight back a flood of feelings and memories that came swimming to the surface; stuttering high before once familiar faces; introducing myself at job interviews before other candidates and wondering if they can sense the nervousness that I'm trying to hide. The eyes of the crowd were fixed upon now me more than ever, because they knew I was ready to speak, and, at that moment, a silence engulfed the whole of city; as though noise itself had ceased to exist; as though every fork in every restaurant had been laid gently upon every table; as though every television had been smashed and forgotten about; as though all the cars had stopped running around their roundabouts, and every breath was baited in anticipation of what was about to take place. I embraced the moment, became it, let it guide me.

As intuition took control and replaced the rational state before it, I felt finally that I had something to say to these people, something about life and death, something about all of our situations, the human condition, our short time here, and what it means to be alive

What I had to say would reach into the souls of each and every one of them and give them something to talk about for the rest of their lives. What I had to say would be so poignant, so beautifully articulated and expressed that it would bring a tear to the ears of all who heard it. It would go down in history books and be quoted in plaques on park benches and the coasters on coffee tables in vapid middle-class living rooms. It would be something so grand that I would get my own mention on quote databases on the internets, my own Wikipedia page, and a thousand different academic exegeses in books fresh off the vanity press. People who did not know how to be honest with their own feelings would use, or paraphrase, my words in some of the most touching rites of passage moments of their own lives; I would help potential grooms down on their knees to express that special something deep within them; I would help those on their deathbeds bequeath verbal legacy to those they must leave behind. I had it on the tip of my tongue. It was a summation of our trials and tribulations and the perfect method for dealing with and making sense of all the horrors of reality.

There was a gasp of anticipation amongst the Crowd as I took in a seminal breath and felt the glare of the street lights lend an intensity to my gaze. Men and women stood side by side in harmony and clasped hands with each other despite race or creed, religious belief, or pasty preference. And, then, some crisp packets blew by us in the wind and they seemed to dance before us, as though beckoning forth the words I was about to utter. And then they were still and everything froze and I realised that we were all united in time and space and causality. And so I opened my mouth and the words were on the tip of my tongue and then:

'MOOOOOOOOOOOOO'.

The Cow had beaten me to it.

At first the Crowd seemed confused. The supplicating expressions on several of their faces seemed now fraught with bitterness and disappointment. If it hadn't had been for a gentleman buried somewhere towards the front of the crowd taking cue, then I can only presume that a full scale riot would have broken out, and that my life would have ended even sooner than I had hoped for it to.

Who this heroic gentleman was I cannot say. The truth be told, I only managed to ascertain his gender by the baritone of his voice. Whoever he was, he returned The Cow's 'moo' with one of his own, and then, by a sort of slow motion ripple effect, the rest of the crowd began to join in too, mooing one by one, until eventually all bitterness and disappointment were effaced from face the Earth itself, and then from the faces of those who had been left wanting for my lack of words.

I gave The Cow a loving pat (and prayed that she didn't give me one in return), and then the chorus continued to ring out through the evenfall, and I felt paralysed by its beauty. The Cow's simple phrase seemed to have encapsulated everything that I had hoped to express and more. I felt a tear in my eye and wiped it away just as soon as another one began to form.

It was getting late now and it seemed that, as the minutes went by, The Fat Man's pull on my heartstrings became ever stronger. You must go, I thought to myself, leave now, you fool! But to allow myself a moment of self-satisfaction, I stood where I was with the light on my face, my bovine superhero next to me, and I listened to the lowing of the crowd as though it were the first time I had ever heard music. I bathed in the glory of knowing that my presence had allowed these people to share this moment with one another - that my actions had served to set them free of their chains. I felt as though I had given something back, returned to society the 'favour' of still being here, and of still being alive.

Despite my goals for the future, I felt at that moment an intense light shining upon my soul, the smile of God perhaps, the pure joy and bliss of being a human being and partaking in all the gifts that such brings with it. There was no unison to their dirge, no melody. Some people didn't even sound like they were 'mooing' - one old lady was positively quacking – but, if this was a competition, there were no judges and so it was of little consequence. What mattered was that these strangers had found a way to feel like a community again, that they had found a common bond to allow them to bewail their pain without looking like madmen.

I took what remained of the money from my pockets and then I threw it to the air as we turned away to the darkness and traipsed onwards and into the final dark night of our souls.

Chapter 35

Alive for another night time, we walked deep and darker into the city. Though we hardly looked back, behind us we could hear that the files and ranks of the Crowd had broken, that a kerfuffle had ruffled the feathers of the kids in the yard, and it didn't take much effort to guess that they were fighting over whatever money I'd had left to throw before their feet. Other members from the crowd must have left and gone on to disperse themselves throughout the city, because down alleys and back ways I thought every now and then that I heard a mooing, and I knew that we had been successful, and that soon everything would be completed according to the blueprints of the master plan.

The Cow was beginning to grow weary and, the closer we got to The Fat Man's place, the more conflicted I felt about having to butcher her in His honour. Murdering her went against each and every one of my instincts, all of the desires to protect and provide. And, so, it wasn't long before I found myself trying to rationalise, looking at the world about me and convincing myself that, if I loved her, if I really felt like I claimed to do and wanted the best for her, then I would have to save her from this place because the world was broken and corrupt, the very opposite of all the things I felt she represented. I told myself that something this perfect and alive, something as snow white pure and virtuous, did not belong in the sinkhole of existence, down here with the scum and the bits of leftover food and mouldy teabags in the sink. I led myself to believe that for every drop of rain that would fall and wash the pain away, there would be another punch or another kick to the teeth to bring it back tenfold. And, then, I told myself I was scared. Because I didn't think she could take it.

But I knew in my heart I was wrong.

Despite all of these thoughts, I knew this ineffable desire to please The Fat Man was the only guiding star on my horizon and that without it there would be only darkness and an eternal ennui to my days. If I failed to please him after all this time I would die a failure, and it seemed to me now, perhaps in the lowest state of my miserable lifetime, wandering the streets of a broken city, mumbling to myself incoherently as the cow on my leash tried in vain to make head nor tail of it all, that I really had no choice. I stopped again in my tracks and, for whatever reason, this seemed to please The Cow almost completely. The poor old girl had become fatigued beyond her limits.

Looking back over my shoulder, at the path we had just traversed, I wondered if retracing our steps would take us backwards ever farther, back to a time when I had once been satisfied with myself. She stood still and stoic, staring at me, and I knew right away that she could sense my betrayal. Perhaps to placate myself and attenuate my guilt, I thought about the arms in which I had been cradled at different stages of my being. The girls who had known me better than I had known myself, She, The One I Loved, married now to a banker on the other side of the planet as I stood here atrophied, tracing paper thin, and lost to all eternity.

It was all too late. All too over. All I had ahead of me now was the long and winding road to The Fat Man's house, his leathery thighs when I got there, and perhaps the broken promises of The Leader in a week or two. I stroked her once again to tell her I was sorry, but she just let out the lowest of all the lowing sounds, dejected beneath her stale breath, and I felt my heart implode.

Somehow, the Old Theatre had sidled on up to us and I found myself hovering like a stench in the doorway where I had once begged for change. With one hand on her leash, because I could sense now that she wanted to escape into the oncoming traffic, I used my other hand to examine the wall for cracks, to determine the mysteries of the darkness I had supposed myself to have slipped into however many days before. I kicked about the cigarette butts and the junk on the floor, more abundant than last time, and, then, inexplicably, I noticed a shoe amongst the rubble, a lonesome leather loser sat there scuffed and withered with a frown upon its face. I paused to look at it, transfixed, wondering how a person could lose only one shoe, unless he was drunk or legless, and I wondered how long it would remain there

Amidst the silence of the evening, I felt certain that I could hear just the slightest echoes of the marching music I had heard all those times before. The tune was familiar to me now and I realised that over the past few days it had been seeping in and out of my consciousness like a summer's breeze through an open kitchen door. I had been unaware of it but, now, standing there, I remembered everything, every little detail, and so I shook myself to my senses as though exhorted. I told myself to forget about my pathetic problems. To focus. To keep moving. I looked at The Cow and her mad eyes. She was staring at me beseechingly. Fire breeze mountains of electric paranoia sent me a-quail. A sudden short glimpse of reality.

I began to wonder what crime I might be committing.

Despite the darkness, days of fervent paranoia and excitement had hardwired the way to The Fat Man's house into my brain, and so I knew that we would make it. Under normal conditions, by which I mean a healthy man with a healthy gait and minus the tired cow, it would take a few minutes and nothing more. But not now, The Cow was beginning to fade ever faster, and, truth be told so was I -my knees close to buckling, a beating broken heart working over my ribcage. In my paranoia, I became singularly convinced that my dwindling breath was in collusion with hers, that, somehow, she was working against me, because she knew of my intentions, and so we both stood there panting beneath the street lights, secretly wishing ill upon the other as we pretended to be best friends and soul mates forever. I flashed forwards to the situation status at The Fat Man's apartment block and I figured that, if we made it, we would probably have to take the stairs. I had seen the lift the other day, tenuous and half collapsed, and so I knew that to try forcing her in there would be a risk to both our lives.

And, besides, I didn't want to die without convincing myself that I had won first.

Just a little up ahead of us was the figure of an old WWII memorial that haunted the streets. Bronze soldier, gun to the sky; a chiselled dignity in his eyes like everything's for a reason and that, with just a little faith, whatever looms over the horizon can be faced head on with courage and impunity. On the old stone plinth, somebody had added the phrase *obedience is boring* with a spray paint stencil. I stood world weary and reflective once again. Wondered if it was true.

Off to the side of it all were some stone lions at the top of some stone steps, not many, maybe about twenty five or thirty, if I had bothered to count, and, at the top, there were a couple of benches for members of the public to sit on and think about their lives and the sacrifices that others had made for them to sit there and think about it.

More thinking was exactly what I needed.

I led The Cow towards the steps. A pool of water had collected in the middle of the street and so I dipped my foot in it to watch the moonlight dance about the ripples. I watched her tongue dart out and lap at the water. She seemed happy to be there and, for a brief few moments, it made me feel good again, like we were happy and free, that everything was golden, just like it was when we first met and we had the whole of our future ahead of us, before we'd experienced all the bumps in the road.

I thought about how far we'd come; about how she'd followed me obediently and without question, having utmost faith in my design for our life and the future, my plan for her being. I thought about how, when we met, it seemed as though destiny had brought us together, as though the universe had aligned itself in that especial way, for our meeting alone. I thought nostalgically about the miracle of life. But, then, I started to think about how she had slowly begun to disobey me, because I had neglected to think of her as a living being with her own design and her own needs. It hadn't occurred to me that she was sentient and intelligent, and that the cornucopia of conflicting choices presented to such creatures mean that the lives of no two beings can ever be perfectly aligned without the sacrifice of some dream or another. I thought about her resisting the pull of my leash. The mirror of my illusion shattered and the golden moment went with it. Once again, I hated her bitterly.

When her thirst had been slaked and a half sparkle had returned to her eyes, we tried to take on the steps. We did it lifelessly, as though we were just together for the sake of it, because we each had nobody better to be with. When she looked at me now, I could see in her eyes that the magic and sparkle had been wiped away like childish images of real life drawn with sticks into the sand. I knew that she was thinking about another man, but I also knew that I had made her need me too much to do anything about it. Her self-esteem had been taken away; her will was no longer her own. To my relief, she climbed the steps without much of an issue, though she struggled a few times to find her footing, and, finally, as she struggled against the last few, I watched my shoes fell away from her feet, tumble down in slow motion, and I knew that was the end of it all, she was walking tall and proud - herself again.

I slipped the battered shoes over my cracked and bleeding feet; my bare skin against the old leather cool and alien in the night air; I took a sigh as I thought I might understand her now more than ever.

We made it up to the benches, feeling as proud and invincible as the stone soldier on his plinth. I sat for a few contemplative minutes looking up at him; a list of names of dead comrades, all strong and good and biblical. But, in the end, I didn't read them individually, just took them as a mass of characters serving as an embellishment. We are all one in death, I thought to myself, trying to force a moment, to distract myself from the vapidity of my relationship. And then I looked around at the world about me, at my generation, at our time, unfolding before my eyes, and hurtling off into an unknown future. Everybody gets a shot, I thought to myself, but only one, and never everything. There is just no way of knowing.

Tired and a-weary, my mind a-clouded. The metallic tinges of anaemia hit the back of my throat and there again was that haze behind my eyes, as though I were suddenly gazing through a dirty window in the rain at something that is already abstract and indistinct. I floated up as though in a dream and tried to lead her back down the steps. I had wasted enough time, I thought to myself. Let's get it over with.

'Let's break up.'

But at the top of the steps something strange happened as I tried to drag her on down. She made a noise - nothing strange in itself - but I could tell that she was giving me orders for a change, that she had finally decided to do things her own way, and that I would never be able to stop her.

Absolutely positively indubitably she refused to follow me back down the steps and I was powerless to do anything about it. I pulled again, a little harder. But, still, she refused to yield, as though this had been elevated from a mere lovers' tiff to an altercation to a battle of the wits. I felt anger welling up inside of myself and it thoroughly confused me, because it was completely removed from the passive version of myself that I all of a sudden felt slipping away. I began to shout, call her names that I am ashamed to let you know about; I said things that I will no doubt regret for eternity - that I had never loved her; that picking her up was a mistake; that I'd seen nicer cows with better spots and bigger udders before. And, as I pulled at the leash, in quick, sharp jabs that I knew must hurt her, I saw her wince in pain, and it made me feel good.

She had resisted me several times before, on the round-about, through the town, but neither of those instances felt as this did like she was mocking me. The cloud colours of her betrayal welled up red behind my eyes. Everything I have done for you, I said, all the things I have sacrificed. I could have been somebody without you; I should've gone it alone. Before my eyes stood an achromatic ingrate and nothing more. She had determined that the respect I demanded was unbecoming of me; I felt like a meek, conservative parent sat at home before the soaps and whose child has just strolled through the front door looking like some slut I don't recognise with a new tattoo that said 'Fuck u' upon some obscene body part.

We stood there staring at each other for an eternity before it occurred to me what might be wrong. It came to me in a flash of insight, another eureka moment that made my head spin. And, so, in honour of this new theory, I went back up the stairs and tried to lead her around the bench area, and, without the slightest resistance she followed me - round the benches, past the names on the statues, and wherever else I might like to go - and so it was that it hit me: *she could go up stairs but not down them.*

I took a deep breath and counted to sixty.

Now it would be easy.

Chapter 36

The Fat Man's tenement building trembled before us as though some crumbling edifice that had cracked at the seams, a great cardboard city about to sink into a bog. And, as the clouds billowed languid, and the wind howled, we stood in a bus shelter just outside, staring up at the blue television flicker through cracked windows and at the chips in the walls. I counted the number of floors: 12.

To the world passing by, I imagined myself stood brave and bronzed, emboldened by the nobility of my quest, but, in my heart of hearts, I trembled, thoroughly afraid that my expectations might only serve to one day disappoint me, that reality was the one and only thing that can never be hidden from, or worse, that the situation would unfold just as fate had led me to believe it would, but I would find that I was not the person I believed myself to be, and so would end up living forever disappointed with myself and alone with my limitations.

I began to suspect that The Cow might be nervous too but, besides relying on intuition, there was no way of knowing. Ever since the stone steps, it seemed to me that she had been trying to dissemble the contents of her mind, locking them away from my pathetic, grasping hands as though some great hermetic secret that I had been deemed forever unworthy of being trusted with. And though I desperately wanted to believe that I was still relevant to her life and that I was capable of influencing it, I began to feel overwhelmed with the uncanny sensation that I was along now as a mere spectator and that whatever might happen next would be completely out of my hands.

The apartment block was the width of the whole street, a soaring slice of identical prefab lines and boxes that reached out for the sky in perfect towering perspective. From outside on the pavement, all I was able to ascertain was that each apartment had been allocated its own window and flower box, and that the window and flower box of each apartment was exactly the same size as windows and flower boxes of all the other apartments, and that all the flowers were dead.

For some reason, upon witnessing the sorry state of these flowers, the pitch of my doubt intensified, and so I began to feel utterly despicable and unworthy. I stood agape as I looked up at the building and wondered whether The Fat Man was really in there, what I would say to him if I was able to find him, and whether he was as ready to see me as I was to see him. Sometimes, it feels as though I could waste my whole life going back over conversations that I've had, or the things that I could or should have said if I hadn't been crippled by whatever force it is that holds me back; the force that keeps reserve, presses that weight upon my chest; the force that makes a prison of politeness and a key master of responsibility. And so, thinking these thoughts, I became deathly afraid that I was not yet prepared to meet my maker and that, come tomorrow, I would be lost in ruminations upon all the things I didn't say instead of those I had.

Perhaps it was time to turn back.

I was musing in this manner when the bus pulled up. No passengers on board, no condensation on the windows, just sad little row after row of empty seats, and lonesome piles of tickets gathered up and down the gangway. Its doors opened with just a hiss as the driver sat staring at us from behind his booth. We stared back. He shook his head.

'You can't come on here with that cow', he said.

Then with another hiss, the doors closed, and we watched him melt away into time and space like so many others had before him.

'People will enter and people will leave but most of them will stay away for good.'

And from that moment on we are truly alone.

As we approached the double-doors of the vestibule they seemed to open for us of their own volition, as though automatic. We slid through them gracefully and found ourselves in the stairwell besides a metal grid of post boxes without names on them and an elevator shaft adorned with a handwritten sign that said 'Out off order'. I smiled to myself at the thought of everything having fallen into place: I needed the lift to be out of order so we could take the stairs; I needed it to be impossible for The Cow to come back down here after her work was over; and most of all I needed to believe that there was no other way that things could have unfolded. It was the only way I could avoid any future sense of regret.

When all of this was over, I needed to crawl away to someplace other and tell myself that I couldn't have done things any other way. And I would take whatever I could to feel that way. I began to feel good and wholesome and giddy, as though my meeting with The Big Guy Upstairs had been preordained throughout all of eternity, as though I were Destiny's Rogue Trader, that all of this would be over soon and I would be able move on, dead or edified, but anyway at least changed for the better.

And then it came. Ricocheting from above us, bouncing off the walls and into our ears; a scream, like some succubus was awaiting and had the taste for our blood. And such was the intensity of this scream that I became at once transported to the colours of my mind and I found myself in a cave of the purest white. Suddenly surrounding me was the rhythmical, steady sound of ice cracking and I became at once convinced that the ceiling might cave in and that would be the end of me. I took a hold of myself and prepared for the worst. I waited, held my breath. But, after a while, there was nothing. So I opened my eyes and I was back with The Cow, the pair of us frozen in trepidation, daring the other one to take the first footstep before us.

We stood in silence and deliberation, as though the effect of the shriek had been to freeze us, and so we could only do what felt natural, which was to remain as still as the spaces between things, as lifeless as the tombstones in the graveyard, as forgotten as the dusty books on the library shelves, and as eternal as the pieces of chewing gum that had been taken from the dry mouths of strangers and stuck to lampposts, or beneath desolate desks so that they could harden and solidify.

Remain.

I looked at her and she looked at me. It seemed to me at that moment that we had become reunited in our fear; that the horrible uncertainty of what might be in store for us had allowed us to reconnect with all that was pure or good about our relationship - if only for the shadow of a moment. We remembered, or so it seemed, that we might still have some simulacrum of a future if we just gave each other a chance, that we might get something mutual and fair out of all this if, just for once, we could be honest with our feelings and each other. But even so, it felt that there was something between us, some horrible, distant thing that kept us separated; two animals of different species that had somehow found themselves hung up to bleed in the same abattoir, destined to eventually coalesce within the confines of the same strange tasting sausage, and thus doomed to be spat out upon the same dirty kitchen floor.

After a good minute or two of silence, when we had convinced ourselves that all was well and that it was safe again to proceed, we took that first tentative footstep together and hoped for the best. But I knew right away that she wasn't in this for 'us', that she had accepted that this was her destiny and that there was no turning back, but that whether or not it was me that was by her side, made little or no difference. And, as we began to climb the next series of steps, the scream rang out again, through the building like a train whistle in a tunnel, trapped with nowhere to go, and so bouncing off of every wall and surface as though an illicit orgasm trapped inside an old shoe box. I put my hands over her ears to protect her, took a deep breath, and said my prayers. I wondered what the future might have in store. Then I wondered who the hell my prayers were for.

Most likely, we could have remained there for hours, paralysed by uncertainty, bathing in the sterile lights of the council flat alcove, until yet another grey morning had arisen and another day of our short lives had been wasted on inactivity. Every time we moved forwards the scream would shiver on down the stairs, and it would make us stop and panic, and a few times I even thought about leaving the building all together. But I couldn't. There was no way.

'This is a test.'

From some place within me came the courage to take a hold of the leash and pull her forwards again. She was tired now more than ever but, rather than be left alone, she conformed, and so we made our way up the stairs and into the scream. With each uncertain footstep it became louder, a tunnel walled by every nightmare and shiver down the spine that ever was, held in place by every clamorous disturbance to have ever ruined my sleep or broken my concentration, by every cacophony of horns in traffic, or the shrill voice of every irritating stranger that had made my fists clench and my heart split with vexation. Her hooves slipped a few times on the narrow steps, but eventually we had made it to the first floor of the building, and I saw down the corridor of blinking and fading lights that there was a peppering of debris on the floor from where somebody or something had punched holes in the ceiling. An endless row of the doors to closed apartments most certainly did not welcome us to the vicinity, and except for the scream there wasn't a sound, just the endless hum of some distant, unnamed machinery.

For a few minutes, we stood motionless, our eyes transfixed on the corridor. The dank crimson carpet sucked in and spat out the light from the ceiling in a way that was almost wholesome, and so, despite the flyblown nature of the place, there was an incongruous and almost homely radiance that put us both at ease. My breath began to regulate. My mind began to steady. Besides the absence now of the scream, I noticed the absence of another sound, and it dawned upon me that my heart had stopped jumping, dwindling back to a beat at last after having chased me up the stairs. I took a hold of her ears, in the very way that she used to like me to. I felt the melancholy gratification that comes with honesty of emotion; just like when we first met and all the world seemed shiny and new to me – an upgrade on the superannuated and colourless existence of beforehand. We continued on our journey.

On the second flight of stairs we heard a BANG, as though a book had been dropped flat against a table, or a gun had been fired, but up we went anyway, feeling braver now and invincible, like we could handle any and all. On the third floor, I heard dogs barking, though not just any dogs - these were the infernal hounds of myth. They had spittle between their bloody teeth, a ferocious taste for human flesh, and no sense of doggy playfulness or mirth (but somehow we picked up the courage to pass right on by).

The fourth floor greeted us with the sound of silence and this was most terrifying of all, because in the corridor was the very heart of nothingness itself, and so it seemed as though the darkness and the silence were conniving at something and my soul became filled with an inscrutable, cold-fingered dread. The fifth floor smelled rotten, as though a thousand suppurating corpses were putrefying behind each of the doors that lined the corridor. But we pegged our noses and ploughed onwards as though it was nothing; a pleasure stroll for link-armed lovers by the beach - a picnic hamper and a blanket and a box of condoms. On level six, we both had to stop to catch our breath and, in between the gasps and the sighs, I thought that I heard metallic peals of twisted laughter, not as a product of jocularity or glee, but indeed borne of something much worse. It came from behind some distant door, and I knew instantly that there was some lonely fool sat behind there cackling to himself, because his mind had cracked, and so we tried to run away, but the trail of his madness followed us up to the seventh floor.

The Cow by this time was confused. It seemed that her surroundings had taken a hold of her psyche and, in the dimming lights of the corridors, I noticed that her eyes had dilated and that her tongue was swinging lifelessly from her mouth like a dead man in the trees. Gone were the youthful hope and optimism that had been there in the good old days, the vivacity and joie de vivre. 'he has aged, I thought to myself, she has withered. My adventures and my musings have taken her beyond her time and stolen away what is most precious.

'Life is a long and losing battle against the forces of nature.'

By the time we got to the eighth floor, I was exhausted, and I supposed that it must be because of the fluid in my lungs and the unprecedented amount of energy I had mustered and abused over the past few days. I stood incumbent upon the banister and looked down at the whirl of stairs below. When I pulled myself up and away from my vertigo, I looked out of a window over the city; down below, nothing had changed, but from behind the double-glazing of the glass it became an image without sound, a movie with the volume turned down, and the taillights of cars and the drizzle and the traffic lights seemed beautiful to me. I reflected on how beauty is available to us even in the worst and most shocking episodes of our short lives; our greatest gift and only saviour.

'Lol.'

The ninth floor was the one that I found to be most distasteful of all, for it seemed to me that behind every flimsy door of every grubby apartment there was a television blaring, and the cacophony of a million different channels battling for airspace set my head ablaze. Increasingly complex patterns and colours attempted to annex my mind's eye as my fingers began to tingle and my toes stiffened; I was forced to grasp at the back of her shanks in order to maintain my balance and only come back to equanimity by staring at the blue lights emitted under the cracks between doors, as though some kind of a moth being drawn into a flame.

Those who give us the pain are most often the same that take it away.

The story of my life. Over and over again.

Another television rerun.

Reason versus faith is the most pressing issue of our times, but despite the odds being against me, I used what little strength I had remaining to pull her to the tenth floor, to try and convince her one final time that my dream was worth following, that I knew it could be done if we just continued to believe in one other. Up there, as though the very heart and soul of the building, the very core of the universe itself, we could see that the door to one of the apartments was open. Inside, listening to an old wooden radio on an old wooden shelf, an old wooden couple sat motionless, oblivious to their surroundings. I stood like a wolf in the shadows as I gazed upon their faces. A room devoid of conversation. No words needed. They have said all that they could possibly share in a lifetime. Perhaps they were wondering who might die first.

As they embraced, I wondered what it would have been like if I had been a normal person with a normal life and a wrinkled hand to hold in my dotage - to have a room full of stuff and cherished pictures of family members sitting on the old sideboard. Anachronous antiquated furniture; an electric heater in front of their easy chairs; warm orange fuzz reached out to the corridor, as though inviting me in, and I noticed that the way the light shines down upon them lends a healthy tinge to their old faces. I smiled to myself as we moved on. They would always be young to each other.

Floor eleven's corridor was lined with cardboard boxes. Rats had gnawed holes in the sides. The boxes were piled on top of each other with an assortment of jumble hanging out and over the sides of them and had marker pens scrawl on the sides of them listing the names of rooms: Kitchen. Dining Room. Bedroom. I noticed with aversion that all the doors were closed and that the whole corridor was enveloped with the same monotonous, mechanical hum as before.

At this stage, The Cow was beginning to seem invisible, as though she had faded away - lost inside of herself completely. Finally an adult, seeing the world for the first time, without the order that we assume it has in childhood, without the feelings of safety and security that we tell ourselves will last forever. It's hard to explain; I felt myself becoming angered once again, this time by her apathy. I felt that this was a special moment in her life and that she didn't appreciate all of the work that we'd put into getting this far. Perhaps it was because I was tired, though that is not really an excuse, but I had to kick her on the back of the legs, to stimulate her into action. She grunted at me and I thought that I heard again within her the tones of disdain towards me, but eventually she followed along and so soon we had made it.

We had found the twelfth floor.

Chapter 37

A mirror image of the darkest dreams of my weakest moments; I had seen myself *here*, slinking down this very corridor with my hands in my pockets, brushing up against the poker-faced doors with broken trails of weakened light streaming beneath them as though grasping hands; retching as I dragged myself down the same old gangway as my nerves began to get the better of me and I question the enormity of my own pathetic delusions. Down the plank and into shark infested waters; a prisoner, transported by horse and cart towards the gallows; the inevitable presence of the end; the futility of it all; the transitory dynamism of a life lived without purpose and the permeating permanence of the sorrow in all things. Somehow, I had convinced myself that all the answers were waiting right around the corner, but still I couldn't be sure that I would ask any of the right questions.

All my life, or so it seemed, I had been seeking these 'answers', utterly convinced that they were the panacea, the nostrum, the elixir, and that somewhere out there was the solution to all of my problems. How to live? How to die? How to find strength in times of trouble and walk proud and tall into the night to face new dawns or sail off into newer, clearer horizons? But what about the little things? As I walked down that corridor, pulling her along like a wraith behind me, it occurred to me, that, though these 'bigger' questions were an issue, it was the 'little' things that made my life unsatisfying and unbearable on a daily basis. And, for these things, I had never seriously considered the questions before. There were simply too many of them.

But these were just doubts. I can say now, in retrospect, that in such a situation as I had found myself feelings of inadequacy are perfectly natural. I had found myself on the cusp of a make-or-break rites of passage, and to step into it with nonchalance, without due care or effort, before God Himself, could have ramifications that echoed like the thud of a boot to my behind for the rest of all eternity.

I stood staring at the floor. I let go of the leash. I was so convinced that she would stay with me now, not out of loyalty, but because she was tired and couldn't get down the stairs anyway, that I felt more at ease than I had in hours, perhaps even days or years. Despite my reservations, I still felt that getting this far had at least marked some minor achievement and so, whatever happened, I would be able to later convince myself of at least some shade of glory, regardless of its nuance. I focused on my feet. I looked and I stared and it hit me that I was tired. I tried to focus on the shoes, cracked and warped from misadventure. I began to sway as though hypnotised, fully enervated and confused and misplaced again in time and space.

For a few brief moments, it seemed as though the heaviness of my eyes would get the better of me, and it is quite likely that I would have fallen dumb down against the wall if hadn't been for the divine intervention of the television blaring, wafting down the hallway towards me, beckoning forth a voice residing deep within my breast that said: 'You will do this. You will survive.' I tried to block it out of my consciousness, pretend it wasn't there. I wanted one more moment of experiencing the sensation of being 'Me', even though I held such disdain for everything that I stood for, even though I had been trying to rescind all the rights and privileges that came with being a living, talking, dreaming human being for as long as I seemed able to remember. My head swayed back and forth and, through half open eyes, I watched the convolutions of the world a-swirl. I began to intuit how thoroughly ridiculous this whole thing had been, how once upon a time I had been relatively normal; how I had sat in office cubicles and made small talk with uniform colleagues, waged dramas and competitions and mind games with other nondescript bipedal entities. Now, I had found myself in a thoroughly surreal world of animalism and pseudo-profundity, a world of quests and adventures, of angst with neither purpose nor reward; just another middle class schmuck who had convinced himself he was working class and now had to pay the ferryman.

I felt eerie in the most normal of ways.

Whatever I chose to do now there could only be one outcome. Even if The Fat Man told me everything I hoped that he would be able to about living, even armed with the knowledge to move onwards and upwards, I would be unable to use it, would be only able to sink back down into the inferno to waste away. I had become consumed with something, or rather some *thing* had consumed me, some idea, some notion, some crazy belief that wasn't fully formed or based on anything rational anyway. I was a goner and there was nothing I could do about it.

Sorry Mother, I'm just another no-hoper.

I must drift listlessly towards the end.

I shuffled down the corridor to where The Cow was bathed in the bluest of night lights and gazing with lust back down the stairwell. She had wanted to go down them, no doubt about it. If she couldn't she would die.

But that was her problem.

I took a hold of her leash as though in a dream or a trance and she followed me as though a helium balloon on a string. Electric television emissions like beckoning fingers, still blaring beyond the doors of empty apartments - there was only one other person on this floor, I could feel it, and behind all other doors now awaited only the emptiness of photon-free space; the all-consuming everything of an unknown future.

The Cow drifted along behind me, a walking cheeseburger, head down like she knows we're in an abattoir, but the moral and ethical implications are too explosive for her tiny brain. And, truth be told, I had lost all pity for her. I felt nothing. Even the memories of the feelings I had once felt, the parental feelings of pride, the intimacy of love and understanding, the fleeting triumph when she cried out in public and I felt we could change the world together. Even those memories seemed like they belonged to somebody else, somebody I had now surpassed in almost every possible way. My mind became abuzz with an electric shock determination, a desire to get to the end of this corridor and put myself in the hands of Destiny, to let somebody else take control of the wheel for a change. The TV beckoned with ever increasing intensity, opened its arms up to me, like an old but fake friend who isn't really that happy to see me. I could see the end of the road and so I released a sweet sigh of relief.

We had followed the contours of the corridors completely now, opened doors and closed them, reached the end of the line. Ahead of us now awaited the terminal door, a touch ajar, and from there within came the fetid smell of dank sweat and a cloud of stale air that made us both wheeze as though seeking sympathy instead of change.

I took a deep breath and counted to seventy before we pushed the door open. Kicking the piles of rubbish out of the way to clear a path, we clambered over the masses of fast food packaging and overflowing garbage bags as we stumbled blind into the terror and the stench before our destiny personified.

For brief moment or two, I felt dream-like and ethereal, as though life itself was too good to be true.

I rubbed my eyes as I let go of The Cow's leash.

There He was.

Chapter 38

When he first saw us approaching he seemed scared and confused. Some of the rubbish that had blocked the gangway to the main room had wrapped itself around The Cow's hind leg; a plastic bag from Tesco, a torn bin bag that had once had rubbish in it and had been reduced to mere rags, and then a variety of plastic microwave-meal trays and their toothsome looking remnants, crashed and scuttled beneath us as though a death rattle announcing our arrival.

We swam through infinite dankness, through the moistness in the air, to the kitchen bedroom get-up. Consumed with mistreatment and negligence, the sinks in the kitchen overflowed and were sullied with stains and dirty dish water. The foisting smell of crap underneath the floorboards reached out for us like sepulchral hands, and then, on top of it all, drifting in and between the flies by the bin and the empty Coke and Pepsi cans, there was the intolerable stench of sweat, the intolerable stench of complacency and smugness and disgusting self-satisfaction. I found myself both repulsed and in awe at the same time; over the moon, transcendent and high on rarefied pleasure, whilst all at once utterly ashamed of humanity and everything we stand have become.

Here he was, just as I had seen him in his photograph, leathery and bound to his legless bed. To the side of him was the window overlooking the city, the room's only source of light, that famous yellow of the street lights floating up and about us like stale air. The dusty wooden floor boards cracked and groaned as we worked our way towards him, but The Cow was getting nervous, I could feel it. Perhaps she sensed the primitive fear of the beast in the bed. Or maybe it was that sweaty nervous tension that filled the air between us all, the jarring sensation of two conflicting realities meeting one another for the first and final time.

For a few moments, we simply stared at each other. I counted numbers in my head, waited for The Big Guy Upstairs to acknowledge my existence. And, then, he did, he said:

'Who are you?'

His voice lacked the stentorian import that my imagination had led me to believe would be its salient characteristic. I had seen too many movies or commercials where the disembodied voice of God is epitomised by resonance and depth. Instead, The Fat Man squealed like a garbage truck being emptied into the city dump. I stared upon his horrible, grease covered face; looked at his myriad chins and analysed the sheets, which even in the limited light, I could see were rancid with stains and a decade's worth of abuse and lacerations.

And, then, I looked deep into his eyes and I felt his pain. And he asked me, he asked:

'Is that a cow?'

So I watched as he struggled to lift his neck into a position where he could see properly, his body inert and ineffective, supine, looking as though he were some piece of complex, fade-away furniture long forgotten. I stepped closer to the window so that he might get a closer look at me. He was considerably meeker than I had imagined he might be, didn't carry himself very well. I tried to rationalise and tell myself that he was a superior being, that he was selfless and without ego. But this was just the first of many disappointments, and so I took a moment to pause, tried to gather my thoughts and my feelings, to figure out what I wanted from it all.

By now, The Cow had started working her way in circles about the apartment and The Fat Man and I just watched her, mesmerised by the simple beauty of it all. He reached out as though hypnotised and grabbed a sweaty handful of some foodstuff or another from some bedside receptacle. Whatever it was, he shoved it in his mouth without so much as even craning his neck, and I watched with revulsion as smatterings of this unknown foodstuff burst across the room like shotgun pellets or pieces of shrapnel in a war movie.

Then there came the chewing sound and it was loud. He might as well have been eating my ear. I gave myself to it; let it wrap itself around me, felt at ease. I wondered if I shouldn't curl myself into the foetal position and let it carry me back home, but then it all came to me. As though by divine intervention.

'I have come to you so that you may teach me how to live', I heard myself saying.

Actually, I shouted these words right at him, verbatim, my own tired voice competing with the massive sounds of his mastication - flatus against a wind tunnel – and, though he could see that I was trying to get something across, he didn't quite get the gist of what I was saying. So I said it again. I said it powerfully and with conviction and, though I tried to sound as though I respected him, I knew that this was simply masquerade because he already disgusted me more than anybody else I had ever known in the whole of my lifetime.

'Why me?', he quite sensibly requested.

And then a silence engulfed the room.

I had been staring at the wooden floor and the fine layer of dust and scum that covered it, but at that moment, after he asked me that question, I locked eyes with him, looked right into his thick face, and told him seemingly all that had ever happened to me or had ever passed through my mind:

'Because you are the only one in this town with all the answers and because the Fates have led me to you', I began, 'Because time and time again I have tried to delay this meeting for fear of what I might find, but around every corner that I turn, beneath every rock under which I seek insects to crush with my boots and treat myself to a fleeting glimpse of superiority, I am told to turn to you.

I am told that you have the answers to all and any of the questions that I might have to ask, told that you are omniscient and wise and that you can help me to come to terms with all of this whatever it is – this *life*. I am here because wherever I turn and to whomever I turn to, it always your face, or your name, that is given in response.

So, you see, I am here because I have no choice.'

He let out a flabby, nervous peal of laughter that set his bellies and then the room ashudder. He reached out his putrid hands and took some more of the food from his bowl. I looked at the biscuit packets and empty drinks bottles swept about the floor, remembered The Sycophant in the supermarket, her Kewpie doll kisser, her fading and withered complexion, and that smile like a skull in the embers.

And, as soon as I thought of her, the fear that I had previously felt towards her suddenly melted away. I felt eerie in the most normal of ways. It seemed to slide away from me in increments, as though I were a sad willow, sick of my leaves, and so setting them free to the winds; it was as if, standing here before this monstrosity, I felt I understood her more. And so I asked him:

'Do you know why somebody might wish for you to be dead?'

And then I thought about the beached whales. I thought about putting them out of their misery.

My question had frightened him and so instead of answering like a person he could only make noises. The city dump again, clear in my mind.

'Do you know an exceptionally well dressed and decent man? One who consorts with a Half Wit?'

251

But he said nothing.

'Do you happen to know what day it is?'

I had been looking for answers since the instant I had entered the room but so far he had only disappointed. I decided to open it all up. I decided to get heavy on his ass:

'I am here to kill you', I began, 'But in return, I request that you teach me how to live. Whether you are a real God or not is irrelevant. What matters is that you are here and that I have been led to your door. You see, whatever you say to me now will shine some light upon my situation, because I will construe it in whatever way I see fit. And, even if it doesn't, or I can't, it will not change anything. I already know everything that I need to move on with.

'The Cow that is walking around your living room is a gift that I bring to you. I wish to sacrifice her in your honour so that you might shine your light upon me. I know that you have never received a gift of such magnitude, so I do not expect you to be able to express your gratitude.'

And then I got down on my knees before his bedside; took a hold of his clammy hands and took them in my own. There were tiny pieces of potato crisps stuck to the fingers as though skin deficiencies and then a fine, translucent phlegm or spittle that reflected the traffic signals in the street and made the window lights dance in his fingertips. I closed my eyes and drew them towards me before planting a kiss.

'I do not understand', He said.

I saw the city dump on fire beneath the purple haze of an orange autumn sundown and all the bin men were crying because nobody liked them. And, in that brief moment, He gazed upon me with a warmth that I could tell that even he himself felt to be alien and strange. It was as though he had apprehended the game that I was playing and had decided to join right in.

And some people say dreams never come true.

'Perhaps it will be of help if I tell you my problem', I said, 'It is a very simple one that essentially boils down to this: All of my life I have been in awe of my human capabilities. By this I mean our abilities to think or feel or to appreciate the mysteries of life and the stars and the sunsets and the swell of the oceans. I have stood in awe of our luminosity and have wanted nothing more than to excel, to make the best of myself, to reach mastery of my faculties and discover the core of my being. But, then, I find myself trapped. I find myself stuck in a situation where both bloom or blossom are forbidden, because all that matters is being just like everybody else, and all that anybody else wants to do is waste away at the quickest possible velocity; to forget that they are alive for only one lifetime and that they only have one shot at it and, that, if you really want, it is possible to find a deeper and more fulfilling purpose. Everybody wants to just get it over and done with and, yet, here I am dying before their very eyes, and still the feeling that I might be 'winning' escapes me.

'Can you see what I am saying? Am I shimmering and brilliant, like a crystal in the mist? Expressing my individuality adequately? I know it's a cliché, but perhaps that means there is a modicum of value in it – or at least was once upon a time. This is my life and I want it to be the most perfect and beautiful thing that it can be. I want to feel the intensity of emotion that I felt in my youth, because I know that it is possible still to feel that way, when I am not beaten down by anxiety or regret, or every other fool's problems or their issues and confusion. I do not wish to spend my days walking from points A to B in a daze when I know that there is a whole world out there and that it is an A to Z of life and love and levity. Ever since I came down to this town, I have been bogged with disappointment and regret as though it is infectious – a viral disease placed on the dinner plate before me by every other Tom, Dick and Harry with a frown on his face and no desire to do anything about it.

'Isn't it true? That I have felt the needy hands of the masses and the confused, dragging me down with them, pulling me under, even though I have resisted as much as I can and ever will do. But I do not wish to live like this for the rest of my lifetime, because this is not living! I can no longer stand to have the life sucked out of me and the need to forget about myself be constantly rubbed in my face. Do you understand what I am saying? I am not 'happy' with my situation and there is no scope for change and I cannot accept it and sometimes it feels as though the whole world wants me to just say that 'fine, I will do as you ask. I will devalue myself in my own estimation. I will give up'. Well, I won't. I can't do it!'

I carried my weight across the room with a sense of pride and dignity. I gesticulated wildly and internationally. The tears in my eyes were not for embellishment alone.

But, still, The Fat Man said nothing – just sat there as though frozen by a camera flash - struck with that same sorry look on his face like somebody had snapped his winkle off and thrown it to the dogs. I stood next to his window with my arms crossed behind my back - a college professor putting on airs, pacing around the room with drama by my side in order that the students might believe this is the first time I've delivered such utterances. I looked out over the city at the Old Theatre and all of my other problems. I wondered when all of this might be over. I tried to figure out, honestly, what the hell was the point in it all.

Then I took a sigh and wondered what would happen next.

'But, then, I look at you - sat up here in your eye in the sky looking over the city. Passing judgement on all and sundry, smug and satisfied and unashamed of yourself... Look at this place! Look at the pig swill that surrounds you! Suck up that stench through your nostrils and burn your brain! Acknowledge the state of your body! Oh, but if you could only see that smile on your face (I said this dreamily, with almost delicious relish)... Even though you are scared, even though you are worried about what I may be about to do to you and what the future has in store, I can see that you are smiling. Your face cannot hide the fact; you are happy to the very core and this only serves to infuriate me more, because I will never understand it.'

'Let me be honest with you furthermore. Because honesty is all that can really ever take things forwards. I think you are disgusting, I find you to be vile and wrong and terrible. An insult to reason and decency! An insult to humanity and everything that we might stand for if ideals were made manifest.... To see a living, sentient creature in such a state fills my heart with pain and breaks it into a thousand different pieces... But why should I feel this way? What is so special about me that I may look down upon you and judge, when I am every bit as crippled and broken and wrong as you are?'

I paused again as he sat looking at me; sitting up now in his bed, perhaps convinced that I was here to stay.

'So here it is, that shimmering honest diamond: I am here to kill you. By the time I leave here, you will be dead, and the reasons are for more than the fact that somebody has asked me to do this to you. I need to see you defeated; the ideas that you embody crushed. I cannot leave the world behind me, knowing very well that you still breathe and exist within it, that you are taking up energy and taking up time and not even all that bothered by the fact. It's too exasperating.'

'You are going to teach me how to live so that when I kill myself I know what I have given up. Because for months, or years, or even decades, I have lost that feeling of having ever even been 'alive'; I have been floating along passively like a paper boat in the sewers, asking for everything and expecting nothing in return – telling myself in my heart of hearts that one day I will make it out free to the oceans – all the time hiding from the shit in the hull that's sinking me under, tricking myself into believing that it doesn't exist and that one day all will be okay. I have looked upon the living and wondered what they had that I did not, and now I have seen a glimpse of it and want you to show me the whole. Tell me why I am unsatisfied. Tell me what I am doing wrong. Tell me why other people seem to be able to live here in this place without wanting to improve themselves or get out of here and why is it wrong to feel this way?'

By the time I had finished, I felt weaker than I had in days and could feel the colour draining away from my face and falling in puddles about me on the floor. The sound of my own breath filled the room and then the city and then my very soul. And I became overpowered by the strangest sensation that I was baring my teeth, almost involuntarily, as though I were an animal with some perfect evolutionary defence mechanism that would take me all the way to the top of the food chain; I could feel them pressing together, the top and bottom sets, with so much pressure, that it wouldn't have surprised me had they shattered and crumbled to my feet in little piles of dust as though tiny islands seen from aerial photographs.

But, still, he didn't seem very impressed, and so I was forced to go for one final effusive burst – a peacock opening its feathers to get some action and bring the summer into swing. I said these words in hushed tones, as though I might actually mean them.

'My whole damn life it has felt to me as though I have been trying to figure out some nebulous, indistinct problem. And all I have been able to do is to tell myself over and over, again and again, that if I just continue to go about my life in the way that I have been, working on it in this or that fashion, letting the answers come to me, then I'll eventually 'get it' and that this mysterious spark of knowing will inspire me with the answers I need to go out in flames before I die. But, don't you know that life takes so much strength? Too much sometimes. So many trivialities; so many things wrong with the world; too many wrong turns to take to let it all just fall into place. Tell me how to be like you. Tell me how to forget about it all and just be 'happy'.'

The Fat Man was staring at me, totally at a loss for what to say or do. His eyes were moving about as though he might be trying to find a solution of some kind, a person to call on the telephone and implore to come rescue him, a special something to say to me that would make me leave and not come back. But maybe that was just my paranoia clouding my vision again. Maybe he was actually structuring an argument in his head, a theorem to be bestowed and which would giveth life. But all he did was mutter between chewing and breathing.

It sounded like he might have said:

'I like your suit.'

And I thought about answering him. I thought about telling him that this was a special moment in my life. I wanted to tell him that I had waited months and months to scale these sorry heights and that I wanted to make the best possible impression, if not for him, then for myself. So what if I was overdressed? Didn't old wives once say that it was always better to be too prepared for something than not enough (or did I dream that)? Maybe I should have told Him that this was the suit I was wearing when I met her, The One I Loved; the suit I had worn when I thought I still had a 'future'; before I'd lost hope.

But I didn't want to think about it.

Instead of answering him, I found myself walking over to the kitchen unit and looking through the drawers and then the cupboards and even the dirty dishwater that reached up to my elbow - for a knife or some utensil that I could use to kill The Cow with. I fanned my hand and spread my fingers through the tea green waters and I could feel tiny particles of spongy food and debris swim in between my fingers, but there was nothing sharp. No kitchen knives. No table knives. No nothing.

I returned to the drawers and took out the first silver, utensil-y looking thing that I could find, and it turned out to be a bent teaspoon with a brown blemish in its centre. So I wiped away the tarnish with some spit on my finger –sanctifying the ritual tools – and then I marched on over to The Cow, my teeth still gnashing, and I could tell that she knew my motives, because she screamed a little, and then she looked at me as though beseeching, begging me to let her live

'You can't even get down the stairs!' I heard myself shouting at her, but it seemed as though the voice that uttered these words was not my own and instead that of some disembodied stranger hiding under The Fat Man's bed. 'Nature doesn't want you to escape.'

The Fat Man looked on goggle-eyed from behind his bed sheets as I clutched the teaspoon in my hands and it glimmered in the moonlight.

Chapter 39

With one hand free to grab a hold of the leash, I took it and dragged The Cow over to the bedside. I put the teaspoon down next to The Fat Man, just out of his reach, and then I tied the leash to the headboard so The Cow couldn't disappear or sneak off behind my back. Sensing something was wrong, she tried in vain to pull herself away, but the corpulent fellow in the bed was too heavy for her, and so all that happened was that the legless bed slid a few inches across the floor, nearly knocking me off my feet and setting The Fat Man's belly a-wobble with the motion. The Cow, exhausted now, gave up and a sense of nervous calm returned to the room.

When I had convinced myself that the rope would not snap or give in, I took a hold of the teaspoon again, and I got down on my knees. I wanted to say a prayer of some kind. I wanted to make the ritual holy. I took a hold of The Fat Man's hands again and He gave them to me passively, without question or resistance. I closed my eyes and took a sigh. I listened to the surrounding silence, the occasional car passing by in the streets below, the gentle splash through tiny puddles that must have been forming in the rain, the subtle roar of the wind. I felt such intensity of life running through my veins that I thought I might explode like a pink firework in the moonless sky.

And, when I opened my eyes again, I noticed that The Fat Man was crying. His eyes were swollen and red and his mouth had curled up like some ancient pressed flower that I might have just discovered in the pages of some long overdue library book. And, then, I found myself staring at the dry skin around the corners of his thick lips. The redness of the sore lent the only touch of colour to his jaundiced face, and, I decided at that moment that, if I were artistically inclined, and it were possible to find a large enough quantity of paint to do his portrait, this would be the area I would focus on. It was almost beautiful.

Still down on my knees, I struggled to bring myself to a more comfortable position. I thought about the religious experiences in my lifetime, the ones I could remember from childhood. I needed to find something, some action to perform, or motion to go through - anything that would make this seem justified and proper. I needed rules to follow and a path to walk, so that I could feel as though I had aligned myself with a tradition, as though I had the prayers and wishes of a thousand more virtuous saints before me, so that the universe would finally hear me out, take pity on me, and restore me to my former state of ignorant bliss.

I remembered being a kid and believing in God and Jesus and The Devil, because that was expected of us.

I remember being afraid.

I remember going to church with the Boy Scouts, being forced to dress up in my least favourite and most itchiest black sweater. I remember standing there bored and bewildered as the collection tin went round, an old brass plate with arcane etchings that didn't speak to me. I remember getting down on my knees.

And then I remembered the day that the Christians came to school and they watched us say the Lord's Prayer and then gave us each a tiny red bible but most of the kids burned them afterwards in the football fields.

But I kept mine, because I was scared.

I remember the day that I found out there was no God, that it was just another concept like 'money' or 'love' or 'Santa Claus'. And I thought I'd done something wrong, because after that the world seemed different, not just as though I'd been betrayed, but as though it wasn't quite as beautiful anymore. I mean, the wind would still blow through the oak trees in the park, and the rain would patter against the windows, and the moons would light the evening. But, somehow, something was lacking.

It was more of an accident and less of a gift.

So I suppose I stopped being grateful for things.

I took my hand and wiped at the tears in The Fat Man's eyes. His cheeks were soft and he smiled at me as I made contact.

'Don't be afraid', I said, 'this will all be over one day.'

And then I stood up and took a hold of the teaspoon and slapped The Cow on her bottom with it. And it made a noise just like this:

PLAP.

But each time that the teaspoon made contact with her thick and impervious skin it seemed to bounce right back at me. So I tried harder and harder, but nothing happened; just a terribly embarrassing frenzy that I am too ashamed to talk about, so overcome with irrationality was I. And, so, I ran around the apartment overturning every piece of moveable furniture and trash should it have some kind of bludgeon hiding beneath it, but my search was fruitless and I felt as though I had failed, and so, perhaps because I was angry, inspired to a rage by my own inadequacy, I turned the teaspoon round so that I was holding its head in my hand, and then I ran and slammed it handle first into the graceful back flank of my lady friend.

It made her wail. It made her scream. And, then, I realised that the teaspoon was no longer in my hand at all, and was instead partially buried in her flesh. And I guess it was because of the pain that she started kicking her legs and pulling with her neck as much as she could. And, because she was doing this, I had to run out of her reach to the other side of the room. And I watched her pulling and pulling with her neck and the bed was shaking violently, even with The Fat Man in it, and he was really screaming with fear – like he genuinely sensed and cared about the end!

And, for some reason, it made me laugh because it all seemed so ridiculous and his voice was so high-pitched and he was waving his arms about and his eyes were bulging because he was worried that The Cow's hooves might kick him in the face.

But then a strange thing happened. The Fat Man started talking. I mean, it came to be that his screams seemed to have the natural rhythm and cadence of actual human language to them, but it wasn't a language that I understood. It was like in movies or documentaries that you find on the internet when people start speaking in tongues because they are possessed by The Almighty and if only somebody else could speak tongues they would be able to translate.

And, even more bizarre, was that the sound of this strange language seemed to pacify The Cow. She had been fevered with pain and anguish, but slowly and as if by magic, I watched as the song of The Fat Man brought her back to a state of calm. Little by little she became less frenetic, little by little she seemed to come back to earth, until at last all that filled the room was the song of The Fat Man – luminous, angelic and inspired.

I stood by the calm of the kitchen window and opened it a little. Water was dripping from the faucet as the rain fell down outside.

Suddenly, The Fat Man's song turned to a cough and he spat out a peanut that had been stuck in his throat.

And it hit the floor with a noise just like this:

PLIP.

Tiny particles of dust and hair stuck themselves to it, as The Fat Man took the deepest breaths I've ever heard, as though he were trying to swallow the moon and the oceans. But, in between these breaths, he gasped in my general direction. And this is what he said:

'I will tell you everything need to know. Everything about life and death. Everything I have learned sitting here and eating and thinking about life, as I look out of this window. But, I warn you, after you hear these words you will no longer be the same.'

He was exhausted, his sweaty face saturated with stink and ill will. I was too afraid to say anything in case he changed his mind, and so I just nodded obediently, like a dog being offered a biscuit, and prayed that he would continue.

'You say you want to be happy? Well you must stop wanting. You must accept whatever fate that has been assigned to you and you must wallow in it, like a pig in its own dirt, or a rat in the alley behind a Chinese restaurant. If you are disappointed, it is only because you have ever had expectations of yourself or the world and what it can offer you. If you are sad, it is because you erroneously imagined that you are entitled to something else. If you are anxious, it is because you know that you are in the wrong place at the wrong time. If you are angry, perhaps you have seen the light but not yet realised that none of us care about your feelings. Perhaps you have bought into the hyperbole with which they sell you your future or tell you fancy tales about what you are entitled to. But you must learn that there is only one cardinal rule to remain sane and equanimous in the modern world and that is this: PREPARE TO BE DISAPPOINTED. Do not expect to be offered the world when you will never even go to the moon. Expect nothing and give nothing in return and you will always be happy.'

He took another stab of breath into his lungs and I seemed to feel my own air supplies dwindling.

'Haven't you heard that 'comparisons are odious'? You talk too much of other people and their problems. If you want to be like me, then you should forget about other people completely. You should use them for your own gain if that is what you need to do, but you should not feel that they are 'better' than you, or that they have more for any reasons that you can control. Do you think I have not been labelled and abused by the rest of the herd? Do you think it impossible that I have never reflected upon myself and the fact that I haven't left this bed for the past decade and half, what other people must think of me, and what it means for me to be this way?

Well, I will tell you this. Whoever you are, all of the things that you said about me being vile or repulsive and stinking – none of these things are new to me. I am perfectly and complacently aware of the facts, but it is exactly this complacently that allows me to accept myself for what I am and to see myself as beautiful and still human – for that is what I am! For a long while, I thought that perhaps I might change myself but then I convinced myself to feel pride– to accept the nature of my being, because what is natural is divine. I do not need to change just because other people want me to; I have made this work for me. I get money from the council and the government; I have a girl who brings me food and another and her mother for entertainment. Everything that I could possibly want from life is provided to me, and this is all because I have learned to accept myself, and to live happily and apart.'

I looked at Him. Then I looked at The Cow. There was still that look of anguish upon her face and it brought me back to those feelings from before, that I was proud of her, that she could very well be the only one to understand all this - that if I was honest with myself, she was all I had in the world. I began to feel happy that I hadn't sacrificed her in honour of this abomination in the bed sheets; all in honour of my pipe dreams.

Somehow, despite the greatest of expectations, The Fat Man's words had not swung me to his way of thinking. Instead of the banquet I had expected, the special treatment I felt I deserved, I had been given nothing more than the dried up core of an old apple. And, to make it worse, he made it sound so simple: accept yourself, become one of the herd; on a purely surface level his commandments seemed sound, but when I looked at him I felt our world's collide

'But what about what you could have been?', I asked, 'What about potential?'

'There is no place for potential in our lives when we are all the same – prune the buds of the flower you think will bloom! Throw them in the fire! When we are homogenous, living in the same sized houses and sharing the same dreams as our neighbours; spending our weekends polishing our cars, or taking the kids to the zoo, there is no scope for diversity. It is a myth! We are all animals, torn from the womb to fend for ourselves, and then start the cycle over again! You are still young and naïve! Asleep! You think that life is some great ride that offers infinite possibilities, but it is not! It is just a system of placing yourself in boxes: a large box at first, this cannot be denied, but then a smaller one, and a smaller one, and so on ad infinitum, until your choices have been narrowed down, if not by society then by necessity, and all that you can do is wait to die, or deliberate about whether or not you should kill yourself, and what TV shows you can watch to fill in the time. Don't you get it? There is no mystery to life! There is no control. There is just us, somehow in charge of it all, bald monkeys that have learned to count on our fingers and charge each other for services rendered! Everybody has these thoughts that are seemingly filling your mind: that they are special, that they are unique, that you are going to change the world. But nobody can plan to do that. You... You may not realise it yet, but you are just like me. You are just the very same. Everybody is with time.'

He took another deep, disturbed series of breaths as I paced about the room. I felt as though a piano had fallen on top of me from out the top of an apartment block and it seemed that all I could hear was the ghost of some dead minor chord that floated about me like the sweat in the room. When I looked about me, at the room, at the stranger in the bed, the cow, I felt as though I were in a dream, as though time and space had once again become nothing, and that everything was dancing out of tune to the music. Life's great symphony. And ,then, the colours came back to me, great waves of sensation in my mind of a million different shades, another underwater oil slick, a crack in the coral reef, chemicals in the river that turned the water lime green and made my head explode.

The man was still talking but none of it made any sense to me. Nothing ever would. I had followed my dreams for months on end, convinced myself that the answers given to me at this moment would be the only ones I would ever need. But, then, when I hit upon the reality of the situation, it seemed to me that all The Fat Man had opened the doors to were the truths that I had been avoiding all along: that I was just another ungoogleable, just another average Joe Schmoe with limited potential and no future; that my life was just like everybody else's; that I didn't belong to myself, but to the human race; that there was no future for anybody, just what life had put on your plate, and you could either pretend to be bigger than it, or get down on your knees before it all and start sucking.

And though I wanted with all my heart to lend no credence to his words, I had an overwhelming sensation in my very being that what he was saying was the truth, and that if I wanted to feel at peace again, I had to give in, roll over and accept the kicking; bide my time until I died.

I looked up at the ceiling from the floor. My arms and my legs quivered with an electric paroxysm, my eyes opened and closed and rolled backwards to my brain, as the shock ramifications spirited me faraway to unknown places away from familiar faces. I think I must have passed out, because I remember the last thing I saw being The Cow's hooves, and, then, I looked up at the teaspoon hanging out of her side and I started to cry. And the more I cried, the more my eyes seemed to glue themselves together. And, in the background, as though another TV through the wall of another flimsy prefab apartment building, I heard the mumble The Fat Man. He was going on strong, regular at least, and so I imagined again the garbage truck being emptied. And, this time, I saw it coming towards me, backing up with that beep that they make, and then the back opened up and I could see all the dirt and the shit and the icky sticky debris falling down right on top of me. And, shaking down there on the floor, I began to feel that I was drowning in the stuff. Then the colours went away.

Forever.

Chapter 40

I must have been out for a while because when I came to I had stopped shaking and the lights of morning had hit the room.

I pulled myself up into sitting position and took a good look around me. The room was just as I had left it, only, now, The Cow was asleep on her feet and was swaying slightly, as though she might topple over. I could see the spoon wound more clearly in the light; it swayed along with her and filled me with shame.

Somehow, The Fat Man was still rambling, as though of infinite resource, but I doubt he had noticed my absence. His words were like a boulder rolling down a hill, gaining velocity and stopping for nobody or nothing in its path. They were a damn that had cracked and broken open; a river overflowed. They were the stream of shoppers bursting through the department store doors on the first morning of a sale and knocking over the till workers.

He was saying something like:

'Why live in imitation of superior beings when you can experience the unparalleled glory of golden inferiority?'

And then I zoned out again and tried to get my head together.

I reached into the back pocket of my suit pants and pulled out the jigsaw puzzle piece and the picture of The Fat Man wrapped in red silk. I wondered what I should do. I was still convinced that I would be leaving it all soon, but perhaps I should pander to the wishes of The Leader, so as to be fondly remembered. Maybe I could leave myself a legacy; a way out of the darkness and into a false kind of light – one that would allow me to at least pretend to be just like everybody else: a wife and a house (maybe); a baby and a dog in the yard. Maybe I really would perform the task that she had asked of me and then skip out into the street afterwards and into her arms.

'When one dream dies we replace it with another.'

I stood up as gracefully as the ungodly hour would allow and was treated to a rush of blood to the head. The blackout made the room disappear, but I soon came back to my senses and stood towering once again over The Fat Man, who looked even more sickly and fetid now that the bleached lights of dawn irradiated his legless bed. I looked about the room in this new light; took in the lurid, tattered wallpaper that had been there since building plans immemorial; I saw the junk overflowing from its bin in all its synthetic glory; I saw the dust on the windows as a metaphor.

For some forsaken reason, he was still yabbering on, his mouth flapping about in slow motion and my ears either struggling or refusing to take the words on board. I just zoned in on the sound, the garbage truck one and forever.

Compounded all the more by bleary-eyed liabilities, I found myself roughshod right over, the room a whirl and his endless mussitation completely entwined with a sickening degree of unwarranted self-importance and misplaced confidence.

I found myself shouting, loudly. Despite the early hour. The Cow sputtered and came back round to attention.

'I have listened to what you have to say', I lied, 'But the time has come for me to *terminate* your contract.'

I felt as though I were on the top of a dusty mountain shouting into the bottom of an infinite abyss.

He paused for a moment and looked at me but I knew instantly that this was purely for effect; he was really trying to focus on clinging onto his trail of thought – as though it were a kite that he didn't want to lose being torn away from his hands and into an electrical storm. He wanted to keep going, continue with his proselytizing, and his empty talk.

He was enjoying himself.

'Contract?', he smiled.

And then he picked up again. Sententiously. Right from where he had left off.

'So you see, it is pointless to believe that self-improvement is even remotely possible, because all of these things rely on concepts of past, present, and future, but all we ever have is the moment. And so how can you be sure that anything else will ever come to you? All we have is the NOW.'

I stood for a few moments gobsmacked, trying to figure out how I could regain control of the situation, and take the upper hand. I began to get the feeling that he didn't think I was serious, despite everything I had taken the pains of going through; I began to feel that he thought I would eventually just get bored and disappear. But he was wrong.

I walked over to The Cow who was still sleeping and pushed at the teaspoon in her side. She awoke with a roar and it pained me, but she didn't know that I was just doing what was incumbent upon me – my duty.

It seemed to me that something had changed. I know I've said that before. But I really mean it. It was as though all this time I had been pretending, perhaps because there was nothing of any real substance inside of me, and so like the actor I had professed to being earlier, I had simply chosen the most convenient part to play for myself and acted it out soullessly and without due consideration. Now, I had reached the elixir; I had found the panacea. If I wanted answers to take back to the elders in the village then I had enough to last me the rest of my lifetime. Except, somehow, it occurred to me, I had lost contact with the village folk, because I had convinced myself I only needed myself and thus become isolated. Nevertheless, I would attempt to make something out of nothing, purely because I had been places, and perhaps they would believe me for having taken the footsteps. But it seemed to me as though the night that had fallen had been the curtain going down on the end of the performance, and that now the new day had arisen, I was free to choose my next role and step into a new character, to become anything that I might desire.

'You come out of the forest with gold and it turns to ashes.'

A blank canvas; I felt empty. The Fat Man had been perched on my horizon for so long that I had never expected him to disappoint. I thought that I would meet him and be filled with radiant benevolence and beatific joy; I had expected him to tell me that I was being tested and that one day I would be rewarded for passing because everything would work out fine; I wanted him to tell me that I was gifted and just; I wanted to hear that all of the fine things I had ever thought about myself and the fact that there would still be a future were true.

Instead, all he had to say was that there was no future. That there was only his kingdom, one in which the flowers of potential never reached the trees, because they had all been cut down as mere sprouts. And all that ever would reign on the earth was more in his vein, more of his kin, until eventually the whole of the earth was consumed, and all that remained were cracked spectacles, and other stolen remnants of the civilised world buried amongst the rubble of fallen buildings.

A depression fell about me, deeper, darker more potent than any previous. It swam on over and about my head, turned my shoes to leaden boots as I tried to moonwalk across the room. My breath turned heavy and my heart ached. I heard it beating in my chest but not irregularly. It beat steadily as though it were counting down towards something. And then I realised that it would all be over soon. I would be free.

As though in zero gravity, I continued towards The Cow. Everything seemed to be moving so slowly, as though the murmuring of The Fat Man had sent me into a stupor, and still he was going, as though he would burst if he ever stopped. And, then, I remembered the indistinct noise that we had heard coming up the stairs, and suddenly there it was again – filling the whole building. And it occurred to me that it had been The Fat Man the whole while, stuck in his bed on overdrive; barely alive, but moving his mouth with such maundering swiftness that it seemed he were the engine of the whole machine, the whole of this town, that somehow he had been turning the wheels this whole time, because, as we have seen, all roads lead to his house, and everybody has been touched by him.

I thought about each person that I had met since arriving; each faceless nest of eyes out in the street or on the buses and the trains. I realised that all had heard his words and taken heed. I don't know how. I know it sounds crazy. But they had heard him, I was sure of it. And, all the while, they had been saying to me:

'Join us.'

And trying to escape them had led me to his door.

Biting contrition and pitiful rue shook me to the core. I could barely move. Now that the colours had deserted me and there was only darkness in my heart, everything was touched with the crystalline pellucidity of blacks and whites only. I looked about me, conscious for the first time now, seeing that I was the mad one, I was the fool. I was the one who had believed in something that would destroy me. And the rest of them had known it all along.

I put my hands to The Cow's cheeks. I begged her to forgive me. I felt the tears sliding down my face and into my mouth again, but they no longer tasted of anything, and were not warm, but as cold as old stones. I took a hold of the spoon in her side. I pulled at it quickly so as to minimise the pain and it came out and she shrieked and filled the room as though in angelic animal chorus to The Fat Man's people rhythm.

'I love you' I heard myself saying to her, 'I would walk to the ends of the earth for you; I would move mountains; eat the moon. I know I have hurt you, but I thought it was what we needed. Believe me now when I say this: I would never sacrifice you, but would sacrifice everything for you.'

Pulling myself closer to her, I grasped at the side of her neck as though I were home after a long time lost to sea. Feeling those warm columns of breath shoot out of her nostrils, I realised that I might have found salvation after all.

But then I heard something that set my soul ablaze. And, when I looked over to the bed, I saw that The Fat Man was no longer mumbling to himself but was laughing at us - right in our faces with disdain and scorn and mocking derision.

Despite the momentary sense of melancholy whimsy I had felt when holding The Cow, the image of him there looking at us like that was branded to my brain and filled me with rage. I became an ocean of emotion boiling at the heart of the sun. I became the demon within. I looked at his twisted, double-chin mouth and at his broken sugar warped teeth. His beady little eyes seemed completely soulless to me and I used this to justify what I intended to do next; because what doesn't have a soul cannot be alive and so does not have a right to be amongst we the living, and if this is the case then we hold dominion over the rest of the earth and everything in it.

The Cow walked slowly because of the wound in her shanks, but she did not resist my lead when I untied her from the bedpost and led her to the other end of the bed. The Fat Man kept laughing at us, but I didn't say a word. I stayed calm and aloof, as though I were back in that hellhole stood behind the till, as though I were getting ready to deal with any other schmuck in this two bit town. He kept laughing, like a drain in every single possible sense of the word. But, as I began to tie the end of the leash around his calloused left foot, he began to settle down. In many ways he looked panicked, almost like a human being. But he couldn't reach down to touch his toes and fight me off, and his limp, dead bones, did not have the power to kick me away from him.

I gnashed my teeth again as I tied the knot and then the Holy Trinity of The Fat Man, The Cow, and Myself set out to the top of the stairs.

Chapter 41

An epic battle ensued.

At first, when I tried to lead The Cow, she struggled to budge, but then I said something, like I believed in her, or I knew that she could do it, and, inch by inch, she managed to pull The Fat Man out towards the door.

I led the way and she followed; once she understood the game plan, she seemed to smile almost, and I was able to let go of her leash without having to guide her.

I walked past the plastic assembly in the hall way; beyond the Tesco carrier bag, which earlier on had wrapped itself around The Cow's legs, and The Fat Man screamed and waved his arms about as, little by little, he was dragged out of his apartment for the first time in years.

The Cow was more tired than ever before, but I could see in her eyes that she was determined to win, and that she would not let me down. She was doing this for herself now; failure was not an option. The Fat Man's mattress had slid along with him as far as the door frame and, as The Cow continued down the vestibule and into the hallway, the mattress became wedged and The Fat Man, somehow, was pulled through the door without it, filling the frame from jamb to jamb, screaming in agony and confusion, as he abused our efforts.

The mattress finally unstuck itself from his back, a snail trail build-up of sweaty negligence, as it unpeeled itself and smashed down in the corridor behind him. It fell to the floor with great resonance, sending dust and random pieces of garbage floating about in the air like the notes to a symphony that had fallen off the page. Then, everything settled into place again, and there was silence, and The Holy Trinity was out in the hall.

I led The Cow through corridors and doorways; I showed her where to go. In some of the narrower parts, she would have to fight not just against her tiredness, but also against the extra friction of The Fat Man's girth caught up against the walls. It was a miracle of science and technology that the leash did not snap. I felt my eyes light up with wonder, the morning lights brighter through the windows. All I wanted now was to get out and into the daylight; I wanted to feel the sun on my face and the wind in my hair.

Humping and greasing and huffing and puffing, The Cow used all of her might to pull The Fat Man. Sometimes she would have to stop and refocus her energies, but she never gave up. I could see deep down in her eyes that she wanted to, but something kept her moving.

His screams turned to sobs. The sheets that had been wrapped around him like a nappy had somehow come untangled and all that remained was his bellies and his wailing and the humanity. Oh, the humanity!

But then we reached the top of the stairs. In our excitement we had forgotten that we were not invincible, that we were mortal. I raced over to the lift and tapped at the buttons, until I thought that my fingers might wear away – but nothing happened, just the unnerving silence that comes after having one's expectations of disappointment meet you like a bottom tickle from an anonymous pervert in an overcrowded train carriage. I ran back to The Cow, forlorn at the top of the stairs, looking down as though into the heart of hell itself; The Fat Man crying out curses upon us behind her.

I tried to think of a plan.

'You can do it!', I shouted out, 'I believe in you.'

And, as I went down ahead to try and coax her, I realised that I had never told her anything like this before; not with conviction. I had always just assumed that she would get the message, but this had only led to her doubting herself.

'I believe in you!' I said again. But this time I held out my arms.

The Fat Man slid along the floor behind her as she moved closer to the top of the staircase. One of her front legs hung suspended in the air; hovering over the top of the steps, a startling, levitating, wonder thing.

I stood beneath focusing on it. It seemed to dangle there for the whole of eternity. I'm sure I saw my life flash before my eyes. But then, finally, the clock started ticking again, my heart still counting down with it, and, as though by magic, her foot came floating down and landed with perfect precision on the next step down the way.

She looked at me as though I imagine a child might that has just learned to ride its bike without stabilisers. I felt like a mother duck who has just taught its ducklings to swim. My heart burst with inordinate love and satisfaction.

But then it happened. She took the next step forwards, lugging and heaving with all her might The Fat Man behind her. And, at first, it seemed as though everything would work out fine, as though it was destined to be. But as she put her second foot down there with the first one, I noticed her legs began to shake, like rotten wood weathered by years of storm. I took a step up the stairs towards her but, before I got there, she went crashing to her knees, and then she rolled down the steps with The Fat Man tumbling after her, and the two of them lay motionless at my feet. If I hadn't jumped out of their way I would have been crushed beneath them for sure.

I started to panic. I took deep breaths to try and calm myself but it didn't work. I found myself waving my hands about like hummingbirds, but this too proved to be inefficacious and so, eventually, I found myself down on my knees, stroking her, touching her, letting her know that I was still here and that I cared and that oh life could be so beautiful if she just knew what was in my heart. Her eyes were only half open; her tongue limp as though it had fallen out of her mouth; and, as though to remind me of the horror of my crimes, the flank that the spoon had once been in faced me like a mirror, and I saw the monster I had become, in a world of blood and pain and anguish.

'Don't go!' I said.

A solitary tear slid down my face and into her half open eyes; I put a hand on each of her cheeks and held her with as much tenderness as I could muster. I thought about the good times that we had shared, even though they were only a solitary blink in the ripped open, eyes torn rest of my life. I wanted to believe that things could be that way again; that in this dead mine of hell and turpitude there somewhere awaited a diamond, and that all I had to do was keep digging.

The Fat Man lay as a heap behind her, breathing heavily, but not saying a word. He could have been deflating.

'Come on, girl' I said, 'Don't you know you have work to do.'

And she looked at me again with that look in her eye – the one that said she understood, the one that said we would've made it in another time and place.

And then she smiled.

I know it is a strange thing to say that a cow smiled, but I am not anthropomorphising. She smiled with the warmth and congeniality of any human person, baring her perfect white teeth, backing it up with an afterglow in her eyes, like the sun going down for the final time; I think I felt the mirror shatter.

'Don't go!' I begged her again. 'We have come so far!'

And then I found that I was standing. I was pacing back and forth in the remaining space between the next set of stairs and the heap of flesh and beef on the floor besides me.

'Look how easy it is!' I said, 'All you have to do is get up. All you have to do is take one more step and then follow it with another and you will come into the full radiance of your being! Don't give up! Don't ever not believe in yourself, don't ever feel that it's too much for you, because that just means that you don't see yourself as I see you – that you don't see the power radiating from every bone in your body and every wrinkle of your skin! I know I didn't tell you before that I believed in you...But that was only because I didn't believe in myself! There are so many things I needed to tell you! But you overshadow; you are all powerful. This whole while, I have followed you and not you have followed me; I have been lying to myself. But I am not the person I thought that I was and you are ten times anything I can ever be!'

I crashed down against the sticky balustrade in exasperation. I stood with my head bent in my hands and my lungs about to fall out of my chest. Everything was broken and wrong; nothing had gone to plan; the sound of my breath filled the dim air. I thought it was all over.

But, then, she started to twitch. And then her eyes opened more fully. Somehow she started to crawl out from beneath The Fat Man, faltering at first but making it in increments, as though she were being poured forth from the womb, covered in placenta, wide-eyed and torn away from all comforts of complacency. It looked to me at first like she might fall again; trembling, brittle, broken. But she didn't. She stood up radiant and strong and determined; inspiring me with awe and making the sun shiner brighter through the windows, pouring down the steps like spring waters, a place to wash our sins away. She stood there as though made of bronze, beneath the dusty communal windows, as though we were in the illustrated pages of a bible story. A new day had dawned and with it had arisen new hope; she took a step forward, unafraid of anything.

The Fat Man slid along behind her, carried with a graceful ease this time, as though sliding on ice or floating on air, moving with such supreme swiftness and poetry of motion that I remember thinking to myself that divine intervention was once again on my side. This could only be a miracle.

I pressed myself up against the wall so they could plough on right by. She made the stairs look easy, as though she had done it a thousand times before. I couldn't account for it if I tried.

And, then, as I watched her go down, the excitement got to me so much that I forgot myself – lost all fear and trepidation. Each flight of stairs that we tumbled down, as though swept away by the benevolence of reality's rapids, with my head a-spinning in the eddies, I found myself running into the corridors and laughing. I slapped the doors of strange apartments with the palms of my hands; I slapped them and ran, and then slapped on the others. And, then, another miracle:

Slowly, the doors began to open, the people behind them nervous at first; sounds of locks on chains and bolts being unbolted. But, still, I kept laughing and slapping, and when their doubting eyes caught glimpse of the smile upon my face, when they saw me skip down the corridors, and on to neighbouring doors, they tumbled out as though from under some stone unturned.

And when I shouted:

'He is coming! Hallelujah!'

They followed on behind with grins from ear to ear, feeling good and whole again, because it was a new dawn and we could each sense that life was what we had originally been promised. Gone it seemed was the dread and the unknown horror that had terrified us on the way up the stairs. Gone was the sound of the televisions blaring and the dogs barking. Gone were the screams. All of this had been replaced by the murmur of voices and exalted chatter; the electric dance in the air as though something good and true were about to happen. And, all the while, The Cow ploughed on ahead of us, her eyes dead set on success, owning the stairs, her heart finally full of a joy and a wonder that filled the hearts of those behind her with the very same.

And, before we knew, it we had made it back outside; I squinted in the lights, high inside myself from lack of sleep and too much adrenaline. The Cow came to a halt outside the automatic doors of the building, down in front of the final set of steps just by the pavement; The Fat Man at rest behind her like so many sacks of potatoes, breathing more heavily now than ever, semi-awake and semi-asleep. I could see that his eyes were unaccustomed to the light, like a mole out of his hole and praying for darkness. The automatic doors burst open for the final time in his lifetime and from out of them poured the residents of the building, hundreds of them perhaps, smiling and laughing and joking, coming to a standstill around the heap, as though it were a bonfire around which we would all learn to find ourselves and share our stories.

I stood over The Fat Man and watched his chest puff up and down. The Cow stood next to him taking in the wonder of her own breath. And then The Fat Man beckoned to me with his finger and so I put my ear to his mouth. Between now and eternity he whispered to me.

'I hope that answers all your questions', he said.

And, with that, he was gone.

I unfastened the leash from The Cow and congratulated her for her stellar efforts. Then I climbed up on top of The Fat Man's belly, as though a beast conquered, resting there on the pavement, and I shouted:

'We are free!'

And everybody around me cheered. And they threw their hats up in the air and, suddenly, the buildings all looked new again, and the flowers in the flower boxes returned to life, and everybody looked younger and more affluent and I knew that I was living the dream.

Chapter 42

We stayed there for a while; celebrating with them, rejoicing in the name of restored liberty and unbridled freedoms. But, soon, the excitement melted away like a waxen candle, and, one by one, as I watched from the vantage point of The Fat Man's dead belly, the people went back to their apartments and rebolted their bolts, retuned their televisions and maxed out their volumes, as if to say 'nothing ever happened' or 'it's always been this way'. Deal with it.

All the same, we stood until their numbers had dwindled almost completely, a few bogg-eyed hangers-on thinking that perhaps we had a plan of some kind, but when they realised that we didn't, all they could do was look at us with malice and spittle-covered disgust. And so, when we left them, we felt that they had been disappointed in some way but that there was nothing we could do about it.

For one splendid and ephemeral moment, I actually felt something as I gazed at the wondrous mass of flesh and bed sheets consuming the road before me. Piled almost poetically amongst the trash in the gutter, I watched with an almost religious sense of abandon, as a procession of rusting cars careened around The Fat Corpse as though some super-sized traffic cone.

Of course, this isn't to say that I hadn't felt anything at any other time; I had felt miserable for as long as I could remember, but as I looked upon the corpulent cadaver that the scene had presented to me, its legs splayed and a peaceful look upon its triple-chinned face, I felt a deep sense of empathy as a melancholy awareness that youth had slipped through my fingers hit me and I realised that I, too, would soon be gone. It hit me that we all only get one shot, to be young and to be free and alive, and it appeared now that I had wasted my youth chasing phantasms, hallucinations that had finally managed to materialise right before my very eyes, a death personified of every dream I ever had and ever thought might have meant anything.

One might suppose that in circumstances that were more 'normal' I would have felt some sort of responsibility or, at worst, some sort of contrition for what I had just taken a part in. But, at that particular moment in time, all I could focus on was the fact that my mind now seemed empty, a void devoid, as though what had once been a shelf chock-a-block full of books was now emptiness itself, and so all that remained was space, free of even air or dust, yet all the more potent for knowing what once was. I felt as though a snake might when it has shed its skin, or like the ship of Theseus, having over time had my parts replaced, one by one, and so no longer knowing if it is still the same vessel that set out upon its maiden voyage. Another existential crisis: not knowing who I was; not knowing what I wanted; I didn't even know what I already had or who I could turn to; just that inner ear twirling pain of the end of the road, slowly realising that, even though it had led to exactly where I thought it might, it was not the place that my heart had been aching for; the people spoke a different language; the climate was inclement and unsuitable for my body type; I didn't like the food and couldn't stomach the smell. I wanted to go home.

The Fat Man's mouth was wide open now, a tunnel to nowhere. I stared into his dead eyes like two almost out-of-date pork pies festering at the end of a long and sweaty day on the Tesco discount shelf, and then pulled his eye lids closed in one final act of reverence and disgust. And, as he lay there like some fallen god – some Disolympus sleeping, I thought to myself that there was an almost regal air about him, a grace and dignity evoked beneath the golden morning sunlight.

The faintest sniff of a breeze made the hairs on his legs and chest stand up and quiver – as though part of him, some immortal force, was still alive. The king is dead, I thought to myself, and then I took a hold of The Cow's leash and decided that it was time to take her home.

As I gave her my attention, she looked at me as though disappointment was an infectious disease I had purposely passed on to her. Despite the fleeting glory of having the masses cheer in appreciation of her deeds, she had realised now how empty they were. No matter how much we tried to console ourselves with the fact that we may have learned a thing or two about each other along the way, and that, perhaps now, we understood the structure of ambition and dreams and reward, it stood as an irrefutable truth before us that the lasting change and happiness that we had expected had only been a fleeting one. All the problems that we thought would be solved still remained. It was the strangest feeling of being a total success but not caring for it. The strangest feeling of knowing that there is no success, only a pale imitation of the realising of our ambitions. The Mona Lisa probably looked a thousand times more perfect in Leonardo's mind's eye; I redirected my gaze to the ground and, with leaden feet, moved forwards.

I began to think about The Leader. It was time to see her again, not because my heart was in it; but because it seemed like the only way to tie up loose ends, and I was still determined to discover the great punch line of life's big joke. When I compared my feelings for her to the one's that I held for The Cow, I realised that everything that had taken place between us had happened out of dumb-eyed desperation. All I had wanted was to get in with the crowd, float along in a world where I didn't have to make my own decisions; all The Leader had wanted was the illusion of love, of undying promises and passion, despite knowing them chimerical. I had known this all along, in my heart of hearts, had just been pretending to feel like I had a shot at being normal, a chance to make my parents proud of their fair-weather son; a chance to pretend that I wasn't dying and wouldn't be dead soon, an excuse to leave a paper-mache imitation of a legacy behind me, instead of the certified, bona fide empty space in which I had once stood.

We set off back the way we had come. I removed my shoes to complete the journey as I had started it, felt the blisters and the cracks and the lumps on my skin tear for the final time against those hypodermic pavements. Everything comes full circle, I kept saying, everything makes sense in the end. And, with that, I let go of the leash, as though I were releasing the ever weakened grip of a man about to slide over the edge of a precipice; as though the ship had sunk and I were about to let my icy-lipped lover sink to the bottom of the ocean; as though the power was out and it would stay that way.

Somehow it was over. We walked past the monuments and the theatre and the city square with the televisions and the town hall. Out of alley ways and backstreets we heard the occasional 'moo' from one of our converts, but instead of being impressed with ourselves we just felt sorry for them. People looked the same as they always did; eyes to the ground; hands in pockets; clothes too big or too small for them. But I felt more lost than every single one of them.

Everything so fleeting and ephemeral and transitory, I found myself looking at buildings as we passed them by, trying to imagine what it might be like fifty or a hundred years from now, when they have crumbled and been replaced. I saw cars on the road and thought about how they can only go so far before they rust and fall to pieces; I imagined houses falling into the ocean because of land erosion; and I saw the storms and the hurricanes and the earthquakes that would sweep the rest of us away. The Fat Man behind me, I realised the futility of my insignificant life and the inefficacy of my ambitions. An Upanishad wet dream, I thought to myself that if nothing is permanent then our evanescent existence cannot ultimately be real. I took comfort in this for a few seconds, told myself that I didn't exist, followed the chain of reasoning, and bathed myself in its revelations. But, ultimately, all I will ever have is 'now', and what I needed now was something lasting and eternal; and there is only one of our actions that can leave us changed forever.

Tired from another night of misadventure and disappointment, I stumbled into a quiet street where the lines of parked cars and rows of sticky-tape street lamps began to flicker in and out of existence, semi-comatose.

Another haze, The Cow followed on behind me, plodding along quite amicably in her state of enervation, and, as I stopped in the road as though drunk and disorientated, she gazed upon me as though a divorcee might her ex-husband in honeyed memory of how things once were. We were getting higher and higher up towards the suburbs – towards the school where I had gone on that first night with the Leader and her sycophantic friend. Behind The Cow, stood the whole panorama of the city, that whole dismal postcard picture of reaching and grasping and trying to pull oneself out of the sinkhole; the clouds on the horizon grey and tumescent. Heaving. Swelling. Moving. Breaking. The Cow plodded on up towards me, simply because she had nothing better to do; there was a crash in the sky as the rain prepared to fall and I wondered where all the people had gone.

I sense that the Leader is close by; I can smell her on the electricity in the air, imagine my fingers through her hair, and the intimate warmth of her cigarette stench breath. But this isn't love, just more of the same: instinctual, unadulterated, emotionally polluted lust. Perhaps upon meeting her, I could make like it was otherwise, I told myself. Perhaps she would play right into my arms. Every happy family is the same, every unhappy family stays home to eat Chinese takeaway and watch the telly whilst mum and dad make love with their socks on and afterwards argue about whose turn it is to wash the dishes. I tried to convince myself that this was what I wanted; to be inimitably unhappy. But I didn't want anything anymore. I wanted out. I didn't even know why I was going to see her.

On top of the hill was an old English phone box, red and rustic and otherworldly. I caressed its door with my fingers, as the sky took deep breathers in preparation for the imminent bombardment of everything beneath it. And, as I looked at dry paint crevices, I marvelled at how 'English' I suddenly felt: standing outside in the rain, an iconic phone box, and an existential crisis caused by locking myself within myself via excessive politeness and deference to the wishes of strangers that didn't care if I lived or died. I opened the door, but only a little, because it was jammed at the hinges. It opened slowly and incrementally, as though I had found myself prying open a tomb that had been left sealed for centuries – as though it shouldn't even be happening, as though a dream.

A visible cloud of stale air drifted out like some exhumed corpse found under the patio and, as I lifted the receiver and listened to the dial tone, I found myself once again besieged by another insuperable obstacle: I had forgotten about commerce, coins and exchange, the cogs of the system. A demonstrable fool, I had given away my money at a time when I most needed it.

'He who fails to plan his own life will find himself becoming a pawn in the plans of other people.'

Despite proclaiming money to be redundant and frittering away what little of it I'd had, I found myself once again at its mercy. The Cow pressed a tired and insensate eye against the graffitied glass of the box windows and watched as I unleashed a haphazard scatter of accoutrements across the floor – various handkerchiefs and puzzle pieces and photographs – things I had become involuntarily attached to; I rummaged through the pile and picked things up one at a time, but, alas, no coins or notes or credit cards.

No longer a member of society, I looked down at my bare feet, tried to ignore the paradigmatic stench of phone box urine, banged my head against the cool glass, and then cursed the day I was ever born. Why me? I wondered to myself, but I knew in the pit of my breast that I had brought all this on myself. So, suck up, Sweet Cheeks, keep on moving.

I took a deep breath and counted to eighty.

The thought of reverse charging the call crossed my mind, but, in my anxiety, I began to imagine the situation in which her single parent might answer the phone and berate me for being irresponsible and disorganised; or, even worse, chastise me for importuning their precious daughter. I could hear them clear as day, shouting and grinding their teeth in sweat-induced rage; the mist of anger sweeping down and clouding about their eyes. I began to tremble. I didn't want them to know that I was just another nobody. Failure was not an option, it was a luxury. I read the call information guide by the receiver.

It would cost me twenty pence to make a call.

Head slumped, feet shuffling, I did the only logical thing that I could do, which was to go outside and beg for change. My mouth began to cake and dry as I rehearsed my lines, as though stepping into a new role for the final, grand performance:

'Have you got twenni pence, mate?'

Inevitable. As though I had been waiting my whole life to allow those words to roll out of my mouth and into the void – as if they had been the first sacred words to bring the universe into being. The Cow stood munching upon sporadic vegetation – the weeds between cracks in paving tiles, gutter remnants blown down by the wind. I looked about the empty streets, pacing between the phone box and a set space circle boundary around it, afraid to go too far away from it because I was an animal and it was my territory; the cave for me to hide in; the rock for me to crawl under; the shell for me to someday return to with my tail between my legs (but what strange animal was I?).

Where were all the people? Where was the sentient somebody with a wallet and a desire to understand my plight? For the longest time nobody came and I was left horribly, painfully alone with only my thoughts as company.

Over and over again, I repeated my lines, as though to distract myself; anything to stop my thoughts from taking hold of me, because I was terrified that they might not let go.

'Have you got twenni pence, mate?'

But all this futile exercise served to achieve was to parch my throat further and I soon felt my heart pounding in my chest as I looked about the rows of parked cars and the lines of unfamiliar terraced houses with their doors closed and not even the slightest signs of life behind the murky taped up windows, besmirched by human hands.

And then it happened: my thoughts gripped me. I convinced myself that I had wasted my entire life. I felt as though there were no excuses for each of the terrible decisions I had made, not even the socially accepted excuses like having been callow, or having been ignorant, or having been misinformed. I felt as though I might not be the person that I had aspired to become or thought I was, or, perhaps even more horrifying, that I was EXACTLY that person, but that such a person had absolutely no value or consequence within the world of men and thus by extension the universe.

'And it's better to be a nothing than a nobody.'

My life was full of holes and I had dug them, but I could at least see now that destiny is just a growing awareness that we are powerless to escape from of some fundamental and unalterable fact about ourselves over the course of our too-short lifetimes.

The door of the red telephone box creaked behind me as I slid down dirty against the floor and started to shiver. I couldn't believe and refused to accept that this was the life I had built for myself. I heard voices outside heading in my direction and then they faded away and turned to nothing and I hated myself for not bestowing upon them those eternal, unshakeable words.

'Have you got twenni' pence, mate?'

And, still, the trail of thought continued to plague me, filling the whole booth with its taunts and its angst and its anguish, as though it were a path into the woods that I knew could only lead to danger or destruction, but which somehow had a hold of me and so dragged me down it kicking and screaming. Hopelessly aware, I started to choke; the airtight booth, a cloud of sulphur, stale and dried out completely, another few seconds would have been the end of me.

I burst through the door with a war cry, took a breath, and then another.

'Recompose yourself.'

As before, the same emptiness of the streets, that same dearth of people, but now, inexplicably, I am overwhelmed with the impression that something else is missing. As though on auto-pilot, I check my pockets for the usual items that I carry upon my person, but they are all as they should be. I look upon the horizon to see if there is some hole upon it. After a few moments of behaving in this erratic fashion, I realise what it might be: The Cow. With a puff of smoke, she's disappeared, and without her the streets seem even emptier and more painfully desolate than ever before. Rows of terraced houses shadow loom over me. Still weakened from whatever anxiety it was that had crippled me moments before in the phone box, I found myself rocking back on my feet. Once upon a time, I had felt certain that I was the only living creature on the face of the Earth; now I was sure of it. I pace back and forth in irregularly shaped circles. Wondered what would become of me. All of the world is an idea.

And, for a moment or two, I thought I had lost her forever; I thought I had finally reached the end of myself. But then, from behind a large removal van that had been parked down one of the side streets, I saw her flanks quivering and my heart beat with joy and satisfaction and I felt whole again. Thus fuelled by a manic joy, I ran up beside her side and embraced her as best I could, almost ready to weep as I pressed my face up close to her once again and felt that warm and wholesome breath shoot forward from her nostrils. She stared off distant over the horizon, chewing upon another mouthful of strange vegetation. And still I couldn't admit how much she meant to me.

Reunited, we stood waiting outside the red phone box for signs of life. Occasionally, a seemingly empty car would pass by or a vacant bus would hiss at us, but there was still that same eerie silence over everything, as if a nuclear bomb had been dropped and somehow, magically, we alone had survived. Despite wanting to be away from people for as long as I could remember, to seek hermetic hideaways, I now found myself praying for them to be sent in my direction. I needed them; they needed me. People need people. I finally saw the light.

Perhaps it would have been wiser to go in search of people instead of waiting for them to come to me, but I felt now that the theme of my life had been passivity, and, as wrong as this was, I saw myself as incorrigible. You can't teach an old dog new tricks, I thought to myself. I would put my tail between my legs and become a supplicant to each and every one of them, each anonymous stranger, each sack of turbulence and emotions and history; I would get down on my knees before them and petition them for saviour.

The two of us stood turned to rock within the clasp of our proverbial eternity, as a commotion of clouds swept about the sky, a grey veil of inferior imitation fabric, a blanket to be placed over the coffin in which I was to be buried alive. Throat still dry, I paced around in languid circles to help me forget about it, but it only served to exacerbate my problems and so, after a few moments of said pacing, I felt the first explicit tinges of thirst and became unable to take my mind off anything else.

Longingly, I stared at the cars, hissing by with their faceless drivers and sedate passengers, and I began to imagine that the hush of their passing was the sound of water falling from some great waterfall. The thirst grew stronger, as though I wanted to drink in the whole of the world, not just its liquids, but indeed the whole of its offerings, whatever I could experience. But I knew it was too late. I had peaked, plateaued and fallen. My cup had overflowed long ago but, instead of appreciating the quality of its wine, I had imbibed without due care or hesitation, and so all that was left now was the disappointment of an empty bottle.

I performed my own interpretation of a rain dance, used the last of my energy to hop from one leg to the next, beat my hand over my mouth for one more ululation, praying for rain, holding my hands out to the sky with such vigorous potency that I thought they might leave their sockets, or fall defeated to the floor like perishing fishes at the shore of some salty lake. I beseeched the heavens, even though I knew that they were empty, even though I knew in my heart of hearts, my soul of souls, that the merest drop would be nothing more than a coincidence; I had learned nothing and still wanted to convince myself that I was still a part of it all. Connected.

The Cow had been munching weeds. Between my hops and my twirls and my howls, I caught a sly glimpse of her, emaciated and afraid. She seemed distant and malevolent, staring at me with once-wide-eyes now full of pain.

Upon our first meeting, she had seemed to me oh so fresh –alive and vivacious and ebullient - happy to be here. But, now, all I could do was wonder what I had done to have her age so much, what it was about this test of her mettle, this journey that we had been on, that had taken so much from her when I had meant for it to give her everything. Seeing her in this state, I tried to convince myself that at least within myself were the remains of the great light. I wanted to believe that I was one of the last of a tradition, the last man on earth, the last man standing, full of life and joy and curiosity.

I returned to the solace of the lifeless rain dance but, still, there were no people in the streets. No pedestrians, no passers-by. Only the inexorable thirst in my throat like a flame climbing up a vine. It burned from my belly and then screamed up the back of my throat. I prayed again for the rain. An empty invocation. I held my hand out in supplication.

'PLOP'.

A single drop had fallen as though the shell of a flower in the centre of my palm. I put my face to the moisture, licked it like a thirsty dog lapping at a dirty puddle. Greedy, wanting so much more, I looked to the sky and held my mouth open, as though expecting life to be that simple, as though expecting nature to satiate each of my needs as and when they arose, and so I stood there for few solitary moments, confused there was not more, until it finally struck me: A single drop was all I deserved. I tried not to look at the sky, focused on the phone box, focused on my immediate needs, tried not to make excuses that would distract me from attaining my goals. Call the Leader. That was the agenda. Keep it in mind. I rubbed my palms together, determined to make a change.

I shouted out loud and clear to the world that I was coming for it and then I pounced into action as Destiny delivered me a belated birthday present.

At the end of the road, stumbling towards me amongst the rows of parked cars and the terraced houses, I saw the silhouettes of an unlikely duo, of two characters I felt certain I had seen before, one lean and with good posture, the other a little more rotund and rocking from side to side with his uneven gait, clinging onto the sleeves of his companion for support and sustainability.

Their uneven silhouettes transmogrified from black to grey, and then finally the colours of life itself, and I realised that it was exactly who I had hoped it might be: The Well-Dressed Man and his Half-Wit sidekick.

The shock of seeing them before my eyes after all this time, after so many gallons of water had passed under the bridge, at first seemed incredibly unreal to me, as though something were not quite right in the world, as if perhaps I were imagining it or had finally gone mad completely. But, as they continued walking towards me, as real as any of the other objects or ideas around and about me, I began to tremble with excitement, as though I had been given a second chance to realise my dreams. I reached into my back pocket and pulled out the jigsaw puzzle piece that I had found on the roof of the theatre oh so many moons ago. I held it out in front of me. I felt certain I would win.

At first, they seemed as though they were going to walk right on by me as I gazed upon the Well-Dressed Man's face, still purposeful and intent, and with the same thick veins upon his neck coursing full of life. He was dressed in a very similar way to the first time that I had encountered him, the fine fabrics, the rood around his neck, and the leather shoes seemingly polished by the hands of God himself, so refulgent and vital did they shine. And, despite the capricious weather, which seemed ever gloomier, the Half-Wit had chosen once again to attire himself in his sports socks and sandals, and from there on up he had about him the same old shorts and T-shirt, accentuated by that smile upon his face, that mile-wide gurn that seemed to take in all the sadness from the outside world and churn it up, turn it out, and reflect it right back on itself with brilliant felicity.

I as the Village Idiot with my trembling hands cast out before me and the jigsaw puzzle piece sat in my palm as though some broken-winged bird that I were attempting to set free. The Well-Dressed Man caught my gaze. I don't think he recognised me, but he could certainly tell that I was about to try and tap into his funds, and as a naturally charitable man, or so I assume, he paused in his tracks, and once again stood looking at me as the Half-Wit stood rocking at his feet.

'Are you going to ask me for money?', asked The Well-Dressed Man.

'Just twenty pence, Sir', I replied.

And then I explained: 'I found your companion's jigsaw puzzle piece. I shall give it to you in return.'

The look in his eyes was one of consternation. I had imagined him imperturbable by most standards, but, perhaps at the embarrassment of not recognizing or knowing what the hell I was talking about, but feeling in some way that he should at least have an inclination, he began to tremble with indignation. He was clearly the kind of man who preferred to know what was happening, to be omnisciently aware of his surroundings, and all that was taking place and unfolding at his feet. So when he asked of me:

'Who are you?'

It felt as though there was a crack in the universe, that somehow things were not as they should be, as if the master blueprints had been scribbled on with the asinine drawings of a drooling imbecile.

And so I was forced to explain: That once upon a time I had met him as a mere thinker and he had explained to me that he was a thinker too and then referred me to the Big Guy Upstairs. I attempted to stimulate his memory by discussing the jigsaw that his friend had been carrying in his shopping bag, and how he was disgruntled because he had lost a piece. Upon hearing these words, he seemed to vaguely recall what I was talking about, but then, as he looked at the tattered piece of cardboard in my hand he said:

'But we found our piece of the puzzle behind the sofa months ago.'

And, as he said it, the Half-Wit, in recollection of the joy that he must have felt at the time, began to gesticulate wildly and swing on his feet with all the vigour and impetuosity of a cat in a fish processing factory.

'Then where is this piece from?', I enquired, utterly defeated, utterly lost to the world of causality and confused reason that I dwelled within.

'I'm afraid I'm unable to help you there.'

And then he looked at me tenderly, as if he found me to be utterly pathetic; as if I were some rare animal crushed underneath the wheels of a car; as if I were a baby born with a limb missing; as if I were a portly man in a suit, sweating on a bicycle, as I tried to cycle up an endless hill next to a stinking, polluted canal in an area thronged by sweaty, doddering tourists. He took a huff and then a hold of the Half-Wits hand and the two of them began to set off down the street. I watched them fade away a few steps into the future. But then I came back to my senses and I heard myself saying:

'Please, Sir!'

And they both turned to look at me with unnerving anticipation in their eyes.

'Have you got twenni' pence, mate?'

A terrible silence prevailed as an ineffable dread wrapped its arms around me as though a chance encounter with a secretly despised ex-girlfriend in a supermarket car park.

I thought that I saw anger rising in the breast of the Well-Dressed Man, but then he seemed to regain the equanimous deportment with which he was associated, and from underneath his robes he pulled out a leather coin purse and marched right up beside me with a look of grizzly determination in his eyes.

'Take these and take heed', he said. 'I will pray for you.'

Into the cup of my hands he poured a thousand shimmering, twenty pence pieces, sparkling and brilliant and alive. I got down on my knees before him and I thanked him a thousand times over. But he wouldn't have any of it.

'I must leave', he said.

Then he took again the Half-Wit's hands in his own and proceeded on down the street as golden sunlight burst down upon us from the sky, as though he had just descended from heaven with the express purpose of leaving me in a state of awe and stupefaction.

But, still, there was still something that I felt I had to say to him, something that had been hiding deep within me, a sense of compunction and regret for all the terrible things that I had done.

'Father', I screamed, 'Forgive me for my sins.'

And, once again, he stopped in his tracks. Once again, he turned to look at me, his eyes bulging, and his mighty arms tensed down to the balls of his fists. I watched the thick veins in his temples throb and pulsate.

'I'm afraid that I might have killed The Big Guy Upstairs', I said with tears in my eyes, 'I don't know what to do.'

And, as I said these words, the intensity of his gaze faded like a flower that hasn't been watered and he said to me:

'But He is alive everywhere, even in our very souls.'

And, with that, he turned and walked away until eventually the vision of him leading the Half-Wit on the path to his destiny became just another silhouette. And so, thus pardoned, I went with my twenty pence pieces to the telephone box and thought about making my call.

Chapter 43

The sun had set by the time I had managed to pluck up the courage to place my call. I rolled her rote remembered number back and forth upon my tongue and then slammed the telephone handle back down into its cradle, hyperventilating and afraid, worrying about inconsequential consequences, unsure of an unwritten future, and each of the myriad possibilities that could unfold within it.

The Cow remained outside, oblivious to my pain, incognisant of what might be about to transpire, unaware of whatever might be about to swallow our world up whole, and put it to bed in its final resting place. And so, once again, I began to resent her indifference, envied her animal lack of awareness, wasted yet another doleful instance of my empty life wishing that I could exist on a more simple and austere level of being, that I could astral travel to some great womb in the sky and forget about it all, suckle upon the swollen teat of eternity until I was comatose on satiation. Is it a part of the human condition to consistently place oneself in one undesirable and hopeless situation after another? Must we never learn? Or, could it be the case that this is the nature of the universe? That life is a hopeless situation? If only I could vegetate in a dark corner somewhere, or curl up in a ball and forget about it all, until I was good and dead and over.

But what would life be without its problems?

The phone began to ring. The sound of it sliced right through me, each note of the tone protracted out into the tenth dimension, ringing out through all of time and space and causality, rubbing my past, present and future right in my nose; all possible universes and reminders of how things could or would've been. I imagined an empty house somewhere in the city, her place, 'The Leader'; I imagined a living room with creased television gossip magazines spread about the floor and a vacant, biscuit crumb broken sofa. Nobody home. Nobody to interact with. If a phone rings in an empty house does it make a sound? How could I ever know?

I took deep breathes, aberration of thought, mind, and sanity; pure unbridled passion and anxiety. I had not been this tense in years. The sound of the phone on the other end of the line rang out into the empty streets as I waited with baited breath, as though some common criminal that is awaiting the gavel to sound and his sentence to be delivered.

A few deep breaths. A pregnant pause. An anxiety attack and a few moments of wishful thinking and rationalisation.

My world is a void and the people are avoiding me.

'Hello', she eventually said.

And then I turned back inwards.

There was another unfathomable silence, as though two strangers had found themselves sat next to each other in the waiting area of a desolate, backwater train station, and were afraid to make eye contact.

I pretended to be reading the phone box graffiti. I stared at it reverentially, as if I had found the panacea after all, as if it had all the solutions to my tiny little problems.

For a good time call XXXXX-XXXXXX

XXX was here XXXX.

This is the worst of all possible worlds.

And then it occurred to me that, through the very act of dialling her number, I had initiated the conversation, that the ball was in my court. It was incumbent upon me to take the next step, and so I began to spit my words out like mouldy milk into the sink. They came suddenly and without premeditation.

'The Fat Man is dead.' I said, 'We are free.'

And then she exploded.

She let out the words I had been waiting to hear. She told me that she loved me. She told me that she cared. She said that we would be together forever and that nobody or nothing would ever tear us apart. She said that we were special. She said that our love was unique. She said that from the moment she had set eyes upon me she knew that this day would come. She said that I was The One.

All my physical, spiritual, and emotional needs would be satisfied, she said. I no longer needed to fear being so alone. From now on, things would be different. It was us versus the world. We were the authors of our own destiny; we were the light shining in the darkness; the only stars in the sky. We were the stolen treasure in the magpie's nest; the wind between the trees; the ripples in the canal; the sunlight on the chimney. This was the start of something beautiful.

I became overawed with joy as her energy and ebullience transmuted the crackles on the phone line into snow drops of the purest white. I could feel the warmth emanating from her smile, even though I couldn't see her; I could envisage the sheen of her white teeth irradiating the room, the town, the city. My heart began to beat, I felt it pounding up against my rib cage, hardly able to contain myself, a momentary sensation of euphoria, of everything being good and just and whole in the world; of life finally being fair and being able to provide me with everything I had ever wanted from it, despite my having previously convinced myself that it were impossible. Then the phone began to beep to tell me that my credit was running out and so I had to delve into my pockets and pull out one of the shimmering twenty pence pieces and start the cycle over again

Reality folded in on itself all around me and I saw the world as though a baby opening its eyes for the first time, taking in each and every sensation as though the newest and most remarkable, shiniest and most beautiful thing in the whole of existence. I let out a cry and she giggled right on down the line.

'Meet me in the scrap yard at the top of town.' She said.

So I slammed the phone down, burst out of the phone box, took a hold of The Cow's leash, and ran off towards our meeting place like my life depended on it (assuming that one considers one's life to something of relative value).

Chapter 44

The Cow and I slid on through the open gates of the scrap yard as though royalty returning to a castle; the rows of trees around the perimeter loomed on heavy in sentry, and, as we watched an old train slink by on the tracks behind the big barbed wire fence, we felt the wind dance in our hair, as we took in the smells of earth mashed metals and destructibility. Here in the final resting place of material things, the sacred home of crushed and tattered machinery, of the iron innards and endless balls of wire, we watched the sun go down behind the sleeping jaws of rusty diggers.

We wandered slowly, with tentative footsteps. The Cow occasionally paused to eat at the grass that shot up between the cracks in the earth; I looked about me at the piles of flattened cars with their cracked paint and the fading colours. Piles and piles of rusted metal as far as the eye can see, cables and bits of thickened wires sprawled before us like the heads of Hydras, broken engines, and ineffable objects torn at the seams by the jaws of yellow machinery.

A magnet in the sky. In one corner, up against another pile of twisted car shells, I see a rusted double-decker bus. Yellow and white, the brown of its rust makes it seem almost stylish, sitting there still as an old Buddha. Drawn to it as though the ocean, I find myself swimming on up beside it. And then I peer through the windows, look at the old burgundy of archaic leather seats. The double doors open with the most delicate of pushes and so I climb on board, leaving The Cow outside to her leisure; she sniffs and chews at whatever vegetation she can find, as I think about sitting in the driver's seat and tricking myself into believing that I still have some kind of control over the direction that my life is heading in.

Slipping into reverie, I imagine that when The Leader arrives she'll climb on board and I'll put my foot down. The old bus will creak into life again, its engine purring like it did when in service, and we'll drive on into the sunset, onto new horizons, occasionally stopping to pick up happy vagabonds and other like-minded souls to join us on our quest for freedom. We'll set the world on fire, be renowned and soulful and in control, live happily ever after until our final days, knowing that we found the strength to get out of this hellhole town and lived to tell the tale.

But, alas, there was no key in the ignition. And when I sat in the driving seat and tried to turn the big old steering wheel I realised that it wouldn't turn anyway. Years of inertia had caused it to rust and stick into place; I imagined for a few moments that we could simply move in a straight line, titillated myself with another shot at pseudo-profundity.

But what is life without twists and turns?

Death.

And now was not the time.

Dejected, I left the driver's seat and headed on up the stairs. The whole interior of the bus smelled damp from where the rain had crept in and I began to feel as unholy as I did unhygienic; as though the simple act of breathing in the stale air would afflict me with another incurable disease. Apathetic, I sucked it up anyway, made it to the top of the stairs, sat in the front seat, and looked out the big window at the whole of the scrap yard. There was The Cow on down below me, still oblivious to what was going on, not knowing or caring where I had disappeared to, and then there was the gate; I kept my eyes on it and waited for The Leader to come.

I took a deep breath and counted to ninety.

The piles of scrap that constituted my junk heap panorama seemed ordered yet confused. I put my feet up against the window. Restive, fully alert yet serene, I kept my eyes on the gate; waiting for her to arrive; waiting for her blonde hair and her beauty to radiate and contrast against the decay and the dirt that surrounded us. And, eventually, she actually turned up, waddling through the gates with that same old orange sweater that she used to wear, only stretched now from nine months of impoverished gestation. She hobbled like a leper, looking at the cars and the dirt around her with the fascination of some wide-eyed child. And, for a little while, I didn't make a peep; I didn't let her know I was here. I wanted to watch her for a while, hobbling along with her bent back and her big belly, her once perfect breasts bloated as though about to burst, that tiredness in her eyes from the pain of expectation.

Her face was caked with make-up. Even from up there in the bus I could taste the cherry red kiss of her lips, and so, as I felt my heart implode, I began to knock on the window.

When she looked over, I saw that she startled a little at the sight of The Cow waiting by the side of the bus. I kept knocking and watching as she took a deep breath and then hobbled on down towards us, past the turned up cars and the wires, past the broken bus graveyard, stopping finally right in front of the bus and looking up at me with her wide, tired eyes. For a few moments, we both seemed anxious to maintain eye-contact, but then, when she finally broke away and tip-toed nervously past The Cow and onto the bus, my heart began to beat again and I knew that we had reached the final level of our game.

She called up to me on the top-deck.

'I can't get up the stairs.'

And so I clambered down the damp old staircase and saw that she was waiting for me on the back seat of the bus, her massive belly hanging the edge of the chair, her cheeks bloated and swollen, her oedema ankles filling the once graceful space between her tracksuit bottoms and her made-in-China plimsolls. I floated on down the gangway and into her arms. And then she kissed me with all the dullness and passion of a beach ball bouncing up against the side of a bus window.

I pulled my lips away and looked at her, wondered what I had been thinking this whole time, wondered why it had to always be the case that things were better in the distance, that nothing can ever align with expectation, or why, if it does, it must only ever serve to display the puerility of our motivating thoughts. Even so, I smiled the whole while my super smile, as though never before happier, nor ever again as satisfied.

The vestiges of the same smile that had once drawn me to her remained semi-etched upon her face, but, when I gazed upon her, it seemed to me as though her true self was hiding tired behind a thin layer of orange paint, and that only very faintly beneath this mask were traces of her original beauty. Somehow, these traces alone were not enough. Somehow, I realised that love is nothing more than the past on a pedestal, that we remember one especially wonderful moment in our lives and pay tribute to it ever after.

I suppose I can only ascribe it to my fear of being alone, but at that moment, despite knowing that she was not the one for me, I felt obligated to persevere, and so I took her cold hands in my own, and got down on my knees before her and once again began to weep. Even though I knew that these actions were a complete betrayal of my real feelings, I felt inexplicably bound to the laws of expectation and result; I felt that this was how things were supposed to be, that I must act accordingly, that the way things are in appearance is the way that they ought to be, and so I should treat the fatality of truth with the reverence it deserves.

For a few pathetic moments there was an eerie silence between us, as though we were two uncaring strangers that had been forced into an arranged marriage by misanthropic parents, as though she did not wish to be with me either, but for some reason felt that she had no choice in the matter, and so had acquiesced to the whims of superior forces. She looked down at me from the back seat of the bus, her huge orange belly between us as though a mountain range to be traversed; and then I remembered that night at the school, the night of purported conception, and I remembered how her T-shirt had hitched itself up for my viewing pleasure, how I had longed to lift it further, how I had planted a kiss on this very belly, before it had been stretched and deformed, before there was this moving, sentient thing preparing itself to crawl out of it.

With the belly still between us, I managed to catch her glance. She was trying to give me the puppy dog eyes, but I knew right away that they concealed the most duplicitous of lies. I knew that she was out to deceive me, but still I kept weeping as though moved by the majesty of it all.

And then the silence consumed all, myself included. And, as I thought about standing and leaving, I realised that I was powerless, that I had been imprisoned by my own weaknesses and desires. I thought about Charles Darwin; I thought about pusillanimous men like myself, conned by vindictive women like The Leader into investing their time and energy into the raising of another man's child. I tried to tell myself that these were just more of those niggling dubieties; I tried to deceive myself, to find a rational way of irrefutably explaining to myself that The Thing was mine, that I had begotten despite having forgotten, and so should live virtuously, according to the laws of social responsibility and conformity.

You could have cut the tension with a knife.

She began to talk, but the words came out lifelessly, robotically. Like some automaton programmed to mimic the very worst of human nature. And the whole while she yabbered on I looked on helplessly, hypnotised by her heaving titties and the cherry red smear of her pumped up lips:

'I always knew that you would be the one to save me...From the moment that I set eyes on you, I knew in the pit of my heart that you were special, that you had the qualities and the skills that none of the others could ever have. I looked at you behind that counter and saw a prisoner of misfortune, a prisoner of providence and ill-tidings, but I saw that light in your eyes, the torch still shining, and I knew that you would light the way to my saviour.'

The depth of her turpitude and the sheen of her chicanery set my brain again aflame. Yet, at the same time, the weakest part of me wanted to believe it, wanted to believe every single word, as though set in stone by the hallowed chisel of God himself.

My breath become heavy as I gazed upon her and, as I did, those lurid lips of hers seemed to return to their previous state of pulchritude, as delicate as the brush strokes on some great work of art, and her face seemed once again to be made of porcelain, as her eyes shone like fire in the sky, and I felt my heart irrupt once again with ridiculous, terminal ferocity.

She continued to speak lifelessly, but somehow I managed to project the qualities of humanity on to her utterances, to imbue them with beautiful meaning and dignity.

'You are my saviour. My big strong man. My little alpha male. My Hercules.'

And though I knew that each word was mendacious and that she had plans for me, I wanted to believe it anyway. I was tired of fighting myself; tired of seeing myself as incomplete and inefficient; I would take whatever comfort I could get, whether a lie or otherwise. It was all the same in the end.

She stopped talking for a while and stared at my face. I could tell that she was looking at my teeth and wondering whether she should ask me how I lost them. Real beneath the weight of her gaze, I took my eyes away and looked down at myself, my suit now torn to shreds, stained and destroyed; my old shoes caked in the mud of the ages, dilapidated and abused. I had finally become The Vagabond.

I turned away and tried to catch my reflection in the bus windows, but all I could make was the dim outline of the dishevelled shock of hair on my head. I sighed in memory and recognition of glory days gone by, mumbled something unmemorable to myself in dejection, and then I turned to face The Leader. I looked her in the eye and I then I asked her:

'The Thing... is it really mine?'

I don't know what I expected. Instead of answering, she lashed out at me in a fit of instantaneous and glorious rage, lunging forwards off of the back seat, and then clawing at my face with her nails (which, I must admit, were remarkably well kept all things considered). And through a torrent of tears she unleashed a scathing and vitriolic verbal attack on me. Her teeth gnashed and foaming at the mouth, she asked me how I could be so goddam insensitive? She asked me how I could ever doubt her loyalty towards me. She said that I must have little faith in our relationship to ever even suggest such a thing, and then she wailed some more, and sobbed something else, until eventually her energy was depleted and she had no choice but to sit back in the chair, panting with vigour and attempting to catch her breath, still sobbing and looking at me with such malice in her swollen red eyes that I felt a shiver to the core.

And, all the while this was going on, The Cow was looking in at us through the window. I stared deep into her bovine eyes through the misty glass, and knew immediately what she was thinking. Despite the vicissitudes of our relationship, despite the fluctuations of our feelings for one another on the course of our long journey, I could see that she was hurting. Seeing me there on my knees in the dirty gangway before another woman, even though neither of them really wanted me, was slowly eating away at her. And, instead of eating at the grass placidly as before, she too began to breathe heavily, almost as though attuned to the suspirations of The Leader. She pressed her big brown eyes up against the windows, and as she did so the columns of breath jetting out of her nose began to steam it up, and I swear that her eyes began to redden, as though on fire, and so I began to feel like I had nowhere to turn. Every which way was an incensed female; static in the air -that fabled female energy swallowing me whole.

I stood inert and conflicted. My gaze on The Leader, my gaze on The Cow, vacillating between two worlds, wondering how much simpler life would have been if I had just decided to accept my fate in the first place and stick to a life of depravity at the bottom of the barrel. In unison, the two of them stopped their respective respirations and began to stare at me, each calling me towards them, begging me to make the right choice.

And so I stared at The Cow as if to tell her I was coming, that my heart belonged with her, but, seeing me do so, The Leader reached out to me and pulled me towards her, like a spider pouncing on a fly and crushing it with its jaws.

Limp, folded over her belly and confused, I was pulled towards her lips and kissed once again, with passion this time, as if she really meant it.

Long, slow and deep, great waves of pheromones and exhilaration swept over me, and when it was over, I instinctively turned to look at The Cow, feeling guilty. The redness in her eyes redoubled, she began to let out a scream, one that pierced the night time and reverberated throughout the scrap yard. She looked at me as though fully betrayed, The Leader laughing the whole while. And, upon seeing this, The Cow did something awful: despite the tiredness she must have been feeling, she began to rock the bus.

Using her body weight alone, she smashed herself up against the side of the bus still screaming. At first, it moved only in increments, but the more it rocked the angrier she seemed to get and so The Leader and I were forced to hold on to whatever we could: she the rungs of the seats and myself the swinging handle bars dipping down from the ceiling. Each time The Cow's body smashed up against the rusty old exterior we would be jolted into anti-gravity, and, sure enough, The Cow's will triumphing over all, The Leader's confidence in the situation seemed to dissipate. Soon it had been replaced with an unadulterated terror, the tawdry lipstick twisted into the quintessence of fear, her flabby titties jiggling with the motion of the bus, The Cow pounding all the while, making the world shake despite my protestations and supplications.

I attempted an escape, doing what little I could to clamber on down the gangway. But, somehow, The Cow had found inordinate strength, as though indefatigable, and so every time I found myself approaching the end of the gangway I would fall to the floor with the shudder of her attacks, sliding down towards The Leader's feet at the back of the bus, which as it happens was perhaps the most unfortunate place to be.

In the heat of excitement, a great puddle of water had fallen from between The Leader's legs, saturating the gangway, and sticking to the hairs of my arms to my skin. As The Cow continued to shake the bus, The Leader began to scream, but no longer out of fear; this time, she was clearly motivated by pain. I watched her from the floor, still shaking with the bus, still sticky from the amniotic ocean seeping about me, as she took her track suit pants off frenzied and screaming. As though in a virgin's wet dream, she pulled off her underpants and cast them aside as though the most insignificant of all the thing in the world. I stood mesmerised as her legs opened up and she began to bellow, her face contorting, her cheeks puffing up and out; deep, laboured breaths, as she clung on to whatever she could find, and the bus continued to shake back and forth.

Best I could, I pulled myself up. A few times I fell, but I persisted and eventually I made it to the window nearest The Cow, banging on it best I could, beseeching her to settle down, telling her that I was sorry and I didn't mean it, tempting her with promises of lush green fields to ruminate in once all of this was over, and begging her to stop. For a moment, she paused to look at me, the silence between us filled with the raucous screams of The Leader at the back of the bus. I broke my gaze with The Cow for a few seconds and turned to look at her; still, her face was contorted with an ineffable expression of pain; still she heaved and pushed as though attempting to push a boulder through an empty toilet roll tube. I thanked the empty heavens it wasn't and would never be happening to me.

Sick. Weak. Knowing that I would never have to put myself through anything like this, I felt great waves of incredible relief. But, at the same time, I felt as though I were witnessing something miraculous, the most natural thing in all of the world, unfolding before my very eyes, our animal nature finally revealed, far removed from hospitals and anesthesia, and all the contrivance and symbolic fictions of the modern world.

I stroked the glass of the window with the back of my hand in the hope that it would somehow pacify The Cow, and then, when it didn't, fumbled my way back down the gangway to The Leader. Outside, the sun had finally disappeared between the piles of junk and broken metal, and now the only light that we could utilise came from an evanescent moon. I took The Leader's hands in my own, told her to breathe like I had seen them do in the movies, and then I put my palm to her forehead, told her that it would be okay, that somehow we might find a way to make it work.

Once we got a steady rhythm, going I heard a laceration form, and then, as though in recognition of such a horrifying sound, she let out the most blood-curdling scream of them all, and from between her legs I saw the incipient bulb of a hairless head; and the more she pushed, the more there was, until eventually there were arms and legs, pushing, screaming and swearing, until eventually there was another living soul amongst us, and a great peace came over us all, there in the back of the bus. I spanked the baby and it let out a cry, its first of many in its lifetime.

For a few minutes, I felt that I had made friends with serenity, a great sense of relief that things had worked out as well as they could do. Perhaps placated somehow by the screams of the baby, The Cow returned to the grass outside, hardly looking at me, but calm, as though the anger she had felt just moments before was merely a hallucination in some distant stranger's dream. I smiled at The Leader. Her face was swollen and her eyes bloated, the very epitome of tiredness, but nevertheless she looked relieved and at ease, as though a war had just come to an end, or as though a great famine had finally concluded and she could smell the homely scent of food cooking in the kitchen after years without it.

The sight of her holding The Baby in her arms made me chuckle to myself, I don't know why. She held it close into her chest, its face pressed up against her breasts. Slowly, it stopped crying, and as silence once again prevailed, I took The Leader's clammy hands and hoped for the best.

Somehow, though I knew I was deceiving myself, I felt a connection to the newly born child. Though I knew rationally that it could not possibly be mine, bearing witness to the turmoil that it had put itself through just to get here filled me with a certain sense of reverence. I wanted it to do well. I wanted it to survive. I began to imagine what I could do to help it grow and blossom, analogous thoughts to those that I had felt upon first meeting The Cow, except that, where I had known The Cow to have limitations, I looked upon this little human as a blank canvas, as though anything were possible, as though it could be moulded and shaped and twisted and reformed into something wonderful, instead of the monstrosity before me. I clasped at its mother's hands with rigorous certainty and determination.

Inexplicably, I began to feel for the first time in years that my life might be worth something, that even though I was ignorant of a great many things, I had enough insignificant information on my side to pass at least something down to the child. And so, at last, I began to feel thankful for each of the mistakes I had made, for each of the slips and errors that had shaped me; I felt gratitude swelling up in my breast, feeling once and for all that I finally understood the simplicity of life, that I finally 'got' what it was all about. Perhaps we know nothing of ourselves until we have children. Though I doubted its genetic authenticity I wanted to feel as though I had evolved.

And so I began to think about the things I could do. I realised that if I had to I would return to the store and the manager and all of the other things anathema to the happiness of my soul. I would sacrifice my dignity and my ego. I would work under the heels of boots again, be demeaned and beaten - black and blue - whatever it would take to provide for this creature in front of me and its mother. Whatever was needed would be provided; I would work and toil and scrape, making use of whatever force I could find within myself to succeed. This is life. I could finally see. Life is the propagation and support of more life. It really is that simple.

I paced up and down the bus aisle as though my feet were on fire. My mind felt utterly alive, a thousand thoughts a minute, electric charge, but still none of the colours which had abandoned me on being subjected to The Fat Man's empty maunderings. Instead, there was only a glorious clarity, as if I truly were on the right path, as if my thoughts and my actions were in perfect unison, as if it were supposed to be this way. I understood not only myself but seemingly everybody I had ever met. Life could be seen as a system of meeting and breeding and delivering, nothing more. Everything seemed so simple and I was a part of the process. I banged on the window until The Cow looked up at me again, dejected and confused and barely even alive. Regardless, I let out a cry of happiness, half school girl giggle half war cry. And then I ran back down the gangway to The Leader and her child and I took her hand. And then I got down on my knees and I said the immortal words:

'Marry me.'

She looked at me with tears in her eyes as that horrible lurid mouth folded itself into a pathetic and blubbering smile. She said nothing, too tired to even speak on account of her travails, but I knew almost telepathically that the answer was 'Yes'; I jumped a little for joy, feeling finally that I had made it, that I had succeeded to be normal, and that, from now on, it would all be downhill and there would be little, if anything, to worry about.

Oh, pity the fool who must never learn.

The Leader lifted The Baby from her chest and passed it over to me. Clear now of the blood and the placenta, and whatever else constitutes the birth cocktail, I could see it clearly for the first time. Perhaps deluded at first, I looked into its eyes and saw all of the clichés: hope, promise, innocence. And so for a few moments I held on to it, laughing and smiling, looking back and forth at The Leader as though in wondrous disbelief.

But, the truth is, that the more I looked, the more disturbed I became, because its pink little face reminded me of something, and, as though watching a photograph develop, exactly what it reminded me of slowly dawned upon me. Where I had first seen promise and potential, I now saw a smug complacency, a greedy glimmer in its eyes ready to have a fat tit shoved in its mouth, the great fountain of life ready and on tap to its every whim and desire. Where I had first seen a loveable chubbiness to its wrinkled face, I now saw a shabby obesity, its fat little cheeks folded in on themselves. Where once I had heard cries induced of turmoil, I heard a demanding scream. And then I looked deep into its beady eyes and I realised the truth. This face was not my face. It was the face of The Fat Man. The very same.

In my shock I almost dropped It. Flabbergasted, I looked around me with my mouth wide open. Once again, the world had come crashing down, and though perhaps you would expect each collapse to be a diluted and easier-to-take version than the prior, it seemed to me ever worse. I felt my heart snap in my chest, lost for words, lost for reason and virtue of anything analogous. I thrust the creature back into The Leader's arms, turned my back on them both, and then collapsed down to my knees, as though a tree cut at the roots, crashing down in the gangway with mighty reverberations and a dull, yet crushing sense of defeat.

But what were the roots of my foolishness? From where did it stem? How could I have gone against every one of my instincts, every one of my inclinations and propensities? How could I continue time and time again to pull the wool over my own eyes? How many more times in life would I allow this naïve optimism to lead me to my own destruction and unhappiness? If our characters are formed by a mere repetition of the same mistakes, then undoubtedly I was accursed with one - but couldn't I ever learn?

The Leader began cooing behind me, the most horrifying sound I had ever heard in my too short lifetime. I turned to face her, rocking like a madwoman in a padded room, the life in her eyes faded away completely now, The Baby looking up at her with its Fat Man face, grinning, completely aware that it would be protected and cared for if not for eternity then forever and that I had just signed a verbal contract to be its lifelong slave, lackey and serf.

But most horrifying yet was that The Leader paid no heed to my mortification. Perhaps she had noticed at some level of her being, to tell the truth, I do not know. But as she caught my gaze she began to smile, still devoid of human emotion, ever more the automaton. And she began to talk of our wedding, of nothing else, as if it was the only ship on our horizon, as if it was written and there were to be no escaping it.

'...and of course, it will have to be in a church with flowers and pretty dresses and even candles. And if we do it in the summer then the weather will be nice and so the photos will look pretty because of the light...And we can eat cake and we can dance... Oh, and we can dress the baby in red velvet, and...'

She continued on and on again, listing, naming and demanding things, as though there were a wedding catalogue in her head, and she were going through each of the pages circling each and every item with my blood. And in between the items on her list, she would look at The Baby and coo some more, her tired eyes oblivious to anything else, and the noise coming out lifelessly, automatically, as though a kettle letting out steam and whistling merely as a consequence. The Baby looked at me and grinned, an evil, twisted smile that suggested some kind of ownership over me, the kind of smile that a cruel master would give to a servant that it didn't like; the sort of smile a waiter would give to you after secretly spitting in your food.

And so once again I began to panic, despite the promise I had made with my marriage proposal, despite the responsibility I had convinced myself I had felt towards the upkeep of a tiny soul. Once again, I vacillated to the other side of conviction. Once again, I looked for an escape route, because even though I was completely unhappy with my life as an unemployed, sick and lonely bachelor, I had become set in my ways and my freedoms. Even though I knew that the path I had been walking would only lead to self-destruction, to evolutionary suicide, and thus oblivion, I was happy to walk it. I looked at The Cow out there in the scrap yard, loyal, true, waiting; asking for nothing in return, but willing to give me everything as long as I looked at her in the right way. And so I began to take steps towards her, hoping that The Leader would let me go; that she would forget about everything that had happened between us. That that would be that.

Slowly, I walked the gangway, a heavy sense of expectation hanging about me, as if some horrible, ineluctable thing were about to happen any moment. I dared not look back behind me, as though a child who simply ignores the Brussels sprouts on its plate in the hope that that they will go away. All the while, I kept my eyes on the prize, focused on the open door of the rusty bus, as if it were the only thing in the whole of the universe and that I were pulling myself towards it.

One step. Two Step. Three step. Four. I felt that if I counted it would prevent me from turning my head back. And, in fact, I almost made it, but then there was that noise again:

'Cooochie cooochie cooooooooooo.'

Increasing louder in intensity and stridency, so much so that I could see The Cow cowering in fear out the corner of my eye, so close was I to the bus door. I put my fingers in my ears to make it go away, once again like a child, this time attempting to block out of existence the truth of its situation, but for some mysterious reason my efforts proved to be fruitless, and the horrible sound became even louder, converse to expectations, filling my soul with its horrible, simpering tone.

Finally, safe at the end of the gangway, I prepared myself for the final step towards freedom, but then, quite naturally, the anxieties took another hold of me, gripping their lifeless hands around my neck so that I almost began to choke, reminding me one final time, that if I went away now, there would most certainly be no turning back.

I began to question my very heart, wonder if I couldn't just trick myself into believing that the child was mine, if I couldn't just plod through life in denial, a Prozac blankness to my fake smile, a synthetic understanding of my own happiness, and an eventual conviction that nothing could have ever been any other way.

I remembered The Leader's smile when I had first met her; I remembered the power that I had felt by just acting free and spontaneous in front of her. Perhaps she would play the Good Wife, fawning before me, acting like my weaknesses are strengths alone, letting me feel like the King of the World, just as long as I continue to bring home pay cheque after pay cheque, and keep that roof up over their heads. I wonder if this wasn't a small price to pay for the alternative; I wonder if I have the strength to follow it on through.

For as long as I could remember, I had been aware of the fact that my solitude would lead to destruction, that I had no home to go to, no other arms to collapse into. But, somehow, my ego seemed to be telling me that it is better to die alone than to die as a pale imitation of somebody else, as a diluted version of somebody else's ideals and expectations, as a phantom form of what was never meant to be.

I delved into my pockets and let the Well-Dressed Man's shimmering twenty pence pieces tumble through my hands as though cleansing them. Still the sound of The Leader's gurgling fell about me and, in another moment of weakness, I turned to face her, one final time, to make certain that I was about to make the right choice.

I was sure to only turn my head around - to keep my feet facing out of the door and into the scrapyard - so that I would not be drawn into her arms again through some mindless machination or artifice. But still, she continued to make that horrible noise:

'Cooochie cooochie cooooooooooooo.'

Looking vacantly into the eyes of her offspring, rocking it gently in her arms with an animal tenderness that I couldn't help but envy. And for a good few moments she seemed oblivious to the fact that I was even there. But then, slowly, I watched aghast as her head rose, until she was staring directly at me, and in an instant I realised that she hadn't been cooing at The Baby at all, she had been cooing at me!

Attempting to torment me with her new status as The Mother, she wanted to let me know that I was still a child in her eyes, one that she could easily manipulate and take control of, win over in the blink of an eye on account of her insight into the great cycle of birth and death and revivification.

I began to tremble on my feet, completely overwhelmed. The smile on her face turned to a smirk, a mocking distortion and nothing more.

'Cooochie cooochie coooo, Little Boy.'

And I realised that I could never be the man that I wanted to be.

I jumped in terror from the bus back to the scrap yard and I took a hold of The Cow's leash as I ran as fast as I could away from all of my problems and back into the heart of the city.

Chapter 45

The Eternal Boy, I marched ever onwards, The Cow following diligently behind, without any real awareness of what had just unfolded, completely tired and bored now, completely uninterested in her surroundings and any of the strange things that had happened to us.

I myself, Me, I felt as though it was all over, that my head were nothing more than a rotten cabbage patch of decaying threads of thought, my ambition spent, and my expectations of what life could offer shattered. If any lesson had been learned, it was that things are never what we expect them to be, not even ourselves, because, even though I had convinced myself that I could dance the great masquerade ball and fake my way to happiness, all I had served to do was build a castle out of sand, one that had been swept away in one prodigious and ferocious moment of intensity, as the great oceans of reality had come crashing down and about me.

Once again, we found ourselves wandering, back into the city, past the same old skies and the same old buildings, tuning into the same old hiss of the same old traffic, as I felt just the same kind of detachment I had once thought myself capable of escaping. Despite everything that had happened, all the superficial changes that had taken place, the shedding of skin, the removal of layer after layer of the onion, it seemed incontrovertible and absolute that the core of me still remained in the exact same state that it had always been, whatever it was, this bundle of anxieties and quirks, this picnic basket full of out-of-date foodstuffs and long since perished perishables.

Despite the death of The Fat Man, the birth of his child and the coming of age of The Leader, the town about me still seemed as it always had. Even that earlier ghost town dearth of people and traffic, up by the red phone box, had come to an end, the sun still shining just as matte grey as ever before, and, once again, that strange feeling of nausea, a reflexive repellence of my environment, haunting me as though the spectre of my own shadow, just like in the bad old days. And, as we reached again the heart of the city, the people still bumbling about in droves, their eyes to the floor, their backs arched, I noticed that none of them noticed me; none of them aware of or even caring about my battered suit body, nor The Cow on a leash; none of them thinking of anything outside their own heads, and their own problems; none of them really thinking anything much at all.

From Hero to Zero.

It began to dawn on me that I had failed to change even the tiniest scintilla of a solitary thing. Perhaps deep down within myself I had changed in the sense that I could finally accept the truth of my situation, that it wasn't really as tragic as I first thought, that every other person has problems to worry about too, that I wasn't a singular being in this or any other sense, just another part of the great absurdity that permeates the nothing that surrounds us; the great bumbling and stumbling and wandering through life as we try to grasp at whatever seems meaningful to us at the time. What I mean is that I had changed nothing externally, or, if I had, it had only been in a completely transitory fashion, the kind of change that only lasts a day or two, beginning as nothing but an empty promise, and then dwindling slowly back to the prior state of being, once this emptiness has been made clear.

It was fair to say that, round about me, there was nothing to say that I had been there previously. I had not carved my name into the bench, nor written it on the wall. I had simply allowed for it to be whispered in the dark and to be forgotten about as soon as the lights came back on.

I stopped in the street, The Cow behind me. I looked into the faces of those passing me by, but received no recognition or connection, no understanding, or tacit expression of humanity. Before me stood nothing more than a bunch of individuals, walking aimlessly through space, and going about their lives; a whole generation of humanity, forgetting about itself and heading into overdrive. And, at that moment, I realised that there was a part of me that would never change, that the central part of the onion was where the tears reside, and that this great sadness that I felt would never leave me, that there was no way for me to open the door and kick it out of my house. And so then I knew that there was only one thing left to do.

I took a deep breath and counted to one hundred.

Perhaps it is right that after a little while we are impervious to change; though it is true that the people and events that surround us express a strange fluidity, the fact that we have different stimuli to interact with does not mean that we have 'grown', or improved, in any sense - it just implies that, at best, we have become more sensible, less curious, more cautious in regards to reaching out for fear of being attacked by the rest of the herd. Our curiosity has deserted us and so we are left only with a head full of burdens and a mind full of dreams left unfulfilled; I looked about the city, this prison that had kept me docile and bumbling for all of these months, and I realised that this prison was my body, but that my mind held the key.

There passed me by a family of two parents and a young boy and a young girl. They drifted on by in their own world, as I stood like some nebulous, negligible hallucination with The Cow at my side. These people weren't rich; they didn't have 'taste'; but they had something that I would never find now, on account of my MTV attitude problem, and the pseudo-neuroticism that I had acquired from books - my desire to have either everything or little in between, all of the world or none of it, and in the end an inescapable emptiness that filled my very being like a cup of swill to the brim.

We walked ever onwards, past all the same old sights. We went by the clock tower and the TV screens, and I remembered my fifteen minutes of fame, standing before the crowd, preparing to deliver my sermon, and convincing myself that I was capable of touching their hearts. Even then, I had said nothing, allowing The Cow to speak up for me, allowing the ambiguity of her lowing to mask the contents of my own heart, crawling back within myself, yet feeling proud of the fact because I could feign responsibility.

I looked at the city and its people, the builders on the construction sites, the machinery tearing into the earth and turning it over, pulling, crashing and regenerating, and I realised that, despite my complaints, this town could have been whatever I had wanted it to be. Despite the wads of spit on the floor and the empty crisp packets dancing down the gutter, this was our tabula rasa, the chance for the flower to raise up through the concrete and shine afresh.

And, then, I began to feel the vague semblance of some intuition: That choosing reaction over interaction, this is where I had gone wrong; I had allowed a fastidious disgust, fed of a yearning for my old life, to preclude a healthy development of the new; I had clung on and judged and now I had been forgotten about.

It was too late for saviour now or then or ever onwards.

In another daze, another fog of a mind, I suddenly realised where I was; I looked about me at the familiar streets, at the throngs of immigrant gangs and drunken underclass; at the hustle and the scatter; the bookies and the fast food joints, and the desolate, boarded up pubs, with esoteric etchings on their walls, and the cheap stench of urine hovering outside their doors.

I stood there with The Cow, clinging on to her leash lifelessly, staring vacantly ahead of me at the store in which I had once worked, at the same old people going about their same old business, at that same long line of mooncalves with their junk under their arms and that thirst in their throats, never to be satisfied. I stood there staring, the world about me. But nobody paid me any attention, as if I hardly existed; they simply floated along with their eyes to the floor, thinking about whatever it is that people in the street like to worry about, forgetting that we are all monkeys in the same forest, and that our lives are just one long yarn of the same old dramas never to be disentangled.

I stared into that shop and I thought about my life. I stared right into that floor, the one that I had once swept. I watched the manager being bellicose once again, as if that's all he was ever capable of doing, and then I watched the world go by and wondered where my life had gone. I took a hold of The Cow's leash and we set off again, listless and non-directional, another haphazard meander through the city, taking it all in for the final time, trying to find something, anything, to 'connect' with - to find somebody or something that would notice my absence, but I had lived irresponsibly, and so there was nothing.

And, upon this realisation, I began to think of myself as my own ghost, walking inconsequentially from one place to another, seen by no one, and touching no other. What difference my life had made, I couldn't think. I only knew that I had been here or been there, done this and done that, and that my life was little more than a bundle of unverifiable and insignificant memories which, even if I continued to live, would fade away with the rest of me, until eventually I had forgotten myself completely.

And so I turned to the obvious and I looked at The Cow, my partner through thick and thin, the only true witness to the tale of my life as it had unfolded. I looked at her and I asked her for validation, wanted to know if she knew who I was, and if there was any point in carrying on. And so I demanded of her:

'Tell me my name.'

But, of course, she just looked upon me blankly, tired now, no longer caring, and naturally unable to speak anyway.

I looked at her for the first time through the lens of lucidity; I looked at her as though any normal person might, as nothing more than an emaciated cow in the high street. And, as I looked upon her in this fashion, I felt my mindset shift, as though the ideas that I had held about her had simply fallen away, like all of the other untruths I had become accustomed to; and, seeing her like this, as some hopelessly, confused, incongruous beast, I became completely overwhelmed with a sense of desperation, as though I suddenly realised that I had somehow found myself in a position of responsibility for this creature and its well-being, but that, because I had entered into this social contract at a time of great confusion and loss, it could not be properly validated, and so I could freely justify a breach of it if I so desire.

Truth be told, in my heart of hearts, I had prayed and supplicated whatever forces that might guide us; I had begged them to endow her with the faculty of speech, if only so that for one mesmerising moment I could have known that my name was known, that I truly existed within the human world of ideas, that this town was a part of me, and that I was not merely the ghost I felt myself to be. I wanted to feel a part of something, despite that fact that I had convinced myself time and time again that I didn't belong; I wanted to feel that I had enough of a soul to efface my ego and bow down to the masses. And I think, should it have happened, that I would have fallen to my knees in gratitude, that I would have forgotten and started afresh, that it would have been my great escape, the fresh rain falling upon the seeds of new life. But I know that I had been asking for the impossible - it would be insanity to think otherwise. I had lost the battle with myself long ago and now all that I could do was to try to deal with the consequences.

Somehow, we had found ourselves in the grey car park behind a supermarket. It was as though we had just sprouted up there from the ground, as if we had always been there, and that anything else outside of such was an illusion. I let go of her leash, and then, like a robot whose batteries were about to run out, I tried to explain to her best I could:

'It was unfair of me to have kept you tied up for so long. Perhaps even it was wrong. And the truth is that I should have known that it could never last between us, that there was never even the most remote of possibilities. And this isn't merely because of our differences, it's the similarities too. You see, I thought that you wanted to follow on behind me, and I guess at the start of all this that you probably did. But that's only because I convinced you that I knew where I was going, even though I was secretly happy to just wander. And so I guess eventually I led you the wrong way; took you down paths and through forests that you were never meant to go down, showed you sights that you were never meant to see.'

She stood chewing something, not even looking at me.

'And the truth is that you saw me at my worst; drowning out to sea with lungs full of water, still pretending that everything was fine and dandy, struggling and clinging, and pulling you down too. I held on. I tried to guide you into the maze, knowing that in many ways you were stronger than me, and the only way that you could follow me is if I lied, if I acted like I wasn't afraid, if I made out like things we're going to work out fine, and that my blind faith in the Great Nothing would somehow save us .'

But still she said nothing.

'And I know it was stupid, I can't deny it. But I wouldn't have done it if I was a stronger or better person. In my darkest moments I knew that it would never work out, but all the same, my naïve optimism led me to erroneously believe that it might do, and that we might make it. And in my darkest heart, I knew that we were from two different worlds, and that we were doomed, because the things that we want and need from life are separated by a world of disparity. For you are happiest when you are chewing upon the grass, but for me, I must convince myself that I was the one who planted it. But, look at you now, wasted and emaciated, tired and confused. If I keep clinging on then I will destroy you, but should it be true that I love you then, I guess I now is the time to let you go....'

And with this I let loose the leash, I let it slip between my fingers and fall to the concrete floor. And it then seemed that the space between us somehow served to unite us, as if we were both aware of its implications, that we had reached the end of our journey together, and all that was left to do was to ensure that this space continued to expand.

Once again, I had hoped that somehow she might find within herself the strength to say something. I crossed my fingers as I stood there beneath that grey sky, looking out the corner of my eye at the housewives unloading their shopping trolleys into the trunks of their cars, at the cloud configurations in the sky, at the ever increased space between myself and the world around me, as I became further and further detached, one thing at a time, from all that surrounded me.

And, as I looked into her eyes for a final time, I wanted to tell her that I was sorry; sorry for trying to convince her that anything was possible, even though I had once believed it. I wanted to tell her that I was sorry for not letting her go in the first place, sorry for seeing something within her that made me believe that it might be possible to hold on forever. Because I realised now that these sensations had been nothing more than a way for me to run away from myself, my fears of being alone, my fears of blending in, my fears of not being loved or adored or respected, my fears of finding out the truth about myself, of being just like every other ungoogleable Joe Schmoe in this two-bit town.

Love is nothing more than the sanctuary for our most innocent deceptions.

We stood staring at each other, I could tell that she was thinking something. I don't know what it might have been, but could tell from her eyes that it was profound and majestic, that if she were capable of articulating the thoughts or sensations that were clouding her brain at that time, then it perhaps might have saved me from what was to come. Indeed, it might have saved us all, because I could see in her eyes that it was a sentiment of great beauty and unquestionable truth, that it was the key to all peace and understanding.

She faltered on her knees, as though weak. And then, for the final time, before fading away completely, she opened that mouth of hers, and she said the only thing that she could say:

319

'Mooooooooooooooooooooooooooo.'

Grounded to the earth, I stood immobile but resolute, watching as she hobbled on down the horizon. The tattered leash dragged along behind her on the ground, twisted and limp, and I watched as she melted out of sight, into the streets of the city, into the darkest regions of my mind, until eventually she was gone and I was alone again, back to my old self, a solitary seeker - only now I had seen everything that the world had to offer me, and I knew for certain that there was little if nothing more. The train had pulled into the station.

And, so, I did all that was left for me to do: I wiped away my tears, and I headed on down to the city, and back to the Old Theatre.

Chapter 46

Alone again, at last; I took desultory steps through the hustle and the bustle of insensate streets, and, as I did so, it began to dawn on me that it is true that we can measure a man by the company that he keeps. And though it is possible for a loner to convince himself that he is some singular, shimmering being, it is also just as likely that he is a nonentity; a thing of inconsequence that can be forgotten about and neglected, the merest of blips, or most minor of ripples, certainly nothing of any lasting value or significance.

The palms of my hands began to call out to me, afflicted with rope burns from holding at The Cow's leash for so long. Now that she was gone, they had become purposeless and soulless; there was no longer any role for them to play, no reason for being; I had chosen to let slip through my fingers one of the only things I ever really pretended to care about.

But, despite these thoughts, the feeling that I had finally reached at least the imitation of a conclusion, the nebulous sensation that somehow something would come along and ameliorate the situation still hung over me like the promise of a broadband technician perhaps coming to visit at some uncertain hour of the day. I still had that feeling, though much vaguer than before, that there was an order to things, and that everything must happen for a reason, even though I suppose I could say that all of the evidence against such was stacked right up against me.

And so I bumbled in between polyester pedestrians. I mumbled incoherently to myself. And, the closer I got to the Old Theatre, the more terrified I became, because the truth was that I did not know why I was heading there, only that there was something down those stairs that had been calling to me, and that, actually, I had known this all along, and that, but for trepidation, I would have been there long ago – face to face with whatever there awaited.

I began to imagine that whatever this thing was, this thing down the stairs, it would somehow bring me peace, and that by finding peace I would have discovered my fate after all, and that if this could be achieved then all that had happened before it had not occurred in vain.

With each step that I took through the city, it seemed to me that my heart rate redoubled, until eventually the sensation of its beating encroached upon my very being, interposing itself with the pedestrian soundtrack of the workaday city. The badinage and the mindless chatter, the hissing traffic and inner-city ruckus, all had gone completely. Instead, I was left to feel terribly alone and inside of myself, convinced that this was it, that these were my final footsteps, and that very soon this sorry excuse for a life would be over and forgotten about.

But, naturally, I was once again besieged by doubts. The evolutionary defence mechanism kicked itself into action, and I began to think of reasons to live, reasons to keep a hold of myself and pull myself together, reasons to unleash the beast and to devour and replicate and propagate. But I also realised that despite whatever false promises I may be able to make to myself as regards the future, by very definition, I would not be able to keep them, and so I simply continued to march ever onwards, under tunnels and over pavements, past buildings and people and statues. Until eventually, the Old Theatre could be seen on the horizon, as though waiting for me, like an old whore in a wheelchair, supported by its scaffolding; a great sense of pride, despite its crumbling frame and the patina of weeds that covered it like scars left by disgruntled punters; the security signs that sat like scabs waiting to be peeled from a wound. It stood there as though waiting for me and, as I felt my breath deepen and my heart tighten in my chest, I danced towards it with tender, dreamlike footsteps.

All the while, I harboured the expectation that perhaps I could meet some kind of distraction on the way, that, for example, I would run in to The Counter, or some other outré soul, and that I could spend my time with them, open up and be real, tell the truth for a change, have one last shot at making that connection, one last attempt at looking somebody in the eye as an equal, attaining that sacred state of animal magnetism that had for too long been nought but sour grapes upon the vine.

Yet, the closer I got, the more acutely aware I became of the inevitability of all things. Every time I had to cross the road, for example, there was a green man at the lights, seeming to appear as soon as I set foot on the pavement besides it. And, then, looming up and above the city skyline, I saw the clock tower, that ever-weather reminder of the futility of it all, of time running out somehow, and then - at the very moment that I looked at it - it began to chime the hour, though I do not remember which, and yet it seemed to me oh so fitting.

Once again, I found myself crossing the road, near the wall where I had once sat taking photographs, by the wilted flower memorials to those that had long since been run over by cars, besides the junk infused alcove where I had once upon a time sat begging for change, and then finally, down the old back alley, where the old green bin had returned and sat awaiting for me to climb upon it. The window I had smashed so long ago was still broken; shards of glass sat upon the soggy pavement, eating out what little sunlight remained, as the sun began to fade, and the sky burst into flames. I held on tenuously to the old red brick walls as I approached, so as not to stumble or falter, and I felt the abrasions of cement between the cracks collapse into tiny piles of dust beneath the pressure of my fingers.

Slowly, I pulled myself up on to the old green bin, saturated with the same old filthy rain waters, and then, as though enraptured within the mindless trance of an empty dance, I pulled myself up and through the window. My heart continued to pound in my chest, but I was not afraid anymore; it was beating now on account of the promise of salvation, beating on the naive expectation of somehow reaching an end and taking all the pain away; I laughed at myself and how terrible I had become.

Standing within in the darkness of the staircase corridor, the only source of light a trickle let through the window, I focused on my breath and my breathing, as if once again my body did not exist, that I was only a mind in a sea of emptiness. And, then, I stood deliberating, knowing that heading down into the further darkness of the unknown was my only real option, but knowing also that if weakness were to dictate my actions that I could crawl upstairs and take a final look at the city.

After much deliberation, I found myself climbing the stairs, because I had convinced myself that I felt nothing but affection for this town, now that I knew I was leaving it. I convinced myself, somehow, that in its incompleteness it was beautiful, and that, if I were a man of any scruples whatsoever, it would be best for me to take one last look, to drink it in with my eyes like ocular wine, express my gratitude with my tears and lamentations, as a kind of ode to all that I would leave behind. And, so, I began to climb the stairs, holding on to the handrails in the darkness, fumbling to find my footing. But, just as I was about to leave, I heard that marching music begin to play, the very same as I had heard before, and I knew that it was calling to me.

Now, perhaps it was because I am naturally of a pusillanimous disposition, or even simply because I am as fallible as any other man, and so when confronted with an uncomfortable truth, will run away from it instead of into its arms. Whatever the reasons, I found my bare feet battered pounding up the stairs in leaps and bounds, taking three or four steps in my stride at a time, panicking as those terrible emanations floated up from below me, as if the musical notes were a swarm of bees my tail.

And so it was in this fashion that I ran and I screamed and I panted until I had reached the top of the stairs. But then, as I found myself at the same door as I had encountered long ago, the same shivering scintilla of light creeping out from beneath it as before, a strange thing began to happen. Instead of the distance that I had put between myself and the abominable music dulling or quieting its call, the distance seemed to have the obverse effect of increasing its volume tenfold, of filling my very being with its ominous exhortations.

In a fit of madness, as though suddenly possessed by a demon, I burst out through the double doors and into the sunlit roof upon which I had once upon a time found the jigsaw puzzle piece. And, as I paraded around its perimeter, taking one last look at the city under construction, at the world unfolding and making do without me, the music increased in volume ever moreso, until eventually I felt as though my ears were about to burst, until eventually, I thought that I would lose myself, that I would explode in a fit of dementia, or that I would simply collapse upon the concrete floor in a fugue, shivering ever eternal in a paroxysm of dead electric confusion and concrete self-abasement; and this was true even if I put my fingers in my ears; indeed, it seemed to me that the more of an effort I made to escape the horrible sound, the louder it somehow became.

In one final act of insensibility, I found myself climbing up onto the crumbling parapet that surrounded the roof. I looked down at the pavement below me, at the people passing by with their suitcases and their polished shoes, at their paper cups full of steaming coffee, their sandwiches in neatly wrapped cellophane. I stood there looking down upon them and I prayed one final time, with such intensity that I thought it would bring me to my knees.

And, all the while, that abominable music obtruded upon my soul like a hand up a skirt, resounding as though my bones might be about to shatter, filling me to the brim with an unbridled, sweat-stained fear that made my clothes stick and rip into my skin, and my legs aquiver as my knees knocked together. I stood there and I thought about jumping, but as I did so, I noticed that a crowd of pedestrians began to gather in the street below me. I stood there and I noticed that they were looking up at me, and I thought to myself, this is it, finally you have been noticed, your pain has been verified as tangible and real. You are going to be okay.

In my euphoria at this recognition, I noticed that they were shouting something up at me. Even over the horrible marching music, it could be heard clear as day, as though waves coming through on a radio receiver. They were looking up at me with a gleaming wonder in their eyes and they were shouting the same two words over and over and again at me:

'DO IT!'

As if they wanted me to fall.

I began to tremble, my knees weak and oscillating, as I wondered to myself whether I should give myself to their satisfaction. I took a step closer towards the edge of the ledge, my head a-spinning with the vertigo, but still they continued to shout up at me, and still, as though I were putting more distance between it and myself, the music continued to get louder, to fill me with dread and self-loathing disgust at making it ever intensified.

But, despite the inclination to fuel the fires of the desires of those down below, I took a step back off the ledge and on to the roof. And, as I did so, the volume of the awful music seemed to have turned itself down a notch. With my fingers still in my ears, I took a final gaze at the city about me, and then proceeded back through the doors and then down the stairs to do what I should have done as soon as I arrived here. And indeed, with each footstep that I took in this direction, the volume of the music became more tolerable. Eventually, I had reached my original point of entry, besides the cracked window, and then I began my descent of the stairs and, sure enough, the music, though still audible, decreased even more so.

I continued in this manner until I had reached the last of the steps and indeed another door, behind which I knew I would find the answer to my prayers.

I had reached my destination.

Chapter 47

My ear to the door, I stood panting and sweating in pathetic desperation. Despite having little choice, I still had reservations, and so I stood there trying to suppress the sounds of my own breath, listening to the ethereal tones of the now soft music; quite certain that from behind the door emanated the empty clutter of momentous activity, the cracking of whips and of drudgery, the brittle swirl of forced commotion and pale excitement, as though listening to an imitation ocean in a shell; an eternity away but oh so close.

All the same, I knew that I had to find the strength within myself to move forwards. Dawdling or faltering at this stage could only cause the intensity of that horrible music to rise up against me like a tsunami, send me supine into a stupor as I cursed myself for being a personality instead of a character, curled up on the floor as I waited for another boot to the face, as I tried to justify it all in a way that absolved me of any blame for my own downfall.

'Natural selection punishes the profligacy of wasted time and effort; if I refused to act now it would all have been in vain.'

And so I pushed tentatively at the door. It opened with a creak. And, upon entering the room to which it led me, I found that, just as I had imagined, I was within the pit of the old theatre, down below the stage, hearing the footsteps of those walking the boards above as, I melted beneath the dim spotlight of a faded memory and the red velvet of the dusty old seats.

My heart stopped upon reflection of what to do.

Notwithstanding the obvious signs of life that stood before me, the occasional cough and splutter, or sounds of heavy breathing, that clatter of unknown activity upon the stage above me, there was no conversation between whoever, or whatever, was up there; just the sound of the same sorry music; a scratched record forever on repeat; the infernal racket that had previously filled my heart with darkness as black as the band pit in which I had now found myself entombed.

I was left to wonder what I might do with myself; I thought about breaking down, but didn't have the willpower; I thought about shouting out, but I was too numb and unsure of myself to go ahead; and then I even thought about turning back, but when I turned about me in the darkness and tried to find the door through which I had entered, I noted that it had disappeared, that no matter how much I felt about or reached out it simply wasn't there. My breathing became heavier in panic, and just as I approached the height of my fear, I heard a familiar voice call out to me. It said:

'We have been expecting you.'

At first, I assumed that it was addressed to somebody else. But then my faceless interlocutor said it again, the very same but a little louder, and, following her utterance, I noticed that a great silence filled the room and the clatters and the bangs began to stop. And, in the silence, I noticed a strange smell, a sweetness that I had not noted upon entering; it filled my soul with its warmth and almost took away the fear that I felt at being called out by whoever, or whatever, waited up above me upon the stage.

However, despite an incremental decrease in the tenor or my fear, I still felt myself rooted to the spot, unwilling and in fact unable to move. Truth be told, just as that diabolical music had increased in intensity the more of an effort I had made to escape it, I noted that the more that I tried to move, the more rooted I felt that I had become to the spot in the band pit. And, then, it occurred to me that the music was still playing, ever so softly now, but still quite audible, and I further noticed that the activity of whatever work was unfolding up above me was going through a revivification, the clicks and sputters and coughs and breathing, returning to life again, the cracking of whips, that ever sweet smell of sugar and dough filling my lungs and bringing about within me a lofty, yet contrived sense of serenity.

I decided to move to Plan B: which was to try and convince myself that I was invisible, as though I were a shy child hiding his face behind his sleeves. I remembered what I had read somewhere or someplace about our thoughts being connected to our being, that if I could somehow find it within myself to merely clear away extraneous or importunate anxieties, that I would bring about existential cessation, that I would crumble to the floor, and into the roots of whatever plant had entwined itself about my feet; I would become a part of the earth; find myself reduced to the elements of which my body is composed, allow my brain to shut down and my soul to disconnect itself – fly away ever free, soar up and above buildings and mountains; finally, feel myself liberated.

But, alas, as is perhaps obvious by now, the more that I tried not to think of anything, the more that I attempted to shield myself behind an invisibility cloak weaved of my own inertia, I became ever more aware of my surroundings. Instead of hiding within myself, another introvert's holiday, I found myself overawed by the darkness of it all, overwhelmed by the mysteries of the Old Theatre, of my finally being upon the cusp of discovering and understanding the punch line of life's great joke.

Instead of seeking flight, I became thoroughly grounded, and I felt that instead of achieving nonexistence, I had found nothing more than a purer and more uncurbed version of its opposite; I felt, somehow, that each of my senses and my sensations, were filled with sensuous abundance; I felt myself tingle with the joys of being alive, that each sound, each smell, each sight about me was the final gift of living, that, before I said 'Goodbye' to it all, I was making the very most of it, feeling good and serene and whole, because I knew that I had made the right decision in coming here, and that I was not attached to anything or anybody; I had unbound and unshackled myself from all of my earthly displeasures.

And so, in this manic state of euphoria, I reached down about my feet and extirpated the roots around them. Still silent, as though some great animal that could not speak but only feel, I found a great strength within myself and used it to extricate myself from the band pit. I pulled myself up with my sinewy, broken arms. Short of breath, it did not bother me. I stood upon the creaking boards of the Old Theatre's stage, ready for the latest and greatest performance of my lifetime, and as I looked out at the dusty old auditorium, over a sea of broken velvet, I noticed with pleasure the vacancy of the building, the desolation of a non-person audience. It seemed so fitting to me that I should go down in a cloud a vacuity, in a vacuum of silence, unnoticed, watched by nobody, witnessed by myself alone, that I couldn't help but wonder if maybe perfection existed in this world after all.

As I stood facing this scene, lost to myself and the tears in my dry eyes, I took a deep and laboured breath, convinced that this was really the end of it all, that this is what it, my life, had amounted to; I prepared my thoughts and reflected upon it all, saw my life flash before my eyes. I thought about the people that I had once upon a time known and the places I had once been; I remembered anonymous streets and buildings, insignificant slices of the countryside, the scenes of swollen oceans besides unknown beaches, and then the faces of parents and other fade-to-grey relatives that had interspersed themselves throughout my lifetime, but were now completely unaccounted for. I caught a hold of my breath. And then, from behind me, came a sound which brought me back to the present:

Cough

It was The Sycophant surrounded by a band of doleful Chinese people; she had a whip in her hand and it looked like they were baking fortune cookies.

Chapter 48

In all honesty, I wasn't as surprised as I perhaps might have been. Nevertheless, I was unsure of what I might be expected to say to her and so I did all that I could think of, which was to stare into those empty eyes of hers, to look as though pleading, to attempt to find some form of recognition, some kind of acknowledgement that we were both sensate and sapient beings, and that, here on this stage, we both had a purpose of some kind.

She stared at me just as she always had; without life, her beady eyes hovering beneath her fringe, as though two tarnished coins left on a church collection tray. The Chinese people stood behind her with baited breath, awaiting her instructions; ready, I could tell, to do whatever she might wish for them to do, looking at her now and again with a complete and wholesome sense of reverence, because it was she that held the whip in her hands and it was her alone that knew how to use it.

I heard a cornucopia of conflicting voices in my head, each painted with an amalgam of contrasting emotions. Though I was unaware of what to say to her, the fact that she was stood here before me, after all of the turns in the road and the obstacles and the great chain of cause and effect that had preceded our encounter, led me to start wondering whether or not she was the one that I was supposed to be with, whether or not it was she, The Sycophant, who all this time I had been waiting for. Right before my eyes this whole long while, she had stood silent and unassuming, and now Destiny, the universe, those age old forces that I was unsure of whether or not to believe in - they had led me right to her door. Everything that had come before, every footstep and every falter, all of it was painted afresh in vernal hues; I saw all and everything in a new light.

'We are our own reasons for being.'

The silence between us all became ever tangible and more real. I stood there at the edge of the stage, worried that I might lose my nerve somehow, and topple back into the band pit. Nobody said anything and so neither did I. The only activity came from a tiny old Chinese man in the corner, writing something onto tiny slips of paper with an admirable penmanship. To prevent the devil in my head, I looked about me, at the creaking floorboards with their age worn abrasions, at the wine red curtain up against the back of the stage. For a brief moment, I turned my back on The Sycophant and her band of merry men; I looked at the rows of empty seats down before me and I realised once again that I was performing for myself alone; that my character and my role and whatever else about me you may care to name were simple constructions of my own will; that I had created myself through the choices that I had and hadn't made and that if I wanted to, here on the stage, I could slip into whichever other role I might arbitrarily choose.

The Sycophant came slowly towards me, dragging her whip behind her as though a tail, her pale face paler in the spotlight.

I thought about speaking. But I didn't wish to be the first because I felt as though this place had found me, and so it somehow seemed appropriate that it would give itself meaning without my having to beg of it.

She opened up her hand and, in her clammy android palm, I saw a red handkerchief. It was just like the one that she had handed me all of those months ago with The Fat Man's photograph inside of it, wrapped in a similar fashion, a golden ribbon around it, and the same attention to detail as regards the neat folds and the intricate knot that had been tied in the bow.

'This is for you', she said. And then she reached out her palm, urging me to take it from her.

Once again, I opened the handkerchief slowly with the reverence that the little package seemed to suggest it deserved. I pulled at the ribbon and watched the rest of the parcel unfold itself, and then, as the four corners fell about my hands like lotus leaves, I examined the contents with a respectful attention to detail and sense of delicacy.

Wrapped in cellophane was a cookie, just like the one I had discovered many mornings before outside of this very building, identical to any of the others round and about me; the ones that formed a mountain over by the table with the Tiny Old Man; the ones overflowing from the boxes on the stage floor; the ones in coat pockets and upon restaurant tables and in takeaways and supermarkets all over town.

I expressed my gratitude all the same.

'Open it', she said.

And so I did.

I took the crescent moon cookie from its wrapper, sniffed at it, and made the appropriate noises to express my supposed delight at the craftsmanship that had produced it. I raised my eyebrows and smiled at the gang of workers, still patiently waiting in a line at the base of the large curtain at the back of the stage, and then I took a bite of the cookie, noting nothing particularly remarkable about its taste, but groaning with delight nevertheless, as though it was all too much to handle.

The Sycophant took the remnants from my hand and removed the slip of paper with my fortune on it. She passed it to me still folded, asked me to read it aloud, and so, excited, as though I might have one last shot at learning something, I opened it with trembling fingers, more nervous than I perhaps should have been, desperately hoping that it would not disappoint. All the while, I looked The Sycophant right in the eyes, still lifeless by most standards, but with a glimpse now of something that I had not noticed before - a kind of bittersweet understanding, a yearning for something that split my heart in two and made her cold face seem warm for one fleeting, ineffable second.

The paper slip shook at my fingertips as I did my best to read it:

'   '

But it said nothing and so I couldn't.

'It's blank', I said.

And, as I noted the disappointment in my own voice, it reminded me that I had slipped inadvertently out of character. I had wanted to play it calm and collected.

'How can this be?'

Without saying another word, The Sycophant turned to the workers at the back of the room and cracked her whip against the floor before them. Instantly, they returned to their work stations around the stage area, baking and shaping and packing the fortune cookies. She took my hand and led me over to the table with the Tiny Old Man.

'This man is writing out the futures of those who cannot decide their own', she began to explain, 'My job is to ensure that there are enough to go around, to ensure that these gentleman work as efficiently and as swiftly as possible.'

'But why don't I have a future', I asked.

Once again she gave it to me straight:

'Because I have been watching you, this whole time. I have seen that you are lost and that you are confused; I have witnessed the terrible things that you have been prepared to do in the name of uncertain love and out of sheer desperation; how you are eager to please anybody but yourself in the name of some uncertain future, just so that you can feel a sense of normalcy, blend in, and efface yourself with the rest of them.'

And, then, she brushed her fringe back and over her head and I saw that she wasn't as hideous or freakish as I had led myself to believe. Though her eyes were still lifeless and she had a whip in her hand, I began to convince myself that there was something beautiful and soulful about her, that she was 'human' in every sense of the word, but that she had somehow become locked inside of herself, just like I had, and that if I could just show her that I knew she was in there she would be able to do the same for me and we would both be free.

'I wanted you to know that there is no future; that you just assume there is because you have experienced time in the same way as any other human being, and so you have assumed that what comes will be meaningful in some way. But this 'meaning' is an illusion. Today seems meaningful only because it is a continuation of yesterday, because we cannot imagine things being any other way. Tomorrow will make sense only because of today, but it doesn't necessarily mean that it is predetermined.'

I told her that I wasn't quite certain what she meant, that I didn't get her gist. She tried her best to elucidate and to drill the point home, waving her arms about with effusive gesticulations, and it reminded me of myself, stood at the foot of The Fat Man's bed, begging him to give me answers, lecturing him at the same time about his complacency and his slave-to-the-self ways and his repugnancy.

At that time, when I stood before him, I had somehow convinced myself that, even though I was looking for answers, I already knew everything that I could possibly need to know. It was almost as though I wanted answers to reaffirm my own opinions and ideas, and now, here was The Sycophant, doing the same thing, and I knew that we were connected in some way.

'I have seen you and I know that you fear the future based on where you are situated and what has happened to you and so you live as though you are doomed.'

And I told her that, yes, she was right, because I did spend a great deal of time reflecting on providence, awaiting the great punch line that would underscore the great travesty of my life. And, when I looked at her, after having said these words, I watched the tension slide away from her face, replaced by a great calmness and vivacity in her green eyes.

'Then I am not alone', she said.

And that was when we kissed.

As though lacking volition, I fell into her arms. I felt my fingers curl around her back, paid extra special attention to the sensuous textures of her crinkled shell-suit bottoms. And then I felt her tongue darting in and out of my mouth, her tight-lipped mouth clamouring for air and carnal satiation. Ultimately, it was an incredibly unsatisfying kiss, but I wanted to believe that it was perfect, I wanted this moment to be real, to be a great catharsis, the summation of all my efforts and meanderings, the great culmination; a globe of ice and wonder and monument to order over chaos.

Whilst we were at it the gang of workers bumbled silently about us, making their fortune cookies, and going about their business. I realised that my eyes had been open for the duration of the kiss, and so I closed them and leaned into her ashtray mouth some more, willed myself to believe that this was what I had wanted all along, that The Leader had just been some foolish pipe dream, that The Cow was a distraction, that The One I Loved had been mere whimsy, and nothing else but this moment could ever really matter.

The Sycophant pulled away and I noted the tears in her eyes; she cracked her whip against the floor and the workers startle; I wondered what would happen next. I didn't have the heart to tell her that I hadn't felt anything.

'Do you love me?' she asked.

'I would like to.' I replied.

And at that moment she pulled a pen from her pocket thrust it into my hand.

'You can write your own future.', she said.

And so I looked at the blank piece of paper in my hand and I began to wonder.

Chapter 49

My eyes remained fixed on the tiny slip of paper in my hand. Its blankness seemed to expand and consume all of the things that surrounded it; all of the problems that had defined the past, all of the showmanship and confusion that emanated from the present moment. I clutched The Sycophant's pen in my free hand; still cold from her fleshless grip, an extension almost of her entire personality, cold and thin and ever present.

Realistic consideration of the future was hardly something that I could consider myself to be experienced in. All I had done previously was moon down about the past and use the passivity that I considered myself to be imbued with to allow me to stumble into some indistinct version of the future; some nebulous formation in a distant sky that had, through random connections and coincidence alone, led me to connect disparate dots, or to put together different pieces of different jigsaw puzzle pictures, to create these incongruous images and shapes etched into my brain like kaleidoscopic banners in the sky.

As I stood there, staring at the piece of paper, at the great unwritten rest of my life, it occurred to me that anything might still be possible, within reason, and that, if I could just process the information that was available to me about the available options, then I could perhaps salvage something of my life. I could remove the jetsam from the stream and reconstruct it into multi-coloured wonder stuff, use what I had been through and had become as a result to my best advantage.

I looked up at The Sycophant. She was staring at me with a great intensity, as though she was willing me to include her in my plans, as though that was the only realistic option, because she was the only one still here.

And, then, I felt the great heaviness of the world upon my shoulders; I realised all of a sudden that each decision we make comes with certain responsibilities, that we cannot be free to do completely as we please, because it is logically impossible. She stood there still smiling; I clutched the pen in my hand and thought about what I wanted from life.

And, as I stared some more at that piece of paper, I noted that the intensity of its whiteness increased evermore. Despite its tiny size, its insignificance in the scheme of things as a whole, I felt as though the slip of paper in my hand were the most important and influential of things in my universe. And then a strange thing happened.

Though once having been afflicted with electric colours and grim sensations at the height of my confusion about the world, I remembered how upon listening to The Fat Man and his maunderings I had been brought around to the collective palette of this town as a whole. I realised that in my initial confusion about it all, life I mean, I had overanalysed and overthought my situation, romanticised and made more overwhelming than it had perhaps needed to be. The Fat Man had brought me back down to earth, shown me that things were more simple than I had considered them to be, that if we are not prepared to fight for what we want, or believe, in, then we truly will become as complacent or as colourless as the others around us. Finally, however, I had found myself here, before the Sycophant, and as I stared at that fabled slip in my hands, I finally lost sense of all colour completely, because I realised now that there was only one choice that we must make within our lifetimes, that it was a simple case of black and white divisions, that all there was for us to choose between was life and death.

I took a deep breath and counted to one hundred again.

And then it hit me.

I suddenly dawned upon me what it was to be alive; it suddenly dawned upon me what was real. I realised that I had spent my whole life looking for perfection, comparing whatever I had to some indistinct paragon in the mental realm. All my life, I had wanted the perfect life, the perfect woman, perfect health, or financial status.

Despite, in my more confused moments, to proclaim myself as being imbued with strength or fortitude, I had failed to accept the imperfection of my situation as real. I had failed to ride with it and learn from it. Instead I had turned to faith, convinced myself that things were going to be 'perfect' again one day, despite having little or no evidence that this might be the case, against all odds and realistic probability. Somehow, deep within myself, I had failed to really understand that there are no controlling forces but, by keeping my faith in such ideas aflame, I had only served to isolate myself from the world, to turn ever inwards down the spiral, to move out of control like a leaf in the wind, blowing whichever way outward forces so compelled me. Despite the internalisation of my thoughts and feelings, hardly letting them out of the cage, I had allowed the randomness of the external world to guide me here, to lead me to this slip of paper, to this final choice, between life on the one hand and death on the other.

All along I had known that it would come to this.

I glared at The Sycophant. I could feel my mouth agape, as though I were truly lost for words, truly unaware of my connection to her or the fortune cookies or the people making them. Whenever I had looked at her before, especially in comparison to The Leader, she had seemed so imperfect, and before this had seemed naturally repugnant. Now, however, I stared at her and her imperfection seemed real. It seemed natural. The animal everything I had craved for, a connection to nature and our evolutionary past, not the far-removed, pseudo-perfection that came caked in orange upon the Leader. Here before me stood an ape in a shell-suit; a lost, lifeless simian with a terrible fringe and dead eyes; yet, for some reason, in the black and white world I had found myself, it seemed to be the be all and end all, every answer to every question that had remained unanswered and hovering in space since time immemorial, every solution to every problem, the great elixir, the great cup from which wine would heal all wounds, and settle each and every issue with swift precision and fierce determination.

The gang of workers stood in file besides the majestic old curtain at the back of the stage. The marching music, so frightful mere minutes ago, began to rise again, as though an exhortation to action, as though begging me to make haste in determining the way that my future would unfold, because I was a human being, a fanciful creature that could make up its own mind, if only it had principles on which to base its decisions, guidelines to follow, or character and dignity.

I considered my available options but it seemed that I was not as free as I had originally thought. Gone was my past life and all of the things that it entailed; gone was the job in the shop with the mooncalves and the junk under their arms and the horrible stench and the sweat-stained manager with the crumbs in his beard. I thought about The Leader in the back of the bus, squirming and gyrating and breathing, that horrible child of hers with its Fat Man physiognomy and its grubby hands. Then, naturally, I remembered The Fat Man, the great disappointment, the promise of answers now forgotten; the cows in the field, the One I Loved overseas. Everyone and everything, gone but not forgotten.

And, as if able to read my thoughts, the line of workers at the back of the room pulled apart the massive burgundy curtain. It burst open in perfect synchronicity with the marching music and when it was finally as open as it could've possibly been I realised what all of this had been building up to. Behind the curtain was a decaying wooden door, not too large or imposing, but as black as the inside of a wolf's mouth on a moonless night. Above it flashed the word 'Exit' in neon green and, perhaps least surprising of all, there was a coin slot to the left hand side. Though I couldn't read its details from where I was standing, I knew instinctively that it was for twenty pence pieces; I fumbled about my pockets for the Well-Dressed Man's coin purse, as the workers stood straight to attention, and The Sycophant stood with her whip between her legs to the other side of me.

Finally, everything had clicked into place; I had reached the final crossroads, and the choice that I was forced to make really was the simplest and most ultimate of them all:

'Do I choose to live or to die?'

Perhaps life would be worth one more shot, I thought to myself. And so I took a hold of The Sycophant's cold hands, despite having felt nothing when I had kissed her just moments before. Though all fear had left me, as regards death, I found myself leaning in for a final kiss, just to be certain. Once again, her mean tongue darted like a worm in a cup, and her cigarette breath and her nervous energy began to get the better of me. I looked into her eyes and wondered if she felt analogous thoughts about me, if she knew that I was imperfect, but that she would accept these imperfections over time and that we would be able to look into each other's eyes for the rest of our lives, safe in the knowledge that the secret shame of our human frailty was buried safe within the breast of the other.

Maybe a compromise is not so bad. Maybe that is all life can ever offer. After all, we are all victims of circumstance and so there is little else we can do if we are to keep on meandering through the maze we call 'life'.

But I knew it was too late.

I knew that I was too jaded now to convince myself of anything but the truth; the truth that I was just another Joe Schmoe; another gene-machine, breeding and pulsating and taking carbon dioxide; another dreamer, with too much time on his hands, and no sense of what to do with it all.

'Do you love me?' she asked.

And this time I told her the truth.

'I can't.'

And that was that.

Perhaps it would have made more sense if she was bothered, but she absolutely wasn't. Perhaps she too had come to me because she had run out of options, because, no matter what happens, to us the clock will keep ticking and life will continue to pass us by. On a long enough time line we all amount to nothing.

And so, as I walked towards the black door, clutching a handful of shimmering twenty pence pieces, I began to think about The One I Loved, the one that I would never be able to have, the only one who I had ever wanted to be with, the only non-compromise, or one that actually meant anything. I thought about the absurdity of it all, I thought about the vagaries of existence. I thought about colour and optimism and virtue.

I turned to face The Sycophant for the final time.

Then I put my twenty pence piece into the slot and I disappeared forever.

The End

Printed in Great Britain
by Amazon

69725764R00200